ABOUT THE AUTHOR

Iain Edward Henn has a background in newspaper and magazine publishing.

Twenty of his short stories have appeared in magazines in England, North America, Denmark, Sweden, Norway, Australia and New Zealand.

His novel, The Delta Chain, was an Amazon Breakthrough Novel Award Quarterfinalist, and has appeared on Amazon UK's Mystery and Thrillers bestseller lists.

Praise for the author:

"fast-paced thriller...hooks the reader in..." *-Publisher's Weekly*

"ensures the reader will turn each fresh page in ... anticipation of the next surprising twist..." *-Renee Washburn, Apex Reviews*

By the same author

The Delta Chain

DISAPPEAR

IAIN EDWARD HENN

SUNFIRE

First published in Australia as 'The Silent Scream,' by Saga Publishing, an imprint of Gary Allen Pty. Ltd.

Revised and updated 2012

Copyright 2012 Iain Edward Henn

This edition published 2012 by Sunfire Publishing

ISBN 978-0-9808493-4-9

Dedication

To my wife, Janne,
for your light and love and encouragement

Each year, in Australia alone, 35,000 people are reported missing. In the United States, it is 900,000, in the UK: 200,000. More than 85% of these return, or are found, within the first two weeks. The remainder fall into the category of the long term missing person. Some have run away to a different life; some have suffered memory loss or illness; some have been kidnapped or murdered. Most are traced eventually one way or another. There is always a small percentage, however, who are never seen or heard of again.

- *Missing Persons statistics.*

PROLOGUE

It was the perfect time and the perfect place for the killing.

The first soft sweep of dawn light, the air crisp. The reserve was a large, sprawling tangle of green, sections of park, sections of natural bush. The running track circled the grounds, obscured from view in several places by overhanging willows and over-reaching ferns.

The jogger's blood lust was running at fever pitch, his senses singing with exhilaration. Most people would wake this morning feeling good to be alive. The jogger had woken feeling reborn, his all-consuming, dark need re- energised. His moment had finally arrived.

The time. The place. And the perfect victim.

For the first time in eighteen years he was free to kill again. The watchers were gone, he was certain of that.

He'd driven the perimeter of the reserve, stopping at random to scan the area with binoculars. No cars in the immediate vicinity. The reserve itself was empty, except for the young woman, keeping to her usual routine.

He joined the track on one of the hidden stretches and began to jog. His timing was precise, so that the woman was a dozen metres in front of him. She covered the ground in long, casual strides.

He couldn't have wished for a finer specimen. Long legs, athletic physique, electric blue shorts in a tight fit.

The urge coursed through his veins like a drug as he closed the distance between them.

He was going to make up for the long years of frustration and denial; of trying to satisfy his desires with fantasies and memories; of practically being driven mad on occasion by the inexplicable restraints.

That was over now.

The woman was almost within reach. He imagined the thin strip of wire looped around her throat, pulling tight, biting into flesh. Her panic; her gasping for breath. She'd be unable to scream, unable to break free of his iron grip.

And then acceptance as her hands fell limply to her sides and her knees sagged, life draining away.

The jogger reached for the wire that lay in the pocket of his tracksuit pants. Its cold steel felt reassuring against his fingers.

The woman was within arm's reach now. He noticed the slight tilt of her head as she became aware of another runner on the path. It was almost time.

For the young woman it should have been the start of one of the most exciting times in her life. She'd woken that morning feeling good to be alive. Instead, it was to be the end of everything.

ONE

Eighteen years earlier

Thunder rolled across the sky, nature's soundtrack to the dark clouds that blanketed the city. The night was lit only by the occasional flash of streak lightning. There was steady rain, not a deluge, just the promise of one, and the wind howled like a pack of hounds.

Hell of a night, thought Brian Parkes.

He'd been stuck on the train for two hours, any hint of rain and the blasted things slowed down. Give them a full blown electrical winter storm and they threw in the towel completely, stopping and starting with a familiar, grinding mechanical wheeze. Then came to a complete standstill.

On a number of occasions during the two hours the train had stalled for up to fifteen minutes at a time, before lurching on a little further. Stop-starting all the way.

At the end of the long journey Brian learned from a station assistant that the delays were caused by overhead lines coming down under the force of the strong winds. Many decades earlier Neil Armstrong had set foot on the moon. But in Sydney, the train system defied the fact that, elsewhere, Man was reaching for the stars.

It was a twelve-minute walk from the station to his home. His umbrella had been pushed inside out by the wind and the metal sprockets had snapped. The thin strands of metal stood upwards, away from the inverted cloth, like a creature on its back with its legs in the air. He dumped it in a roadside bin as he ran, pulling the collar of his coat tighter. He sprinted the first two blocks, and then slowed to a walk for the third. After all, what was the point of racing? He was already soaked to the bone. He wasn't going to be any less wet when he walked through the front door.

Was it just his imagination or was the rain driving harder since he'd left the train? That'd be right. It pounded the pavement like a battering ram. He broke into a run again as he rounded the corner into his street.

Inside number forty six Claridge Street, Jennifer Parkes watched her husband as he stepped into the front alcove. She felt herself tingle with contentment. She loved the rumpled look of his young face with his easy smile, snub nose and pointy chin. His curly brown hair was plastered to his head by the rain, but the lines of water that ran down his cheeks didn't detract in the slightest from those handsome, cherubic features.

Their eyes connected and Brian beamed.

'Hi, baby.' He eased out of the wet jacket and ambled towards her. 'I was starting to worry.'

'Train packed up. Been stuck in a carriage for two hours.'

She winced. 'Poor thing. Hot cuppa? Hot bath?'

'Yes please. The works.'

She melted into his arms. The feel and smell of her made Brian's senses soar. The firm swell of her breasts through the light cotton of her blouse, pressing against his chest, the gentle warmth of her body, supple and slender, fitting snugly against him. He brushed his fingers through the dark hair, shiny ebony black, centre-parted, that fell below her shoulders.

'Cuppa first. I'll make it while you get out of those wet clothes.' She pulled away, headed for the kitchen.

'In a sec.' He flopped down on the lounge, shivered, reached for the packet of cigarettes in his shirt pocket. Flipped it open. 'Damn. I'm out of fags.'

Jennifer's head popped around the corner of the kitchen doorway. She made a face at him. 'Silly, aren't you.'

'Bloody silly.'

She looked at the rain lashed window, then back to him. 'You're not going out in that again?'

10

He shrugged. 'It's only a coupl'a minutes to the corner store. Bill will still be open.'

Jennifer gave him a despairing look. 'Good night to give them up.'

Brian shook his head. 'No. Bad night to give them up.' He retraced his steps to the door, pulling his coat back on again.

'You'll catch a chill.'

'I'll hop straight into a hot bath when I get back. Promise.' He paused at the door, looking back at her. The dance of the rain on the roof became suddenly louder. 'Of all the days to have the car in for service.'

'One day we'll look back on this and laugh. Or at least I will.' She smiled again, winked at him, and he marvelled at how her smile lit the room .

'Love you,' he said.

'Love you too. Be quick.'

'Real quick.' He blew her a kiss and stepped out into the storm.

'Wait!' she called. She took her small yellow umbrella from the hook on the hall wall and ran to the door, passing it out to him. 'Take my brolly.'

'Thanks, hon.'

Jennifer went back through to the kitchen to check on the vegetable stew. She placed four bread rolls in the oven to heat. This was going to be just the meal for a night like this. Despite the cold air outside, she felt warm and cosy in here. Before she knew it, twenty minutes had passed. It was only a five-minute walk, three if you ran, to the local store.

She went to the front door, opened it, and peered out into the rain. She couldn't see a thing. What was taking Brian so long? Probably standing in that shop, dripping wet, chatting with Bill. *Men.* She went into the living room, placed her open palms in front of the electric heater, and waited.

Another fifteen minutes dragged by and she began to worry. *Brian and his damned silly cigarettes.* Where was he? She went to the door again and looked out. The rain had eased off considerably. A full moon glowed through a break in the night clouds and the wind had stopped.

Jennifer pulled a jacket on and marched off along the street towards the shop. The store was closed when she reached it but a light was still on inside. She banged on the front door and half a minute later it swung open.

Bill Clancy was a large, round, red-haired Englishman who, despite his ten years in Australia, had not lost any of his pommy accent. 'Ullo, luv. Lucky you caught me. Just closin' up, I was.'

'Hi, Bill. Sorry to disturb you but I'm worried about Brian. How long since he left here?'

'Left here? I'm afraid you've lost me, luv. When're we talkin' about?'

'He hasn't been here for a packet of cigarettes?'

'No, luv. 'Aven't seen Brian at all today. 'E say he was comin' 'ere, then?'

'Yes. He left home forty minutes ago.'

Bill lifted his arms in a gesture of bewilderment. 'Doesn't make sense.'

'You've definitely only just closed up?' Jennifer asked.

'Yes, luv. Look, maybe he decided to try another shop. He's probably back home now, snug an' dry an' all.'

'No Bill. You're the closest shop by far. Why would he go somewhere further?'

'Well, let's go look for 'im then.'

'No.' She hesitated. 'It's all right. I'll just go home and wait. I'm sure he'll turn up soon enough.'

'Bound to be a reasonable explanation,' the shopkeeper said.

'Of course there is.' Jennifer waved as she headed for the door. 'Thanks anyway, Bill.'

'Let me know if there's anything I can do,' he called after her.

Jennifer walked back home and noted that the storm had passed. Suddenly she was annoyed with her husband. He'd probably changed his mind, gone to a different shop and got held up for one reason or another. *Didn't he realise I would be worried? Why didn't he think?*

She arrived back home to an empty house. Normally she liked the quiet, but now the silence of their home seemed menacing. 'Brian!' *How silly of me, to call his name as if he were here.* Then again, maybe he was. Anything was worth a try.

'Brian!' He's snuck back in, she speculated, and he's hiding somewhere, playing a game. Stupid bloody game, not like Brian at all. The silence, in reply, was deafening.

She sat down to wait. An hour inched by and Jennifer had no doubt it was the longest hour of her life. She went to the laptop, accessed the local directory, and called the Hurstville Police Station. The senior constable on duty, Ken Black, listened as she explained the situation.

'I'm sure it's nothing to worry about, Mrs. Parkes,' he said, 'we've seen this sort of thing before. Hubby decides to sneak down the local for a coupla' beers.'

'My husband doesn't drink,' Jennifer protested, inwardly aware that she needed to keep her cool. 'He went to the corner shop for cigarettes. That was almost two hours ago. He was wet and tired. He could be lying somewhere, hurt ...' Her voice trailed off.

Forced to put her fears into words she realised all of a sudden the reality of it: Something was wrong. Terribly, horribly wrong.

'Very well, Mrs. Parkes, I understand,' Constable Black said. 'Please stay calm. I cannot list your husband as officially missing until he's been gone for twenty-four hours. But I'll take down the particulars from you, and drive by the area as soon as possible, keeping an eye out for anything unusual.'

'How long is as soon as possible?'

'Twenty minutes or so. Now, let me take some details. Your husband's full name, Mrs. Parkes?'

Jennifer gave him the details. Height, weight, hair colour and so on. Then all she could do was wait. Again.

After a while the rain began falling heavily once more. Jennifer, restless, walked out to the covered garden rockery that stood immediately outside the back door. She and Brian had spent much of the past few weekends out here, building the rockery, planting the flowers and ferns. Roughly hewn bamboo cross-beams held up the green tinted, clear fibreglass covering.

She listened to the steady rhythm of the rain. Normally it had a calming effect on her. Not tonight though. She felt a great, deep, dark chasm opening up inside. She was nauseous.

What's happened to you, Brian? The thought buzzed inside her mind like an annoying insect. *Something must have happened because it just isn't like you to go traipsing off for hours without saying something. That just isn't you.*

She wandered over to the rock pool she and Brian had fashioned out of rockery stones. The moonlight, tinged by the green tones of the covering, glinted off the dozens of five-cent coins that lay on the bottom of the tiny pool.

It had been Brian's idea on the first day they'd completed the rock pool. 'I'm going to make a wish,' he'd said, and had tossed a coin into the water.

'A wish?' Jennifer giggled.

'This is going to be our own private wishing pool,' he pronounced. 'My first wish is that you and I will always be together.'

'That won't work, will it? Telling someone aloud what your wish is.'

'Why not? Our pool. We make the rules.'

'My turn, then,' Jennifer said. 'Got a coin for me? My purse is inside.'

Brian handed her a five-cent piece and she dropped it into the water. 'I wish for our love to keep on growing and never stop.'

He screwed up his face. 'Corny.'

'No cornier than yours.' Jennifer laughed and punched him lightly on the shoulder.

Standing there, staring into the pool, always made her feel good. There'd been so many good times already and they'd hardly even begun.

She rummaged in her skirt pocket and, to her surprise, found a lone five-cent coin. Maybe not such a surprise, she realised. Since Brian had started this wishing pool thing she'd got into the habit of leaving the coins in her pockets. There was no particular reason for always using five-cent pieces. Just another one of Brian's crazy "rules." There had to be rules, he'd insisted, for the magic to work.

She and Brian had often strolled out here, impulsively, and made their wishes. It was fun.

She dropped the coin into the pool. *My wish is that nothing has happened to you, Brian. Please, please, come home safely to me.*

TWO

'Come round and take a seat, Mrs. Parkes,' Senior Constable Ken Black said from behind the long, wide front desk. Jennifer nodded and went through the narrow front opening.

It was 11.30 a.m. on Wednesday morning and the suburban police station was a hive of activity. Two or three calls at a time lit up the switchboard. Each being handled swiftly by a feisty, no-nonsense woman, middle-aged, who wore a constable's uniform.

Jennifer realised she'd never been inside a police station before. From the open doorway of the radio room, a few feet away along the left wall, came a non-stop series of garbled messages over the police radio frequency. Every voice seemed to quote a series of numbers, tens and fours and so on, a kind of numerical shorthand that reminded Jennifer of the many police drama shows.

She took a seat facing the senior constable.

'As I told you on the phone,' Black said, 'normal procedure with adults, is that twenty-four hours must elapse after a person has vanished before they're listed as officially missing. The exception is when it's immediately probable that a missing person may be in danger.'

Jennifer nodded. 'My husband isn't the kind of man to go off without telling anyone, Constable Black.'

'I'm sure he isn't. Hence our decision to move early and bring in the Missing Persons Bureau.' He turned towards his PC. 'I'm going to take a statement from you, and I'll need all the particulars on your husband.'

'Didn't we cover that on the phone last night,' Jennifer said. Her eyes felt as though they had knives sticking through them. She hadn't slept. The constable's return call the previous night, around eleven, had advised her that his drive around the area had revealed no sign of Brian.

'Yes, but we're going to need a great deal more than that with which to initiate a thorough search.' Senior Constable Black typed, firing questions at her as he went along. He took down Brian's physical description, hobbies, interests and personal habits. The questioning included the names of Brian's family members and personal friends and, where possible, contact phone numbers and addresses.

Jennifer answered the questions mechanically. In her mind's eye the words "thorough search" flashed on and off like a neon sign on a garish, night-time city strip. How could this be happening, out of the blue, to her and Brian? *Missing Persons Bureau ... thorough search ...*

'Who does Brian work for?' Black asked.

'He has his own accountancy practice. He set up an office in the city just a few months ago.'

'Do you have access to his office?'

'Yes, I have a key.'

'I'll arrange for you to meet me there later, Mrs. Parkes. The Bureau will want a list of his clients and any other business associates.'

The questioning continued. Medical history, family history. Was theirs a happy marriage? Had there been an argument the previous night?

'Please understand that I have to ask some highly personal questions,' Black explained apologetically.

'All right.'

'Does your husband have a drug dependency, or had he ever to your knowledge?'

'No.'

'Do you and your husband have financial difficulties of any kind?'

'No.' To her own ears, Jennifer's voice sounded like a watered down version of itself, swept away by a torrent of fears.

Meg Roberts was sitting on the steps outside the house when Jennifer arrived home. 'I thought I'd hang around in case you weren't going to be too long,' Meg said, springing to her feet as Jennifer came up the front path.

'I've been with the cops.' Jennifer unlocked the front door and Meg followed her through to the living room.

Jennifer was moving as though in a trance. Going through the motions. The police had run a thorough check on all Sydney hospitals. No one matching Brian's description had been admitted. She'd started to wonder if she was partly to blame. Perhaps she should've phoned the police earlier. Why had she waited so long?

Brian had only gone to the local shop, just minutes away. If she'd acted sooner Brian might've been found.

It had been close to midnight when Jennifer had phoned Brian's parents. They lived on the Central Coast, north of Sydney. The anguish in Brian's mother's voice had stayed with Jennifer through the long, sleepless night.

'Jen! I thought I told you to call me. That I'd go down to the cop station with you.'

'It's okay, Meg. I'm handling it.'

Meg looked closely at her friend. Jennifer's eyes were dry but glassy; her face set rigid in an expression of firm resolve. She's mustered together all her reserves of strength, Meg thought, and steeled herself to face the trauma and get through it. That, in Meg's opinion, did not mean she was handling it okay. 'I don't want you handling it on your own. I'm here for you. Okay?'

'Okay,' Jennifer conceded.

Meg felt like rolling her eyes. Jennifer was her oldest, closest friend, and she was always insistent, no matter what came along, that she was "handling it."

'So what are the police doing?'

'They took down a lot of details. Just about everything you could think of.'

'And?'

'Checked the local hospitals and emergency services. Nothing. So they've called in the national Missing Persons services.'

17

'They'll find him, Jen. There's bound to be a reasonable explanation for all this.'

'Maybe.'

'This is not the time to get pessimistic on me. Fashion designers are positive, forward thinking people, right? That's what you told me.'

'Point taken. What would I do without you?' Jennifer gazed gratefully at her old friend. Meg Roberts had always had a bright, breezy personality. She was a pleasantly plump girl with large, expressive eyes, a wide smile and reddish brown curls.

They had been close since their school days, despite the differences between them. In comparison to Meg, Jennifer was often seen as quiet and intense.

Meg grinned. 'Don't go getting all buddy buddy now. I don't think I could stand it. And it's way too early for alcohol. How about coffee?'

'Make it strong.'

'I don't make it any other way, honey.' Meg went through to the kitchen and placed the kettle on the stove. 'So how's the dress designing coming along?' she called out as she reached for the coffee jar.

Jennifer sighed. 'Slowly. I'm still picking up a bit of freelance work with that small fashion warehouse at Surry Hills. There's not a lot around at the moment.'

When Meg returned to the lounge she found Jennifer, head in hand, crying freely. Meg dumped the two steaming hot mugs on the table and sat down beside her friend. There was so little she could do to help. So little anyone could do. Except wait.

'It's good to let those feelings out.' Meg placed her hand on Jennifer's shoulder. 'Cry it all out, babe.'

'Where is he, Meg? What on earth could have happened to him?'

'He'll turn up, Jen. Has to. Whatever happened, he can't be too far away, surely.'

Jennifer wiped the tears from her eyes and took a deep breath, an attempt to regain her composure. 'There's something Brian didn't know. Now ... he may never know ...'

'What could he possibly not have known?'

'I think I'm pregnant,' Jennifer blurted out. 'I'm two weeks overdue. I've got a doctor's appointment in the morning for the test.'

'Listen honey, with any luck your old man will be back and he'll be able to make that doctor's appointment with you.' *Yeah, so why don't I feel convinced,* Meg thought, and she hoped her doubt didn't show. She hated this feeling, the same one she was sure Jennifer had, that Brian wasn't coming home.

THREE

One foot after another hit the pavement in quick succession. There was an acquired art to this, for the sole of each foot to touch the ground only lightly and briefly, the result of the powerful sweeping strides of the runner. One movement passing fluidly into the next.

Jogging in the early mornings and evenings had long since become a popular pastime. Exercise and nutrition had swept the youth culture of the western world, a fad to some, a serious concern to others. These days it was a multi-faceted industry. It suited the jogger's purposes nicely.

He wore a blue tracksuit lined with a single white stripe. He had matching gloves and sports shoes with thick rubber soles. His sports cap, with rounded peak, was pulled down low on his forehead and with his head tilted downwards as he ran, his face was mostly obscured.

The thin, pliable piece of wire was looped round and round itself, wound into a compact ball, and stuffed into his pocket.

It was a cool, clear morning, one of the last days of winter. Six-fifteen. The jogger had been here for a run on two previous occasions that week, to get his bearings. This wide, leafy reserve in a semi-rural district north west of Sydney was ideal. A narrow path ran along the perimeter of the reserve, amidst hedges and trees that looked as though they'd been there forever.

The jogger had noticed the young woman on both of those previous visits. Fair-haired, plump, wearing a tee shirt and slacks. He noticed her running had improved. She had an easier, more natural pace, a rhythm she'd lacked before.

He'd passed her and now she was several metres behind him on the track. After a while he slowed his pace, allowing her to gain on him again.

He thought back to the previous kill, two weeks before, picturing the quiet street in the nearby suburb. An attractive, middle-aged woman had arrived home in the middle of the day. She carried her bags of groceries into the house. There was no one else on the street.

Plenty of trees in the front yard for cover.

He simply walked, unseen, into the open side door of the house, twenty seconds or so behind her.

He had stood behind the open door between the kitchen and the lounge room, the thin stretch of wire at the ready in his hands. He felt the flood of excitement. Blood coursed through his veins, pounding in his temples. Not too soon, he thought. Control it. Concentrate on the task at hand.

He'd always been this way. Feeling pleasure while inflicting pain on others, though it was getting out of control and he was aware of the need to be careful. The time lapse between each of the past few kills had been less and less and he felt he should taper back.

After this one, he decided.

The third time the woman passed through the doorway, the jogger pounced. His method was always the same. He struck suddenly and swiftly from behind, snapping the looped wire around the neck of the victim, and then pulling tight. The deceptively smooth, thin wire cut into the flesh of the woman, an ugly red welt at first, then a pencil thin crevasse, weeping with blood as she fought for breath.

Now he felt the blood coursing through his veins like an electric current, igniting every nerve end with its voltage, as though stretching out every fibre of him with the power.

He wanted to scream out, for release, at the sheer ecstasy of it.

Strangulation by garrotte didn't take long. Sometimes, when the jogger could regulate the flow of strength through his arms, and manipulate the struggling of his victim, he made it last longer, which lengthened his enjoyment of the act.

At the surprise of the attack, the woman's shock gave way to an overpowering fear so strong it was like an odour in her nostrils. She

21

could neither scream nor run though she tried desperately to find a way to do both. As the seconds ticked by her horror became an anchor in the pit of her stomach, plunging down, ripping apart the fabric of everything she had ever been. She began to weaken, her strength slipping away as the world around her darkened, her terror so great that even tears would not form in her eyes.

Afterwards the jogger left the house as he'd entered, unseen, by the side. His car was close by.

He pushed those memories, as exciting as they were to him, from his mind. Control it. Concentrate on the task at hand. The young woman was adjacent to him now on the narrow path.

She glanced in his direction and caught his eye. 'Hi.'

'Hi.'

'You're a sucker for punishment. Third time this week, isn't it?'

'Yeah.'

'I'm here every day. Determined to get in shape for summer.'

I know you're here every day, you stupid bitch.

She moved ahead of him. He slowed his pace further, shifted his position so that he was directly behind her. He allowed the pace of his stride to match hers.

Same speed, same rhythm.

He was certain their breathing and the beats of their hearts were in tandem and the idea thrilled him. She was his.

For two weeks he'd longed for this moment. The exhilaration soared through him like a mad, demonic song. Savour it. The jogger knew he was different, he'd always known that. He simply couldn't help himself.

The two runners approached a bend in the track, which was completely hidden from view by hedges on either side. His hand slid into his jacket pocket, removed the ball of wire, his fingers deftly allowing it to uncoil. The young woman was oblivious to him. He was close enough to hear the pant of her breath. He ached inside with the irresistible urge.

Now.

He lunged forward. One simple, single movement. He looped the wire around her neck, pulled it tight, heard her gasp, heard the air expunged from her lungs.

22

At first, the jogger didn't know what the cold, clammy sensation was on the back and side of his neck. He was pulled backwards in a swift, savage movement by what he now realised was a large, meaty pair of hands. Another arm came from the side in the same instant, delivering a karate blow to his knuckles, destroying his grip on the wire. It fell from his grasp and he became briefly aware of the young woman tearing it from her throat, coughing, then falling to her knees.

Two large men in dark, nondescript gear had attacked him. One man kept him restrained, pinning his arms to his sides. The other man stooped to pick up the wire, pocketed it and looked towards the woman.

'You okay?'

'I think so.' She gulped in lungfuls of air.

'Then go. Get away from here.'

'But ...'

'Get out of here. Now.'

The woman stumbled to her feet, paused momentarily as she glanced wide-eyed at the three men, then ran off along the path.

The man holding the jogger released him, and with a powerful lunge pushed him off his feet. The jogger sprawled in the scrub at the edge of the path. He looked up at his two assailants. Who were they? Passersby? Police? He didn't expect what happened next.

The men turned and strode quickly away across the reserve towards the street.

The jogger rose to his feet and sprinted back to where he'd left his car, several blocks away. He drove cautiously, one eye fixed on the rear vision mirror to see if he was being followed. He'd broken out in a cold sweat and it stung the recently shaved area of his neck.

It didn't take him long to regain his confidence and he cursed aloud the strangers who had foiled his plan. Inside he ached more than ever with his need. He would have to forget about that woman now and seek a new victim in a new locale. This process normally took a couple of weeks. He would cruise the outer lying areas of Sydney, choose a convenient place, and commence looking for someone - anyone - who had a routine he could get a fix on.

This time, however, he would need to fast track his selection process. He wanted to strike again, within days.

It was three days later when the jogger attacked again.

Late evening.

A middle-aged, pot bellied businessman was leaving his office late, as he had the previous two nights, walking towards a flat, open air parking lot at the back of the suburban office block. It was deserted. The businessman reached his car and placed his key in the door. As he turned the key a wire was looped violently around his neck and pulled tight.

Once again the intended victim was saved by the arrival of two large men. Once again the killer was restrained until after the shaken businessman had driven away, warned off by the mysterious figures.

The two men then strode off into the darkness, shadows eaten up by the night.

'Who are you?' the jogger screamed after them. There was no answer, just as there wasn't the next time or the time after that.

At first, it seemed impossible to the jogger that these shadows were watching him and following him day and night. Yet that appeared the only possible way they could always be on hand to stop him whenever he undertook a murder.

Who were they? How did they know about him? Why did they always walk away and leave him free, unharmed?

None of it made any sense at all.

The jogger was in his apartment, his lean frame settled into the centre of the three-seat lounge, feet spread out on the coffee table in front. The ring of the doorbell startled him. He wasn't expecting company. He opened the front door and surprise showed clearly in his expression.

The girl on the doorstep couldn't have been any more than sixteen but she had a hard look that was decades beyond her years. The short, short skirt, low cut lace top and provocative stance made her profession obvious.

The jogger glared at her, confused. 'Yes?'

A half smile, half sneer stretched across the girl's face but there was no expression in her eyes. Just a dull, glazed look. 'It's party time, mate.' She strode confidently into the apartment, pushing past him. 'Where's the bedroom?'

'What the hell is going on here?'

'I told you, lover. Party time. For you, anyway. And don't worry. It's all paid for. You've got me 'til midnight. But that's not the good news.'

'Oh?'

'The good news is you get to do whatever you like to me. With a few exceptions.'

The jogger stared at her, speechless. She was beautiful, with long auburn hair that fell below her shoulders. Her lips were of the thick, sensual kind and they were in a permanent pout, even while she spoke.

'Well, don't you want to know what the exceptions are?'

'Okay.' He decided to be cautious, watching the girl closely. He had no idea what this was about and he didn't like being caught unawares.

'No broken bones. No cutting me. If I even think you're going to try and kill me I'll scream and, quicker than you think, two big bozos - I believe you're familiar with the type - will come crashing through that door and pulverize you. Got it?'

The jogger looked towards the door.

'Yeah,' the girl said, 'they're out there.'

'Who sent you?' he asked. His gaze returned to the girl's face, watching her, sizing her up. He could imagine himself doing all sorts of vicious things to her. The thought of it excited him.

'Wrong question, mate. Can't tell. Let's just say it's someone who knows you're frustrated. Knows you need an outlet for your ... uh ... needs. So I'm it.'

'They must be paying you a lot of money.'

'That's none of your business. Well, I'm ready when you are, big boy.'

'Take off your clothes,' he said.

'Hey, original.'

He glared at her. *Smart-mouthed bitch.*

The clothes seemed to slip away from her body as though cast off by magic. The jogger reached out and ran the tip of his finger down the

25

middle of the girl's flat belly. Her skin was smooth, like satin. She had solid thighs, a slim waistline and large, round breasts.

'Remember the rules, sweetie?'

'No breaking bones, no cutting or killing,' he replied matter-of-factly. 'Bruises are okay?'

'Within reason. Otherwise, anything goes. Like, y'know, sex - remember that one? - is fine. Preferable, actually.'

The jogger grunted. He raised his right arm, his palm open, and swung it towards the girl, slapping her hard across the face. She reeled backwards, began to topple, and then regained her balance quickly.

His heart was beating rapidly, the thump, thump, thump, hammering in his ears. 'Get down on the floor,' he commanded. He felt the electrifying rush. He was going to rape her as violently as he knew how. Beat her.

What he really wanted, though, was to kill her. But he knew that was the one thing he dare not try.

FOUR

Present Day

Rodney Harrison was eleven years old, a freckle-faced kid with a shock of curly, red hair. He had always wanted to have his own delivery run and today was his first day on the job, distributing leaflets to letterboxes. He was thrilled by the thought of having his own money, which he'd earned himself, to do with as he pleased. He intended to save up enough to buy an Xbox.

It was Wednesday morning, seven fifteen, and Rodney hoped to get in an hour both before and after school, five days a week, to complete delivery of his allotted number of leaflets. He rode his bicycle around the corner of Meson and Claridge in the southern Sydney suburb of Hurstville, the fifth street corner of his run, when he saw the man sprawled on the side of the road.

'Hey mister, you okay?' He braked, bringing the bike to a stop alongside the man. The body lay face down on the asphalt, and his coat appeared to be very damp. Rodney thought that was unusual, it hadn't rained for weeks. 'Mister?'

No sound or movement came from the man. Rodney was worried. Should he do something? He stepped from his bike and reached towards the man. 'Hey mister, wake up.' He shook the man's shoulders. The body was heavy and didn't budge. 'Can you hear me?'

Rodney stooped down closer and his heart began to beat rapidly. Dead? Was the man dead? There was something eerie about the man's stillness. Rodney walked around to the other side of the body, where the man's face was partially visible. The eyes were open, unblinking, unseeing.

A car came along the street, driven by an elderly man. Bill Hartland was on his way home after an early morning trip to the newsagent. He pulled over to the side of the road when he saw the boy waving frantically to him. The kid was clearly in some kind of distress. It wasn't until he eased himself out of the car that he saw the man's body.

'He's dead,' Rodney called, his breath coming in short, sharp bursts. 'His eyes are wide open, like dead people in the movies.'

Thirty minutes after the message had been radioed through, Detective Senior Sergeant Neil Lachlan arrived on the scene. At the age of thirty-nine, he was in his fourth month with the New South Wales Homicide Squad, and was working out of the Hurstville Police Local Area Command. People would have laughed, he imagined, had he told them he found the Homicide work less stressful than his previous position, so he kept the thought to himself. It wasn't a form of black humour, however, just a simple fact considering that he'd spent the previous ten years with the Drug Squad. Ten years of traumas, late nights, undercover work, waging war against users, dealers and organized vice gangs.

He'd demanded the transfer after the irretrievable breakdown of his marriage but he knew the transfer would come through too late. The job was the reason a wonderful relationship had turned sour. He realised, at that late stage, that if he was to have any life of his own, he needed the change.

Lachlan didn't know why his mind was sifting through those memories now, as he stepped from the police-issued Holden Commodore. Then he realised it was because of the freckle-faced kid. The delivery boy stood on the fringe of the cordoned off area, watching the forensic team make their on-site inspection of the body. The boy was fascinated and watched with a naked curiosity. Lachlan figured the lad was a similar age to that of his own boy.

The local cop walked over and offered his hand. 'Rick Crayfield. Glad to see you.'

They shook hands. 'Neil Lachlan. What have we got here, constable?'

'A hit and run, according to the forensic boys.' Crayfield handed a black leather wallet to Lachlan. 'The body had plenty of I.D. Local fellow, lived just up the street.'

Lachlan flicked the wallet open. It contained a driver's licence and a local club membership badge. He took the licence out. The date of issue and the expiry date indicated it was close to almost two decades old. Lachlan checked the details. The address was 46 Claridge Street, Hurstville. The victim's name was Brian Parkes and the birth date indicated the victim should be aged in his mid forties, though the picture on the licence was much younger.

Lachlan scanned the licence several times but kept returning to that date. Weird. Surely no one carried around an old driver's licence for that long. Did they?

Crayfield noticed the detective senior sergeant's quizzical expression. 'Problem?'

'Just that it's an old licence,' Lachlan told him. He didn't elaborate. 'Have you run a check on him yet?'

'Yeah. Still waiting to hear back.'

Lachlan approached the senior forensic man.

'Lousy night,' Tim Baldwin said, yawning. 'My three-year old. Toothache.'

'Had a few of those nights myself. What's the verdict?'

'Gashes and contusions on the back and left sides, consistent with a hit and run.'

Lachlan peered over Baldwin's shoulder at the corpse. 'He doesn't look smashed up badly enough.'

'No. It seems internal damage is minimal. He was damned unlucky to croak.'

'No other signs of possible cause?'

'We'll know better after the coroner does his thing.'

'Time of death?'

'Less than twelve hours ago. Early stages of discoloring. Of course, the autopsy will give a more precise time.'

Lachlan took a closer look over the body. He noticed the label on the man's trousers - StyleSet. They'd been a successful and trendy label for some years, but had gone bust at least fifteen years earlier. Lachlan knew because he'd had some StyleSet gear himself. *Funny the things you remember. Way out of date now.* He'd worn that style in the days when he'd met Marcia. Reminiscing again. *Enough.* He pushed the thoughts of the past from his mind.

'I want you to include in your report the make and year of manufacture of the victim's clothing,' Lachlan told the forensic man.

'Sure,' Baldwin said. 'Unusual request.'

'I've got a feeling it's going to be a day for 'em,' Lachlan commented. 'There's something weird about this body.'

'How's that?'

'His driver's licence is more than a decade out of date. His pants label is just as old but these trousers aren't all that worn.'

'Nostalgia buff or maybe he was going to a retro party,' Baldwin said drily, 'some guys take that shit very seriously.'

Lachlan couldn't have missed the cynicism in Baldwin's tone. Another forensic cop who'd seen too many strange and wonderful things to be surprised any more. Neil Lachlan had come across a few of those. 'Maybe,' he replied. He'd always made a point of exhaustive investigation of any and every small detail that puzzled him during a case. He'd been known for it throughout his years in the Drug Squad. Homicide work was no different in that regard. The license and the clothing simply didn't make sense.

Crayfield approached. 'An old fellow phoned in to alert us to the body. I've got his statement.'

'He's gone?'

'Yeah. He was pretty distressed so I sent him home. The boy over there was first on the scene.'

They strode over to where the boy, wide-eyed, had been watching the action.

'Hello, mate. What's your name?' Lachlan asked.

'Rodney Harrison.'

'I'm Detective Senior Sergeant Lachlan.'

The boy eyed him suspiciously. He saw a tall, lanky man, broad shouldered, with sharply etched features, a lived-in face, a wide grin.

'Why haven't you got a uniform?' was the first thing that came to Rodney's mind.

'Because I'm a plain clothes detective from the Homicide Division.'

'Really?' The boy sounded incredulous.

'Yes. I am.' Lachlan cocked his head towards the spot where the body lay. It was now being removed, draped in a cover. 'This must have been quite a shock for you, son.'

'Shock? Well, yeah.'

'Are you feeling all right? Nothing to be ashamed of if you're not.'

'Oh no, I'm fine. It was real cool finding a dead body. Just like in the movies. I mean, it's not so cool for the man, not really but ...'

'I know what you mean, Rodney. Not the sort of thing that happens every day.'

'No.'

'Why don't you let me stick your bike in the boot and I'll drive you home?'

'In the police car?'

'Yes. In the police car.'

The boy's excitement was obvious. 'All right!'

Lachlan was certain his own boy would have reacted in just the same way. He placed his hand on Rodney Harrison's shoulder and walked with him to the car.

The plaques lining the reception area wall were a chronology of success. Australian Excellence In Fashion Awards from various intervals over the past ten years. The carpet was a burgundy plush pile, the walls a montage of pastel shades and strips of polished redwood oak that matched the reception desk. Cindy Lawrence swept past the area and along the adjoining corridor to Jennifer Parkes' office.

Jennifer was at her desk, returning her phone to its hook. 'That was Freddie Jamieson at Myers,' she said, 'he's just ordered ten thousand of the new range of *Bellisimo!* skirts and tops.'

'Great,' Cindy enthused.

'Don't say great, say when.'

'When?'

'By the end of the month.'

'Impossible.'

'Since when did we start saying that word around this place?'

'Just thought I'd give it a try.'

'He has to have them. And he'll pay full factory floor, no volume discounts, if we can deliver.'

'We'll deliver. I'll get right on it.'

'If Ken doesn't think the factory can handle the full order, even with overtime, tell him to look at farming some of the work out,' Jennifer instructed. 'It shouldn't be a problem with the market the way it is right now.'

'Tell me about it.' Cindy retraced her steps to the door, paused. 'Oh Jen? It's eleven o'clock. You wanted to be reminded.'

Jennifer followed Cindy out of the office. 'That's right. Come and watch.'

'More on Kaplan's?'

'Yes. A judgment is expected this morning.'

At thirty-nine, Jennifer was still tall and slender but the girlish gawkiness had long since been replaced by the graceful carriage of an independent woman. The innocent, wide-eyed look was more focused now, her features more pronounced, knowingly serene.

The LED screen was built into the wall of the oval shaped meeting room. Cindy reached for the remote on the conference table and the screen flicked to life with the morning news program. Familiar theme music and the electronic logotype came together with a series of well known recent news scenes, then altered just as quickly to the presenter. 'Minutes ago in the Macquarie Street courts, Judge Roland Hetherington handed down his judgment on the crumbling fortunes of the Kaplan Corporation. The decision came as no surprise to the business community. The financial empire founded by Henry Kaplan has been declared insolvent. Judge Hetherington appointed chartered accountant Warren Stokes, of Parkhill Stokes, as receiver.'

Jennifer gave a long, low sigh. 'I never thought I'd see the day.'

'Despite everything that's happened over the past twelve months?' Cindy queried.

'Despite everything. If you'd followed Henry Kaplan's career as long as I have, then you'd understand. He had an answer for everything, and he always bounced back from every possible predicament.'

'Do you think he will this time?'

'See what he has to say himself,' Jennifer said, indicating the screen. The image of Henry Kaplan strode defiantly down the steps of the courthouse, flanked by aides. At sixty-one, he still cut a dashing figure, as robust and dynamic as he had been twenty years before. Broad features, tanned, with the attractive roughly hewn lines that age brings to some men, doing them even greater justice than in their younger days. The iron-grey hair was perfectly cut and styled. He could have been a statesman or a legendary actor. Perhaps the millionaire businessman was a bit of both, Jennifer thought, and more.

Despite the bankruptcy, Kaplan beamed at the cameras, not at all flustered by the dozens of TV and radio microphones pushed towards him.

'Any comment, Mr. Kaplan?'

'Is this the end, Mr. Kaplan?'

'Do you have anything to say to your shareholders, sir?'

The questions came thick and fast.

'They really don't want answers,' Jennifer commented to Cindy. 'They just want to be heard to have asked the question.'

'The same old questions,' Cindy added.

'Oh yes. The same. No wonder Henry always knows the answers.'

Both women laughed. God, thought Jennifer, am I really this cynical at thirty-nine? Then she heard Henry's reply to the media and she smiled inwardly. Just what she expected.

The irascible old devil.

'I'll be back,' he declared triumphantly. 'Down for the count but certainly not out.' He waved as he and his aides clambered into the back of a waiting limousine. A moment later it sped away like a knight in shining armour retreating from the battlefield.

'I think we both knew he'd treat this as only a temporary set-back,' Cindy said. 'What do you think? Can he come back from this?'

'I'm sure he can.' Jennifer's tone was reflective. 'And if there's anyway I can help him, I will.' She gestured to indicate the business

33

around them, 'After all, he's the one who made Wishing Pool Fashions possible.'

'Excuse me, Jennifer.' The receptionist, Carmen Tucker, was at the doorway. 'There's a Detective Senior Sergeant Lachlan here, asking to see you.'

'To see me?'

'Yes.'

'Send him through to my office, Carmen. I'll be along in a moment.' Jennifer exchanged a curious glance with Cindy.

'No idea what it's about?' Cindy asked.

Jennifer shrugged. 'None.'

'Something to do with this Kaplan thing, perhaps?'

'I doubt it. Kaplan's had no financial stake in Wishing Pool for years.' Jennifer headed out of the room. 'You'll handle the Myers order?'

'You just leave that with me.'

Neil Lachlan stood just inside Jennifer's office, admiring the view her window afforded of Hyde Park. It was a clear day, no clouds. A flock of birds moved swiftly over the treetops of the large city park, a patch against the distant blue. The birds were too far away for Lachlan to tell what kind they were.

Jennifer strode in and offered her hand. 'Good morning, detective.'

Lachlan took her hand. 'Sorry to disturb you, Ms Parkes.'

'Quite all right. What can I do for you?'

'I'm here to ask about your husband, Brian Parkes.' Lachlan referred to his pocket notebook. 'I understand he was listed as missing eighteen years ago and has since been declared officially deceased.'

'That's correct.' Jennifer was incredulous, so much so that she could find no other words. What on earth was this about? Now. After all these years. She glared at the plainclothes policeman, waiting for him to continue.

'A man answering the description of your husband was fatally injured in a hit and run accident last night, Ms Parkes. I understand this must come as a great shock, but we need you to assist us by identifying the body.' Lachlan wondered whether he sounded as uncomfortable as he felt. He'd done this many times before but it never got any easier – not for him, anyway. This was one of the worst tasks for any police

34

officer, asking the spouse of a deceased person to help with identification. There was more to this, though, an eerie feeling of ... displacement. It wasn't as though this woman had last seen her husband the night or day before.

'I think someone must have their wires crossed,' Jennifer said. 'This hit and run victim can't possibly be my husband. He would have died a long time ago.'

Lachlan reached into his coat pocket and withdrew the wallet. He handed it to Jennifer. 'This was found on the victim. Do you recognize it?'

Jennifer flicked through the contents of the wallet. The color drained from her cheeks as she glanced over the drivers licence. 'This can't be ...' Her voice trailed away, lost.

She felt a sudden stabbing pain in her temples.

'As I said, Ms Parkes, I know this is an enormous shock. Perhaps it's best to clear the matter up as soon as possible.'

Jennifer nodded, slowly. She felt numb all over, simply numb. Part of her mind insisted that this was a ridiculous, dreadful mistake; but another, deeper part had always known that this day would come. It should have come eighteen years before. Not now.

Why now?

Jennifer had done her grieving for Brian a long time ago. So why did she feel a stinging, watery sensation at the corners of her eyes.

I was over you a long time ago, Brian, wasn't I?

At the city morgue, Jennifer was ushered into a large, nondescript room. Long, flat tables and metal cabinets jutted out from odd corners and rows of small metal doors lined the far wall.

The attendant opened one of those doors and pulled out the tray containing a covered body. Jennifer was oblivious to the attendant. Her eyes were fixed on the body. She took a deep breath as the cover was folded downwards, revealing the face.

Eighteen years had passed since Jennifer had seen that face. The memories came flooding back. She felt a catch in her throat and a shiver ran down her spine like a lone teardrop, lost in the wrong part of her body. Eighteen years, yet his face was just as she remembered.

'Is this your husband?' Lachlan asked gently.

'It looks just like him,' Jennifer said.

'I need a positive ID from you, Ms Parkes.'

'It can't be Brian, Detective.'

'But is it?' Lachlan carefully retained the gentle quality to his tone. He could imagine how difficult this would be for any man or woman.

'Of course not, detective. If he'd been alive up until yesterday then Brian would have been forty-three years old. This man looks to be in his twenties. Mid twenties.'

Lachlan nodded in agreement. 'I can see that.' *This is the age Brian Parkes was on the night of his disappearance.* He regarded Jennifer. The same thought must have been running through her head. 'So, apart from the age discrepancy, this man appears to be your husband?'

'Yes.'

'Any distinguishing marks you can recall?'

Jennifer thought for a moment. 'A mole,' she said, 'right in the centre of his shoulder blades.' She remembered telling Brian that he should have it looked at; that she thought it was getting bigger. 'Everyone has funny little moles that look like they're getting bigger.' That had been so typical of Brian's gentle, cheeky humour. 'I've only got one so you just leave it alone.'

Lachlan gestured to the attendant, who turned the body over and lifted the sheet further. A mole rested in exactly the spot described by Jennifer. There was a slight drop to her jaw, and a gasp, but she said nothing.

Lachlan escorted her into the adjoining office and invited her to sit. He took another seat, facing her across an interviewing table. He noted that her eyes were glassy, her expression unmoving, as if cast in stone. 'Going by the physical description, and the personal effects he was carrying, it seems certain that the deceased is in fact your missing husband. I realise the shock-.'

'But the body in there isn't forty-three years old. Nowhere near it.'

'I agree. Rest assured, I'll be looking into that. I'm certain there's an explanation. In the meantime, a match of dental records will be completed by this afternoon and, given your comments, I'll wait for those records before finalising the identification. The dental check will confirm one way or another whether that man was your husband, or an imposter.'

An imposter, thought Jennifer, that must be it. Someone who looked just like Brian had. But why would a look-alike be carrying Brian's wallet? Where would he have got it? Why had he been run down on the same street where she and Brian had lived way back then?

'You'll let me know the result?' Jennifer asked.

'As soon as it comes through.'

Jennifer left the building. She wanted to put as much distance as possible between herself and the morgue. She felt a dozen tiny shivers, like icy pinpricks, stabbing at her insides. None of this made any sense and she expected the dental check wouldn't help, confirming that the body on that slab was Brian.

Deep inside she knew it was Brian. This didn't make any sense at all.

And what would it mean to her daughter Carly, born almost eight months after Brian's disappearance, to learn that the father she'd never known had been alive, somewhere, all these years? Carly, the living proof of Brian and Jennifer's love for one another, the single greatest treasure that Jennifer had been blessed with these past eighteen years.

How would Carly react to news as devastating as this? The thought made Jennifer shiver with an old despair.

FIVE

Roger Kaplan, at forty-two, was a younger version of his father. Not as handsome, nor as athletic, or as suave, but with the same characteristic traces of all three. What he lacked most was the inner fire, the charisma that made his father, up until now, one of Australia's most successful businessmen. Roger flashed an insipid smile at his father's secretary as he strode across the office and into the spacious corner suite.

Henry Kaplan stood at the window, arms behind him, surveying the view of Sydney Harbour. The sunlight sparkled across the water, clusters of tiny jewels riding the swells. A helicopter flew over the Sydney Opera House. This suite of offices was the Australian headquarters of the Kaplan Corporation.

Kaplan turned when he heard the footfalls at his doorway. 'You weren't in court.'

'I don't get my kicks parading around courthouses in front of TV cameras,' Roger said. 'That's more your style.'

'I didn't enjoy it any more than you would have.' Kaplan's tone echoed disdain. 'As the Chief Executive in Australia, you should have been there for the decision.'

'It wouldn't have made any difference. The decision was made; it was made months ago.'

'I never should've allowed you to extend our credit on Fenwicks and Sharvin Glass. They were never strong. You should have sold our holdings in those companies.'

'So it's all my fault, is it? Wake up, Dad. Blaming me isn't going to wash anymore. You've been paying six figure salaries for years to a bunch of financial advisors who've warned you to stop diversifying. You haven't listened to a bloody word they've said.'

'It's the local operation that's let us down, Roger. Reduced profits, expensive loans. Your financial status reports have been bullshit for years. I should've seen it coming.'

'And what do you call Southern Star Mining. That was your baby. Fifteen million borrowed from Hong Kong. That's what brought the whole thing crashing. Or don't you read the comments in Business Weekly anymore?'

'The financial journos can write about companies but they can't run them. They can't even manage their own petty cash accounts. Southern Star was the victim of the GFC and erratic high interest rates.'

'So if anything's a success around here it's because of you. If anything fails it's because of a stock market correction and greedy banks. The great Henry Kaplan's recipe for business acumen.'

Kaplan exploded. 'I've had it up to here with your blasted sarcasm. I've given you a million and one chances. You've never lived up to one of them, not one.'

He made a visible attempt to control his fury, sucking in deep breaths. He turned his back on his son, looking once more to the magnificent view of the water and the coat hanger shaped bridge that was famous all over the world. 'I called you in to ask if you had money put aside for yourself; money the receivers won't be able to trace.'

'I'm touched by your concern. Yes, you know I have.'

'Whatever you've done to keep your money hidden, I suggest you do doubly from now on. As officers of the corporation you and I, along with Johnson, Kopins and Masterton are personal bankrupts, or will be if the appeal fails. All our known and traceable assets will be frozen.'

'I know that.'

'The receivers and the corporate affairs people will be watching us like hawks in the meantime.'

'What about you?'

'Don't concern yourself with me.'

'What's next, then? What does Masterton think can save us? A break up and sell off of the companies?'

'That won't come anywhere near clearing the amount of debt to discharge the bankruptcy. The only chance we have is Southern Star. A buyer for the mining operation will put us back in business.'

'You could've put Southern Star on the market a year ago.'

'I'm doing it now.'

Roger sat on the three-seat leather lounge in the corner of the office. 'Do you think we can come back from this?'

'Can and will,' Kaplan said gruffly. 'I called you in for another reason as well. I need you to work closely beside me and the other directors, to project a united front. I have a potential buyer for Southern Star. Blue Ridge Corporation, the Canadian mining and munitions operation.'

'Of course. Conrad Becker's mob.'

'Becker and his chief executive, Wilfred Carlyle, are flying in late next week. They'll spend a couple of days here, speaking with our accountants and with the receivers, and specifically going over the details of buying out our holdings in Southern Star. After that we'll fly them up to Queensland to look over the mines and meet our key people there.'

'You think this will go through?'

'It has to. Everything hinges on this sale. Everything.' The phone on Kaplan's desk buzzed. He picked it up. 'Yes?'

'Excuse me, Mister Kaplan,' said Jodie Lenton, his secretary, 'I have a Ms Jennifer Parkes on the line for yourself or Roger.'

Kaplan beamed. It was a long time since he'd spoken to Jennifer. Speaking with her would be a refreshing change on this, the worst day of his life. 'Put her through, Jodie.' He covered the mouthpiece momentarily. 'Jennifer Parkes.'

Roger nodded. 'I thought she'd get in touch when the news came out.'

Kaplan switched the incoming call to conference mode. Jennifer's voice boomed out clearly over the loudspeaker. 'Hello, Henry?'

'Jennifer, always good to hear from you. It's been too long.'

'Must be close to a year. You're never in the country these days.'

'I wish I hadn't been today,' he said, an intended joke, only he wasn't smiling. 'Roger's with me, Jennifer. I've got you on loudspeaker.'

'Hi Roger.'

'Hi, Jennifer. Thanks for calling. As you can imagine, things are a little gloomy here right now.'

'I know this is lousy timing,' Jennifer said, 'but something has happened. I knew you'd both want to know.'

Kaplan and his son exchanged a worried glance. They'd both noted the anxiety in Jennifer's voice. 'What is it?' Kaplan asked.

'They've found Brian.'

Roger exchanged another glance with his father, only this time it was one of confusion. 'When?' he asked.

'This morning. He ... he died last night. A suspected hit and run.'

'Hold on.' Kaplan screwed his face up, totally perplexed. 'You mean to tell me he'd been alive somewhere all these years?'

'Apparently.'

'You don't sound convinced. Are they sure ... are *you* sure that it's him?'

There was no reply.

Roger voiced his astonishment. 'It wasn't like Brian to do something like that. Disappear. Tell no one.' He muttered half to himself. 'He just wasn't like that.'

'I suppose none of us know what anyone is really like,' Kaplan said.

Roger recognised this as something his father had said many times before, usually in conjunction with business matters. 'That's hardly the point, Dad. Jennifer, where are you calling from?'

'My office.'

'Stay put. We're coming over to see you,' said Kaplan.

'No, Henry. You and Roger have enough on your plate right now.'

'Blast what's on our plate.' Kaplan was insistent. He'd adopted his familiar and persuasive style, the one that came so naturally to him. 'This is a hell of a shock for you. For all of us. We'll be across town in twenty minutes or so.' He flicked off the conference line switch.

'Well, what do you make of that?' he said, thinking aloud. 'Eighteen years ago I spent fifty thousand dollars on two separate private detectives trying to trace Brian Parkes.'

'I remember. There was no angle they didn't follow up on.'

'They came up with nothing.' Kaplan shook his head in amazement. 'Not a single solitary clue. Everyone, including the police, was certain he'd been killed and buried somewhere.'

'Except Jennifer, Dad. She never gave up hope.'

'Oh, I think she did. She knew he was gone.' He winced. The memory of Jennifer's despair was still painful to him, even now. 'She'd never admit it, not even to herself, but she knew.'

'But we were all wrong.'

Kaplan didn't reply. He grabbed his coat and headed for the door, gesturing for Roger to follow.

Jennifer was at her desk, deep in thought, when Cindy came in. 'Carmen said you were back.'

'I've just been talking to Henry and Roger Kaplan. I wanted them to hear it from me.'

'It *was* Brian?'

'Yes.'

'I'm so sorry, Jen. To have to go through this now, after so long.'

Jennifer didn't appear to have heard. Her face remained impassive. 'At least, it looked like Brian. I don't really know who it was.'

'What do you mean?'

'The face on the body looked just as Brian did at twenty-five. It couldn't really have been him. Must be a look-alike.'

Cindy tried not to show her alarm. Jennifer wasn't making sense. Was she rambling? 'But you identified the body as Brian's?'

'I think I did. I'm not sure now. So confused. The police wouldn't listen. They said it must be him, pushed me a little. The dental check will prove it one way or another.'

'You said you spoke to the Kaplans. They knew Brian?'

'Yes. Roger Kaplan was one of Brian's best friends. They went to university together. Rich man, poor man, that was how Brian used to refer to Roger and himself.' Jennifer smiled at that memory; her eyes taking on a faraway expression.

Cindy realised that Jennifer was back there, re-living it.

Jennifer continued, 'Brian came from a poor family. He actually got into uni to study accountancy on a scholarship.'

'And Roger was the rich one.' It was more a statement than a question.

'Yes. Even then, Henry was a well-known go-getter. He owned a string of companies in the industrial and manufacturing fields, but you never really knew what. He was always buying and selling. He put Roger through Business Administration so that he could assume managerial roles in his companies. After they graduated Roger and Brian remained firm friends.'

Cindy thought back over some of the things Jennifer had told her during the two years they'd worked together. 'Your husband started his own accountancy firm, didn't he?'

'Just a few months before he vanished. It was his dream. He set it up on the strength of projects assigned to him by the Kaplan Corporation, from the divisions Roger ran at the time. Brian didn't rely on that, though, he made sure he had other accounts as well.'

'What about Brian's parents, Jen? Are they still living?'

'No. They've both passed on.'

'Oh.' Cindy shuffled her feet. She felt awkward. She wanted to console her friend and colleague somehow. She wanted to tell Jennifer that Brian must have been a wonderful man. If that was the case, though, then why had he walked out of the lives of everyone who knew him?

'They never got over it, Cindy. They were shattered.'

Cindy took Jennifer by the hand, clasping it tightly. 'As big a shock as this might be, you can't let it drag you back over old ground. That part of your life was over eighteen years ago.'

'I know. I'll be okay. Really. And there's no need for Henry and Roger to come charging over. I don't see that much of them these days, anyhow.'

Cindy squeezed Jennifer's hand and gave her a reassuring smile. She could see that her friend had been dragged back across the years. And what was all this Jennifer had said about a look-alike and dental records for proof of identity?

Cindy only knew that a shiver passed through her when she looked into her employer's eyes and saw the haunted expression.

Drew McIntyre had been in the Coroners Department for fifteen years. In that time there wasn't much he hadn't seen. A short, pudgy man, with puffy eyes and a comfortable smile, he was leaving his office when Neil Lachlan crossed his path.

'Just on my way out,' McIntyre said. 'Something I can do for you?'

'Dr. McIntyre? Detective Senior Sergeant Neil Lachlan.' He offered his hand and the two men shook.

'Seen your name on a few documents just lately.'

'I'm still one of the newbies in Homicide. Used to be with the Drug Squad.'

'Well, it's always good to put a face to a name. I've got to rush though, sergeant, I'm due in the lab for an autopsy.'

'I realize your report on the Parkes case isn't complete, but I've scanned your initial findings. It would help if I could run through a few things with you.'

'Walk with me,' McIntyre said. Lachlan fell into step beside him as they headed down the corridor. 'This is the hit/run? The man missing eighteen years?'

'That's right,' said Lachlan. 'Your estimated time of death was approximately six hours before the body was found, around one a.m.'

'Yes. Very minor cellular damage. Rigor mortis and discolouring barely started.'

'The widow said the body looked exactly as her husband had looked eighteen years ago, when he disappeared aged twenty-five. She said he couldn't look the same now.'

'I saw that in the paperwork. Nevertheless, the dental check has confirmed the identity.'

'I called for the dental charts because Ms Parkes thought the man was too young. I needed to rule out the possibility of a look-alike.'

'The youthful appearance is puzzling.' McIntyre shrugged. 'On the one hand it's an unusual case, but on the other it's straightforward. The body's been positively identified and the cause of death is clear.'

Lachlan pressed the point. 'But the widow is adamant. If it is her husband then he hasn't aged from that day to this. What do you make of that?'

'Nonsense, I'm sure you'd agree. Just because the man looks young doesn't mean he hadn't aged. And determining exact age in a situation like this can be a very tricky thing. Let me elaborate –

'Up until the age of twenty-five, dental development is very consistent. From that alone we can be accurate in determining the age of a child or a young adult. Likewise with older people. There are pathological changes such as arterial degeneration and arthritis. And from the early forties sutures of the skull vault begin to close at a standard rate. This affords a reasonable degree of accuracy in determining age.

'The middle adult years are the most difficult. There's minor organ deterioration, if any, and this - along with physical appearance - varies widely from one person to another. It's strange, of course, for a fortyish man to pass for mid-twenties, but it's not impossible. For goodness sake, Cliff Richard looked boyish until he was in his fifties.

'So, we can't guarantee accuracy in that age group. I certainly can't support some woman's claim that her husband hadn't actually aged. That's preposterous.'

Lachlan conceded the point with a nod. Technically, McIntyre was correct in his observations. But Lachlan had seen the body of Brian Parkes and he didn't believe it belonged to a forty-three year old man. 'There was nothing in your internal physical examination to suggest a discrepancy in the age?'

'Only in the bones. You see, certain skeletal changes take place between thirty and forty. This man did not show any of the changes that I'd expect to see happen by the age of forty-three. But once again, this isn't definitive enough to contradict his known birth date. It's rare, but a freak hormonal condition could slow skeletal changes, just as in some people it could accelerate them. Can't be ruled out.'

'What about plastic surgery? That could explain Parkes' youthful appearance.'

'No surgery of any kind.'

'Drugs? Unusual substances in his system?'

'Nothing unusual. Only nicotine. The autopsy showed none of the things you're looking for, I'm afraid. Apart from the injuries sustained in the accident, Parkes was in excellent condition and good health. The question of age doesn't concern me, detective, it's something else entirely that jumps out and will be in my report. One highly unusual fact. I found a surgical puncture mark to his right jugular vein for which there's no rational explanation.'

'His jugular? That would cause fatal bleeding.'

'Not in this case. The puncture was made post mortem, so no bleeding.'

'You're saying someone came along while the guy was dead in the street and stuck something in his throat?'

McIntyre shrugged. 'That appears to be the case. I'm afraid I can't shed any further light on that, other than the incision was made by someone with surgical know-how.'

'But it had nothing to do with the cause of death?'

'No.'

Frustration gnawed at Lachlan. 'What will your official summary be, doctor?'

'Death due to injuries sustained in a hit/run, with a person or persons unknown interfering with the body afterwards.'

'What about a coronial enquiry?'

'That's up to the courts. However, with evidence as flimsy as this, it's hardly likely.' They arrived at the lab. 'Sorry I can't help more, but I must get on with it.' McIntyre disappeared through the double swing doors. 'Good luck with your investigation.'

'Thanks for your help.' Lachlan didn't think the examiner had been much help at all. He'd raised even more questions without coming up with solutions, which reminded him that coroners dealt with facts, not fantasies. And, as McIntyre had said, the known facts to this case were mostly straightforward.

He pondered the Parkes mystery as he drove back to Hurstville Police Station. The dental records matched so the body had to be Parkes. Didn't it? If that was the case, why was there no sign of ageing?

And how the hell did he get a post mortem surgical incision to his jugular vein?

Why had he turned up now, in the exact same place from which he'd vanished years before?

Lachlan cast himself back to the discovery of the body. He'd looked into the face of Brian Parkes. There had been no fear, no pain, no indication of what Parkes had seen or heard in his final moments.

Just the ordinary face of a young man who seemed to have grown no older.

SIX

Henry Kaplan embraced Jennifer and hugged her tightly. 'You look marvellous,' he said, 'and I see you're still doing wonderful things with this business. Six stores now, isn't it?'

'Boutiques,' Jennifer corrected him, 'and yes, six.'

'Plans for more?'

'No. I'm happy with the size we are now, and the current economic climate is not the time for expansion.'

'Expansion was our undoing,' Kaplan reflected.

Watching Jennifer, Kaplan noted that age suited her. *She's one of the lucky ones.*

Her face, with serene blue eyes and finely chiseled cheekbones, was untouched by lines except for those that ran in slight creases beneath her eyes. But these were hardly crow's feet - instead they were true laughter lines, soft shadows that crept playfully across the top of her cheeks, magnifying her natural warmth. The medium length hair was still raven black, parted a little to the side, the style shorter than when he'd last seen her and perfect for accentuating those eyes.

Kaplan recalled that he'd always regarded her slender figure as that of a dancer's, and this view remained unchanged. If there was a difference it came in the distribution of her weight, so that she was now shapelier than he remembered.

Roger had entered the office behind his father. He leaned towards Jennifer to kiss her on the cheek. 'It's been a week for bad news all round.'

'Yes.' Jennifer leaned back against the side of her desk, arms folded, gazing at the two men. So long since the three of them had been together like this. She could see how much Roger's physical appearance had followed that of his father. The thickening eyebrows, the cleft in the chin more pronounced now than when he was younger.

'How's that gorgeous girl of yours?' Kaplan asked.

'Carly's fine, Henry, and not so little now.'

'You sounded uncertain on the phone. About the body,' Roger said.

'He looked exactly the same as the night he disappeared. The same clothes, the same wallet with the same driver's licence. It's as though he stepped through a hole in time from that day to this.'

'Nonsense,' Henry Kaplan said. 'I'm sure these things were mere coincidence. And don't discount the idea. I've observed over the years that coincidence plays a part in all our lives. Happens every day in dozens of ways, big and small.'

'But his *face*, Henry.'

'Perhaps you saw him the way you remembered him. It was the shock. I'm sure that's what it must have been.'

'But are you certain it was him?' Roger asked. 'Could it have been someone else who looked like him?'

'I thought that must have been the case. But the police just phoned. The teeth on the body match Brian's old dental records.'

'You need to get out of here,' Kaplan said. 'We all need a breather at the moment. Let Roger and I take you to dinner tonight.'

'I'd love to, but an old friend is coming around later. Meg Tanner. I phoned her last night with the news.'

'Meg Tanner? Was that Meg Roberts?' Roger asked.

'Yes. Her maiden name.'

'I remember her. She was a great comfort to you back then.'

'You all were.' She focused her attention on Henry Kaplan. 'You've done so much to help me over the years. Getting me started in this business ...'

Kaplan waved away the praise. 'Bring Meg Tanner with you. We'll all dine together.' He strode over to Jennifer's desk, picked up the phone and held it out to her. In control, as always. 'Call her now. We'll make arrangements to meet at Eduardo's.'

Jennifer smiled. Henry Kaplan's style of command always made the recipients of his attention feel secure. 'If you insist.'

He grinned back at her. 'I always insist. It's what I do'

Soft, muted lights gave the French restaurant an old world charm. An Edith Piaf record played softly in the background, adding to the Parisian air and the Gallic decor. Grainy black and white photographs of the landmarks of Paris, circa 1920's, adorned the walls in gold embossed frames.

Meg arrived at seven-fifteen and the waiter, dark hair, dark eyes, tight black trousers with velvet sash, showed her to the table. Jennifer handled the introductions.

'A pleasure to meet you,' said Kaplan. 'We've just been hearing all about you.'

'Don't believe a word.' She took her seat and nodded to Roger.

'We've heard only good things,' Kaplan told her.

'Like I said, don't believe a word.'

Kaplan laughed.

'It's been a long time,' Roger said, 'we met a few times, many years ago, at Jennifer's place.'

'Of course.' Meg moved quickly to change the subject. She didn't want the discussion focusing on the past, when Jennifer and Brian had been newlyweds. 'You'd think, both being friends of Jennifer's, that our paths might have crossed a little more often.' She grinned. 'Perhaps she's been deliberately keeping us apart.'

'Wouldn't put it past her.'

Meg laughed at his joke but moved quickly again to change the subject. 'I'm sorry to hear about your business troubles. Awful news.'

'The last few years have been the toughest on business in a long time,' Kaplan explained. 'Of course I'm not telling you anything you didn't already know. It's been a struggle for everyone. In retrospect, we should have adapted faster. The GFC changed the financial landscape. We're a corporation with our fingers in lots of pies, stretched too thin for too long.'

'Like us, a lot of corporations with diverse interests and large debt have fallen into trouble,' Roger added.

Kaplan shot a nondescript look at his son. 'We were particularly over exposed with debt in our Australian based companies.'

Roger glanced at his father but said nothing. He simply lifted his glass of wine to his lips and sipped casually.

Jennifer noticed Roger's glance. It confirmed her suspicion that the life-long antagonism and rivalry between father and son was still there, bubbling under the surface, consistently coming to a head. It had been like that years ago and even then it had been something she could sense.

She'd never known the real reason for it. Kaplan was a self-made man and Roger, like too many rich sons, had taken the money and prestige for granted. Roger had coasted through university, an average student, secure in the knowledge that a senior management position awaited him. Jennifer suspected that was the core of Henry Kaplan's resentment and frustration. He knew his son was lazy and arrogant. However, Kaplan's pride made him intent on having his own son and heir inherit his business empire.

For the past decade, Kaplan had been building the corporation in North America and Canada while Roger steered the local divisions deeper and deeper into debt. At least, that was the impression now given by Henry Kaplan. Jennifer was well aware that for the past few years the Kaplan Corporation had been rocked by one financial crisis and panic sell-off after another. The troubled fortunes of the proud family had shifted from the financial sections to the general news pages of the print media. It was one of several drawn-out corporate collapses throughout Australia.

The waiter arrived to take the dinner orders. He scribbled down the ladies' orders first. Then, as he turned to Kaplan and Roger, Meg directed her attention to Jennifer. Both sipped their wine. 'You're holding up well,' Meg observed.

'Being out with you lot helps. I don't know how I'll be later. I was feeling a little ... weird ... last night.'

'You sounded strained when you phoned.'

'Trying to take it in, make some sense of it. I was stunned.'

'You can't let it get to you, Jen. It was a long time ago, another life for you. For both of us, actually.'

'I know. I remember that day, after Brian vanished. You were waiting by the house when I got home from the police station.'

'Was I?' Meg squinted her eyes and made a face, trying to remember.

'You stayed with me, made lots of pots of tea, and a few strong scotches, while I cried.'

'That's right. That was the day you told me you thought you were pregnant.'

'How is Carly?' asked Roger.

'Rebellious, obnoxious and incredibly beautiful.'

'Still the same, huh. She must be ... what? ... seventeen?'

'Yes.'

'Still shacked up with that guy?' Meg wondered. 'Willy? Wally?'

'Rory.'

'Right. Rory.'

'She's still with him. Still doing a spot of modelling.'

'And still hanging around with Rory's radical, weirdo, socialist friends?' Meg supposed.

Jennifer took another sip of wine and frowned. A hint of resignation crept into her voice. 'I really don't know what to do about that.'

She had mental flashes of the years spent as a single mother.

It hadn't been easy, raising a daughter alone. She'd had to work to support them, and her burgeoning fashion career offered her the best opportunities. The downside had been the countless times she'd left Carly with babysitters and relatives. Too many nights and weekends when a mother should've been with her daughter.

There'd been so many times when Jennifer's own feelings were reflected in Carly's sad little eyes, watching her leave the house.

I didn't put motherhood first, Jennifer thought.

But Carly had been a good child. It wasn't until the teenage years that she'd become increasingly difficult.

'You're talking about Carly?' Kaplan wondered out loud, interjecting after the waiter had left with the orders.

Jennifer nodded.

'The last time I saw her she was this high,' Henry Kaplan said, using the outstretched flat palm of his hand to indicate the height. 'A cute little tyke with braces and pigtails.'

'That cute little tyke is seventeen going on twenty-five,' Jennifer replied. 'A straight A student at school, she dropped out to go and live with some creep. He's filled her head with nonsense about the corruption of the capitalist system, which of course puts me in the realm of the public enemy.'

'Sounds like a throwback to the sixties,' Roger commented.

'Worse,' said Jennifer.

'Apparently, though, Carly doesn't mind earning cash from the very capitalist business of modelling,' Meg added.

'What makes my blood boil,' Jennifer confided, 'is she's giving most of her money to radical groups suggested by Rory. It seems it's okay to use capitalist income to help further socialist causes.'

Kaplan grunted. 'How did this happen?'

'I don't think I was a very good mother.'

'Rubbish!'

'Perhaps we should change the subject,' Meg suggested. 'After all, this dinner is supposed to help us all forget our worries for a while.'

'I'll drink to that,' Roger agreed and he raised his glass. The others followed his lead.

Jennifer smiled weakly. No one would agree for a moment that she'd been a bad mother and over the years she'd certainly never thought of herself that way.

She felt differently now.

On reflection, she knew she hadn't been there enough for her daughter.

From the time Kaplan loaned her the money to set up Wishing Pool Fashions she'd directed most of her energy to her work. Later, when the insurance money from Brian's policy had finally been paid, she'd repaid the loan and bought out Kaplan's share in the business.

He was happy to let her have total ownership of the company to which she was so devoted. She had named the business Wishing Pool Fashions, in memory of Brian and the quaint little wishing pool rockery at the old house. She felt that a part of Brian - of the life they'd never had together - was the legacy of her company.

Such a stupid damn notion, she realised now.

I had Carly. She was the legacy of Brian and myself. I should've been spending more time with her. Oh, she had everything she ever needed - clothes, dolls, friends, nannies - she just didn't see enough of her mother.

There were so many nights when Jennifer had been away on business - cocktail party functions; fashion shows; late nights at the factory when they'd had huge orders to fill. As a child, Carly never complained.

On those occasions when they'd been together, Jennifer had always felt close to her daughter. Looking back now, she remembered the plaintive expression in Carly's eyes when she'd told her she'd be home late that night.

'Can I wait up for you, Mummy?'

'Of course, dear. But I'm going to be very, very late tonight.'

'I can stay awake!'

She never did.

Jennifer's own mother had been the same. Her father had been a solicitor, her mother a sales manageress for a cosmetics company - a career woman in an age before it became fashionable. Loving parents who were always so busy, *too* busy.

Kaplan had drifted into small talk with Roger and Meg. They were startled when Jennifer suddenly announced out loud, cutting across their conversation, 'I was never there for Carly.'

Kaplan and Roger looked bewildered.

Meg understood that Jennifer was still fighting a flood of memories. She reached across, took Jennifer's hand in hers, and gave it an affectionate squeeze.

Henry and Roger had each taken their own cars to Eduardo's. As Jennifer had caught a cab from her office to the restaurant, Roger jumped in first and offered to drive her back to her office car-space.

'I still think about you often,' he said as he drove. He was glad for the chance to have a few minutes alone with her. 'I sometimes wonder how things might have been.'

'You shouldn't. It was a long time ago.'

'You ever wonder? About us?'

'It's in the past, Roger. We've both moved on.'

'You're right, of course. You always would've thought of me first as Brian's best friend.'

'And you always would've seen me as Brian's widow. Brian meant too much to both of us for it to have been any different.'

'Did you ever come close to marrying again?'

'No. Not close. You?'

'The same.' He drove on for a short while in silence. 'I've had some good relationships. But there's a point in every romance where you have to be prepared to ...' he searched for the right words, '... make a deeper commitment. I always seem to go wandering off around that time.'

'I can't criticise you on that. I've been exactly the same.'

Roger parked the car outside her office block. 'I meant what I said earlier. About helping.'

'I know.' Jennifer touched his arm to register her thanks.

'When Brian disappeared and you really needed help, well, it was Dad who stepped in, took command, did everything. As usual I was left trailing behind. But I really wished I could've done something.'

'You did. You were a friend to me as much as you'd been to Brian. So don't sweat it, okay?'

'Okay.' He smiled awkwardly and they embraced.

'If there's anything you can do to help I'll let you know,' she assured him before saying good-night and stepping from the car.

Driving home in her own vehicle, Jennifer thought back to the months following Brian's disappearance. Roger, like his father, phoned regularly to see how she was coping. He'd met her for coffee once or twice a week and they'd gone to dinner once a fortnight.

At first they'd discussed every possible aspect of the disappearance and the failure by police and private investigators to unearth any leads. As time progressed, they began to speak of themselves and what the future held - Jennifer with her pregnancy and her fashion world ambitions; Roger with the pressures facing him in the family empire.

After Carly's birth Roger had become serious, revealing the depth of his growing feelings for Jennifer.

Initially, Jennifer responded in a positive way to Roger's overtures. He had a sensitive side to him. They had a shared grief over Brian. But before long she realised her attraction to Roger was based more on familiarity and friendship than it was on anything deeply spiritual or physical.

They'd almost made love once, if you could call it that - an awkward tumbling about, the necessary spark failing to ignite for either of them.

Jennifer told him that whilst they'd always be friends they'd never be lovers. That it would be best if they saw a little less of each other and sought romance elsewhere. Sheepishly, he'd agreed.

Poor, sweet Roger. Still lost. Thought of in some quarters as the wealthy, aimless playboy but that wasn't totally fair. He wasn't as lazy or as arrogant now as he had been when younger. He'd never be the dynamic leader his father had wanted him to be. But at the same time, Roger had a quiet, caring quality that was quite different to anything she'd ever seen in Henry Kaplan.

And, for the first time, she did wonder what it might have been like if things had turned out differently between her and Roger.

SEVEN

It was two months since he'd first suspected he was free of the shadows.

Over the years the jogger had become sensitive to the fact he was being watched whenever he was out and about. Although he rarely saw the watchers, he knew they were there. They'd never gone away. A long time ago he'd become adept at noting the figures following him in a crowd, or driving behind him at a discreet distance. If he dined at a restaurant, or went to a movie, he usually had a reasonable idea who the watchers were.

Of course, he could never be certain. There was never a familiar face, never a give-away look in the eye; and while he was suspicious of large, powerfully built men, that was no guarantee.

Once, many years before, he'd attempted to draw these shadowy figures out. He drove to a lonely bush setting in the early morning, left his car by the side of the road and hid in the bush with binoculars. He trained his sights on the road. A car stopped further back, within sight of his own vehicle. There were two men in that car. Waiting. Watching.

Who the hell were these people? Clearly their mission was to stop him from killing. They had succeeded at that, but they left him free to go about his business. His only release in inflicting pain came with the prostitutes who visited him each month. Always a different girl, always with the faceless, nameless minders waiting outside the door.

Even when the jogger had travelled interstate or overseas, or changed address, the watchers were there.

This had been going on for eighteen years. In the early days he thought it would drive him mad. How had they known about him? If they wanted him stopped, why didn't they turn him in to the authorities? Surely that made more sense than running a twenty-four hour, seven-day-a week surveillance. Who, or what, could do such a thing?

He tried to bribe the prostitutes and their minders. Tell me who sent you? Tell me why?

The men outside never spoke. The girls too could never be budged on the subject, they never told him anything at all.

The jogger's next step was to hire a private detective, six months after the surveillance had begun. He sought out a seedy character from Sydney's notorious Kings Cross district. Carstairs was an ex-cop with underworld connections. His assignment was to find out who the people trailing the jogger were.

The jogger didn't tell Carstairs about his own dark secret. There was no need for that.

A week after Carstairs commenced work, he vanished. The jogger went back after seven days to find that the private detective had closed his run-down office and left town. Had he been scared away? Or paid off?

The jogger wondered if he was part of some obscure criminal justice experiment? From time to time he tried to research that subject, but he never found anything remotely like the situation he was experiencing.

No, this wasn't some bizarre experiment.

The strange thing was that the jogger began to reluctantly accept his predicament. After all, what could he do? He couldn't risk going to the police. As the months turned into years he grew accustomed to the invisible surveillance, as a prisoner gets used to the confines of his cell. He stopped looking for victims; stopped stalking the streets in the lonely, quiet hours.

He still jogged, he had come to enjoy it, but only for fitness.

Perhaps, if he lived like a saint, then the strange vigil would end. Month after month, year after year, he hoped the watchmen would decide he was cured and leave him alone. He went as far as playing it straight with the prostitutes. Eventually, he realised the ploy wasn't going to work. Five years had passed and the shadows remained. He started treating the girls rough again. It was the only satisfaction he could get.

It wasn't enough - there were times when he felt sure the frustration would tear him apart. There was even one dark, prolonged period when he considered suicide.

In time, all of that passed. He learned to live with the frustration; with the watchers; with the maddening curiosity of who they were and how they managed to maintain their endless vigil.

Life went on.

When the jogger first suspected the watchers had left him, he did nothing. After all, it was just a feeling. He sensed the eyes were no longer upon him. He hadn't picked up the now familiar signs of a follower in the crowd, or a car always just within view.

It must be my imagination.

It was a funny kind of delusion to get after all these years. But this sense that something had changed persisted.

He decided to put his feelings to the test. Why not? He had nothing to lose.

He rose early and drove to a long stretch of road in a country area. He remembered having done this once before, many years ago. He found a vantage point in the bush and scanned the road with binoculars. He'd suspected all the way out that no one had followed him but he couldn't be certain. The watchers were brilliant at staying out of sight, moving as though they were part of the surrounding landscape.

No car. He stood and watched for half an hour, swinging the sights of the binoculars in every direction. No lurking cars. No followers.

No one watching, waiting.

The electric surge of excitement began then. The desire exploded violently inside him; fantasies filled his mind.

He drove home and wondered about returning to his old ways. The thought was delicious. It can begin again, he thought. At long last. Fulfilment. Real fulfilment.

Later, he worried that he was getting carried away too soon. What if it was some kind of trick? An attempt to draw him out one last time so he could be caught red-handed by police.

Why? Why do that after all this time?

He decided the best course of action was to play it safe. Another three weeks passed. Every day and every night the jogger's head was filled with his vicious dreams. The thrill of it; how he had missed the savagery, the all-powerful sensation of exerting command over life and death.

Twenty-seven year old Trish Van Helegen was a second generation Australian, the daughter of Dutch parents who had settled in Sydney in the late 1970s. She always woke instantly when the pre-set radio alarm clock switched on at 5.45. This morning she opened her eyes to the solid rock beat and melodic swirls of Michael Jackson's *Dangerous*. She sat up, stretched, and then elbowed her slumbering boyfriend in the side. 'Today's the day, lover,' she said.

The young man mumbled and shifted position. Trish smiled to herself. All his talk of getting up and jogging with her in the mornings, all his promises. He never budged. This time, though, they had a bet. She was going to make sure she went through with it, partly for fun, and partly to teach him a lesson about making promises and not keeping them.

She placed her hands on his shoulders and shook him vigorously. 'Today's the day,' she repeated, 'the day you leap out of bed and join me on the run.'

'Not today, hon,' he drawled, still half asleep.

'Don't forget our little wager,' Trish reminded him. 'If you don't jog with me today, no sex for a week. Remember?'

'Hmm.' He rolled over, buried his face deeper into the pillow.

'You don't think I'll make you do without, do you?'

'Not today, honey. Tomorrow. I promise.'

'Last chance. Get up.' She slapped his backside through the blanket. 'Come on. Or no slap'n'tickle for seven whole days and nights.'

There was no response.

'Trent!'

He stirred slightly. 'Tomorrow, hon.'

Trish laughed to herself as she went through to the shower. The hot needlepoint of the water sprayed over her. She could barely wait to feel the brisk, dawn breeze lift her sandy hair as she jogged around the narrow path of the nearby reserve.

The funny thing was she'd started her period the night before, so sex was out anyway for the next week, or near enough to it. She wouldn't tell Trent, not for a few days at least. She would keep up the pretence. It would teach him a lesson - and hopefully result in his joining her for the runs. She would love to have Trent jogging alongside her, sharing the exhilaration and the freedom.

She stepped from the shower recess, towelled herself dry, slipped into shorts, tee shirt and running shoes. She would need another shower - a proper one - when she got back, but she always loved that initial, brief burst of water rushing over her when she first woke. With any luck, she thought, I'll be able to drag Trent into the shower with me when he finally starts getting up earlier. Then she thought, maybe that's not such a good idea. She giggled, imagining those long, loose limbs, sinewy and sleek. She wouldn't get any jogging done if she started the day in the shower with Trent.

It was a four-minute drive to the reserve, a large, leafy stretch of green at the far end of the semi-rural suburb.

She had lived in the apartment with Trent for the past two months and so far it was working out well. From the moment she'd met Trent at a party six months before she had the suspicion that, finally, she'd met the right man.

Trish parked by the side of the reserve. The path ran the full perimeter of the park and was ideal for joggers. In total, it was a run of two kilometres. One lap was just right for Trish. It kept her body trim, her muscles nicely toned, without wearing her down to the point of exhaustion.

She started out slowly, as she always did, building momentum as she went. It was early spring, and over the past few days she had noticed a considerable warming. This morning there was a stunning blue sky. The sun was already hot, unseasonably so, nature's preview of the not too distant summer.

Trish loved this parkland. The air was always fresh and clean here, even though she could sometimes see a brown haze lingering over the city skyline in the distance. It was the main reason she liked living outside the suburbia of Sydney, away from the smog.

She'd been jogging for fifteen minutes when she saw the other runner on the path ahead of her. A man, dressed in a blue tracksuit with white trim. He was also wearing a cap. It occurred to her that he was still dressed for the colder weather and moving slower than her. It wasn't long before she passed him on the narrow track.

'You'll work up quite a sweat in that outfit,' she called out as she glided by.

His face, looking down as he ran, was mostly hidden, the cap pushed down low on his forehead. It had a long, broad brim. She caught the flash of a grin as he waved in response. If he said anything Trish didn't catch it as she sped by. She was really moving now. She felt energised.

Up ahead was a familiar curve in the path, a spot where the surrounding trees and hedges of bush obscured the path from view. Trish slowed down as she rounded the bend.

Never return to the scene of the crime. That was how the old saying went. It amused the jogger that he'd returned here, even though this wasn't actually the scene of any crime. It was the scene of the crime that never was. The first time the watchers had appeared and foiled his plan; a day he would never forget.

He wondered what kind of life his intended victim had lived over the past eighteen years. He recalled that she was a fair-haired, plump young woman. She'd been so close to death, the thought excited him. So close. Had she any idea how lucky she was to be saved? Wherever she was now, did she ever think of that morning, so long ago?

It was a brilliant stroke, the jogger reasoned, to return here for his rebirth. And that's how he thought of this, his return, his freedom. His resurgence. He couldn't believe his luck when he found that this beautiful young female jogged here every morning. Alone.

This was perfect. A dream come true, as though it was meant to be. Of course, he told himself, that's it.

Fate. This is meant to be.

The girl was pulling further away. The jogger increased his pace, came up behind her, the coil of wire unravelling in his hand. All of a sudden he felt as though he'd done this only days ago; the long years of frustration melted into nothingness.

He was exploding inside with his need. Adrenaline surged; the dark power gripped him and rocked him feverishly. It seemed so natural, felt so right. He lunged forward swiftly, slipping the wire around the girl's neck, pulling the loop tight.

Trish Van Helegen gasped for air. The wire cut into her flesh and squeezed the breath from her throat. Despite the shock and the sudden searing pain, her mind snapped to the alert. She swung her elbows back, searching for her attacker's rib cage, but the jogger easily sidestepped her arms while maintaining his vice like grip on the wire. This one was going to fight.

He kicked his leg forward, smashing into the back of Trish's knee, causing her to lose her sense of balance. Her hands went to her throat now in a vain attempt to loosen the garrotte, but the thin steely band was imbedded in the skin, blood seeping from the gash.

The jogger pushed her to the ground and straddled her from behind. He released the tension on the wire slightly. He knew he was playing with fire - after all, this one had guts - but he wanted to play. He deserved to prolong his pleasure after waiting almost two decades.

Trish was weak, disorientated and barely breathing. She felt the loosening of the wire and somewhere, in her mind, came a flash of understanding, a ray of hope. Got to fight this, a voice screamed inside her head. *Got to ...* She tried to push herself up again, using her knees while simultaneously raising her hands to her throat. Her assailant snapped the wire tight once more and pushed his knee into the small of her back, forcing her further toward the ground.

Now she began to writhe, a curious gurgling, whining sound escaping her lips as her body jerked in a series of spasms. They were violent, desperate movements. Then they stopped, her body limp.

The jogger's excitement was at fever pitch, his own breath coming in short, deep gasps. Still straddling the corpse of his victim, he felt as though he was going to explode. He whipped his head about. The reserve was empty, as it had been on the previous two mornings he'd come to survey the scene. It was early, little chance of anyone happening by.

He pulled the girl's shorts down, ripped her panties feverishly with his bare hands and thrust himself roughly into her. He shivered with the sweet sensation of relief as the morning light strengthened, streaming through the crossbeams of the branches in spidery patterns.

EIGHT

Todd Lachlan stepped from the car and waved as his best friend, Mark Harris, and Mark's father drove away in their brand new Holden.

It was late – eight-thirty-five, almost his bedtime. The air was balmy, the first real taste of spring. He bounded up the front steps and through the front door of the modest brick and fibro home.

His mother, Marcia, was vacuuming the lounge room. She smiled and called out to him over the roar of the appliance, 'How was soccer tonight, love?'

'Soccer *practice* Mum.' Todd shrugged, walking into the kitchen. 'Fine, I guess.' A bright, energetic ten-year old, he had an impish grin and a mess of curly brown hair.

'I'll be finished here in a minute,' Marcia called after him.

Todd poured a glass of coke and sloshed it down. Just a couple of days to the weekend and this one he spent with his father. It seemed longer than almost two weeks since the last one and he was longing to spend time with his dad.

The drone of the vacuum cleaner stopped and Marcia Lachlan came into the kitchen. 'I've a thirsty little man here, have I?'

'Mmm.' Todd took another mouthful.

'Bedtime,' Marcia said, indicating the wall clock.

'Uh huh.' Todd grimaced and placed his empty cup on the counter top. His mother placed her arms around his shoulders and they went into his bedroom.

'I've got some news, good and bad,' Marcia said.

Todd was curious. 'Yeah?' He pulled his soccer shirt off over his head.

'Your Grandpa is quite ill. He's in hospital with bronchial pneumonia.'

'What's that, Mum?'

'It's a serious infection in the chest, love. A bit like the flu, but much worse. That's the bad news. Anyway, we're going to Brisbane to visit him. We may be there for a week or so. That's kind'a the good news, because you get a trip away and a few days off school.'

'When?'

'We're going to fly up tomorrow, darling.'

Alarm bells rang in Todd's head. 'Tomorrow! But, Mum, that means I won't be here for the weekend. I'll miss seeing Dad.'

'I know, dear. I know how disappointed you must be, but sometimes these things just can't be helped.'

'Mum, I don't want to miss seeing Dad.' Todd's voice rose. The one thing that made his temper flare more than anything else was the anxiety he felt over his parents' separation. 'Can't we see Grandpa next week?'

'Todd, don't make this any more difficult than it already is. Grandpa is sick now. When you're going somewhere to support a family member who's ill you can't just put if off.'

'I don't care. I'm not going!'

'I won't enter into an argument over this, Todd. We're flying up tomorrow and that's that.' Marcia headed for the door. 'And if you're going to make this so damn hard for me then you can get ready for bed on your own.'

'You just don't want me to see Dad,' Todd screamed after her, 'because you hate him, don't you?'

Marcia paused at the door and glared back at her son. 'You can be terribly cruel sometimes. Of course I don't hate your father, how could you say such a thing?'

'Yes, you do. You hate him and you don't want me to see him!'

Marcia slammed the door behind, tears stinging her hazel green eyes. She feared there was some truth to what Todd said. She wanted what was best for her son, but was it true, did she always jump at any chance to stop him seeing his father?

A large part of Marcia Lachlan wanted desperately to start a new life. That was so hard, though, when she was still tied to her ex-husband by their son. A father and son deserved to spend time together. As a result Marcia found it difficult to break out and begin afresh. She felt as though she were in a rut, working part time five days a week at the local leagues club and sending Todd off to be with Neil every second weekend.

Todd always came home telling her what a fantastic time he had. The weekends spent with Neil were one long boys own adventure. Playing and watching sport, lunches at McDonalds, trips to the movies. Then it was back to her and the drudgery of school, homework, brushing teeth and taking baths.

It damned well wasn't fair, Marcia thought. She went to the bathroom mirror, wiped the tears from her eyes with a tissue and brushed her long, brown hair. She was thirty-eight years old, carrying a little too much weight around the hips and she didn't like the hard lines developing around her mouth. She'd met a man at the club, a local electrician. He was an old fashioned type, solid and reliable, a tall man with a big, hearty laugh. She knew he liked her.

She wanted to start again but it was so damn hard ...

Much later, Todd crept from his room. The house was dark. He peered into his mother's bedroom and saw that she was asleep. He watched the slow, rhythmic rise and fall of her chest, listened to her breathing, low and steady.

He returned to his room and called his father's number on his cell phone. He glanced at his bedside clock as the dial tone hummed in his ear. It was 11.20.

Earlier, Lachlan had arrived home and listened to the TV news from the adjoining room while he fixed dinner in the kitchen. He lived in a small, one bedroom apartment, first floor, tiny balcony crammed with pot plants left behind by the previous occupant. Lachlan had made an attempt to look after the plants but he had no experience with gardening and he suspected they were beginning to wilt. It was a furnished rental, the furniture of a streamlined, angular style, considered modern ten years before. Now it looked dated, not to mention knocked about.

The news broadcast made no impact on him. The mystery of Brian Parkes' corpse had been imbedded in his mind all day and it wasn't going to go away, no matter how hard he tried to shut it out.

He decided on a treat for himself tonight and cooked a pasta, with meatballs, and tomato and basil sauce. He deliberately made it extra spicy. Lachlan had always enjoyed cooking. He found it satisfying and relaxing, the total antithesis of the stress in his job, and probably the last thing anyone expected of a homicide detective.

He'd always got a kick out of cooking for the family on weekends. *Yes, on the weekends when you're home, hardly ever,* he could hear Marcia's taunt, and he was filled with the same sense of sadness that he felt whenever his memories ran free. He thought: at least I didn't run away for eighteen years like Brian Parkes.

But had Parkes run away? Lachlan fixed himself a Scotch and dry, while he waited for the pasta to boil. From the other room he heard the Channel Nine newscaster launch into a story on the fallen business tycoons from Australia's history - Bond, Skase, Goward.

And now, post-GFC, the enigmatic Henry Kaplan.

Had Brian Parkes been in financial strife? Lachlan gulped down large mouthfuls of the Scotch and decided to make some garlic bread while he was at it - going the whole hog tonight.

He had put two separate streams of his investigation into place. The first was to find out where Parkes had been in the intervening years. That wasn't going to be easy. All the items on the body suggested he'd simply stepped from the distant past to the present day in the blink of an eye, and been run down.

Lachlan had circulated Parkes' photo to every police station in Australia and to the offices of Interpol overseas. If Parkes had been photographed by police for any reason over the years, regardless of what name he might have used, then the computers would match the photo to the police image they had on file. That would yield the first clue to his whereabouts.

If Parkes had vanished for criminal reasons, if there was a side to him his wife knew nothing about, then possibly he'd been in trouble with the law at some time or other. Nevertheless, Lachlan knew it was a long shot.

The second stream of his investigation focused on the instrument of his death. The car. Lachlan was waiting for a detailed forensic breakdown of all substances found on Parkes' body. A trace, however microscopic, of the car's paint could help identify the make and model. The layer pattern of paint was often confined to just a few models manufactured between certain dates. The police laboratories kept those paints and patterns on file. Lachlan would then trace any such models stolen prior to the hit and run.

There was no certainty the car had been stolen, it was simply another angle to try. So far this case relied heavily, too heavily, on long shots and that fact made Lachlan wince.

Then there was the question of Parkes' youthful appearance. So far he'd drawn a total blank on that. And the coroner's office wasn't going to be any further help. Without conclusive evidence, that was to be expected. But he wasn't satisfied about the question of Brian Parkes' age. And the out-of-date driver's licence and the post-mortem incision played on his mind.

After his meal he fixed another Scotch and dry and listened to a retrospect of 60's music on an FM station. So many evenings he should have spent like this with Marcia, feet up, listening to music, one or two drinks. He noted the bitter irony that now he'd left the narcotics work and was keeping more regular hours, he was spending the evenings alone in a rented flat in the inner city suburb of Glebe.

He looked forward to the weekend and his time with Todd - the one thing that would take his mind off the job, help him to relax. He missed Todd and the one thing he hated most, the thing that tore at his insides, was when he and his son parted again at the end of each of these alternate weekends. Lachlan tried to push away the memory of the last such time, but the image was too strong and once more it took centre stage in his mind.

'Can't you stay this time, Dad? Please.' Todd's voice was plaintive, touched by a sadness no ten-year old should feel.

'Wish I could, tiger.' Lachlan punched his son reassuringly on the shoulder.

'Why don't you talk to Mum, make up or something. Couldn't you do that, Dad? Couldn't you?'

'We have talked, Todd. Too much water under the bridge. But I'll see you at your soccer game next week, and the week after that for the whole weekend again.'

'But I want you to stay with us now.'

'I'll always be around, Todd. Even though your Mum and I aren't together, we'll always be your parents, we'll always be there for you.'

'Todd?' From inside the house came Marcia's voice. Footsteps. The exterior light flooded the front porch, and the door opened.

'Hello, Marcia.'

'Hello, Neil.'

All so formal now, Lachlan thought, like two acquaintances whose children happened to go to the same school.

'You take it easy, tiger,' he told Todd. 'I'll see you later.' Their eyes connected, a mutual resignation between them, and Lachlan left, waving to both of them. In the car, driving home, he fought back tears.

He felt tears well up in his eyes again at the memory. These past few months had been the only times he'd come close to tears since his childhood. The one thing, in all these years, to cut him so deeply was the sad, lost little boy who didn't understand, nor accept, that he couldn't have both his parents with him, as a family.

And it's all because of me, Lachlan thought.

Lachlan was sipping a late night Scotch when the phone rang. At 11.15 at night he didn't expect to hear his son's voice on the other end of the line.

'Dad?'

'Todd? What's up?'

'Nothing.'

'You sure? It's very late for you to be up, making phone calls. Where's your mother?'

'She's asleep.'

He sounds distressed, Lachlan thought, and he realised he wasn't helping matters. He wondered whether his words were slurred. 'It's always good to hear from you, tiger, no matter the hour. But I get the impression something's bothering you. Can I help?'

'Mum says I can't spend the weekend with you and it's our turn, y'know.'

'I know. Why did your mother say that?' Lachlan tried to sound positive, assured. His kid needed at least that much from him. But deep inside he was feeling the same as Todd. He didn't want to miss out on his weekend with his son. What had Marcia cooked up this time? Why was she doing this more and more lately?

'We're going to Brisbane to see Grandpa. He's sick. Mum says he's in the hospital.'

There was a lump in Lachlan's throat. 'I'm sorry to hear that about Grandpa. Your mother's right about going to see him, he'd love to see you both right now ...'

'But we'll miss being together.'

'These things happen. Sometimes we just have to put up with them. I'm going to miss you like crazy, sport.'

'But why can't Mum and I wait 'til Monday? It's only a few more days.'

Lachlan wasn't sure how serious the matter might be. He hadn't heard from Marcia with regard to her father. 'I'll tell you what, tige, how about you and I have two weekends together after this, to catch up?'

'You said that last time and Mum said no.'

'Yes, but that was then. This is the third time we'll have missed our weekend, so I'm sure we can work something out.'

'No, you won't!' Todd was on the verge of tears, the rage building within him. 'You never do 'cause you don't want to have more arguments with Mum, so you give in. And Mum will say no, I know it, I know it!'

'Todd, mate, listen ...'

'No, I don't want to listen to you any more!' The crash of the phone being slammed down boomed in Lachlan's ear.

He hung up, feeling helpless. There was no point calling Todd back; there would be no talking to the boy while he was like this. He wanted to talk to Marcia about the situation. No doubt she would have phoned him the following morning, but Todd had beaten her to it. You wouldn't think a quiet night at home could be so lousy. He decided to pack it in, knowing he needed to sort out the problem as soon as possible the following day.

Hours later, though, he still lay wide-awake in bed. His temples ached. He longed to hold Todd close, comfort him, tell him everything was going to be okay.

But it wasn't. *Nothing* was okay. The future was uncertain, his son was hurting, and his sense of failure was like an anchor, pulling him down.

NINE

You never get used to the sight of a dead body. Joe Caseli's first sergeant had told him that. Now a sergeant himself, Caseli had been called to the scene of a murder only a few times in his twelve-year career but on each occasion he remembered those words. They were the truest he'd ever heard.

He and Constable Lewis Harrap strode across the leafy reserve in the northwest suburb of Dural. The path circling this reserve was a popular one with runners and another jogger named Cal Birkenshaw had made the discovery. Birkenshaw had brought the local police to this spot, but stood back alongside the police car, pointing in the direction where he'd seen the body.

He didn't want to go near the corpse again. His pale face and watery eyes were testament to the fact he might throw up at any time.

Not in the squad car for Chrissakes, Caseli had thought on the drive over to the park. He wondered whether his own appearance became pasty on these occasions.

The woman lay face down in a manner Caseli had seen before. He glanced across at Harrap, a solidly built nugget of a man the other constables called Bulldog. Caseli noted that he didn't look like a bulldog now. He looked the same as any young cop who'd seen his first murder victim. Ashen faced. Nauseous.

'You gonna be okay?'

'I can handle it, sarge,' Harrap assured him.

Caseli knelt beside the body. The woman was sprawled like a broken doll, arms all askew. Her shorts and panties were down around her ankles. Caseli didn't need a forensic report to tell him that the victim had been viciously raped as well as garrotted.

He turned to Harrap. 'Get the area cordoned off,' he said. 'But first, call the lab. Tell 'em to get their boys over here.' He turned back to the body, checked the pockets of the shorts. 'No ID. We'll be relying on missing persons reports to identify her.'

'I'll make sure a bulletin goes out on that, sarge.'

Harrap was a good man, Caseli thought. Solid. Reliable. And handling this well. It didn't change Caseli's opinion, minutes later, when he saw Harrap vomit into the bushes on his way back to the patrol car.

The previous morning, Trent Dowding had woken with a start at 7.45. *Damn! I'll be late for work.* He shaved and dressed quickly, wondering why Trish hadn't woken him when she'd come in from her run. He was in such a hurry he didn't notice the telltale signs. Normally, when Trish returned from the run, she left her sports gear on top of the bed.

The shorts and tee shirt weren't there that morning.

Trent couldn't understand why Trish hadn't woken him. Getting even with him for not getting up earlier as he'd promised? Perhaps, but that wasn't really like her. She didn't have a cruel streak. He pondered the question on the train as he headed for his clerical job in the city.

Later than morning he phoned Trish's place of work. Alarm bells rang in his head when he was told that Trish hadn't arrived. Had she come in from her run after he'd left? That was it. She was feeling ill and she'd stayed home. He phoned the apartment and allowed the ring to continue for several minutes.

Where the hell was she?

'Probably gone home to mother,' one of his workmates said cheekily. 'I'm only surprised it took her this long, after six months with a slob like you.'

'Very funny,' Trent said, but silently he worried that there might be something in it. Was Trish pissed off with him over something? Would she up and leave like that without a word?

Arriving home that evening, he spent two hours phoning her parents, her friends, a few of her workmates. All to no avail. Trish's parents were concerned and began making phone calls themselves to Trish's friends.

None of Trish's friends were too concerned. Maybe she'd simply tired of Trent and was returning to her older, wilder ways. She'd been one hell of a party girl a few years back. They considered Trent Dowding to be, in one girl's words, "wishy washy", but they didn't say too much to Trish about that. They didn't want to spoil her happiness. Despite these comments, Trish's parents weren't convinced.

That night, Trent lay awake for several hours, agonising over whether or not to call the police. He would look bloody silly if he did, and then Trish turned up.

He searched his mind - had Trish told him she had something else planned for a day or two and he'd simply forgotten? She was always complaining that he didn't listen properly to her, and she was right. He made a mental note not to make that mistake in future. He didn't want to lose Trish Van Helegen. He was in love with her.

By the time he reached the office the following morning, he knew the only option was to call the police. His mouth went dry when the Dural police sergeant, Joe Caseli, told him that his description of Trish matched that of a young woman whose body had been found earlier. Caseli asked him to come in to the station as soon as possible.

Lachlan arrived earlier than usual at his office. He intended to phone Marcia straight away to discuss the problem with Todd.

Superintendent John Rosen, who was coordinating special projects between the various squads of the State Crime Command, was waiting for him. Rosen, normally operating from the S CC at NSW Police HQ in Parramatta, was currently working from Sydney's local area command in the city.

He'd made a special trip across town to see Lachlan.

'Hello, Neil. I thought I told you to keep in touch.'

Lachlan laughed heartily and shook the hand of his old friend. 'John! Haven't I been keeping in touch?'

'Only if you call a rushed phone call every few months being social.'

'You're old enough to make a call yourself, you old bugger.'

'One better. I'm here in person. So how're you finding homicide in the suburbs?'

'I'm happy with the change.'

'I was sorry to hear about you and Marcia,' Rosen adopted a serious tone, 'if there's anything I can do to help, Neil, shoulder to lean on, that sort of thing.'

'Thanks.'

'I have another reason for this visit.'

Rosen was a ruddy-faced bear of a man who always struck Lachlan as something akin to a military figure with his clipped moustache and greying, silvery hair. A commanding figure, he spoke in a rich baritone, more like an international diplomat than a policeman.

'I'm here to discuss a sensitive matter. This Parkes case. Hit and run. Been missing twenty years.'

'Eighteen.'

'Whatever. It would be a fairly straightforward case if not for the widow's claim her husband hadn't aged. You've drawn considerable attention to that in your report.'

'Right. Something bizarre about the state of the body, including the incision to the throat.' It was clear to Lachlan that Rosen had been over the HQ copy of the report. That was standard procedure. This visit wasn't.

'I have a small unit of special investigators at HQ who work on unusual cases. Like this one. I'm taking the investigation away from the Homicide Squad, Neil, and assigning it to that unit. Your squad commander will inform you officially, of course. I wanted to tell you in person myself, though, because it's got nothing to do with you personally or the squad. This is purely about the sensitivity of the case.'

'There's nothing sensitive about this case.'

'The word from above is, they want this one kept under wraps. And I agree. We don't want the media getting hold of it. The way your report reads we're dealing with an accident or murder victim who's stepped through time, or who has a Dorian Gray type painting stacked away somewhere. Imagine if the reporters get hold of something that gives that impression, there'll be widespread curiosity. Half the community will believe it, the other half will think the widow and the police force have gone balmy. Next think we'll have a flood of UFO sightings and haunted house reports in the area.'

'I can keep a lid on my investigation,' Lachlan insisted.

'I know *you* can, Neil. But you're working out of a suburban station, with people in and out, phone calls overheard, local news guys hanging about desperate for angles. It wouldn't be unusual for something to get out.'

'Aren't you over-reacting, John? After all, there's nothing speculative in the autopsy papers. It's routine. The coroner wasn't prepared to dispute the fact that Parkes was forty-three years old.'

'No reason a coroner would buy into something like that, not without conclusive evidence. Only make him look stupid. As you know, they can't say for certain what age a body is.'

'No. But they can determine if a body is closer to thirty than, say, forty. McIntyre wasn't even prepared to do that for the record. Only to say the body's condition prior to death was excellent for it's age.'

Rosen nodded. 'I'm inclined to agree with the coroner's assessment.'

'But it isn't just a matter of the body's appearance. There's the clothing. The eighteen-year-old driver's licence, still in pristine condition. The fact that he re-appeared in the same spot he went missing.'

'Which brings me back to the original point. These are all details the press could get hold of.'

'You really think there'd be a circus over something like this?'

'The big boys at SCC have seen it happen before, mate. They don't want anything that rocks the boat, not after the recent corruption and efficiency enquiries. You know that the force is going through a cleansing and rebuilding phase.'

'I still think it's an over-reaction. After all, it's just another case. The sooner it's solved, the less chance of speculation and ridicule.'

'There are hundreds of unsolved cases, much simpler than this one,' Rosen pointed out.

'You don't think this will be solved?'

Rosen sighed, frustration showing in the droop of his cheeks. 'I hope it can. I want to find the driver who ran Parkes down. But the puzzle over his appearance will be difficult, especially with the coroner ruling out plastic surgery. As you said, it's bizarre. Answer this: what kind of explanation can anyone come up with? You think this guy had a Dorian Gray picture tucked away somewhere?'

'Of course not.'

'You think he did a H G Wells and stepped through time?'

'Those aren't rational explanations.'

'And there may not be any. But those are the sorts of things people will speculate about. The media will make a home grown version of the X-Files out of it, if they can.'

'So what's the point here, John? The big boys want to sweep the whole thing under the carpet?'

'Not at all. My HQ special investigations unit will be calling in opinions from the boffins, and following up on those points concerning the make and model of the hit/run car, and any international crime records relating to Parkes. We just want to keep all the details under wraps for now. Access to information on the case will be strictly classified.'

'Limit any possibility of a leak.'

'Exactly. You understand, Neil. There are always some cases they want handled that way. And it's the sort of thing my special unit deals with.'

'I understand.' Lachlan cast his eyes over Rosen's features, still sharp and clearly defined even though he was approaching sixty-five. 'You're concerned that I don't take the moving of the case as a personal affront.'

'Damn right. Hell, how long have I known you? Must be twenty years since I coached you on the academy rugby team.'

'Twenty years,' Lachlan confirmed.

'You've had a hell of a rough time lately. You're still the new boy on the block in homicide. Didn't want you getting the wrong idea.'

'I haven't.'

'Word is you're creaming it here.'

'I needed a new challenge. And the pace here is right. Busy, but I get to go home occasionally.'

'Good. Actually, I blame myself partly for your troubles at home.'

'How's that?'

'I should've been on to you years ago, made sure you didn't spend too long in narcotics. I've seen it burn up too many guys. But I made the same old mistake. Got out of the routine of staying in contact.'

'It wasn't your responsibility, John. You're a superintendent with a wide brief at SCC, not a guardian angel.'

'I'm talking about the personal side of things, about being a friend.'

'I appreciate that, John. You'll keep me informed on the Parkes case?'

'Of course.'

'As you can imagine, my curiosity has been piqued.'

'And mine.'

'There's a widow ...'

Rosen nodded. 'Jennifer Parkes. I'd like you to explain to her that a special team from HQ will be undertaking the investigation. Also take her through the autopsy result, persuade her to accept the known facts. From there on, I'll see to it she's kept advised of our progress.'

'There's one thing you haven't told me,' Lachlan said, as Rosen stretched his legs, preparing to leave.

'What's that?'

'What's your take on this, on why Parkes doesn't appeared to have aged? On the apparent interference with the body post-mortem?'

A grin spread across Rosen's face, a grin Lachlan remembered well from the old academy football days.

'Most obvious case of alien abduction I've ever seen. But don't quote me on that.'

Lachlan gave a half-hearted smile. 'Wouldn't dream of it. We don't want this turning into a circus.'

After Rosen left, Lachlan ambled over to the coffee machine and poured himself a cup. Everything John Rosen said made perfect sense. Why then, did he have the feeling he'd been deftly manoeuvred by a master manipulator?

He returned to his desk, sipped at the steaming hot liquid, then remembered his need to contact Marcia as soon as possible. Her phone rang and rang, until finally he hung up in frustration. Glancing at his watch, he realised Rosen's visit had caused him to miss her. She must have already left to take Todd to school.

Carly Parkes was an early riser. It was the one thing, she speculated, that she had in common with her mother. 'It's the sign of an achiever,' her mother had told her repeatedly when she was young.

5.45 a.m. Early spring. The first rays of dawn, warm and ethereal, filtered through the partly open floral curtains. It gave the bedroom an old-world ambience, all the surrounding colours soft and muted, welcoming.

Carly slipped out from beneath the fawn coloured quilt cover, the short, creamy negligee clinging to the slender lines of her body. She went to the vanity unit. Her hair, raven black like her mother's, had a tendency to develop knots while she slept. She loved this part of the morning, the serenity, the soft light, so she sat at the vanity unit mirror, combing the knots from her smooth, fine hair, all the time watching the man who had slept beside her.

Carly had left the corner of the cover drawn back from him, and, as she did every morning, she watched the rise and fall of his chest. She loved the look of his suntanned skin, and the firm, oval shape of the muscles in his long legs. She loved to watch him in the early mornings as he slept. She could feast her eyes on his body without him being aware, without her feeling self conscious about her lust. And that, she knew, was exactly what it was.

At six o'clock his clock radio came alive. The chirpy, high-speed voice of the FM breakfast DJ resounded around the room, bouncing from the walls. Rory stirred, one eye opened first, then the other. He focused on Carly. She rose from her stool, reached across and switched the radio off. 'Can't stand it so early in the day,' she said.

Rory sat up, yawned and stretched, sending ripples across his shoulder blades.

'Hi,' said Carly.

'Running?'

'You ask me that every morning.' She grinned.

'And you always say no.' He wiped a thin seam of sleep from his eye.

'So you know my answer.'

'Typical.'

'I get plenty of exercise from my aerobics classes.'

He made an exasperated face. 'Aerobics.'

'It's my one vice,' she pointed out.

'Point taken ...' He yawned again. 'Well, not the only vice.' He laughed, his voice still husky from sleep.

He had dark hair, longish, dark eyes and a lazy droop to his eyelids. His boyishly handsome face was very 1960's Paul McCartney, but his dry wit and arrogant resolve were pure John Lennon at his most rebellious. They were both into retro, and were Beatles fans. She had said that to him once - McCartney look, Lennon spirit - and he'd laughed, making a face and dismissing her comment as childish, her views tainted by commercial pop culture imagery. She suspected that, secretly, he'd been flattered. She liked to flatter him, it was one of the ways she could exercise influence over him.

Normally he was totally in control of his life and his emotions, always the organiser, the decision maker. She liked that, up to a point. He was thirty-five, seventeen years older than she was, but she often felt that his zest for living and his passion for social issues were those of a much younger man. Rory was her soul mate. She wished she had his knowledge, his maturity, his ability to translate his anger at the injustices of the system into clear, concise lines of attack.

'What's on today?' she asked.

'I'm meeting with Harlan later this morning,' he replied. 'He wants to discuss another assignment with me.'

'Great.'

'You?'

'Catwalking again,' she said, turning her eyes upwards, disgusted, 'it's really not me, not what I'm about.'

'Keep it up a little longer, baby. The organisation needs the money. What better place to get a little help, than from the purses of the idle rich, the miserable bastards who care for nothing but themselves.'

'You're right, of course.'

He stood up, naked, yawned again. Carly rose from the stool, allowed the negligee to slide from her shoulders and fall. She wiggled out of it as she moved towards him. 'You're not really going to go for that run this morning, are you?'

81

'I need my exercise,' Rory protested. His tone was definite, but his eyes, taking in her body, told a different story.

Carly placed her open palms against his chest and pushed. He fell backwards across the bed, pulling her down on top of him.

'You're getting sexier and sexier,' he said, his breath heavy.

'You've created a monster.' She lowered her lips to the skin stretched taut across his belly, swept her tongue lightly over the matted hairs, felt the shiver that passed through him. Then she pressed her tongue firmly against his flesh, dragging it downwards, following the shiver to the point where all his senses gathered, ready to erupt. The groan that escaped his lips, a grunt of true ecstasy, was music to her ears.

Later, they lay with limbs entwined, light headed, catching breath. The phone rang, a rude intrusion.

Carly glanced at the bedside clock. Seven a.m. 'Who,' she wondered aloud, 'at this hour ...?'

'I'll get it.' Rory ambled out to the lounge room, picked up the receiver. 'Hello. Oh. How are you? Sure.' He covered the mouthpiece, called to Carly. 'It's your mother.'

Carly came out from the bedroom, pulling a white robe around her. Rory handed her the phone. 'Abrupt,' he commented, frowning.

'That's entrepreneurial businesswomen for you,' Carly replied, cynically. She lifted the receiver to her lips. 'Hello, Mum.'

Rory padded his way to the adjoining kitchen alcove, filled the kettle. From out of the corner of his eye he noticed that Carly had gone rigid, her eyes glazing over, her face emotionless.

'You're sure ...' she began, but the words stopped, an apparent interruption from the voice on the other end.

Rory caught her eye, held her gaze. 'Something wrong,' he mouthed the words, but Carly gave no response. The phone seemed glued to her ear. She remained silent, listening.

'Okay, thanks for the call, Mum.' She replaced the receiver.

'What is it, Carls?' Rory asked, concerned, shifting as he sometimes did to his sweetheart name for her.

'My father ...' Once again the words dried up. Carly sat on the sofa, clearly shaken.

Rory sat alongside her, touched her arm. 'Carls?'

'Mum said she called yesterday but we were both out and she couldn't raise me on my cell. She phoned early to catch me before I left for the day.'

'Bad news?'

'Strange news. My father has been found.'

'Your father? You told me he disappeared yonks ago.'

'Before I was born.'

'Alive?'

'Dead. Hit by a car the night before last.'

Rory's expression was one of amazement. He'd never been good dealing with emotional situations on a one to one basis. What words were needed? What actions?

'How's your mother taking it?'

'Okay, I think. She's had a day to adjust. And after all, I expect she got over him a long time ago. It's just that ... it's so unusual. He was found in the same street where he and Mum used to live.'

Rory shook his head. 'Weird.'

Carly wasn't listening. Her mind was crowded with thoughts and emotions that made no sense to her. 'He's been alive all these years,' she said, more to herself than to Rory, 'and I never knew. He never tried to contact me.'

'Perhaps he was looking for you when he was knocked down,' Rory said. 'That would explain why he was in the same street.'

'Would it?'

Rory didn't reply. Ever since he'd known Carly she'd held a resentment of her mother. The distance between them was so strong it was almost physical in intensity when they stood together in the same room. This was the last thing Carly needed right now, to discover that her father, living somewhere all these years, had deliberately shunned her.

Then something occurred to him, something Carly hadn't considered. 'If he vanished before you were born,' he said, 'then I doubt he ever knew he had a daughter.'

Carly nodded slowly. 'Maybe,' she replied, 'but why did he vanish like that? Mum always said she and my father were very, very happy. Still in the honeymoon mode when he disappeared. If he was so happy, then he wouldn't have taken off like that.'

'I guess not.'

'I have to find out, Rory. I want to know what really went on between my mother and my father. And why he disappeared the way he did.'

The curiosity was overwhelming. What Jennifer really wanted to do was go to the office, get on with her career, her life, and simply stay in touch with Detective Senior Sergeant Neil Lachlan for information as it came to hand. Let him pursue the case, do the digging, find the answers. He'd had less than two days to get the investigation under way. Nevertheless, she wanted to know if there were any further developments, and whether any conclusions had been drawn from the autopsy.

She'd accepted that the body on the slab was Brian. The dental records left no doubt.

Accepting it didn't cure her restlessness. It merely led her, this morning, to Neil Lachlan's office at Hurstville Police station. It was her second deed of the day, the first being her earlier phone call to her daughter.

She felt a sense of deja vu when she walked into the station, which was unnatural because this was a different building - the police had moved premises in the years since the disappearance. But the deja vu persisted. She realised it wasn't so much the place itself but the act of visiting the police in this locality. A part of her would never forget the aura of this suburb, where she'd spent such happy times with Brian.

Lachlan rose from behind his desk when Jennifer appeared in his office doorway. 'Take a seat, Ms Parkes.' He waved her to a chair. 'I'm glad you called by, I was going to phone you.'

'News?'

'No. Not as such. It's still early days for any developments, I'm afraid.'

'I see.'

Lachlan had already decided how he would handle this. 'I had a visit from one of the State Crime Command superintendents, this morning. He's taking the case under his supervision at Sydney HQ. He has a special investigations unit there that will be working on it.'

'Oh.' Jennifer wasn't expecting that and it didn't mean a great deal to her. 'Is that good?'

'Yes. We're bogged down in cases here, so the investigation will get specialised attention.'

'You won't be working on the case?'

'No. I'll be very interested, though, to know the outcome and I'll be keeping in touch with the superintendent to see how things progress.'

Jennifer felt a twinge of disappointment. She realised that, subconsciously, she'd had a sense of confidence in Neil Lachlan's abilities from the first time they'd met. She mulled over his comments. 'You would have given the case your individual attention,' she said. It was clearly more a statement than a question.

Lachlan shrugged. He agreed with her, despite John Rosen's comments half an hour earlier. He'd been the first detective on the scene. He'd seen the body, met the widow, he'd conferred with the coroner's office. He'd always believed that the man who began an investigation had an affinity with a case, far more than someone who came in later.

However, he didn't want to expose Jennifer Parkes to HQ's sensitivity to possible publicity of the case, the real reason for the move.

'I would have,' he agreed, 'but not as much as the unit in town can. Really, it's in the best interests of the case.'

'I see.'

'The man who'll be keeping in touch with you,' Lachlan said, taking a notepad from his desk corner, 'is John Rosen. This is his number at the Sydney LAC.' He wrote on the page, then ripped it from the pad and handed it across the desk. 'You're getting very special attention, actually. Not everyone gets this unit on their case.' He smiled at her, a warm, easy smile from the attractive, slightly rumpled, lived-in face.

She returned the smile and found herself responding to his gentle authority.

'What I want to do before handing over to Rosen, however, is to go through the coroner's report with you.' Step by step Lachlan explained McIntyre's findings.

At first, Jennifer said nothing. She absorbed the information, but as she did her calm demeanour hardened, her serenity turned to steel. 'I can't believe I'm hearing this, detective.' Her gaze was intense. 'You saw my husband. I don't think there's any doubt there was something eerie about his appearance. How can this coroner ... ignore that?'

Lachlan went over the post mortem with her again, this time stressing the point that while the body's pathology could not be conclusive about age, it didn't alter the fact that the ID was positive. The coroner had no reason, no definitive proof, to support a theory that the body had not aged. Lachlan was insistent on this, while at the same time making certain he remained sympathetic.

Jennifer shook her head in frustration. She wanted to argue, but what the coroner had said made sense. She suspected, however, that the real reason the police accepted the body's appearance, and the ID, was that it was simply too baffling to contemplate otherwise.

'Then I suppose we have to leave it at that for the time being,' Jennifer said tersely. She rose to leave. 'The coroner's report doesn't do any more than state the obvious. And makes no attempt to explain this…incision in the neck.'

Lachlan wanted to agree but he bit his lip. He had to be careful how he handled this.

'Thanks for your help, detective. I'll take the matter up further with Superintendent Rosen.'

He offered his hand and they shook. 'Best of luck.' He felt a twinge of disappointment that he wouldn't see her again. She was a striking looking woman. She had a blend of fragility and command that he'd noticed in some other businesswomen, but in Jennifer Parkes the contrast was stronger, and therefore more interesting. Her finely sculpted bone structure attracted the eye and held it. He wondered why she'd never remarried.

He knew next to nothing about Jennifer Parkes, and he had the feeling he would like to know more.

86

TEN

First Letter

Dear Mother,

I had an intriguing thought today, one I wanted to share with you.

Just think of the crimes - all the crimes committed by all the men and women throughout history.

The killings, the thieving, the tortures, the deceptions. Imagine them all strung together as one long, endless sideshow.

What a bizarre carnival it would make.

I'm part of it, you see, the next hawker along the alley with a product no one really wants or needs - except that I want it, and why shouldn't I get a little of what I want?

Everyone else does.

I don't get the chance to share things with you. I can't tell you about the things I do, or show you, but I can write about them. You read my letters, don't you?

I want you to know all about me.

It's a long time now since my first time, and I've never told anyone, not a soul. Hard to explain how it felt. Kind of like the first time I slept with someone, only much, much better. I was young, too. Thirteen. If you'd been around then you would have known Vince Martinelli. Italian kid, real airhead in my class at school. He was a friend of mine, except I never really liked him. I always knew he used me to get the things he

87

wanted, like money 'coz I always had a little more than he did. Once he talked me into giving him a whole pack of footie cards I'd collected. He was going to give me a metal ring with a skull and crossbones emblem in return, except he never did, and sometimes he assured me I would get it - eventually - and other times he taunted me, flashed it at me, called me gullible.

He was the first one I killed.

It was fourteen years since he had written this, the first of dozens of letters to his mother. He remembered how it began.

Those first years of the strange surveillance had been the most frustrating of all. The prostitutes, the erotic magazines - and later still the pornographic and violent videos - none had actually helped him overcome the frustration. They weren't the same as the real thing, the physical act of destroying human life, of wielding the ultimate power.

Writing the letters and posting them helped a little, giving him an outlet. As he revealed his secrets on paper he re-lived them for a while.

The glory. The excitement.

He found a certain satisfaction in imagining the revulsion the reader of these letters would feel. The bitter taste of vengeance, like acid drops in his saliva. He swallowed hard, the lump in his throat pushing against his Adam's apple like a sexual urge.

The jogger often took copies of the letters and leafed through them, choosing one at random to read. It was a long time since he'd re-read this, the first letter. As is often the case with the first of anything, it was his favourite. He sat cross-legged on the floor of this secret place, the lights low, the large, empty space around him silent and dark, and he continued reading:

It was after school one afternoon, we were walking home. Just Vinnie and me. Vinnie had a knife, a switchblade that he'd discreetly removed from his older brother's bedroom. I've no idea why his brother had it in the first place: some macho teenage thing, I suppose.

Vinnie was a smart-ass and that afternoon he decided to stir me about the ring, flashing it at me. Only this time he drew the knife as well, acted tough, daring me to try and get the ring from him.

Do you believe in fate, Mum? I do. You see, Vinnie was all brawn and bluster, and he could be very clumsy. He dropped the knife and my reflexes were faster than his. I stooped down like lightning, picked it up and ran off. He chased me into an alley that ran between the newsagent and the delicatessen. It led to an old, gravel parking station behind the mall.

That was where it happened. Out of breath I stopped and turned around, panting. Vinnie was just about on top of me, laughing, actually. Probably thought it was a good game, loads of fun. I struck out with the knife, swished it through the air and the sharp steel edge sliced into his throat.

An expression came onto his face that didn't make any sense to me. He looked puzzled, and his eyes seemed to grow larger. I thought they were going to pop. The blood was gushing from his throat, soaking into his shirt.

That's when I first felt the elation. An exciting tingling sensation pricking at the hairs on the nape of my neck. That's why I think it was fate. If Vinnie hadn't dropped that knife, I would never have run into that alley with it and cut his throat, I'd never have felt the wonder and the power of it - and later the craving for more.

I remember stepping back, watching him crash to the ground. Luckily no blood splashed onto me, and no one had noticed Vinnie and I together that afternoon. I was never questioned, certainly never suspected. One of the advantages, I guess, of being thirteen years old.

Of course, I can't rely on luck or fate now. I have to plan. I need to be prepared.

But the thrill of it, Mum. The exhilaration can last for days. I never cease to be amazed at the pleasure it gives me, the sexual urge that erupts throughout me. And the heady, giddy feeling of power. And total control.

Isn't that what any of us really wants? Control.

I kept the knife. It's still packed away somewhere, a memento. I've never used it since that day, but one day on a special occasion, I will.

I took the ring of course. I knew no one would miss it and, it was such a silly childish thing. I soon tired of it. And the football cards. I took them from his school satchel and I felt good. I had everything I wanted.

Before long I knew I wanted to kill again, but it was a long time before I did. I was scared of getting caught. I never forgot the enormous amount of publicity that surrounded the discovery of Vinnie's body.

Police at the school. The talk amongst the kids.

I caused it, Mum. All that. I began to wish for another opportunity, the right set of circumstances so I could do it again.

By the time that happened I'd long since forgotten the pirate ring and the footie cards. All I remembered was the extraordinary surge of adrenalin that made me harden with desire, panting for air, glistening within and without with the sweet, forbidden juices I'd never dreamed existed.

ELEVEN

Eleven years before, when Brian Parkes was officially declared dead, Jennifer felt the need for a memorial service, something small and brief. She had approached the local Chatswood Reverend Mark de Castellan to conduct the service.

There had not been a proper funeral. No body, no declaration of death, and therefore no chance of a proper and dignified farewell. In its place had been a long term, lingering doubt, a grief that slowly sank into the routine of life. An unwelcome intrusion, one that offered no memory of goodbye.

Father de Castellan showed an understanding of this. A bearded, dark haired man, fortyish, he had a face of friendly lines and folds that generated an air of hope and inner peace. His voice, deep and resonant, clothed the listener with its warmth like an invisible barricade against the world's ills.

Now that Brian had been found, his body had to be laid to rest. Now, eighteen years too late, there was need for the funeral.

De Castellan had moved on from Chatswood a few years before, to a country posting. Jennifer had liked him very much but she'd lost contact in recent years. She wanted the same man for this new service and she had discussed this with Meg on the evening of their dinner with the Kaplans.

'It's probably a bit silly of me, going to the bother of doing it like that, following on from that earlier service,' she'd said to Meg.

'Not at all. It's the natural step, the logical conclusion. You can't let Brian's body be buried without a service.'

91

'Can't I, Meg? This is the man who walked out on me a lifetime ago.'

'I don't believe for a minute he walked out on you, Jen,' Meg protested. Her tone was definite.

'How else do you explain it?'

Meg shrugged. 'I don't know. But I knew Brian. He was besotted with you. Totally. He never would've left, not of his own accord. And what's more, you know I'm right. Deep down you know, don't you?'

Jennifer hesitated. 'I guess I do.' Something Meg had said stuck in Jennifer's mind. *Not of his own accord* ...

'So you're doing the right thing,' Meg said. 'I remember the music you requested for that service ...'

'Berlioz's Requiem,' Jennifer reminded her.

'It was beautiful. Touching.'

'Yes, it was. I've loved it since I was a child. My grandfather requested a requiem service for my grandmother's funeral. That was the first time I heard it.'

'A lovely service. The reverend was terrific. What was his name? De something or other?'

'De Castellan.'

'Why don't you let me arrange the whole thing?' Meg offered. 'You're busy enough, playing superwoman and all that.'

Jennifer raised her eyebrows dramatically. 'Ha. I'm no superwoman.'

'You really don't need to go through all the preparations again. Let me help. Let me plan it.'

'Okay.' Jennifer smiled warmly at her friend. It was nice to have someone who stepped in, unasked, to lift the weight from her shoulders occasionally. 'That would be great.'

Meg contacted de Castellan the following morning. He was delighted with the idea of a proper burial, at long last, for Brian Parkes, a service that followed on from the earlier one, a second requiem.

After her early morning visit to Detective Sergeant Neil Lachlan, and her catch-up with Meg, Jennifer went straight to her George Street office and phoned the number for Superintendent John Rosen at Sydney

Police HQ. The secretary explained that he wasn't in and asked that she try again late morning.

Despite the events of the past few days, this was another typical day in the life of a fashion label's owner/designer.

'All set for 11 a.m. at the Rosegrove Shopping Centre?' Cindy asked, pen and pad in hand, efficient and forthright and exquisitely dressed as always.

Jennifer's brow creased into a distinct furrow. 'Bring me up to date, Cindy. My mind's been a little hazy lately.'

'Understandable. 11 o'clock today is the first of our daily shopping centre fashion parades.'

'Of course,' Jennifer said, 'I just didn't realise it was upon us so soon. The next fortnight's going to be busier than ever.' Jennifer had never been one to sit and wait for things to happen. That was part of the reason for her success. With retail slow to regain momentum after the GFC and its ongoing aftermath, she'd decided to mount her own fashion parades in a different corner of Sydney every day for two weeks.

Sales at the boutiques were still dropping off, the big retail chain orders were down, so she was taking her line to the streets. There was nothing new about parades, of course, but the style of these would be something that had been missing from the city and suburban retail complexes. A light show, moody and modern, would engulf the stage, electronically keyed in to the pulse of the recorded music. As well as the models, the parades would feature a back-up three-piece male dancing troupe. Glamour. Excitement.

In addition, a number of tables would be erected around the stage, manned by casual sales staff, from where the actual items of modelled clothing could be bought.

'You've done an awesome job, pulling this whole thing together.'

Cindy leaned forward and knocked on the polished cedar wood top of Jennifer's desk. 'Don't say that. It hasn't all come together yet.'

'It'll be all right on the night,' Jennifer quipped and then winked confidently.

'It's good to see the old Jennifer Parkes back,' Cindy commented. She'd been worried about her boss. This morning, however, she noted that Jennifer's usual air of command had returned.

93

The fashion show was a success. Long legged women, tall, graceful, moved regally across the catwalk as though they were floating just above the stage. Their movements showed off every angle of the range. There was a section for business dress, for casual gear, formal wear, swimwear and underclothes.

Instead of the thumping, electronic rhythm of disco and rap, often the norm at these affairs, there was something different to characterize each section. Billy Joel's 'Uptown Girl' for the evening gowns; Ravel's 'Bolero' for the underwear.

The parade attracted a large crowd and the numbers swelled further during the twenty-minute performance. After that the tables were busy and sales flourished.

At 11.50 a.m. Jennifer slipped away from the action. From a quiet area, she pulled out her cell. John Rosen was still unavailable. This time she left a message. She thought back once again to her conversation with Meg.

'The police are bound to uncover what this is all about,' Meg had said. 'There's a reason why Brian did this, and why he died. The cops will find it.'

'What if they don't, Meg?'

'Knowing you,' Meg laughed, 'you'll be on their backs until they do.'

I suppose that's been my way, Jennifer thought, ever since I got wrapped up in my own company. Always pushing staff and suppliers to do better; stretching myself to manage the business more efficiently, open new stores, design new clothing lines. And neglecting the only child Brian and I ever had ...

Harold Masterton was a tall, thin man, earthy in manner. He had bright blue, piercing eyes and a thatch of red hair that looked as though he needed a scrubbing brush to comb it. He'd been Henry Kaplan's right hand man, advisor and financial controller since the early days, an ambitious young accountant of twenty-four when he'd first met Kaplan. Thirty years, hell, where had they gone? At the time Kaplan, at thirty, had already made his first million, starting out with a discount food store that he'd expanded into a chain.

He'd retained Masterton's small accountancy practice for various financial services. Kaplan had been impressed by Masterton's business savvy and efficiency and had offered the accountant a full time position. Sensing success for both Kaplan and himself, Masterton accepted the offer provided he received a parcel of shares as part of his package. The first takeover bid they worked on together was a resounding success, the first of many.

Two decades later, with both he and Masterton spending more time overseas, Kaplan had groomed his son to step into his shoes and to run the Australian network of companies.

Masterton had never thought too highly of Roger Kaplan. He knew the tycoon's son wasn't the best man for the job. Masterton himself would've done the job better - but he'd always been regarded solely as the right hand man, the number cruncher. Mr. Fix- it.

Roger hadn't been responsible for any innovations, for any growth. For a while the corporation succeeded in spite of him, as he'd made one blunder after another.

Roger was the one weakness Henry Kaplan had shown.

Masterton blamed himself partly for recent events. Prior to the GFC, with so much money available to so many, he shouldn't have turned a blind eye, shouldn't have allowed the borrowing and the expansion Roger had undertaken in Australia. Masterton had been too distracted, working alongside Henry in New York.

The final nails in the coffin had come with the enormous amounts swallowed into the black hole of the Southern Star Mining venture, and now the appointment of a receiver. Masterton was confident their appeal would buy more time. But for now he and Kaplan were due to meet the receiver, Warren Stokes.

'Do you know Stokes?' Masterton asked Kaplan as they sat in the spacious, elegant boardroom.

'Met him once or twice,' Kaplan replied. 'Arrogant little bastard. Gets his kicks winding up other people's firms. Couldn't run a business of his own if he tried.' Kaplan's voice seethed with anger.

Minutes later, Kaplan's secretary ushered Stokes and his colleague, a junior associate named Mike Davodivich, into the boardroom.

'Nice to meet with you again, Mr. Kaplan. I'm sorry the circumstances aren't more favourable to you.'

'I'll bet you are,' the entrepreneur replied gruffly.

'Just doing my job,' Stokes said, 'nothing personal. What we want to do is to get the fairest possible outcome for your employees and your shareholders.' Kaplan was certain that Stokes was suppressing a smug grin.

Kaplan restrained himself throughout the meeting, allowing Masterton to handle the bulk of the discussions. He hated seeing his corporation carved up, even if it was just on paper at this stage. His mind wandered, unusual for him, and he found himself thinking of Jennifer Parkes. The sight of her, more mature and even more beautiful, had touched a chord within him.

He wanted to help her. He'd offered to pay for the requiem service but she'd refused, pointing out that she was financially secure and able to cover her own costs. He wondered how it might've been if they'd stayed in touch over the years, become closer ...

He knew Roger had been interested in her at one stage. But he also knew nothing would come of it. Roger had been too vague, too flighty, drifting from one half-hearted romance to another. He'd been too young for commitment, whereas Jennifer was focused, committed.

Kaplan snapped himself out of his reverie and tuned in on the boardroom conversation.

There were so many times, in the past, when he'd snatched success back from the jaws of failure. This time, above all times, it was essential to do it again.

Back at her office, Jennifer rang John Rosen's office again and this time, third time lucky she supposed, she was put through to the Superintendent. 'I'm very anxious to know how things are progressing, Mr. Rosen,' Jennifer stressed. 'This has been hanging over me for a long, long time.'

'I understand perfectly, Ms. Parkes. I have the best possible team here working on the case. I do have some news for you. The coroner is ready to release your husband's body to your funeral director.'

Jennifer was quick to tell Rosen her view of the coroner's findings, repeating comments she'd made earlier to Neil Lachlan. Rosen heard her out, then gave the same re-assurances she'd already heard from Lachlan.

She queried Rosen about the strange incision mark. 'I'm not going to mislead you, Ms. Parkes, that mark, along with the other particulars of your husband's body, have us puzzled. I have no leads at this point. But, let me assure you, no stone will be left unturned in finding the answers.'

Jennifer thanked him and then rang off, despite her growing frustration. She next called Meg to ask her to contact the funeral directors, Morris and Sons.

Meg called back later in the day, confirming that the service could be held in two days time.

Jennifer put in a call to Henry Kaplan, advising him of the time and place for the service. She asked him to pass the details on to Roger, and while she had him on the phone she updated him on the police investigation and the autopsy result.

After the call, she reflected on her conflicting emotions. On one hand she felt good about the upcoming service, about finally putting Brian's body to rest with dignity and prayer. On the other hand she was haunted by the lack of answers to the mystery of his death and his missing years.

I'll find the answers, my darling, she thought. I'll find out what happened and why and I'll see that justice is done.

She needed no five-cent coins to drop into wishing pools. This was one wish she'd make certain came true.

For Roger Kaplan there'd been no sudden pang of despair over his impending insolvency. Like his father and the other directors of the company he'd been living under that shadow for the past few years. The first attempts to place several of the individual firms into receivership happened after the GFC, by one bank and various other companies who were major creditors. They'd been unsuccessful.

Other attempts had followed in recent years. These looked like being successful but after Kaplan Corp. did the rounds of the appeal courts the moves against it were stopped. Kaplan stayed solvent by making alternative loan arrangements with its backers, and extending credit further overseas. The acquisition of the mining project in Western Queensland had helped to allay the fears of the bankers, and the international business community followed the ongoing saga closely.

Henry Kaplan had always been a private man, rarely heard of outside the financial sections of the newspapers. The constant bankruptcy proceedings alerted the general news media to the story. Like vultures they began to circle, swooping in at the slightest scent of further drama. They took an interest in Kaplan's marital history - three ex-wives - and speculated over his more recent lady friends.

Roger didn't like the limelight either and avoided the press as much as possible. The journalists could find out very little about the equally private Roger Kaplan. What they saw was an unmarried man in his early forties, good looks, easily cast as the wealthy playboy.

Roger arrived at the office that morning well aware that he was late for the meeting with the receivers.

First, a drink.

He fixed himself a stiff whisky, swallowed it quickly, fixed another, and reflected on the events that had led to this week's judgment.

Am I really prepared for the inevitable?

He lounged against the corner of his desk, eyes on the window, his gaze roaming over the city skyline.

At the insistence of his father, Roger had long ago established his own private family trust - despite the fact that he had no wife or immediate heirs. He had a little over a million dollars stashed away in overseas accounts as part of that trust. His escape fund. In the event of bankruptcy there'd be enough to live on, in style. It was money he'd gone to great lengths to ensure the receivers never found.

He knew his father and Masterton and the other directors had done the same. He also knew his father and Masterton had been involved in other illegal financial practices within the corporation. He'd turned a blind eye, but now he wondered whether he could be implicated if the others were found out.

Roger straightened his tie and went to the elevator. He would join the meeting, watch and listen closely, keep abreast of developments. If worse came to worse he wanted to sense it in advance. His nerve ends were on edge. He was beginning to wish he'd walked away from it all years ago.

When she responded to the doorbell's ring at 2.30 p.m. the last person Marcia Lachlan expected to see was her ex-husband.

Lachlan was on his way back to his office, after interviewing a number of people in the western suburbs over another case he was working on.

'Neil? What's going on?'

'I wanted to talk to you while Todd's at school. I phoned earlier but missed you.'

'Come in, then.'

He followed her into the living room. Both stood awkwardly. She crossed her arms and waited for him to speak. Lachlan made an effort to keep his tone reasonable. 'It's about this trip to Brisbane.'

'How do you know about that? I was going to phone you, actually, this afternoon.'

'Todd called me last night.'

'Todd called you ...' A glint of understanding came into her eyes. 'Late. After I'd turned in?'

'Yes. He was practically having hysterics. I tried to calm him down but he hung up before I could get any sense from him. How was he this morning?'

'Withdrawn. He's making a big deal about this. It's just for a few days.'

'It could be longer.'

'So you've come here to complain, have you? To take his side, gang up on me. My father is sick for Chrissakes ...'

'No. I agree. You and Todd should go.'

'You do?'

She sounded wary. *Why is she like this?* Lachlan wondered. Always defensive. *It's not as if I've been giving her a hard time.* 'Of course I do. But we have to consider Todd's feelings as well. Our separation's put him through an emotional wringer.'

'I know that, Neil.' Her tone was icy, ready to pounce.

'I know you do. That's why we have to work this situation in with him.'

'How? I can't stay the weekend. I need to be with Dad as soon as possible.'

'You go. Let Todd spend the weekend with me, as he expected. I'll bring him up to Brisbane Monday morning. I'll fly up with him.'

'What about your job?'

'I'll take the day off. It's only one day, after all.'

'You never felt that way while we were together. The job was more important.'

'Marcia ...'

'Now you're a new man, it seems.'

'Is there any point in going over all that again? I didn't come here to cause an upset. Just to talk about Todd.'

She shrugged. 'Okay. I suppose it's a good idea.'

'You'll tell him?'

'As soon as he gets home. I don't want him moping all night, laying some blasted guilt trip on me.'

'Is there something else bothering you, Marcia?'

'I need a life too, Neil. I haven't had much of one these past few years.'

She won't let go of the anger. But now it seems worse. 'I'll pick him up, usual time, tomorrow?'

'Sure.' She turned, arms still folded, went towards the kitchen. No good-byes.

'See you tomorrow night.' Lachlan left, wishing he hadn't had to make the visit, but glad that Todd would be with him on the weekend. He drove to the office, recalling many of the darker times during the last years of his marriage. The steel in Marcia's eyes and the edge in her voice had brought back the memories.

He made an effort to block them out and, to his surprise, found himself thinking about Jennifer Parkes instead.

The office of small, independent newspaper People Power was housed in a ramshackle building in the poorer district just outside the central business area of the city. The inner walls, once a brilliant white, were dull grey now, peppered with stains and rising damp, the carpets too worn, the light bulbs naked.

Rory McConnell, dressed in denim jeans and jacket, white Reeboks with blue trim, entered the building and made his way to the cluttered, smoky room at the far end of the ground level.

Harlan Draper sat at his desk, shoulders hunched, poring over a spread of layouts. A pipe rested comfortably in the left corner of his mouth. Rory was certain, always had been, that the pipe was like the endless stream of French cravats and designer sportswear – there for effect more than anything else. Part of the image Draper enjoyed projecting: socially minded, eccentric founder and editor of an independent publication that championed the rights of the underdog.

Draper had launched People Power at the tender age of twenty -one, way back in the anti-Vietnam, flower power days of the early 70's. On the wall behind him hung a montage of photographs and front-page tear-sheets from over the years. The largest photo, at the centre of Draper's do-it-yourself mural, was a blow-up print showing Draper on the streets, selling the very first issue. He'd been surrounded by an assortment of hippies, complete with love beads, multi-coloured flowing garments, all offering the then fashionable V-shaped peace sign to the camera.

Draper, unrecognisable back then, was the pivotal figure. Full beard, shoulder length black hair, dark coat and dark trousers, open neck shirt with an Eastern symbol medallion glinting in the sun. Very Beatle-esque, circa The Maharishi.

Draper looked up. Rory, hands in pockets, slumped down in the weathered chair opposite him. 'Were you a guru back then?' Rory glanced at the photo, then back to Draper. It was something of a ritual,

Rory with his irreverent comment, as cheeky as possible, every time he came in.

Draper, though tired of the ritual, joined in the banter. 'Gurus were taken seriously back then.'

'When did the flower children stop hanging on your every word?' Rory grinned widely. 'When the hair went? Or when you kept smoking cigars in the office after it became illegal.'

Draper snorted. 'What the landlord doesn't know, doesn't hurt him.' These days he was clean-shaven. The hair, thin and vastly receded, was combed across his head in lonely strands. But his eyes still had their youthful vitality, a piercing messianic stare that had travelled the revolutionary road with him from the student protests of the sixties to the fight for the environment in the twenty first century. 'The reason I put up with you, McConnell,' he said, 'is because I like the ideas you keep coming up with. The latest one has potential.'

'Which one? I pitched five article ideas to you last week.'

Draper's hand skimmed across the papers on his desk. Effortlessly, he plucked Rory's sheet from the mess. 'This thing on that damned plunderer Kaplan. I like the angle. The mega-yuppie who ravaged the capitalist system that created him, causing one of the most drawn-out corporate crashes the country has seen since the days of Skase and Bond.'

Rory smiled inwardly. He'd known Draper would go for that one. 'And I've got the inside track. My lady's mother is an old friend and ex-business partner of the Kaplans.'

'Yeah. You say she was heavily influenced by Kaplan. Turned out hard headed and caring only for business, like him, which caused an estrangement from her daughter.'

'The human side of the super capitalists, Harlan. Showing just how screwed up their families are.'

'Juicy. You think you can dig up some dirt on Henry Kaplan?'

'Sure of it.'

'Okay, go for it. Usual set-up. Advance plus expenses.'

On his way out, Rory parodied the hippies in the photograph. He gave the V sign to Draper. 'Peace, brother.'

'Fuck off, McConnell. Just give me an article that makes sure Henry Kaplan doesn't get any peace at all.'

Henry Kaplan put down the phone. The news from his lawyers was what he'd been hoping for. He picked up the phone and spoke to his secretary, 'Jodie. Have Roger and Harold come to my office.'

'Yes, Mr. Kaplan.'

He reached for the console that brought the radio to life. The news broadcast was seconds away and he expected the radio people already had the latest on his case. The familiar signature tune introducing the report filled the room as Roger entered.

'News,' Roger began.

'We've got our breather,' Kaplan confirmed. 'Listen.'

'The Harry Houdini of Australian business, Henry Kaplan, has done it again,' the male broadcaster announced. 'Less than a few hours after the receivers moved in, the Kaplan Corporation has been granted an injunction against any immediate liquidation proceedings. An appeal against the bankruptcy finding, handed down earlier, will be heard in ten days. Financial analysts believe the stay of execution is a temporary one, with bankruptcy proceedings to continue as soon as the appeal is overturned. In the meantime, Henry Kaplan has less than two weeks to pull the proverbial rabbit out of the hat to save his ailing empire.'

Harold Masterton had entered the office during the second half of the broadcast. Like Roger, he beamed at the news.

'Well done, Henry. Little do the pundits know we do indeed have a rabbit, and his name is Conrad Becker. Provided he signs on the dotted line for Southern Star next week then we have the projected cash flow to win the appeal.'

'And if he doesn't then we've played our last card,' Roger surmised.

'He will,' Kaplan insisted. 'But on the practical side, gentlemen, in the event that the appeal is lost then we have two more weeks to ensure we've each made all the private preparations, financial and otherwise, to cope with life in the aftermath. Understood?'

Roger and Masterton nodded.

Kaplan gave both of them an intent stare to further drive home the point.

There was a hidden meaning to his words, one that only he could know.

The world believed his salvation lay in the result of the court appeal. In fact, financial disaster was the least of his worries.

The real stakes were much, much higher.

TWELVE

It was an early service, 9.45 a.m., squeezed in to fill a gap in Reverend de Castellan's schedule. De Castellan, mournful eyes, dark robes, was more animated than some people might expect of a reverend. There was a sense of drama to his movements as he took his place at the podium.

He cast his eyes over the small group. Jennifer sat in front, flanked by Meg Tanner and Henry Kaplan. Roger was in the row behind, seated beside Cindy Lawrence, Carly Parkes and Rory McConnell.

'Eleven years ago I conducted a service for Brian Parkes,' de Castellan began, 'which was long overdue even then. And although it is now eighteen years since he was last seen, that passage of time doesn't discount the importance of today's service. Today we commit Brian's body to the earth and his soul to the Lord. This is a proper, holy farewell and a special remembrance of Jennifer's loving husband, a father young Carly never knew.

'For today's service we shall listen to Berlioz's Requiem. Firstly, though, I shall read from Psalm twenty-three as we pray for a place in heaven for the spirit of Brian Parkes.

'The Lord is my shepherd; I shall not want. He maketh me to lie down in green pastures: he leadeth me beside the still waters ...'

There was a timeless comfort to the words of this piece, Jennifer thought. De Castellan had read the psalm at the earlier memorial service, and commencing with the same piece now provided a bridge from that service to this. She allowed herself to be transported back to that earlier time. Carly had been six, elfin smile, head of dark curls. Jennifer pictured the little girl sitting beside her, tiny hands clutching her mother's fingers, not fully understanding the event but knowing it had something to do with the father she'd never met.

Jennifer tilted her head, eyes cast back to where Carly sat. The dark hair was straight now, like her mother's, a serene beauty masking a volatile spirit. They exchanged glances, acknowledging the solemnity of the occasion. They had spoken briefly, outside the church, before the service had begun. *What must she make of all this?* Jennifer wondered.

Rory was beside her, dressed smarter than usual. He had smiled politely at Jennifer a number of times; he seemed different today, more reserved, and it struck Jennifer it didn't suit him. Was it just because of the funeral, the boyfriend being supportive? He'd never appeared that type to Jennifer. She wasn't sure why but she'd never trusted Rory McConnell. Something about him didn't ring true.

'... He restoreth my soul: He leadeth me in the paths of righteousness for His name's sake ...'

Carly, Roger, Henry and Meg had all been at that earlier service. Many others weren't here today. Jennifer's and Brian's parents, since deceased; friends and clients of Brian's, long since scattered by the winds of time and change.

Brian. Where were you all those years?

'Yea, though I walk through the valley of the shadow of death, I will fear no evil ...'

Several kilometres away, on a popular bike track, which ran through a section of a national park reserve, Park Ranger Jane Montague reached the bend the young bushwalker had directed her to.

'Down there, in the scrub along the slope,' the bushwalker said. He was twentyish, wide-eyed, scraggy haired, a large backpack dwarfed his thin frame. *Like a tortoise shell*, Jane had thought to herself as she'd followed him along the trail. The genuine, concerned type. He'd gone to the ranger's office to report his sighting. Looks like a body, he'd said. He wasn't certain; he hadn't gone too close. Didn't want any trouble. He was a traveller, he told Jane, originally from Western Australia.

Jane inched down the slope. She was an athletic young woman, short brown hair, lots of freckles.

106

The backpacker was right. It was a body. At close range she saw it was a teenage girl, slim, fair-haired, dressed in jeans, jacket and boots. Another bushwalker. A canvas shoulder bag lay beside her.

Jane looked back up the slope where the young man watched with inquisitive eyes. 'A girl,' Jane called out. 'I'm afraid she's dead.' She watched the backpacker cross himself. *Catholic.*

She knelt down beside the corpse. The girl's skin had a ghostly pallor and there was a bluish tint to the lips. An ugly red welt circled her throat. Her eyes were open - and bulging. Jane's attention returned to that red line. It had a clean, straight look to it, like a ring around the throat. Had she been strangled?

About to spring back to her feet she noticed the bracelet around the girl's wrist. It had an inscription on the metal plate. Jane remembered she'd had a similar item of jewellery when she'd been a teenager. She felt a twinge of curiosity. She lifted the girl's arm and read the engraving. 'Monique. All my love, Craig.' There was an inscription of a date, eighteen years earlier.

Eighteen years ago? This girl didn't look old enough to have been born then, let alone have a boyfriend.

Jane pushed herself back up the slope. 'I need the police,' she said. 'Looks like a murder.' She was surprised at how calm and authoritative she acted. She'd never had to deal with a situation like this before and never would've believed she'd handle it so well.

'Murdered?' The young man was aghast. 'God, no.'

They hiked back along the trail, a twenty-minute trip back to the ranger's office. They were half way there when the word Jane had been searching for popped into her mind. 'Garrotted,' she said.

'What?' asked the bushwalker.

'That poor girl's been garrotted.' It was a chilling thought and there was a sense of unreality to the whole scene. Murdered teenage girl, here in the midst of a beautiful, peaceful sweep of natural countryside.

The queasiness came suddenly, erupting from the pit of her stomach. 'I'm sorry. I think I ...' She darted into the surrounding forest, buckled over. The young man watched helplessly as she dry retched again and again, until finally a thin stream of liquid trickled from her mouth.

' ... For thou art with me; thy rod and thy staff they comfort me. Thou preparest a table before me in the presence of mine enemies: thou annointest my head with oil; my cup runneth over. Surely goodness and mercy shall follow me all the days of my life, and I will dwell in the house of the Lord forever.'

There came a momentary pause as the Reverend de Castellan allowed the weight of the words to settle into the hearts and minds of the gathering.

He turned, nodded to the pianist at the side of the podium. The musician, a middle-aged man, commenced playing a passage from the Requiem. Mournful, lilting, aching with the bittersweet nuance of melody, it filled the church.

Jennifer was inwardly pleased at the skill of the pianist. This recital was full of emotion, an appropriate passage that contained a dramatic element. To Jennifer it signified the high and low dramas of life, as remembered by those left living. She had always believed in recalling the special moments, and was reminded of that philosophy now.

The wishing pool at the house she'd left so long ago, was at the heart of those memories. Jennifer reflected on the wishes, the five-cent coins, the laughter, the romance. She was both surprised and pleased by the positive swell of her feelings - she had no anger towards Brian, no bitterness that he'd been alive all that time. *That's not how it was*, she thought. *He didn't walk out on me. Not of his own accord ...*

The police would find out where he'd been - and why - and unravel the reasons for his sudden return and death. She'd make sure of it. She needed to ascertain that Brian wasn't responsible for his actions.

For the rest of her life, Jennifer wanted to go on remembering Brian with the same fondness she had these past years - without this blemish, without the inexplicable question mark.

At the conclusion of the musical piece, Reverend de Castellan resumed his eulogy. 'We are all aware of the mystery surrounding Brian Parkes' re-appearance and death,' he said, 'but I do not wish to dwell on that. Nor should you. He is in the house of the Lord now. He rests. It is Brian's life - his love of his wife, his good nature, and his value as a friend - that we remember, and which we rejoice in. Those who knew him are better for it.

'Please bow your heads then, in prayer with me, and rejoice in Brian's life, the light, not the dark, as I read from The Prophet, by Khalil Gibran, one of Brian's favourite pieces : "You would know the secret of death. But how shall you find it unless you seek it in the heart of life? The owl, whose night-bound eyes are blind unto the day cannot unveil the mystery of light. For life and death are one, even as the river and the sea are one.

'In the depth of your hopes and desires lies your silent knowledge of the beyond "...'

Detective Sergeant Morris Glenfield, northwest Sydney region, ran his finger down the information listed on the computer printout. The subject's name was Monique Brayson. She had been officially listed with the Missing Persons Unit almost two decades ago. She was described as 120 centimetres tall, of slim build, blue eyes, blonde hair. Eighteen years of age.

He stopped pacing, placed the printout on his desk and sat down. He cast his eyes for the tenth time over the girl's personal effects. The bracelet with the inscription. The purse, which contained her library card, still in mint condition, no discolouring, no dog ears. Issued eighteen years before. The lipstick, in the purse, Glenfield had identified as a brand that had ceased manufacture in the early 2000's.

Only a few minutes ago the bushwalker and the park ranger had given him their statements. The young man had left. Jane Montague had gone to the Ladies. She was back now, standing in the office doorway.

'I'm on my way, then, Detective Glenfield,' she said. 'You will let me know what you find out?'

'I'll be in touch. Thanks very much for your help. Will you be all right to see yourself back to the park?'

'I'll be fine.'

'Terrible shock for you. Finding the girl like that.'

'Yes. I feel that I'd like to ... know more about her.'

Glenfield didn't intend revealing that the girl had been missing for many years. He smiled politely. 'Of course,' he said, and the woman left.

The corpse would be at the coroner's lab by now. Glenfield picked up the photos taken at the crime scene. He was totally mystified. He was looking at the face and the body of a teenager. Monique Brayson should have been thirty-six years old. It can't be the same girl, he thought. But if not, then who? Some street kid who'd rolled the real Monique and stolen her clothes and possessions?

Glenfield looked up from the pictures as Constable Jeff Hyrose breezed in.

'The mother died four years ago,' Hyrose said. 'But the father is alive, still living in the area.'

Glenfield rose from his desk and sighed. 'We'd better go see him.'

' ... "And like seeds dreaming beneath the snow your heart dreams of spring. Trust the dreams for in them is hidden the gate to eternity. Your fear of death is but the trembling of the shepherd when he stands before the King, whose hand is to be laid upon him in honour" ...'

It was amazing, Roger Kaplan thought, as he sat and listened to those words, how clearly he pictured Brian Parkes in his mind's eye; and how untainted his memories remained.

Roger wondered how different things might have been if Brian were still around. Throughout their Uni days, he and Brian had been a couple of knockabout lads. Brian was a brilliant accountant, a wizard with figures. When Roger had gone to work as a senior executive with his father's corporation, he'd relied on Brian to formulate financial structures for new business development plans. Those structures worked well and had won praise for Roger.

But Brian had done most of the work. He had a vision. With his father's blessing, Roger employed Brian's fledgling accountancy practice to work on specific projects.

After Brian's disappearance, Roger was on his own. There'd been no more financial coups. Would we be in this mess now, he wondered, if Brian had been here, consulting me, when the times got tough? The long and pronounced recession had called for a financial whizz like Brian. Someone with his nous ...

Roger had relied on his father's right hand man, Harold Masterton, whom he believed had his finger on the financial pulse. But like all the others, Masterton had missed the signs of impending disaster. Roger realised now that Masterton didn't have the entrepreneurial flair that Brian had shown.

His focus drifted back, through the haze of memories, to the reverend's words, ' ... "Is the shepherd not joyful beneath his trembling, that he shall wear the mark of the King? Yet is he not more mindful of his trembling? For what is it to die but to stand naked in the wind and to melt into the sun" ...'

A police officer sees cruelty every day, in a dozen different ways. Morris Glenfield knew it was something you learned to deal with. But how did anyone deal with this? This was cruelty with a timeless quality to it; a rotten, ravaging thing that kept coming back to eat away at everything decent and pure.

The poor man was seventy years old. Frail, shrunken, white haired, suffering from MS. Thomas Brayson had been a widower for four years, after thirty-five years of marriage. Now he was being led into a mortuary to identify the body of his long lost daughter.

All the grieving he'd done years before had been brought back again. No escape. No respite. No one, Glenfield thought, deserves this.

'I'm only glad my wife, God bless her soul, isn't here for this sad day,' the old man said, ashen faced. 'Our little girl coming back to us, after all this time, only to have her life snuffed out.'

'It is your daughter, then, Mr. Brayson?' Glenfield asked.

'It's as if she died twice,' Brayson mumbled, fixing his gaze on the detective.

He's rambling, Glenfield realised. 'Can I get you something, sir? A cup of tea?'

'Yes ... oh, yes. That would be nice.'

Glenfield led him into the outer office, brought him tea. 'You're quite certain it's your daughter?'

'Oh, it's her all right. It might be eighteen years but I've looked at that face every single day. Lovely photograph we have of her, Mr. Glenfield. It's always had pride of place on the mantlepiece at home. She hasn't changed a bit ... not a bit.' He coughed, sipped at the tea, coughed again. 'She was a very beautiful girl, our Monique.'

'Yes, she was, Mr. Brayson. But your daughter would be much older now than the girl in there.'

'Should've been.'

The old man didn't seem concerned about that. Is he partially senile? Glenfield wondered. He looked to be a million miles away.

'Of course, we can have a proper funeral now,' Brayson continued, 'I would've liked my wife here for that. Say good-bye proper-like. But, then, I guess they're together now, aren't they?'

Together now, Glenfield thought. But where had the girl been for almost two decades? And if the corpse wasn't really Brayson's daughter, then who was she?

After the funeral the small group reconvened to Jennifer's home for refreshments. The get-together lasted an hour and a half, until Roger was the only one left. He joined Jennifer on her back balcony for a final drink.

'Dad told me you'd received the autopsy results but he was a bit vague on details. I gather you're not happy.'

'No.'

'I don't know if this is the best time to talk, but if you want to ...'

'The coroner couldn't, or wouldn't, verify the age difference. We already knew the cause of death. So nothing's changed, really.'

'What's this business about a small hole in the neck?'

She told him about the incision.

Roger leaned against the timber railing and appraised her. 'I've seen that look in your eye before. It says you're going to take charge and get results.'

'I have to do something, Roger, or I'll go crazy. The police seem to be moving so slowly.'

'What can you do?'

She shrugged. 'I'm not sure. Maybe I can follow up on this cut to Brian's neck. I want to speak to some independent medical experts, get some alternative opinions.'

'I can help you with that.'

Jennifer's eyebrows rose in an expectant arc. 'How?'

'Brian and I knew a medical student at Uni. I dated her a few times. I still play squash occasionally with her brother. Katrina is now the surgical resident at St. Vincents. I'm sure, as a favour to an old friend, she'd meet with us.'

'I'll call her.'

'Leave it to me. I'll organise something. Just one thing - stick to the known physical aspects of the coroner's report when you're talking to her. Don't ... insist that Brian hadn't aged.'

'Why?'

'I'm just worried that, if you do, she might not take our other questions seriously. It is, after all, a way-out concept for a doctor to consider. Especially when they haven't seen the body themselves.'

'Point taken. I'll take care how I broach the subject.'

'I hope you didn't mind me suggesting that.'

'Of course not. And you're right. The question of Brian's unnatural appearance needs to be handled carefully. Perhaps that's where I've gone wrong with the police. I don't think they're really taking my view seriously. Certainly the coroner isn't.' Jennifer's focus on Roger became more intense. 'What about you and Henry? Do you share my view that Brian hadn't aged at all?'

'Well, it's not something I could tell from glimpsing him in the casket, not with all that make-up. But I believe in what you saw the morning after his death. I'm going to do everything I can to help you get to the bottom of it.'

Sleep wouldn't come. Jennifer's mind was too active, awash with thoughts of the day. She'd hoped for a long, pleasant talk with her daughter. Perhaps it could've been a chance for her and Carly to get close again.

It wasn't easy for Jennifer: accepting that Carly had left school and moved in with Rory. But she determined to accept it, for the time being, and to work at improving their relationship. She'd been disappointed at the funeral. Carly was very curt - polite but distant, with a questioning look in her eyes. She said she had questions to ask, but it wasn't the time or the place.

Rory, on the other hand, had been more pleasant than usual. Jennifer had always found him insolent - a ridiculous trait, she believed, for a man in his thirties. A sign of immaturity. Today, however, he'd been relaxed, courteous, and far more talkative than Carly. Why? What was he up to?

Jennifer gritted her teeth. There I go again, suspicious, thinking the worst of him. There's probably nothing all that wrong with him.

She'd been warmed by Roger's attentiveness and his offer of help. He seemed changed from his younger days. Perhaps it was just that maturity suited him. The idea of seeking input from an independent medical source appealed to Jennifer. Could there have been some aspect to Brian's pathology the coroner had missed? Perhaps a more imaginative approach was required?

She tossed and turned. Finally, despairing of ever getting to sleep, she slipped on her robe and sat in the closed-in balcony with a cup of cocoa, watching the moonlight touch the trees in the garden.

It was far from over. She knew that deep inside. Brian wouldn't truly be at rest until the mystery of his disappearance and death had been solved. Someone was responsible for what had happened to him. Justice had not been done. Until it was, there could be no rest for her either.

She recalled the reverend's reading of the psalm: ' ... though I walk through the valley of the shadow of death I shall fear no evil,' and found that the words filled her with an inner strength. Today, surrounded by so many caring people in that church, feeling their combined love as she had, she felt empowered by something special.

She remembered something her mother had said to her many years ago: love and strength come to us in many different ways, through many different people. Jennifer smiled inwardly at the gentle thought of her late mother. She felt a longing to see her again, to talk, and that old desire, from when she'd been growing up, to have spent more time with her.

It took her a long time to get to sleep.

THIRTEEN

The constable breezed by Lachlan's office, placing the inter-departmental memo on the desk. 'Another garrotte victim,' he said just before he rushed away along the corridor. 'The northern boys'll be busy ...'

Lachlan, already immersed in paperwork, glanced over the bulletin. A teenage girl, strangled by something that left a shallow cut around her neck. This could get nasty, he speculated, recalling the bulletin, only days before, regarding another garrotte victim. Trish Van Helegen. Also northside.

Lachlan scanned the details. The victim, Monique Brayson, had been reported missing eighteen years ago. This was now being checked further, pending the report from the coroner's office, although the girl's body had been identified by her father.

Missing almost two decades? Lachlan felt a lump in his throat. He picked the memo up, read it again. Initial findings suggested that the style of strangulation matched that which killed Trish Van Helegen. There was no other apparent connection. Van Helegen had not been reported missing years before. Her disappearance had been on the morning of her murder; her body found within twenty-four hours. Lachlan read on further over the report on the Monique Brayson murder. He read and re-read the details of the girl's personal effects. The bracelet with the inscription. A purse, which contained her library card, still in mint condition. A tube of lipstick identified as a brand that had long since ceased manufacture.

116

Monique Brayson should have been thirty six-years old. The body in the morgue was that of a teenager.

Could it be coincidence that two people, missing for eighteen years, had turned up this week, both murdered?

Brian Parkes hadn't been strangled by wire, whereas Monique Brayson and Trish Van Helegen had. Parkes and Brayson were long term missing persons, Van Helegen was not.

The pieces of the puzzle didn't fit.

Nevertheless, Lachlan's gut told him there was a connection. He phoned Sydney LAC in Goulburn Street, asked for John Rosen. The receptionist informed him that the superintendent was out, due back late. Lachlan left a message he'd called. Although the Parkes case was no longer his, he wanted to stay close to it, discuss the similarities with Rosen.

It was a day for catching up with paperwork, of endless calls from court officers about upcoming trial dates. Mostly, though, he concentrated on Todd. He'd already decided to take his son to a movie on Saturday night, after the boy's soccer game, and into the city to Luna Park on Sunday. He'd fly up to Brisbane Monday morning with Todd, then straight back and be in the office late Monday.

Jennifer's weekend would have been quiet, if it hadn't been for two Saturday afternoon calls. The first came from Henry Kaplan, insisting she join him and his lady friend for lunch on Sunday at a seafood restaurant overlooking the harbour in the eastern suburb of Double Bay.

'You're spoiling me,' Jennifer said, 'just like you did when Brian first vanished. You don't have to do it all over again, you know.'

'It's a role I slip into easily,' Kaplan chuckled, 'I'm only sorry I haven't been more consistent at it over the years. You'll join us?'

'Love to.' She hung up, and wished she could return some of the favours to Kaplan, especially now that he faced such enormous financial difficulty. No chance of that, though. By comparison, Jennifer was a small businesswoman. Her company a mere insect alongside the lumbering giant of the Kaplan Corporation.

She thought of Roger. How must he be feeling? The Kaplan Corporation had been there all his life - his only employer. Now it was disintegrating. Despite that, he'd stayed behind at her house after the service, lending a supportive ear, offering his help in contacting his old uni friend. Jennifer hadn't thought to ask him how he was coping with the tumultuous events in his life.

Now, after her conversation with Henry Kaplan, she felt like cursing herself out loud. Immersed in her own problems, as usual, she'd been no comfort to either Henry or Roger at the one time they were at their lowest ebb. They had been the ones consoling her.

What is it with me? It was an angry, lonely, frustrated thought. *I'm always focusing entirely on my own concerns - Wishing Pool Fashions, the awards. Never on my daughter, my friends, my relationships. Am I really that shallow, that self-centred?*

She'd only had one serious relationship since Brian - she didn't consider her friendship with Roger a "relationship" in that sense - and that was in the early to mid 2000's, an on-off affair with a photographer she'd liked very much. It had been an uneasy romance. Mark Russo complained endlessly that she always put her work before him; that she never made the concessions he did. They argued, more and more frequently, until she'd ended the relationship.

I have to change. Somewhere along the way I went from soft and naive to too self- reliant and inflexible. Good God I'm thirty- nine, old enough to wake up to myself.

The second phone call, from Rory McConnell, surprised her. Once again the warm and solicitous Rory, not the insolent one.

'I've a favour to ask, Jennifer. I'm working on an article for People Power about the way the capitalist system can turn on its own, as it has with Henry Kaplan. It would be a great help if I could talk with the man himself, have access to his organisation. And, as you're a friend of -'

'You've got to be kidding.'

'No. Please don't misunderstand. This is no exposé on Kaplan, just the opposite. The positive side of these high profile entrepreneurs. I want to focus on the good things Kaplan has done, things that don't get publicity. Such as his donations to charities, which have been substantial, right?'

Jennifer hesitated. 'Yes.'

'And the employment he's generated through his various enterprises.'

'I'm not getting the point of this, Rory.'

'The point is, the man, and Kaplan, the corporation, have done a lot of good. It's not his fault it's all going down the toilet. It's the recessed market, skyrocketing bank rates, all that economic fallout stuff that the average man doesn't really understand. Our system shouldn't be tearing someone like that apart. I want Kaplan and his people to suggest how that could change, with Government intervention, new trade regulations, a supportive economic structure rather than a dog eat dog one.'

'This doesn't sound like the usual People Power rant and rave stuff.'

'You obviously haven't read us for a while. We haven't been like that for ages. The old greenie bring-down-the-establishment-at-any-cost days are long gone. These days we're about changing the system from within. The modern day radical knows that rebellion can only work systematically by introducing change from within, through strategic planning, organisation, and "selling" of the ideas.'

'I'm impressed,' Jennifer conceded.

'Then you'll help?'

'I'll help. Actually, I'm having lunch with Henry and his lady tomorrow. Why don't you and Carly join us? It's a chance for me to get together with Carly, and Henry would love to see her again. Anyway, you could meet him, discuss your idea.'

'We'll be there with bells on. Thanks, Jennifer.'

'You're welcome.' She hung up the phone, wondering whether she'd done the right thing.

Look for someone with a routine. A routine at a quiet time, in a quiet place.

119

The jogger was on a high; thirsty for the kill. His common sense told him it was too soon after the Van Helegen woman, but like a starving man who has tasted a morsel of food he'd become ravenous for the feast.

Saturday night. 9.15 p.m. For the second night in a row he jogged the suburban streets of East Gosford, in the Central Coast region, north of Sydney.

A beautiful place in which to run, with wide open streets, lots of trees, maples, willows, great sturdy redwood oaks and cypresses that flourished in the clean air of this satellite city. Sea breezes from nearby Avoca Beach and Green Point gave the air a refreshing tang.

This part of the suburb was old, established. The jogger had identified three potential targets, each of whom he'd sighted the night before, and now, again this evening. A young woman, early twenties, also a jogger, both nights at around six. A regular, before-dinner run. Unfortunate. Even in a quiet area like this, there was still activity at this early hour. Cars in and out of driveways. Other walkers.

A little later, at around 8.30 p.m. a middle aged woman walked her dog. Second night, same time. Routine. It was not a large dog, though, a terrier with a peaceful, docile expression. The jogger knew that these dogs could become vicious when excited - especially if their owner got into trouble.

No. The third creature of routine seemed the most likely. At 10 p.m., a man of around sixty, tall, slightly overweight, thick grey hair, also walked his dog. It was late to be out walking a dog, the killer thought, but then some people are night owls.

The dog was small, weedy looking, more like a child's plaything than an elderly man's companion. It was harmless, that was the main thing, and it would be fun to let the animal live, let it run around whimpering while its master had the life snuffed out of him.

The timing was just right. On both evenings the jogger observed no one else on the street, no cars coming or going. Most of the household lights were out. Perfect. All he needed was for this man to keep to his routine.

The jogger would be back Sunday night, primed and ready. He felt the anticipation rise from within like an electric current, throwing off sparks.

This feeling of freedom was extraordinary, and it kept getting better. He had one deep fear, though, which returned to haunt him as he jogged back to the place where he'd left his car. What if the surveillance on him began again? What if the shadows returned to watch, to restrain him? Was there a chance they'd been alerted by Trish Van Helegen's murder?

Perhaps he shouldn't have garrotted the girl. They, whoever *they* were, would know it as his trademark. He liked garrotting best because it gave him a thrilling closeness to his victim. It allowed him to feel the dark power flowing from his fingertips, totally controlled by the strength in his arms.

No, it really didn't matter. However he killed, the shadows were bound to find out - if they were going to find out at all. If he'd ever been able to find out who they were, he might have been able to stop them, or devise a way to avoid them. It was the most frustrating and damning thing of all - being powerless to stop them.

He only hoped and prayed to whatever devils drove him that his freedom was here to stay, that the mysterious sentinels were gone forever.

'We're doing what?' Carly Parkes' tone was hostile. Her pearly blue eyes were wide open, angry, the penetrating gaze demanding an explanation.

Rory armed himself with his ready smile, confident and reckless at the same time. The carefree charm had always come easy to him. 'Temper, temper. No need to sound off the sirens.' He was in the kitchen, fixing a late night snack. Crackers and pate. Irish coffee. He chuckled to himself. This was the best time to break the news to Carly. He glanced at the clock. 12.45 a.m.

She'd been out all evening with a gaggle of girlfriends, fellow models. Now she lounged in front of the television, a glass of white wine in hand, chatting and half watching an old Hitchcock movie.

'You've got no business making arrangements like that without checking with me!'

'Carly —'

121

'Don't cut across me. I'm surprised at you. Kaplan isn't your style. What's this all about, anyway?'

He walked into the living room, plaintive look, shrugged. Playing it his way. 'If you'll let me explain, baby ...'

She glared at him. Challenging him to soften her mood. 'Go on.'

'I told you last week about the articles I planned for People Power. Harlan wants this series on Kaplan. If I can gain some access to his people and his firms ...'

'While there's still something left.'

'Exactly. I'm a journo for Christ's sake, meeting the Kaplans of this world is my job. Journos use the connections they have, in this case your mother. Besides, she wants us to join them for lunch. And you have things you want to ask your mother.'

'I can make my own arrangements with my mother,' Carly said.

Rory noticed that some of the fire had gone out of her. Always a master at timing, he inched forward, came round behind the couch, reached down and massaged her shoulders gently. 'Sorry, babe. I didn't think it would be such a big deal. I just thought, y'know, two birds with one stone. Lunch with your mother and broach the idea on this article to Kaplan.'

She didn't reply. Just pouted. Rory kept massaging. 'How's that?'

'Good.'

'Listen, we don't have to go to this damned lunch, if you're dead-set against it. I can ring, call it off, say I'm ill.'

'No, we'll go.'

'Sure?'

Carly shrugged. 'I need to ask her about Dad. Perfect chance, I suppose.'

'It isn't going to get too heavy?'

'No. It'll be fine.' She allowed her body to relax and enjoy the massage. She couldn't see the smug, satisfied expression on Rory's face, nor the cold gleam of intent in his eyes.

The seafood restaurant was on the shores of Sydney Harbour, elevated, with a glorious view of the flotilla of boats - all kinds, yachts to

122

cabin cruisers. A clear, calm day prevailed, strong sun, and the gentle roll of the ocean was dappled by brilliant speckles of sunlight.

Henry Kaplan had arranged a table on the open-air balcony. He introduced Carly, Rory and Jennifer to his live-in girlfriend, Helen Shawcross.

Jennifer knew he had a young lover but was shocked to see how young she actually was. Twenty-five, Jennifer guessed, and a classic beauty. Long, long legs, hourglass figure, toothy smile, blonde hair. Helen wore a strapless, blue cotton dress, very short. She worked as a cosmetics consultant for one of the department store chains, promotional work, moving from store to store.

'I keep telling Helen she should be a model,' Kaplan said, directing his comment to Jennifer and Carly. 'You two should have an opinion on that, you're in the business.'

'I think that's up to Helen,' Jennifer said pointedly. 'She should do whatever she wants.'

Helen nodded towards her in silent approval.

'Touché,' Kaplan conceded the point, allowing himself a chuckle. '*The Sisterhood*. I left myself wide open for that one.' He focused his attention on Carly. 'I hear you're doing some modelling. How're you finding it?'

'It's not a long-term thing. I really want to do something more worthwhile.'

'What would you do that was more worthwhile?' Helen reached casually for her wine glass, staring Carly down with her large, blue, cat-like eyes. Something in her tone made her question more of a challenge than a simple enquiry.

'Perhaps writing for a publication that has a concerned voice, as Rory does,' Carly said, 'or working with an organisation that has a strong social agenda.'

'And you think you could do that?' Helen Shawcross' tone was cool, the inference one of belittlement.

'Whatever I do, it will be something with more substance than fashion,' Carly snapped. She'd picked up on Little Miss California Dream's attitude, and she wasn't about to be talked down to by such a vacuous glamour puss.

Kaplan seemed to enjoy the exchange. 'Oh, come on girls, relax, drink up and be merry.' He wore a wide grin as he picked up the bottle of chardonnay and re-filled their glasses. 'Always a small fire whenever this little capitalist,' he angled his head toward Helen, 'gets together with someone whose ideals are strictly left of centre.'

Rory saw his chance. 'Speaking of the political left,' he said to Kaplan, 'there's something I'd like to put to you. An article, very leftish I'm afraid, but not at all unsympathetic to your organisation, and others like it.'

'Sounds different,' Kaplan said. 'Go on.'

Rory outlined his idea. As he did, he couldn't help his gaze being diverted from time to time to Helen Shawcross. She watched him, flickers of agreement to his points showing in her eyes. Nothing innocent about this one, Rory thought. Her body language was unmistakably seductive. It wasn't hard for Rory to return the vibe, smiling back occasionally with a casual, seemingly innocent wink. Warm glances, friendly chatter - but a silent invitation to something far more intimate.

While the People Power article was discussed, Carly spoke to her mother, her voice low, her expression intense. 'There's something I've wanted to ask you. The funeral wasn't the right time for it.'

'Ask away.' Jennifer was glad Carly had a question. It would serve as an icebreaker, help to get them talking. She realised, very quickly, that this wasn't the question that would serve that purpose.

'You always told me things were fantastic between you and my father. That he never would have walked out.'

'That's right.'

'But he did, didn't he? He was alive all these years, yet he never contacted you - or me.'

'He wouldn't have vanished voluntarily,' Jennifer replied. 'I'm certain of that. There has to be some other explanation ...'

'What could have stopped him contacting us for eighteen years? There has to be more to this than you're telling us.'

This is the reaction I feared most, Jennifer thought, the idea that if Brian walked out on me then I must be holding back on something. *How do I respond when I'm just as much in the dark myself?*

'I want the answers more than anyone, Carly.'

'I don't believe you.' Carly's eyes flashed early warning signs of her anger. Her voice rose. 'Something was wrong between you, wasn't it?' She felt the frustration rising up from deep inside. Her mother always had pat answers to everything. Now she was giving pat answers to this.

'No, Carly-.'

'Why are you holding back on this? I never knew my father, and now he's been killed, back in the street where you used to live. He must've been looking for you.'

Kaplan, becoming aware of the conversation between Jennifer and Carly, interrupted his dialogue with Rory. 'Whoa,' he said, holding up the palm of his hand. 'This doesn't sound good.' The comment was directed towards Carly. 'Carly, what's this all about?'

'It's about what really happened between my parents. There's more to this whole damn thing than meets the eye. I think I've a right to know.'

'Then let me assure you your mother doesn't know any more than the rest of us. I know that much. I employed two top-notch private investigators for two years to find out what happened to your father. If he'd been in contact, during that time, with anyone he'd known previously, including your mother, the investigators would've been on to it. There was no trace of him. Nothing, until he was run down on Claridge Street last week.'

Jennifer's eyes met Carly's, and she held the gaze. 'The police are giving the case special attention,' Jennifer assured her. 'I'm determined to get to the bottom of this, for both our sakes. Be with me on this, not against me.' To herself she thought: Oh Carly, if only you could see that I'm feeling the same frustration as you, the same anger as you.

A lone tear formed in the corner of Carly's eye. She shrugged, averting her gaze to look out over the water, willing the moment to pass.

FOURTEEN

Bill Dawson liked to keep busy. That wasn't hard, his garden flowerbed had produced three award-winning petunias in as many years - and then there were the three small dogs he groomed and trained for the district dog shows. The wall of his study boasted certificates for first and second places in more than a dozen shows.

At sixty, Bill had taken early retirement twelve months before, bringing to a close a forty-three year career in the printing trade. These days, gardening and his canines absorbed most of his energies.

His wife, Beatrice, stepped into the back yard with a lunch tray. Open ham sandwiches, salad bowls and coffee. She set it down on the timber garden table. 'Are you going to take a break from that and eat?' she called out.

'You betcha.' He tossed aside the clump of weeds he'd extracted from the soil and ambled over to the table. 'The sun is magnificent today,' he commented, reaching for a stick of celery as he sat down.

'It always feels best this time of the year,' Beatrice said matter-of-factly, sliding one of the plates towards Bill. 'Are we working with Max this afternoon?'

Bill munched on a sandwich. 'Yeah. Take him through the motions. We've got one week to brush up on his routine before next week's show.' Max gave a high-pitched yelp from his fenced-in area of the yard. He pranced around in a perfect circle, the born poseur, and then strutted into his kennel.

'I swear that dog knows when he's being talked about,' Beatrice said.

'You bet he does,' Bill beamed with pride, 'and I tell you, come next Saturday, he's gonna be a winner. I feel it in my bones.'

Two streets away, on Palms Avenue, sixteen-year old Dianne Adamson arrived at her boyfriend's place, having walked over from her home five blocks away. Taking advantage of the warmer spring weather, she wore a light cotton blouse and denim shorts. She was slim and dark-eyed with skin that always gave the impression she'd been out in the sun.

Ryan Paisley bounded out the front door, grinning from ear to ear. 'Hi.'

'Hi.' She leaned towards him, gave him a peck on the cheek. 'Your olds home?'

'No. They're out 'til late. Real late. I got a stack of DVD's. Popcorn. The works.'

She followed him into the house.

'And I got these.'

He flashed a packet from his pocket, returning it so quickly she didn't see it, just the blur of colour. But she knew what they were. She wasn't sure how to react. 'Great,' she said uncertainly.

'You're okay about it, aren't you?' Ryan asked, aware of her coyness.

Dianne shrugged. 'I guess.'

He stepped towards her, placed his long, sinewy arms around her tiny waist. 'It's gonna be okay. I promise. And you don't have to do anything you don't want to.'

'I know.'

'Let's pig out, eh, and watch a movie. What do you feel like seein'?'

'What have you got?'

Ryan flicked through the stack of rentals beside the TV. 'Terminator Two, Predator, Die Hard, Transformers ... any of those appeal?'

She winced. 'Ah ... no. I kind of had in mind ... well, something a little more romantic, y'know.'

Ryan frowned. 'Oh.' He fumbled around in the stack. 'How about this one? Sleeping With The Enemy. That's got romance, hasn't it?'

Dianne pouted. That was hardly the romantic mood setter she had in mind. 'No. Look, Transformers will be fine.'

'Oh yeah,' Ryan grinned, glad to be back on familiar turf. 'Megan Fox. Good one.'

Dianne sighed as she sat on the sofa. Ryan loaded the DVD, then dropped down beside her, awkwardly placing his arm around her shoulders. His breath was hot on her face, and Dianne realised she had completely lost the excited, elated sensation she'd felt on the way over. She'd dreamed for weeks of being alone with Ryan, of having a place to themselves. The thought of losing her virginity had made her tingle all over with anticipation. But now she was here she felt anxious and confused. Being alone with Ryan just wasn't what she'd expected.

'Feelin' okay?' Ryan asked, taking a handful of popcorn from the bowl on the armrest.

'All good.' But she knew the monotone of her voice betrayed her real emotion. Maybe I'll snap out of it, she thought. Maybe I'll feel better as the afternoon wears on. Then she felt Ryan's fingers groping at her breasts and she tensed up. 'Not yet, Ryan.'

'No worries. No rush.' He reached for another handful of popcorn.

Early evening. The last, fading strips of light retreated towards the city skyline like ghosts in the twilight. The jogger paced his home, glancing at the view each time he passed the glass doors of the balcony.

All his senses were heightened in anticipation of what was to come. Tonight. Around 10.30 p.m. He knew he was tempting fate, a second murder within a week of the first since his resurgence. At the same time, he needed to fuel his blood lust after so long.

This would be the last killing for a while; it was necessary to lay low from time to time. Not only that, it was becoming difficult to find the time to seek out his prey. It had been easier before, when he was younger, when his time had been more his own.

He had a couple of hours to fill before he drove to the Central Coast. He was in the right frame of mind to write to his mother. Several months had elapsed since his last letter.

For the first time in a long while he had something to tell her.

He'd wanted to write since the morning he'd killed Trish Van Helegen, but a shortage of time and the overwhelming desire to seek a new victim had stalled him.

Dear Mother,

It can be a frustrating thing, this need to inflict death, because it is such a secret thing, one that can't be readily shared. I have to be careful: so much can go wrong, and the smallest detail can give me away. In many ways it's a curse. The curse was doubly so during the years I was watched. I've written to you about the girls before, but they were never enough to fully satisfy my urges.

Well, Mother, this was one of those weeks when it all seemed worthwhile. Something extraordinary happened.

None of us really know the meaning of freedom until we've had it taken from us, and then returned. This week, I regained the freedom to kill.

I don't know why. Perhaps I'll never know. But I'm free again, and I can't begin to explain the sheer, unadulterated elation of it.

I know it must be hard for you, receiving these letters, but you're the only one I can confide in, the only one I can trust. It feels good, sharing this with you. I just wish there was more we could share.

Do you have hidden sides - secrets - that you long to share with someone?

Tonight, I'm going into the dark again, to run with the other creatures of the night.

Wish me luck, Mother, I'll be thinking of you.

It was getting late, and after an hour of kissing and hugging, Dianne Adamson allowed Ryan Paisley to remove her blouse and slip the bra strap from her shoulders. The moulded white cups dropped away, revealing the soft white skin of her breasts. Her nipples hardened, petals ripe and about to burst, as Ryan's hungry hands firmly caressed her.

It isn't working for me, Dianne thought. I don't know why. I like Ryan and I've tried to relax but I keep tensing up. The feeling isn't there.

Ryan removed his shirt and pressed his body harder against hers. 'Ryan,' she whispered in his ear, 'slow down a little ...'

'Slow down,' he kept his own voice low, responding to her whisper with a whisper of his own. He brought his arm up to face level, glanced at his watch. 'We've been together since this afternoon,' he protested, 'we have to get on with this, Di. My parents will be home in another hour or so.'

'Oh.'

He kissed her again, thrusting his tongue anxiously into her mouth. Her tongue was not as pliant as before. She was tense. His left hand stroked her breasts even more vigorously. With his right, he began groping at the button on her shorts.

'Ryan ... I'm sorry. I can't.'

'You'll be fine, Dianne. I promise. Just try and relax.'

'No. I don't know why but I'm just ... not ready, not tonight.' She pushed his hands away.

A lock of sandy hair fell across his forehead. His face took on a brow beaten, puppy dog expression. 'But this is our big chance.'

'There'll be other chances.' Dianne reached for the bra, eased it into position and fastened the clasps from behind in fast, practiced moves. Instinctively she knew there wouldn't be another chance. Not with Ryan Paisley.

'You're just nervous. I understand. I can fix that.' Ryan put his arm around her.

'Ryan. No.' Her voice rose, filled with urgency. She attempted to disentangle herself from him but he persisted.

'We both want this, Di,' he said. His attempt to be seductive and forceful was, instead, clumsy and uncertain.

'No. I don't.' She was angry now. How many times did she have to make her feelings obvious to him?

She pushed him away forcefully, rose to her feet and pulled her blouse on as she headed for the door. 'Look Ryan, I'm sorry, okay? I think it's best if I go now.'

Ryan jumped up and followed her. 'Come on, Dianne, don't over-react. Let's try again.'

'I'm going, Ryan. We'll talk tomorrow.'

She was at the door. Ryan trotted along behind, confused, anxious. The anger started to come. 'What the hell is all this? You've never been the sort to lead me on before. What's got into you?'

'I don't want to talk about it now.'

Ryan took hold of her wrist. 'Well I do.'

She jerked free of his grip. 'Piss off!' She turned hard on her heel, flung the door open and ran down the front porch steps. Tears sprang into the corners of her eyes.

Ryan charged out of the house behind her, fuelled by his own fury. 'Dianne!'

Dianne kept running. She didn't want another confrontation with Ryan tonight. They both needed time to cool off. She rounded the corner at the end of the street. Marcos Avenue, long and winding and lined with trees, stretched before her. Wide, gnarled tree branches, awash with canopies of leaves, obscured the full glow from the streetlights. There were many deep wells of darkness along the way.

She knew how headstrong and petulant Ryan could be. Halfway along the avenue she diverted her direction and stepped over the front fence of a large brick house. No lights shone from within. She planted herself beside a sprawling rose bush, hiding herself from view.

I'll wait awhile, until the coast is clear, before I start out again.

From behind the bush she peered out onto the street. There was no movement, very few house lights showing. From further along she heard the barking of a dog, followed by the sudden, sharp meow of a cat, then silence.

Minutes later she heard footfalls on the pathway. She held her breath, expecting to see Ryan. Instead, a lone jogger glided by.

Half a block around the corner, Ryan stopped at his front gate, fuming, debating whether to follow Dianne back to her place. He decided against it and went back into the house, slamming the door behind him.

At precisely 10 p.m. Bill Dawson, a creature of habit, left his house with an eager Max prancing in front of him, straining at his leash. Every day Bill took Max for a twenty-minute walk in the morning, the early afternoon, and finally last thing in the evening. To train a show dog, routine was an essential part of the day, and that went for relaxation as well as for teaching and practicing tricks and movements. Bill enjoyed these walks as much as Max did. He loved the peace and quiet, and the sky full of stars.

Bill paid fleeting attention to the figure in a tracksuit and sports cap, jogging along the footpath on the opposite side of the road, heading back in the direction from which Bill and Max had come.

At the end of the block, the jogger crossed the road, then resumed running. This time heading back the way he'd come, quickly closing the gap between himself and the old man.

Bill Dawson heard the footsteps approaching hurriedly from behind and threw a casual glance over his shoulder. He saw the jogger. He chuckled to himself.

These fellows are keen. And why not? Good for the health.

His dog, trotting along happily in front of him, also glanced back. The dog reacted differently. It stopped, began barking.

'You are excitable tonight, aren't you?' Bill yanked at the leash. 'Come on, matey. Stop making a fuss.' Sudden shock gripped him as the coil of wire snapped into place around his neck.

Immediately he was choking. His whole body throbbed with sharp pain as the metal cut the thin flesh of his throat. The end of the leash dropped from his fingers as he vainly attempted to raise his arms to his throat. He staggered back, barely conscious of the strong male presence that pressed against him from behind.

His thoughts, in those few final seconds, were chaotic. His lungs were about to burst, his mind on fire, his vision unfocused and blackening, slipping away. The jogger! He pictured the runner, a blurred mental image.

Why doesn't he help me? Can't he see ... what's happening?

The obvious answer didn't register with him.

Max flung his tiny body at the feet of the attacker, barking wildly, teeth bared, jaws snapping at the jogger's ankles. The killer threw his left leg out, the side of his foot pummelling the dog square on its underside. Max reeled back, stunned.

From across the road, behind the rose bush, Dianne Adamson watched in horror as Bill Dawson's limp form crashed to the ground. Her gaze followed the man in the tracksuit, pocketing the coil of wire, continuing his run along the street. The killer looked about briefly as he ran. Satisfied he was alone, he rounded the next corner without another backwards glance.

The dog scampered around the body of its owner, whimpering, rubbing his nose up against the corpse.

Dianne's breath came in short, ragged bursts. Fear paralysed her. When the barking dog had alerted her, minutes before, she had peered out from behind the bush. It took only seconds for the shadowy scene before her to fully register - one man attacking another - but by then the lifeless body of the elderly man was dropping. There was a fleeting instant in which the jogger, beginning to move again, glanced about. The glow from the nearby streetlight touched his face. That brief moment was all she needed to see the firm jaw and the shape of the mouth. The upper half of the face remained in shadow, obscured by the cap's peak. Then he was gone.

Dianne steeled herself against the plummeting sensation in the pit of her stomach. She forced herself to her feet and crossed the road. Several streams of blood were lazily forming into pools around the body. Bill Dawson had fallen on his back and his ashen face, illuminated like a ghostly visage under the neon, was frozen into a grimace of sheer horror. The eyes were wide-open, bulging, pleading.

Dianne ran to the nearest driveway and fell to her knees. She vomitted. She vaguely wondered why lights weren't turning on inside the houses? Why people weren't running out onto the footpaths, raising the alarm. The reason, she understood later, was simple. There had been very little noise.

The man in the tracksuit, she later told police, moved swiftly and silently, like a panther, taking his prey completely by surprise. The actual act of killing was very fast, and then the killer went, like a phantom, into the darkness.

There had only been the bark - and then the whimpering, of the victim's pet. For years to come, that was what Dianne Adamson remembered most about that night - the soundtrack to all her nightmares.

The pathetic, mournful whine of that small dog, grieving for its master.

FIFTEEN

The murder of Trish Van Helegen, just a few days before, made the early news sections of the Sydney newspapers. Reported on the evening TV news, on balance, it received no more or less than most other violent crimes that are, sadly, commonplace in a city of several million people. Bill Dawson's murder by identical means changed all of that. The front page of *The Telegraph* screamed to the city in bold banner headlines that a madman was on the loose. Two identical murders in less than a week.

Society needs to rid itself of these monsters, proclaimed the editorial. *Why is it that in the last fifty years there seems to have been more and more of these mass murderers? It is clearly a phenomenon of our age, and it is not restricted to the cities of Australia, America or Britain. The serial killer knows no boundaries, no restrictions with language or race or colour or age. He, or she, could be anyone, anywhere.*

The editorial closed with a prayer that this was not the work of a serial killer - that there would be no more killings.

9.15 a.m. Monday morning. At Mascot Airport, Neil Lachlan read the newspaper reports quickly. There had been another garrotte killing since Monique Brayson. He'd seen the internal police circular on Friday about her. There had been no media reports of that over the weekend. Had a shroud of secrecy formed around Brayson's death, as it had for Brian Parkes? If that was the case, then why hadn't the same been done about the death of Bill Dawson?

Todd was standing at the wall-length window, watching the runway. 'Hey Dad, look!'

Lachlan joined his son at the window. A 747 Melbourne bound flight was hurtling along the runway. It lifted effortlessly off the ground, nose pointed skywards.

'That is ace,' Todd said excitedly.

'Ace,' Lachlan agreed.

'Will we be on a plane like that, Dad?'

'I'd say so.' Lachlan's mind wandered back to the news reports. Random killings. There appeared to be no connection between Bill Dawson and Trish Van Helegen. If the murderer struck again, anyone, anywhere could be the next victim. It was the stuff policemen's nightmares were made of.

For what reason might Monique Brayson's murder have been kept from the public? The difference struck him. Like Brian Parkes, the girl had been missing for eighteen years. The other two victims had not. He had to assume there was some significance to that.

'I won't be a minute,' Lachlan told his son, 'just going to make a phone call.' He flipped open his cell. He hoped John Rosen could satisfy his curiosity.

The pleasant female voice over the loudspeaker interrupted his thoughts. She was calling for passengers to board the 9.50 a.m. flight to Brisbane.

Todd grabbed hold of his father's sleeve. 'Come on, Dad, that's us!'

Lachlan grinned. The boy's enthusiasm was contagious. The phone call would have to wait.

It was an hour since Jennifer had spoken to John Rosen on the phone. She had sensed the man's reluctance to meet with her. Nevertheless she'd pushed the issue and he'd agreed to "squeeze her in" at 9.30 a.m.

'We have a situation developing here,' Rosen said, ushering Jennifer into his office. He gestured at the spread of newspapers fanned across the large oaken desk. 'It's all hands on deck. We believe this killer will strike again so you'll understand I'm pressed for time.'

Jennifer gave a slight nod but chose not to acknowledge Rosen's comments any further. Why was he being so evasive? There may be a killer on the loose, she understood the urgency of that, but at the same

136

time she deserved some input on the case concerning her husband. After all, the unusual circumstances surrounding Brian's case had caused this man to assign the case to his special investigations unit.

'I want to know if there's been any progress with my husband's case.' There was no mistaking the edge to her voice.

'As I said on the phone, Ms Parkes, nothing further at this stage ...'

'It's been almost a week.'

'Ms Parkes, a murder investigation can take weeks, sometimes months ...'

'This isn't just a murder investigation. There's something extraordinarily strange about my husband's disappearance and the physical condition of his body. I wasn't sure at first but now I'm certain the whole thing is being handled with kid gloves. Do I have to run to the media to get any action?'

'Turning the investigation into a media sideshow isn't going to help you or us,' Rosen said. 'Please, I understand your frustration.' He raised his hands in the air and, with a shrug, illustrated the enormity of the problem they faced. 'I'm sure you understand just how difficult this is. There's no rational explanation for your husband's missing years, his death or his unusually youthful appearance. We have established for certain that he was run down and killed the evening prior to being found. We're currently going back over old ground, cross checking information with the Missing Persons Unit, checking overseas records, trying to establish where he was. But we have nothing, absolutely nothing to go on.'

Jennifer knew she was going round in circles, covering old ground. She felt she was going to burst a blood vessel and her voice rose sharply. 'Why do I feel I'm getting the runaround?'

'It's hard, very hard to have patience in a situation like this. Believe me, Ms. Parkes, I do understand that. Because this case is so unusual, and lacking in any leads at all, it may be a long time before we get any results.' It wasn't the first time Rosen had given such a speech. He'd faced anxious relatives before whom he'd needed to placate. Jennifer Parkes worried him, though. She had more resolve than many of the grieving relatives in difficult cases.

'I'm not the kind of person to be a cowering, whimpering victim in all this, inspector. That was my problem eighteen years ago. This time I intend to ensure every possible avenue of enquiry is sought. Look, I'm practically going crazy just trying to imagine an answer. Maybe what that means is that we have to think this through laterally ... take a different approach ...'

Jennifer cast an unrelenting gaze over the senior policeman. She sensed she was wasting her time, but it felt good to make her feelings clear. She moved to the doorway. 'I'd appreciate it if I could be given a daily update on how the investigation is progressing, and I'll be taking whatever other steps I feel are necessary to advance the investigation.'

'Ms Parkes ...'

She strode out abruptly, not wishing to exert any more energy where it wouldn't get the necessary response. That had been her credo in business. That was the way she felt about this Superintendent. She wished that Neil Lachlan, who'd been genuinely intrigued by the case, was still working on it.

She drove across the city to her office. What could she do? She had an appointment, this coming afternoon, with Doctor Katrina Wells. With Roger. That was a start, but it was hardly enough.

Cindy stood in the reception area, chatting with office coordinator Carmen, when Jennifer arrived. 'Morning, boss lady,' said Cindy with a mock salute. 'Don't look so serious. The good news is that it's all systems are go on the GB's order.'

'We're going to make it?'

'We're going to make it,' Cindy confirmed. 'I've just got off the phone from the factory. They don't think they'll need to call in outside suppliers.'

'Terrific.' Jennifer exchanged a wave with Carmen. She hoped she was hiding the fact that her enthusiasm for the business had all but evaporated. She trod the familiar corridor to her office, reached for the phone and called the Hurstville Police Station. 'Detective Senior Sergeant Lachlan, please.'

'He's out of town this morning,' came the reply, 'due back this afternoon. Can I take a message?'

Damn, Jennifer thought. 'Yes. Ask him to call Jennifer Parkes.' She replaced the handset, noticing that the additional lines on her phone system were lit up with incoming calls on hold.

Cindy entered the office, her arms laden with documents. Jennifer reminded herself she had a business to run, whether she felt like it or not, and resolved to get on with it. People were depending on her.

She had no idea what she was going to say to Neil Lachlan, anyway. As the day progressed her mind kept returning to Brian's body on the morgue slab the previous week. She saw her hands turning over the wallet, and the driver's licence with the long-ago expiry date.

Eighteen years earlier, Henry Kaplan had hired a private detective to search for Brian. This time, she had the money to hire a private investigator herself. She decided that was the only course left for her to follow.

Depression descended on Neil Lachlan, like a dark cloud eclipsing the sun, whenever he returned Todd to Marcia at the end of a weekend. The feeling came - a churning sensation in the pit of his stomach. This was worse though, ten times worse.

He waved to Todd and Marcia. He watched as Marcia's car rounded the bend in the road, quickly becoming obscured by traffic.

Lachlan walked back into the terminal at Brisbane Airport, to the lounge and downed a beer as he waited for the next flight to Sydney.

He was breaking one of his strictest rules, drinking during the day when he would soon be on duty again. He'd hoped it might help to dull his pain, but instead it seemed to bring on a headache. He'd only ever been a social drinker - except for that one period when he'd been consumed by the Narcotics Squad work and his marriage had begun to fail. Lachlan had seen other coppers drift into alcoholism, and he'd been determined not to make the same mistake.

His flight was called and his head swam through murky waters as he boarded the aircraft.

Deputy Police Commissioner, Ed Razell, was a burly, ruddy-faced man with a gravelly voice and a gruff speaking manner. He was also articulate and persuasive, a diamond in the rough type who meant business and inspired confidence. He strode with an air of purpose to the podium, flanked by squad commanders - John Rosen amongst them.

'We're looking for a man of indiscriminate age,' Razell said to the gathering of detectives. 'Let me describe him to you. He's reasonably fit and lean. He wears a tracksuit and running shoes, and most probably a peaked cap pulled over his forehead. He could be out for a run at any time, day or night. That was the part he played when he killed Bill Dawson, thanks to the testimony of an eyewitness. The fact that we have an eyewitness description is strictly confidential at this time. The media mustn't get wind of it. We don't want to alert the killer that we're on to his physical description and his M.O., otherwise he'll change both. If he strikes again, there's a good chance he'll use the same disguise, the same ruse, jogging. We contend he used that method when he murdered Trish Van Helegen days before. Catching him in the act, or while he's stalking a victim, is the best chance we have of stopping him.'

A murmur broke out among the men and women gathered in the operations room.

'Forensics confirm that a wire object was used to garrotte the victims,' Razell continued, 'so we're specifically looking for a male jogger carrying such an object. As you know, Superintendent Rosen will head up the investigation.' Razell turned to Rosen. 'Superintendent?'

Razell moved aside as Rosen stepped up to the podium. 'The first murder occurred early in the morning, the second late at night. Both in quiet areas. We can't rely on that, but it does give us an insight into when and where the killer may strike next. We'll have round the clock shifts of two person teams, in car and on foot, all over the metropolitan areas on the north side and the central coast. Seek out the quiet times and the quiet places. I expect that's where we'll find our man. Any lone male joggers fitting the general description are to be stopped and questioned and their particulars passed on to the command centre.'

Lachlan stood at the back of the room, having arrived just as the briefing session began. When he'd arrived at his station, earlier that afternoon, the head office circular had been on his desk. The homicide detectives from all branches were required to attend the Parramatta meeting for a full brief from Razell and Rosen. It was clear the Deputy Commissioner took seriously the possibility that a serial killer was on the loose, intending to strike again and again. He didn't want an outbreak of the panic that resulted from other mass murder rampages, or the criticism sometimes levelled at the police work. Especially not so soon after the reign of the elderly man who had killed several aged widows.

There was no mention, however, of the other garrotte murder victim. Monique Brayson.

At the close of the briefing session, Lachlan pushed his way through the crowd towards the podium. Razell and Rosen were leaving the room by the large double doors to their immediate right. Lachlan stuck his arm past a throng of shoulders, tapping John Rosen on the upper arm. 'Got a minute?'

'Sure.' Rosen looked around for a quieter spot. 'Over there.' He pointed to a far corner. 'We need a larger room for these things.'

'Tell me about it.' They edged their way to the corner. 'The bulletin last Friday about the Brayson girl's murder. That was a garrotte killing. Why no mention?'

'Could be a coincidence that the murder method was the same. Regardless, at this point in time it's being treated as a separate case, by the same guys I've got following up on Brian Parkes, because both had been missing for such a long period. And before you ask - yes, the girl still appears youthful.'

'You've never been one to believe in coincidence,' Lachlan pointed out.

'If it's connected with the Van Helegen and Dawson murders, then the special unit boys will find the connection and then it will become part of this broader "jogger" investigation. My guys are assisting with the search for this jogger as well, so they're well aware of the similarities. I don't want *every* cop on the investigation in on the Parkes/Brayson thing - no need at this point.'

'You still want to keep it classified because of the disappearance and the condition of the bodies?'

Rosen's eyes darted about, scanning the immediate surroundings.

Lachlan got the impression Rosen didn't want their conversation overheard.

'Precisely, and I've already been over those reasons with you. Razell is aware of the secrecy surrounding those investigations. A follow-up circular was emailed this morning to all stations, advising that the special unit will be handling the Brayson case.'

'Still buried in my Inbox,' Lachlan supposed. 'Just got in from Brisbane and saw the bulletin about this briefing in time to get over here.'

'Razell is very edgy about these latest killings,' Rosen explained. 'Has a bee in his bonnet about Sydney becoming some kind of crime capital. He's driving hard to have the city cleaned up, street violence, break-ins, underworld activities - and now he starts getting these blasted thrill killers.'

Lachlan changed the subject back to the Parkes case. 'Has the Brayson murder shed any new light on the Brian Parkes disappearance?'

'No. And I don't expect it will. In both cases there's absolutely nothing to go on. I believe there have been cases like this before, Neil, cases that appear to deal with a range of ... inexplicable phenomena. They're classified top secret, investigated by special units. Eventually the files are closed. Unresolved.'

'Phenomena?'

'I don't like to say it, but the only obvious fact or clue we have is one that makes no sense. Can't officially be considered by the department. Parkes and Brayson simply appear to have slipped through time in the blink of an eye, like characters from a H.G. Wells novel.'

Lachlan had watched episodes of the old Twilight Zone TV series, but such things had never been to his taste. A practical man, he hadn't considered the realm of inexplicable phenomena in relation to Brian Parkes' body.

Movement through time. Immortality. These were ridiculous concepts, the stuff of Todd's comic books and computer games.

He was back at the Hurstville Police Station, sitting at his desk and immersed in paperwork. He ran his fingers through his hair, it needed trimming. He was tired. It had been a long day, a lot of travelling, the beer and the headache hadn't helped.

An obvious thought occurred to him. What if there were others like Parkes and Brayson? Looking for similar cases would provide a starting point. What if, despite Rosen's comments, there was a connection between the murder of Monique Brayson and the garrotte killings of Trish Van Helegen and Bill Dawson? Lachlan decided to do some digging of his own, starting with Parkes and Brayson, without the involvement of Rosen's special unit.

Something about the case was nagging at him.

This kind of digging meant delving into the archives, into files long buried in the memory banks of the police computers.

It was a while since he'd been in touch with Teddy Vanda. If he remembered the joke correctly, then his mate at the Head Branch Data Communications division owed him a favour.

Henry Kaplan welcomed Conrad Becker with a firm handshake and a wide grin, beaming with the air of a world-beater - not a bankrupt staving off the final blow.

'How was the flight?'

'Too long,' said Becker with a conservative smile that suited his cautious nature. His smooth and suave style was evident from the cut of his tailored suit to the controlled, bass tone of his voice. Everything about Conrad Becker was perfectly balanced. He was physically attractive because nothing about him was too large or too small. His nose and chin were prominent with a rugged manliness, but not overpowering to the smooth, firm flesh of his cheeks or the expressive green eyes flecked with hazel. 'Long plane trips can be a waste of vital business time.'

'Not if used to do homework on potential purchases.'

'We've already done our homework,' Becker assured him. He introduced Wilfred Carlyle, his associate, to Kaplan and Roger.

143

There were two other men with Becker - minders, Kaplan assumed. Becker didn't introduce them. Kaplan acknowledged their presence with a nod, but offered nothing further.

'Come through to the board room,' Kaplan said. 'We've light refreshments and Roger is set up to talk us through the screening of a short video on Southern Star. It's a good, capsuled history of the project.'

They took their seats. One of Kaplan's aides poured the coffee. Lights were dimmed for effect and the video flickered onto the wall mounted television screen. 'Our corporate communications division compiled this video especially for your visit,' Roger informed them, 'using existing footage together with new material filmed just a few weeks ago.' He enjoyed being the focal point. Earlier that morning, his father had strode into his office, wearing a determined expression.

'You and I have to project a united front from now until the sale is made,' Kaplan had said. 'You, Harold and I are going to be solid, persuasive, organised. I don't want either of you out of my sight for any longer than necessary.'

'I hardly think that's necessary.'

'If I say it's necessary, Roger, then it's necessary. The three of us, when we're with Becker, will be a show of strength. It's essential we're in complete unison every step of the way, and if that means living in each other's pockets, then that's exactly what we do. This is one deal we have to close quickly. It's our salvation. And when we're not with the Canadian, we'll have our heads together, analysing his responses, drawing up contingencies for any aspect of the sale that's not looking good.'

As always Kaplan was convincing, even to the son who'd heard it all before. He'd always been able to instill motivation and enthusiasm in Roger, if only for a short while.

'I don't want this whole thing hinging on me,' Kaplan continued. 'You and Harold are to play vital roles in the talks.'

'You don't want them to think that Kaplan Corporation is a one man affair.'

'There's that. And something else. I don't want it to come down to just Becker and myself. The more players on both sides, the better. We need to get all Becker's "yes" men on side, as well.'

Roger relaxed as the video began. Like his father, he would be sorry to see their stake in Southern Star Mining relinquished. But the sale was worth four hundred million, enough to pay the required installments to creditors, stop the bankruptcy proceedings, and cast their other divisions in a stronger light. The corporation would be a shadow of its former self - but that was better than having no financial future at all.

The video's opening shot was an aerial view of the mining operation.

'It is only twenty-four years old,' the commentary began, a familiar voice over the montage of pictures, one heard dozens of times over television commercials and corporate films, 'but in that time Southern Star Mining has become listed in the top five hundred companies on the Australian stock exchange. It is one of the South Pacific region's largest coal producers. Amongst other things it has caused the founding of an outback town with a population of five thousand people.

'Most of Southern Star's output is for export, and even with the rise of new, green energy initiatives locally, the international market for coal is strong.'

News footage filled the screen, taken twenty years before. Tractors roaming a large site, turning rugged earth into a quarry buzzing with men and machines. Interspersed were shots of men in wide brimmed hats, even wider grins, captured during light-hearted moments. 'Coal deposits at Mount Ginger in north-western Queensland were discovered in 1970 by the prospecting team of a small mining exploration company, Western Allies. They formed a syndicate with three other local mining operators, and with large amounts of capital invested by Japanese and American interests, the Southern Star Mining Group was launched ...'

In the space of a few minutes the video drew its small audience through more than forty years of development and growth. 'By 1974 there were haulage roads and preparatory earthworks for the crushing plants. A small, thriving community of workers and their families had sprung up on the level ground to the east of the mines, at the foot of the mountain's western slopes ...'

'... the first contract shipment of coal, an encouraging 30,000 tons, was transported by freight train to the coast in 1976 ...'

At the end of the film, Roger explained that in 1995 the Kaplan Corporation had acquired controlling shares in Southern Star. Those shares had risen steeply in value in the years since, and were now being offered at a bargain price.

Kaplan took his cue then, bringing in the senior accounts people. They were armed with documents and presented the financial structure of the share arrangement.

There were many times when Henry Kaplan had purchased a company at a premium price because the buyer was being forced to sell. On every occasion he felt like an avenging hawk, swooping in for the kill. The urge to take advantage of his opponent's situation was irresistible. He knew the Canadian entrepreneur would feel exactly the same. Kaplan had made certain that everything presented to Becker underlined the desperate need of the Kaplan Corporation to sell under market value in order to survive. Kaplan expected this ploy to make the sale a certainty.

After all, Becker was just another greedy scavenger, brimming with blood lust for his prey, anxious to move in for the final feed.

SIXTEEN

Lachlan strode through the swinging glass doors of the data communications room - a large, oval space with a dozen workstations, each with its own partially closed-off area. Every time he came here Lachlan was struck by the thought that this was the quietest, cleanest part of Central Crime Command at the Parramatta HQ.

The rest of the building he perceived as being in a state of organised chaos. If there was organised chaos in *here*, he reflected, then it was inside the collective memory of the desktop computer units, deep within the intricate bowels of the mainframes.

Lachlan stuck his head around the third cubicle to the left of the swinging doors. 'Hi Teddy.'

Edward 'Teddy' Vanda looked up from his screen, swinging round in his swivel chair as he did so. 'Lacho! Long time no see, no hear. No evil. No way!'

'No time is more like it.'

Teddy laughed. For a computer whizz, Teddy didn't fit the stereotype of the scrawny, bespectacled nerd. He was a big, broad shouldered twenty-eight year old with a wide, toothy grin, an irreverent gleam in his eye, and a thick brush of dark hair, razor short. He spoke in the lingo that had become prevalent in the male youth of recent years - part urban dude, part old time ocker. A curious and infectious blend that had always amused Lachlan.

'Any chance of a favour?' Lachlan asked.

'For you. Always.'

'I need some info on missing persons.'

'We have info on missing dudes and dudettes you wouldn't believe. What are you after?'

'People who've been listed as missing who've subsequently been found murdered.'

'Man, are you kidding? I could run you a printout that's a mile long. It would take you a month of Sundays to read it and you still wouldn't be any the wiser.'

'We're going to be more specific than that. Anyone reported missing seventeen to nineteen years ago, nationally, who's been found murdered in the past twelve months.'

'Now we're cookin'. I'll run a search program first thing this afternoon. Sorry, but the mainframe's chock'a'block until then.'

'That's fine. And Teddy?'

'Yeah?'

'The favour part. Keep it just between us. Okay?'

'Uh-oh. One of those. Internal politics or something equally as smelly.'

'Equally as smelly,' Lachlan replied.

'No problem,' Teddy assured him. 'After all, I owe you.'

'Big time. Make sure I return the favour sometime.'

'Already in my diary, Sherlock.'

Lachlan gave his young friend a harmless punch on the shoulder, then left. Over the past few years he'd asked Teddy for more favours than he could remember. He'd never been asked to repay one of them. Teddy always said he owed him, but in fact he'd never owed him anything at all. It had started out as a joke, now it was part of the repartee between two colleagues who had a healthy respect for each other.

Two men who knew that politics and bureaucracy sometimes got in the way of a man doing the job he was meant to do.

Jennifer made half a dozen calls to contacts within the fashion industry, and two of those she called mentioned Stuart James. He was a registered private investigator who had undertaken assignments for both those contacts.

148

'Always good to get referrals,' James said, 'not that I get much work from the fashion business. Most of the work I do is on missing persons.'

'That makes you ideal for this brief,' Jennifer commented.

James flipped through the notes he'd taken while quizzing Jennifer on the case. 'Most PIs get a lot of missing persons work,' he commented, 'and most of that work entails teenagers from wealthy homes who've left home without a word. Your husband ... quite a different kettle of fish.'

'What do you think?'

'I can't make any promises, you understand, but I'll dig around, see what I can come up with. I gather that's more than you're expecting from the coppers.'

'Seems so.'

'Not unusual. That's why PIs pick up so much missing persons work. The coppers don't have the time or manpower. And in the case of your husband's murder after so many years missing ... well, this is both a cold case and a new case all rolled into one.'

'I have a feeling there's more to it. That man, Rosen, was ... evasive.'

James smiled and held up his hands in a mock gesture to hold back further comment. 'Please. I hear a hundred and one conspiracy stories a day as it is. No more.'

Jennifer half grinned, conceding the point. 'Understood.'

She liked Stuart James. He was a charming, articulate, effusive character, not at all what she expected when she had phoned for an appointment. He'd agreed to see her almost straight away.

'I'm just around the corner from you, Australia Tower, seventeenth floor. If you come by in twenty minutes you can take the place of a cancelled appointment. I don't have long, though - fifteen minutes, so we'll have to talk fast.'

That presented no problem to James, who spoke in fast motion, spitting out words in an endless stream and constantly flashing looks at his Rolex. He was of solid build, with warm, round features, mid-forties, impeccably well dressed. He could have been a real estate salesman for one of the elite suburbs; there was nothing dark or moody or mysterious about him. His offices were modern, relaxing, designer-style, but functional, not overly expensive looking.

'You're certain about your husband's appearance,' James asked, ' he hadn't aged at all?'

'Not a line on his face,' Jennifer said. Once again the vision of the body on the slab crashed uninvited into her mind.

'There are certain possibilities, Ms Parkes - for instance, plastic surgery might allow a fortyish man to pass for mid-twenties, it's just that not too many Aussie men go in for it, at least not yet.'

'The coroner's autopsy showed there'd been no plastic surgery.' Jennifer filled him in on her talks with Lachlan and Rosen.

'I see. Well, I'll check the autopsy result as a matter of procedure. But in the meantime, tell me, was there any indication from the coroner of other surgery, anything at all?'

Jennifer told him about the unexplained post mortem incision to the throat.

James nodded as he listened, but he made no comment. When she had finished, he leaned forward, adopting his down-to-business face. 'I charge a retainer of $150 an hour, plus expenses, minimum start up fee of $500. But, I won't keep taking your money if I don't think I can help you.'

'That's fine.'

'My focus will be to find out where Brian was during those missing years. Answer that and I know we'll find the solutions to the other questions. You know, Ms. Parkes, you may have heard the expression, from the police world, that the dead can talk to us from beyond the grave.'

'Yes...I have.'

'What it means, exactly, is that the circumstances of a victim's body - where it's found, how the person died - can yield clues that ultimately lead to the person's killer. I want you to think of Brian's reappearance in a similar way, perhaps not speaking to us from beyond the grave but crying out to us from the limbo of those missing years. And that something about his reappearance is going to lead us to the answers.'

'Okay.'

'Now, first, I want to look into your husband's business activities. Do you know if his accountancy records still exist?'

'There's been no reason to keep them, but they've never actually been thrown out.'

'They're with you?'

'Yes. In boxes. Buried somewhere in the clutter at the back of my garage.'

'The Missing Persons Unit checked them at the time?'

'Yes. They didn't find anything unusual.'

'I'm looking for something that may not be unusual or obvious,' James pointed out, 'but when accountants are murdered you can bet your bottom dollar it's got something to do with money. I have a gut feeling I might find something useful in those records.'

Jennifer wondered if she'd kept the records all this time, subconsciously suspecting this day might come. She'd always been skeptical about things like that, but this past week was fast changing her in that regard. She had begun to think perhaps nothing was as it seemed.

Could there be something about Brian, something related to all of this, that she had never known?

'How's it going with the Canadians?' Jennifer asked as she entered Roger's office.

'Hard to tell, they don't give much away,' Roger replied. He gestured to the lounge against the wall of the office. 'Sit down for a moment. Masterton and my father are showing Becker and his men the building. We're taking them to dinner tonight and I'm double checking the reservations.'

Jennifer sank comfortably into the pliable welcome of the sofa's cushions. 'With everything that's gone on over the past week I haven't actually asked you how you're handling the problems here. You seem to be holding up okay.'

'I'm holding up. The odds are in our favour that the Southern Star sale to Becker will go through.'

Appraising him, Jennifer reflected once again on how much Roger looked like Henry. The dark hair was just beginning to show flecks of grey. 'It's a wonder Henry didn't take this step much sooner.'

'He wanted to avoid this. Buying into that mine was a pet project of his, you know, big time coal magnate and all that. Doesn't give a shit about all the anti-coal environmentalism going on, sees a world market for it with fewer players. Maybe he wanted to be another Lang Hancock along with everything else.' He shrugged. 'Who knows? We simply reached the point where there was no choice - this sale represents the one chance we've got to stay afloat. And we're better off out of the old energies anyway. I'd be going solar if we were in any position to be taking up new investments.'

'I've got fingers and toes crossed for you guys on this. I just wish I could do something.'

'Just being a friend helps, Jen,' he said, echoing her earlier comment to him.

'I'm glad we've always remained friends. Brian would've been happy about that.'

Roger nodded in agreement. He wondered whether now, after all this time, she might be prepared to allow that friendship to blossom into something more. He allowed himself a subtle admiration of her. The years hadn't dimmed her beauty, quite the opposite. She had an inner glow that came from maturity and experience. No longer just a pretty face and gawky young wife of years before, now she had the warm, intimate allure of a confident woman.

'How's the investigation going? Any further word from this special unit you spoke of?'

'No. I've begun to doubt whether that will change. I know it's still early days, but my feeling is they're stumped, and they're busy enough with dozens of other cases. So I'm taking matters into my own hands.'

'That sounds dangerous.'

'Not at all. I've hired a private investigator.'

'Did you speak to Dad about this? I'm sure he could help.'

'He's got enough to worry about. You both have. This is something I have to do for myself.'

Roger nodded his understanding. 'If you're sure.'

'Nothing may come of it,' Jennifer added realistically, 'but I have to try. And this guy comes highly recommended. The first thing he asked to see was Brian's old business records. He wants to go right back to the source.'

'You still have them?' Roger sounded surprised.

She explained that she did.

Roger made the call, confirming the dinner reservations, then rose hurriedly from his chair. 'We'd better get going if we're to make the appointment on time. You know, it'll be strange seeing Katrina after all these years.'

'I expect it will.'

They headed across town in Roger's car. As he drove, Roger confided, 'There's still times when I miss Brian, Jen. I've never had a close friend like him since.'

Jennifer knew exactly what he meant. A part of her had never stopped missing Brian. She smiled warmly at Roger and looked deep into his compassionate eyes. Minutes later they arrived at St. Vincent's Hospital for their meeting with Doctor Katrina Wells.

The phone rang, shrieking across the quiet apartment in the mid afternoon. Rory turned away from his female companion, sat on the corner of the bed and reached for his cell phone. 'Hello.' He didn't pull a sheet around himself as he spoke. He was unconcerned about his nakedness.

'Rory, got somethin' special, really special,' Hughie Johnson's thin voice cackled over the line, a multitude of street noises fighting for equal volume in the background. 'Dug this up from the public prosecutor's file at the Queensland courts. Back in the nineties, a dozen ex-Southern Star miners claimed medical damages against the mine.'

'Medical damages?'

'Asbestos poisoning,' Johnson leapt in excitedly. 'Case dragged on, no one particularly interested in the plight of these guys, y'know, the way things sometimes are. None of them could afford legal help, and Southern Star used a battery of lawyers to drag the thing out.'

'This isn't news, Hughie. There are industrial cases like that everywhere. Sob stories for the current affairs shows, not what I'm looking for.'

'I know. There's more.'

'Then get on with it.' Rory muttered an obscenity under his breath. He'd used Hughie Johnson from time to time for fieldwork in the northern state. The old timer was a stringer for a suburban newspaper group in Queensland, lowly paid, always chasing the big story, never getting it.

'Henry Kaplan buys the mine mid-Nineties, right? Suddenly the cases are rushed before the courts, half the prosecution's files containing key evidence go missing. The judge clears the mine of any negligence. Inconclusive evidence, right? Rumour mill says the judge was paid off by Kaplan Corp. and that the files were nicked by Kaplan's thugs.'

'Nasty story. But proof? Any proof?'

'Nothin' concrete. But I done some more diggin'. This judge is some turkey named Edsell. Checked with the credit register, the Corporate Affairs people and one of my mates in Tax. Seems that six months after all this, Judge Edsell buys a little holiday home in Vanuatu. Worth a cool million. No one knows 'cause no one goes 'round checkin' on judges. Why should they?'

'You've got documentation on all this?'

'Yep.'

'Email it to me. The details will fit in nicely with the first installment of my series on Kaplan. Have you a contact at the Corporate Affairs Commission up here?'

'Sure.'

'Tell him what you've got.'

'No problem. He'll be very interested. The whole thing stinks.'

'I'll visit the Industrial Court tomorrow. I'll tell them the info has been given to the Corporate Affairs people. With any luck, a low-level inquiry will be underway within weeks. I'll ask them if that's the case and I expect they'll say "no comment".'

Johnson laughed. 'And you'll print that quote in this first installment. All of a sudden a low-level inquiry becomes a high-level one, and we're riding the crest of a major, breaking story.'

'You got it. Great work, Hughie. Thanks.' Rory rang off. He hadn't expected something so substantial so soon. And not from Hughie Johnson. It just went to show you could never pick where the breakthroughs would come from, you had to keep all your options open.

He turned back to the woman on the bed. He'd been about to mount her for the second time when the phone had rung. Helen Shawcross wasn't any more concerned about her nakedness than Rory. She was in a sitting position, her knees pulled up, revealing the dark patch between her legs. Her arms were folded across her knees, pulling them in tightly against her breasts. 'Sounded interesting.'

She shook her head, tossing back the mane of blonde hair. There was a creamy texture to her olive skin, one that tempted Rory, siren-like, to taste its surface, as a child might lick cream from a bowl.

'Interesting? Oh, yeah. One of my northern contacts has some heavy duty stuff on Southern Star.' He crawled across the bed, head low, and when he reached her his tongue flicked out, trailing her arm, her shoulder, the side of her neck.

Helen watched the smooth shift of the muscles in his calves and thighs as he leaned across her. She ran the tips of her fingers in a straight line down his skin, from the matted hair on his chest to the solid flat belly. The nearness of him, the touch, the musky scent of his manliness, aroused her all over again. She had known at the luncheon the previous Sunday that she wanted to go to bed with Rory McConnell as soon as possible. There had been an immediate physical attraction to Rory; and an immediate contempt for his girlfriend, Carly Parkes. Spoilt little rich girl who fancied herself an urban revolutionary. Helen wanted Rory, and she wanted to spite his silly little piece of fluff.

And there was something else.

The danger of it.

Rory's girlfriend was the daughter of one of Henry Kaplan's friends. Helen knew it was no coincidence that her dalliances were always with someone she met through Henry - her rich, powerful, dynamic boyfriend and provider.

But she was her own woman, she made sure of that. Maybe one day she'd deliberately let him find out, just to prove it. Oh yes.

She loved the danger of it.

She tingled all over as Rory's tongue slithered down her body, each touch of his flesh against hers erasing any last, hidden vestiges of

155

innocence. 'Northern contacts,' she repeated. 'You have been busy. Is that all I am? One of your contacts for information on Henry Kaplan?' Another woman might have been offended, but Helen Shawcross found the idea appealing.

'If you want to be,' Rory said. Carrying on the conversation didn't distract him in the slightest from giving her pleasure. His tongue was joined now by his fingers and he knew all the right places to tease and caress, making her gasp in delight. She stretched her long, lithe form over the bed and Rory moved eagerly into position over her.

'You want to know about his previous wives?' Helen said, a reference to an earlier conversation.

'There were three,' Rory commented, almost absent mindedly, his attention more focused on their lovemaking. 'We never hear anything about them. What about the first? Roger's mother. You'd think she'd be around somewhere.'

'This northern contact of yours,' Helen said, 'male or female?'

'Male.'

'I suppose he gets paid for his efforts?'

'The publisher looks after that.'

'Who's going to look after me for my investigative work?'

'Me.' Rory's head tilted lower, his tongue pushing deeper and harder.

Helen sighed. 'Oh yes. There. Right there.'

'The second wife accused him of bashing her,' Rory continued, 'but dropped the allegation when a very large financial settlement was agreed to as part of the divorce.'

'I know.' Helen found her voice, in between the heavy breaths. 'He told me. Henry told me all his wives were bitches who didn't understand him. That I was the first woman who was a real soul mate to him.'

'You believe him?'

'I couldn't care less one way or the other. I won't be hanging around long enough after our marriage to find out.'

Rory was incredibly aroused by the fact that Helen Shawcross was a shameless gold-digger. 'The third wife,' he said, 'appears to have been a diversion he tired of just as quickly. The first wife?'

156

'He never mentions her,' Helen said, 'but I can change that. Get him talking.' She smiled mischievously, like the cat that got the cream. 'If the price is right.'

Rory's tongue moved again, exploring secret places. 'Oh yes, yes,' she cried out.

'Then you'll be finding out lots of things for me, Mata Hari,' Rory said. He shifted the weight of his body so that his limbs moulded with hers. 'Because the payment has only just begun.'

'I've run a printout for you,' Teddy Vanda said, lounging back in his seat at the computer console.

Lachlan scanned the sheet. Teddy's cross-reference search had spewed forth the names of four others, missing for over eighteen years until recently found. They had been discovered at intervals of between three and four weeks apart, over a period of a few months. Always in the northern or north-western districts of Sydney, the same general area where Monique Brayson had been found. Each had been strangled with wire.

There was no other information. The individual files had been flagged as classified by the HQ Special Unit, access therefore being denied on the general police database. But Lachlan had no doubt that in each case, the victim would have appeared to be the same age now as when they had disappeared.

He felt his flesh crawl. He hadn't experienced a sensation like this since his childhood. A film about zombies had made his skin tingle the same way. The film had been a TV rerun of one of those laughable B-grades from the 1950s but it had brought real horror and revulsion to his young, impressionable mind.

Together with Trish Van Helegen and Bill Dawson, this brought the number of garrotte murders to seven. Five of them, like Brian Parkes, had been long term missing persons. Two had not.

The sixth of the newly discovered missing people was Brian Parkes. There were two notable differences. He hadn't been killed by garrotte. And he'd been found in the southern suburbs, not the northern. Otherwise, the similarities were consistent.

157

Whenever the long term missing people had turned up - deceased - John Rosen had been on the scene within twenty-four hours. He'd taken the cases under his wing, assigning them to his special team.

Lachlan guessed that Rosen's team made enquiries, filed reports, followed the official line to the book - but with nothing to go on they ran up the same dead ends. The cases remained open. Relatives were kept in the dark as much as possible. Few details were released to the media. Various coroners had been called in to establish cause of death - quite likely, they hadn't been aware of any age discrepancy - and the autopsy results were quickly removed by Rosen and absorbed by his unit, along with the investigative reports.

And Rosen had revealed none of this to Lachlan.

'I have to admit,' Teddy said, 'I didn't expect the search to come up with anything like this.'

'I'm not sure I did either,' Lachlan confided.

'The details on all these cases is classified. But you knew exactly when and where to run the search,' Teddy noted. 'Without that input at the data entry stage, the computer wouldn't have turned up these names.'

'I saw a connection between Brian Parkes and Monique Brayson, but not enough. Needed more.'

'Now you have it. So what's the story, Neil?'

It was the first time since he'd known Teddy that Lachlan detected a serious tone to his voice.

'Every one of these cases disappeared into the special unit at HQ.'

There was no question that John Rosen, aware of a connection between these disappearances and killings, had moved swiftly and covertly to ensure the connection didn't become general police or public knowledge.

'Keep it under your hat for the time being,' Lachlan said, 'until I've had a chance to look into it further.'

'You know I will.'

Lachlan studied the printout again, not wanting to believe his eyes. With many homicides being documented monthly, it was unlikely anyone else on the force had discovered the similarities in these murders. And, no one had reason to question John Rosen's orders.

Lachlan was reminded of the 1980's Yorkshire Ripper case in England. There had been investigations into the Ripper murders by different detectives in different areas over a period of a few years. Peter Sutcliffe had been interviewed by various officers - on eight separate occasions - but this obvious link throughout the paperwork had gone unnoticed. Sutcliffe had eventually been arrested after he'd been seen acting suspiciously, not because the link had come to light.

Centralising information on computer had come a long way toward ensuring that couldn't happen. But in this case John Rosen had manipulated the computer system for the opposite effect.

Lachlan had known Rosen for twenty years. In his younger days he'd regarded Rosen as a father figure. To Lachlan, Rosen represented all that was honest and dependable about the police force. Now, in a single moment, Lachlan felt a storm of doubt unlike anything he'd known before. He felt as though he were being torn apart inside. Confronted by these details, he simply couldn't ignore the implication: John Rosen didn't want these crimes investigated.

SEVENTEEN

Tall and huskily voiced, Doctor Katrina Wells had a warm presence that put Jennifer at ease immediately. Appraising her, Jennifer found it hard to picture the much younger Doctor Wells with a younger Roger. They didn't seem at all suited.

The woman appeared genuinely pleased to see Roger. She shook his hand firmly and commented that she was aware of his successful career with his father's company. Jennifer caught Roger's wince at the words "his father's company."

Jennifer gave the doctor a run-down of the autopsy result. 'I understand it's rare for an operation to require entry via the jugular vein.'

'That's true,' Katrina Wells confirmed, 'unless all other relevant veins in the patient have collapsed. But, from what you tell me, Brian hadn't had any operations and this - incision - was made after his death.'

'Yes. The police can't make anything of it.'

'I'm not surprised. I don't believe I've heard of anything like this before.'

'The incision mark was surgically precise,' Jennifer said, 'which is the reason for our visit today. I wanted to get a broad medical overview. I guess I'm trying to get a handle on why such incisions are made generally, and the kind of doctors called to make them. Is there any other reason the jugular is opened in surgery?'

'Yes. In a major operation a drip would be inserted into the jugular. It is after all, the most efficient artery for introducing substances to the body. Not that any of that is relevant to a cut made post mortem.'

160

'I expect the police will investigate the possibility,' Roger said, 'that the person who inflicted the cut after Brian's death might be a doctor.'

'Doctors save lives,' Katrina frowned, 'they don't take them.'

'Who else would have surgical know-how like that?' Jennifer questioned.

'Could be an ex-medical student who didn't make the grade, or even an enthusiast who'd taught himself. Stranger things have happened, but this really isn't my field.'

'I can't help wondering, Doctor Wells-' Jennifer began.

'... Katrina.'

'Katrina ... If there's some other purpose, for which doctors might make such incisions. If not for surgery for ... well, I don't know, something experimental perhaps?'

Katrina considered this for a moment. 'There are, of course, new procedures being developed and experiments in surgical techniques. Nothing that I know of, in Australia, but once again it's not my field and there could be something overseas. The person to answer questions on such things is Doctor Stephen Gleitzman, the senior consulting surgeon at the hospital. He also writes and lectures on the expanding medical frontier and has a particular interest in youth preservation and life extension practices.'

'Youth preservation?' Jennifer's body stiffened and she exchanged glances with Roger. 'What exactly does that mean?'

'It's a growing field - alternative lifestyle and medical beliefs. It's been boosted by scientific breakthroughs overseas, in such fields as surgery, biogenetics, nutrients, exercise and diet plans. That sort of thing. There's been a trend in the US for instance, for people who believe in prolonging life and preserving youth, to form into active groups.'

'I believe I've read something about this,' Roger said, 'don't these people call themselves immortalists or something like that.'

'That would be one of the terms.'

'This doesn't sound like the kind of thing the medical world embraces,' Jennifer observed.

'You'd be surprised. In America over a dozen institutions are solely devoted to research and study on anti-ageing, and there are at least thirty journals that report on all aspects of age prevention and life extension.'

'When's the best time to get in touch with Doctor Gleitzman?' Jennifer asked.

'You've just missed him, I'm afraid. Left yesterday for a week in the US. Massachusetts. He's attending an international surgeons conference. He's back in seven days and then you could phone him here at the hospital - though I'm not sure what interest that will be to you, in light of your husband's case.'

'When I saw Brian's body ...' Jennifer paused, choosing her words carefully, 'his appearance was much more youthful than I would've expected.'

'I see. Well ... this certainly is an unusual one. Look, if you'd like some information in the meantime on these life extensionists - that's the term I prefer - I'll phone down to the hospital's PR division. I'm sure they'd loan you a copy of Doctor Gleitzman's book, and the DVD of one of his recent lectures on the subject.'

After picking up the book and the DVD, Jennifer and Roger went for a cappuccino in a small café further along the street.

'You're going to call this guy at his hotel in Massachusetts, aren't you?' Roger predicted.

'You're getting very good at reading my mind.'

'I'll take that as a compliment. You were never that easy to read. Well?'

'I think so. After I've viewed his DVD. I guess it depends on what I learn about all this living longer, looking younger stuff. I already feel as though it's another dead end.'

'It's not like you to sound so defeated.'

'I'm just tired. Really tired.'

'There could be something in this, you know. It's amazing what's going on these days. Special skin creams, collagen injections, calcium injections - I just didn't realise the extent of it.'

'Neither did I. Nevertheless, these enthusiasts are still a minority, and not the kind of thing Brian was likely to get involved with.'

162

'I wish I could watch that DVD with you but I've got this damned business dinner with the Canadians.' He sipped on his cappuccino. 'Once all this business with Southern Star and Becker is settled,' Roger said, 'I plan to get out of the company. Or what's left of the company.'

'You're kidding.'

'No. It's been at the back of my mind for a while. A long while, actually. Dad's business is the only place I've ever worked. Always been the heir apparent. Except I've only ever been a puppet, going through the motions while the great Henry Kaplan made the real decisions.'

'You don't need to be so hard on yourself. For goodness sake, Roger, you're the MD of Kaplan Australia.'

'Hear me out. Fact is, I've never felt comfortable with it. I enjoyed the prestige and the lifestyle when I was younger but that wears off. I've never had the chance to try something different.'

'This sounds like one of those mid life crises.'

'Be fair, Jen. You've had the chance to run your own business your own way. You bought out Dad's share years ago so you could be independent. You're doing what you chose to do.'

'What would you do if you went out on your own?'

'I'm still thinking about that.'

Jennifer gave his hand an affectionate squeeze. 'It's my turn to offer my help,' she said. 'If I can help you with your decision, or if you just want to talk, anytime.'

They shared a smile. A brief, relaxed moment. But then their conversation returned to Brian, to the investigation, and the anxiety haunting Jennifer cast its shadow once more.

Daniel Furrow was a short, squat man with a shock of thick black hair and an unseemly swagger. He liked to be known as Danny The Pimp - he thought this sounded "classy" - but his girls referred to him, behind his back, as the "Danny The Pig's Ass."

His girls did as he told them because they thought he was the big boss - but he wasn't. Like them, Danny was an employee. He'd been hired to manage the three inner-city brothels and escort service because he was a bully without scruples - a vicious thug who, ultimately, was terrified of the man who pulled his strings.

Danny had an office behind the largest of the three joints and he was sizing up the pouty, busty redhead who'd been shown in by the brothel's madam.

'There are certain clients who have - shall we say - *special needs*,' Danny told her. He stopped and cleared his throat, a loud and irritating habit to all who knew him. 'You unnerstan'?'

'What sorta needs?' the redhead asked defiantly.

Danny sized her up, taking his time. 'Arrogant little bitch, are we?'

'Call it whatever you like.'

'What's your name, sweetie?'

'Vonnie.'

'Let me spell it out then, Vonnie.' He emphasised the last word with a spitting sound. 'We like to keep certain clients happy. Expect a few bruises, a fat lip, some very rough sex. You may have to do a bit o' squealing and begging, for effect. Get the picture?'

'I didn't come here to put up with this crap.'

As she turned for the door Danny's right hand shot out and grabbed her in a vice-like grip. 'You'll put up with whatever crap I say.' He released his grip and she stared back at him, her face marked by loathing. Danny liked that. 'If it wasn't for us you'd be starting a nice, long term in the joint. But we got you off the hook. And we can just as easy lay the evidence on the cops and have you sent away for a long time.'

'Bastard.'

'That's my middle name. You'll be one of the girls that services our - deviants.' Danny laughed out loud at this. 'But don't worry, we do have some rules. They aren't allowed to cut you up or kill you. After all, we're a classy operation.'

The redhead's shoulders slumped in acceptance. 'I suppose it's as good a deal as any.'

'Then let's get started, eh? I've a client waiting for you across town right now. Two o' my boys'll drive you, and they'll wait outside while you work.' She was at the doorway when he called out. 'Oh, and Vonnie?'

She looked back, glazed eyes, soul-less expression.

'This fellow's one o' the nastiest. And he hasn't had one o' my girls over to see 'im for a while.'

Afterwards, Vonnie Michaels cried. But only briefly. She snapped herself out of her self-pity and splashed cold water from the bathroom basin over her face.

Her bottom lip was cracked and swollen, her cheek bruised, her right eye puffy and turning purple.

When she'd arrived she'd hardly believed this urbane looking man could be so brutal.

Hans Falkstog was an athletic man with a commanding presence. Even in a relaxed state he exhibited an air of power and arrogance. 'Well, what are you waiting for?' he had said. 'Strip off. The bedroom's through there.' He took great pleasure exploiting their positions - customer and whore. He'd used those very terms during the sex.

Afterwards, as she emerged from the bathroom, a more composed Falkstog offered her a Scotch.

'Why not?' she said with a shrug. She took a long swig from the glass. 'I hope I don't run into anyone like you in a dark alley.' This was her only form of comeback to characters like Falkstog, to hint at what the rest of the world thought of them.

He laughed. 'Oh, I'm as safe as houses out there - in the alleys of the real world. Respectable. Because I get to act out my fantasies, well, most of them, on the likes of you.'

He laughed again and Vanessa shivered. She wondered how many creeps like Falkstog were clients of Danny The Pimp.

'Another drink, Vonnie?'

'No. I have to go.'

'Of course. You're a working girl.'

Heading back to Danny's office, she kept hearing Falkstog's words. 'I'm as safe as houses out there ... Respectable ...'

A chill ran through her. How could these men with the souls of monsters pass for normal in the outside world?

The DVD wasn't the best quality, having been filmed "live' at a symposium. Doctor Stephen Gleitzman stood at a podium with a series of large, colourful charts behind him as visual aids. He would have been of fairly nondescript appearance if it hadn't been for one of the cutest moustaches Jennifer had seen on a man.

Jennifer sank into the comfort of her favourite lounge chair, remote in hand, and watched.

'The ageing process is not as cut and dried as many people believe,' Gleitzman began, 'you don't have to look your age at forty or fifty. You don't have to be old at sixty or even seventy. Medical researchers have known for years that there are a number of inter-acting processes at work in the ageing of our bodies. Today, I'm going to show you how to slow down and in some cases *reverse* that ageing process.

'How can this be? I imagine you're asking. Has this medical practitioner gone out of his mind?' A ripple of laughter erupted from the audience. Gleitzman clearly fed on it. 'Not at all! And I'll prove it by taking you through the medical secrets of rejuvenating your skin, your bones, your heart and your mind. Armed with the right knowledge, and the right attitude, you can begin to start getting younger immediately.'

This man wasn't just an enterprising doctor or a progressive thinker, Jennifer noted, he was also a super salesman. He went on to speak about the newly emerging science of longevity in life and youth preservation - and the growing number of people generally referred to as immortalists who pursued it.

This was a hybrid field - a mixture of genetics, biochemistry, cell biology, medically approved drugs, special diets and exercises. Gleitzman's philosophy was broad. He had no qualms about combining the best strategies of alternative health practices with the latest advancements in mainstream medicine.

Gleitzman used a pointer to indicate the first chart. 'I'm going to describe the nutrients and vitamins that help regenerate the cells of our bodies. There are two ways to absorb these. The first is in our diet, and the correct diet is an essential part of our youth preservation plan. Later, I will discuss the injection of these vitamins, along with hormones and specific amino acids, directly into the bloodstream ...'

166

Jennifer paused the DVD for a moment and thought of the incision to Brian's jugular. Could there be a connection even though the cut had been made after his death?

The following charts were for exercise, surgery and rejuvenating skin - the latter involving the use of vitamin based creams. Retin-A was the best known of these - it could rebuild the deep dermal layers of the skin. 'The creams rejuvenate the cells, making the skin smoother and less wrinkled,' Gleitzman said, showing before and after photographs of people who'd been applying the creams for several years. Jennifer admitted these people appeared to have maintained, and in some cases improved, the state of their skin. There was no evidence, however, that it could work to such an extent for a period of eighteen years.

Jennifer thought of the Brian Parkes she'd known. He'd hardly ever been to a doctor. He'd certainly never shown interest in alternative medicines - or alternative lifestyles of any kind for that matter. Perhaps, as she'd wondered earlier, she hadn't known her husband very well at all.

The police were adamant there was a rational explanation to all this, despite their inability to produce one, and despite the coroner sidestepping the issue. If that was the case then these youth-enhancing alternative lifestyles were a logical line of enquiry.

When she contacted Gleitzman overseas, Jennifer would ask for a list of all the youth preservation groups or societies operating around the world. Then she would have Stuart James follow up by sending a photo of Brian to every one of those groups to ascertain whether he'd ever belonged to one.

In Jennifer's view, the practices of these immortalists didn't explain Brian's totally unchanged appearance. Certainly, it didn't touch on the fact that he'd been wearing the same clothes, the condition of the clothing still the same, as though no time had passed.

Jennifer clung to Meg's earlier observation that Brian would never have vanished of his own accord.

She felt the chill rising up her spine.

EIGHTEEN

Dear Mother,

There is a moment when the wire snaps in to place around the throat of the one I've chosen, and it feels good because I know I have the control - for once I have real control.

There's an enormous adrenalin rush, like a drug, and once you've had the high you need it again and again. I know it's hard for you, but please try and understand. This is the kind of power I need.

The victim struggles but the grip is too tight, the wire cuts deep, the air is closed off. There is a moment, I can sense it, when they know they're going to die. They know they're powerless – they know that the power lies with me.

Me.

That's the moment of ultimate control.

I could release them, and then walk away. The choice is mine. The choice over life and death. Who lives. Who dies.

History in the making.

I remember, when I was very young, they taunted me at school. I wish I'd known about the power then. It wasn't until later, with Vinnie, that I discovered how to take control. I found I could be the one in charge, have things the way I wanted them.

I used to keep a collection of newspaper clippings on murders. All sorts. I recall wishing I was the one doing those killings and being the one the police were trying to find. It would have been my secret identity. The mysterious killer sought nationally by the police but anonymous in

168

any crowd, possessing the dark power while at the same time knowing it couldn't be seen. No one who knew or met me could possibly suspect.

I wondered how it would feel to harbour that kind of hidden notoriety.

Now it's happened. More by accident than design.

The coppers know that the young woman and the old man were killed by the same method, the same person. They know an enemy's out there, somewhere amongst several million people.

I can walk up to any copper in the street, ask directions. He can look me in the eye, talk to me, without knowing.

It's happened because I've been set free for the first time in so long. I'm like an alcoholic turned loose in a grog shop. I killed twice in the same week - and left the bodies to be found. I'm no longer concerned with the secrecy the way I once was.

There's a fear out there in the community now and it's like a living thing. I can feel it. I can feed from it.

The phone rang. The jogger, hunched over his desk, writing feverishly in long hand, rolled his eyes and threw down his pen. Was there no peace? So much was happening in his life. He rose from his desk, giddy with excitement and the anticipation of it all, picked up the receiver, placed it to his ear.

It wasn't a call he expected. The voice on the other end of the line was distant, muffled, but nonetheless threatening. It was the one call he'd hoped he would never receive.

NINETEEN

'You're to stop what you're doing,' the voice on the phone said, 'or the police will be told all about you.'

The jogger said nothing at first. The sound of his heart, an inner thunder, crashed against his eardrums. He felt the terror of discovery well up from within.

'Do you understand?' The menace in the voice was unmistakable.

The jogger found a resolve he hadn't known he possessed. He was desperate to retain his freedom and there was a fighter inside who wasn't prepared to give up that freedom easily. 'What are you going to tell the police? You have nothing on me. No evidence,' he said, buoyed by the determination in his own voice.

Something occurred to him. The owner of the voice on the phone was part of the surveillance of so many years. Whoever they were, they were still out there. They knew he'd killed again. Yet the shadows hadn't returned to stop him.

Just this warning over the phone. Why?

'The police will investigate you. They'll find you have no alibi for the time of the murders this past week.'

'That isn't evidence. It's nothing and you know it.'

'They'll watch you, wait for you to make a move.'

'Then I won't make a move. I'll lay low for a while. After all, I managed it for eighteen years, didn't I?' The jogger chuckled to himself. He thought: I'm handling this well. This time I'm the one calling the shots.

'You can't help yourself.' There was anger in the mysterious voice. 'You'll do something to give yourself away.'

'It isn't going to work. Tell the cops what you want. I'll be a real good boy. And when they give up on me I'll be back, but I'll change my methods.'

'Bastard.'

'Of course, you could always start up the round the clock vigil again. But you can't, can you? Something is different. What? Did I outlive all your people?' He laughed aloud at the thought. 'So tell me, who are you? Who the fuck are you?'

'The police will be told,' the voice said, calmer now, the anger subsiding. 'We'll make sure they stop you. That's a promise. The choice is yours - stop, or we'll make sure you're caught.'

The frustration in the jogger's breast exploded. 'How many of you are there?' he shouted down the line. 'Why have you been doing this all this time?' The line went dead. The jogger hurled the phone into the air. It fell with a resounding crash.

His worst fear had been realised. His faceless nemesis was back, only not as he expected. No shadowy sentinels this time. A threat of exposure to the police instead, the one thing they had not done before.

How could he fight an enemy he couldn't see, couldn't find? They knew him though.

They know everything about me.

The jogger had to control his rage. He knew that. He sat down in the darkness. No lights. It was quiet. A good time to think. The minutes ticked towards midnight. Even when he'd travelled overseas, they'd known. The eyes had been out there, watching, waiting. Angels with all the time and resources of the heavens themselves. Was that it? Were they something otherworldly?

No. There was a very mortal element to the whole surveillance operation. And now they were no longer there to physically overpower him. He sensed they wouldn't do that again. Therefore, he was free to fight back. The first step, he decided, was to trap his enemy into revealing who they were.

They know all about me. They must be close enough to observe me.

171

Once he discovered who they were he would set out to eliminate them.

Someone close.

All of a sudden he was struck by an extraordinary idea. Could it be? Surely not. And yet ...

He was amazed he hadn't considered the possibility before. The idea sickened him. This time the nausea tore through his insides like the sharp edge of a weapon. He raced to the bathroom, dry retching as he flung his head over the toilet bowl. He knelt there for some time, trembling.

The thought stuck in his mind, an ugly intrusion, and with each passing moment it seemed to gain credence. Could it be?

TWENTY

For the past twenty-four hours, eighty-six police on the beat, working in pairs, stopped and questioned twenty-seven male joggers of varying ages. They discreetly watched and followed another twenty. Most of this activity occurred in the early morning or the evening.

None of the twenty who were watched were considered worth pursuing further. The names and addresses of the other twenty-seven were taken down - routine matter, the police said, asking, 'have you seen anything suspicious?' All were thoroughly checked out. None were suspicious. There were no likely contenders.

The senior men on the force had seen this sort of thing before. A line of enquiry that had to be followed, a watch that needed to be kept. They didn't expect anything to come of it, though. Too much of a longshot, unless they got very, very lucky.

All police had been instructed not to let on they were specifically looking for a male jogger acting suspiciously. Not even over police radio. Razell and Rosen were adamant that they wanted no chance of leaks.

In this respect, the investigation was successful. The reporters didn't get wind of it. They could only surmise that the police were following leads. There was no mention of the eyewitness, Dianne Adamson, who had seen Bill Dawson's death. The commissioner was pleased. That meant the killer didn't know his pursuers were looking for a jogger in sports gear. There was no reason, therefore, that he wouldn't continue to adopt that role when he went out to kill.

It was becoming increasingly apparent to Razell that this one piece of knowledge was their only hope of finding the murderer.

It was unusual for a senior detective-sergeant to arrive at Sydney HQ, demanding to see the deputy commissioner. Lachlan had been persistent, making an issue of the fact that he had highly sensitive material in his possession. It may have seemed unusual for Razell to agree to see Neil Lachlan at such short notice, but in fact it wasn't. He'd made a point to make himself available to all the men on the force, regardless of rank. Something like this allowed him to prove it.

It was early evening, the building still a hive of activity.

Razell listened patiently as Lachlan explained the situation. He leaned forward across his desk and cast his eye over the computer printouts. He felt some irritation to Lachlan's maverick approach, but showed it only in the trace of rebuke in his voice. 'Sit down, Lachlan, let me explain a few things to you.'

As Lachlan sat, Razell rose and strolled to the window, hands clasped behind him. 'Back in 2004, I sat down with all the division heads, including John Rosen, and we decided to form a special unit to handle cases that simply couldn't be successfully assigned to the normal channels.'

He returned to his seat and leaned back in the large, leatherback chair. 'There are similar units in Britain, the US, some of the European countries. We often consult with those units, seeking information or documentation.'

'I'm well aware of the unit, sir.'

'Of course you are. It's no secret. But it's also given a very low profile on the force. Let me level with you, it's the intention of the unit to kill public focus on certain issues. For that reason it's possible to get the idea that someone in the unit, Rosen for example, is up to no good when it simply isn't the case. There are two types of cases the unit specialises in. Firstly, politically-sensitive hot potatoes that are investigated quietly. A recent example was the investigation into a number of senior police and public servants involved in a computer fraud.'

Lachlan nodded, recalling the outcome of that case. The deputy commissioner had paused for effect, something he was known for, stroking his chin and jowls with thumb and forefinger. He grunted, cleared his throat. 'God, I feel like a cigarette.'

'I didn't know you smoked, sir.'

'I don't. Gave it up, finally, three years ago after many attempts.'

'You still get the urge?'

'Every day of my life. But I won't turn back now, I've come too far.' He cleared his throat again, signalling a return to business. 'The second type of case the unit handles, Lachlan, is the one with a bizarre element to it. We may not get results on such cases. Nothing unusual about Rosen keeping these particular cases under wraps if he feels there will be wild media speculation about people who don't age or some such nonsense.'

'But you're kept fully informed of the unit's work?'

'Of course.'

'There's a connection between these recent garrotte killings and the six missing persons cases taken on by Rosen. He hadn't acted on that connection and when I queried him I got the impression I was being stonewalled.'

Razell cast his eyes over the printouts again. A lengthy pause ensued before he spoke again. 'I hadn't been made aware these particular missing persons cases involved garrotting.' His irritation subsided. He recognised that Lachlan's concerns were well founded.

'Five had been,' Lachlan corrected him. 'The sixth, Brian Parkes, was run down. Isn't this connection something you'd expect John Rosen to bring to you?'

'Absolutely.' Razell continued to read through the information on the sheets of paper. 'Simply doesn't make sense,' he said presently. 'But Rosen is a good man. And you and John go back a long way.'

'Yes, we do.'

' I've no doubt he knows exactly what he's doing and has good reason.'

'How are you going to handle it, sir?'

'I'm going to look into the matter myself. Immediately. In the meantime your suspicions don't go beyond these four walls. I don't want rumours. I don't like unnecessary and unfounded speculation. When I came to this position, Lachlan, I promised to purge the force of corrupt officers, malcontents and bunglers. A passion I share with the Chief Commissioner. We've come a long way down the path towards that. And the community is reacting favourably.'

'You don't want that blown away.'

'You're damn right we don't want it blown away. I appreciate you bringing your concern to me, and I'm going to let you know my findings as soon as possible.'

'Sir, I'd like permission to continue my own investigation into the missing people and their possible connection with the current wave of garrotte killings.'

'I thought you'd get round to that. Very well, you clearly have a handle on the case. I expect you'll need some back up. I'll advise the men in Rosen's unit that you'll be handling the Parkes case and that they're to assist where required.'

Lachlan raised his eyebrows. 'Rosen?'

'Rosen, like his special unit men, will simply be advised they've been given extra manpower. And that you're it, on a temporary basis, because of your prior involvement with the case.' Razell then shifted the focus of the conversation back to the specifics. 'Tell me more about this theory of yours, that the clue to these recent garrotte murders lies with these long-term missing people.'

'One of them in particular, Brian Parkes.'

'Parkes?' Razell referred to the printouts.

'The only one not garrotted. Parkes was a hit and run victim. That's not the kind of murder this killer likes to commit.'

'But you believe it is the same killer?'

'More than likely. All the other details are too similar to be coincidence.'

'Report directly to me on this, Lachlan. Every morning, seven sharp, I want a full rundown. Here's my direct line.' He wrote the figures on a pad, removed the sheet and pushed it towards Lachlan. 'If you think there's an answer there, bring it to me.'

After excusing Lachlan, Razell spent the next few hours on the phone. First he spoke to the men in Rosen's unit. Then he spoke with the various local officers who'd discovered the missing people, before Rosen had stepped in and his unit had absorbed the cases.

Then he referred to the specific details of the recent garrotte murders. Like Lachlan, he couldn't ignore the similarities. Or the fact that Rosen had kept the missing persons details under wraps. Razell didn't like the pattern. The next painful step was to interview John Rosen.

Jennifer arrived home late, exhausted. Running from her business affairs to the private detective, wedging in her visit to Roger, the endless phone calls, the fashion shows, the huge order from GBs. She felt wrung out and realised she'd been operating on sheer nervous energy.

Her Chatswood home was a large, solid, rambling four-bedroom brick and sandstone house, originally built in the 1920s but totally refurbished throughout in recent years.

The interior style was modern, open plan, spacious. Jennifer's favourite area was the family room at the back of the house with its glass walls looking out across the lush, multi-level terraces of the garden. During the days the room was filled with natural light. On a clear night, like this one, with the drapes parted, Jennifer could gaze upwards, through the web of greenery, and see the stars.

The chimes on the front door resounded through the house. Jennifer went to the front to find Carly on her doorstep.

'Been at a shoot all day, wanted to stop by briefly on my way home.'

'Of course. Come in.'

Carly stepped inside. She followed the front hallway as it curved into the main lounge room.

'Won't stay. It's about my father. I want to find out what happened to him.'

'No more than I do, Carly. Believe me.' They stood beside the lounge, neither wanting to be the first to sit; a mother and daughter forced by the anxieties of their past meetings to square off against each other.

'I want to help.' Carly's manner was flat, straightforward. No hint of her tone from the luncheon, but no remorse either. Jennifer chose not to raise the emotion of their previous get-together. She was thrilled enough that her daughter had come to her, prepared to work with her on a common cause.

'I'd love you to help. What's more I've already started. I've put wheels of my own - our own - into action. I've hired a private detective named Stuart James.'

'What can he do?'

'I'm not sure, Carly. It's too early to say.'

She told Carly about the ideology in Gleitzman's book and DVD. Jennifer had managed, very late the night before, to track the surgeon down at his Massachusetts hotel room. Although pressed for time, he indicated he'd like to discuss Brian's case when he returned from the US. In the meantime he'd emailed a list of known immortalist groups to Jennifer's office. She, in turn, had passed them on to Stuart James for investigation.

'James has some good ideas of his own,' Jennifer continued, 'beginning with your father's old business records.'

'Those ancient boxes in the garage ..?'

'Yes. I was resting up, but after that I'm going to pull the boxes clear of everything else, sort through them, make them accessible for him.'

'I'll help you.'

Jennifer flashed a wide, toothy grin. 'I was hoping you'd say that.' She thought: Come on, Carly, smile back. Open up a little. When is the daughter who started vanishing two years ago going to come back?

Carly's expression, however, was all purpose and determination. 'I'll go out and start now. I'm anxious to do something.'

'I know the feeling ...' The phone rang, cutting Jennifer short.

'I'll be in the garage,' Carly said. She headed for the side door.

Jennifer answered the phone and recognised the voice of Neil Lachlan.

'Sorry to disturb you in the evening, I was interstate when you rang yesterday, I've been tied up since then ...'

'Thanks for returning the call. When I phoned I had some things on my mind. But it's okay now.'

'Sure I can't help? It's about your husband's case?'

'Yes. But I've hired a private investigator to assist me with that.'

'Your prerogative, of course. But there's really no need.'

'I beg to differ, Sergeant Lachlan,' she interjected. 'I was disappointed with the feedback I got from the special unit. I know it's only been a short time, but with something like this isn't it important to move quickly?'

'Yes ...'

'That man, Rosen, was hard to contact, and when I spoke with him he was too negative. Seemed to me to be acting cagey. I know the public can't expect to treat the police force like a department store where you go in, expecting service on every aspect on their daily investigations, but as the widow of the victim, I did expect to be kept abreast of what was going on – not to be deliberately kept in the dark, and patted on the head with platitudes. '

'The trouble with policemen is that we make lousy diplomats. Some of us could use more training in how to deal effectively with the public. I'm sure you simply caught John Rosen at the wrong moment.' Lachlan suspected that wasn't the case here but he could hardly say otherwise.

'Be that as it may, my mind is made up about the PI.'

'I have some news,' Lachlan said. 'As of now, I'm taking over once again on the investigation.'

'What's going on?' Jennifer's suspicions were raised further. Her tone made her annoyance clear. 'It doesn't sound normal to keep switching a homicide case from one detective to another.'

'It isn't. This is a highly unusual situation. Superintendent Rosen has become embroiled on another case so I'm stepping back into the fray. But I'll have the resources of his special unit at my disposal. Let me assure you, Ms Parkes, I'm determined to get answers on this.'

Jennifer was glad Neil Lachlan was back on the case, but she was in no mood to praise the police. 'I see.'

'It will help, of course, if I compare notes with your private investigator.'

'I imagine it would. His name is Stuart James. He's coming by in the morning to sift through my husband's old business records.' She also told him, briefly, about Doctor Gleitzman's list of youth preservation groups.

Lachlan conceded this was an interesting development - and he knew of Stuart James. 'He has a good reputation. I'll keep in touch with Mr. James and, of course, I'll be in touch with you further. I'd like you to have a good look over the clothes your husband was wearing when he was found.'

Jennifer agreed to this, then hung up. She lingered for a moment before heading out to the garage, sensing Lachlan had been holding back when he'd spoken of John Rosen. Why? What were they hiding from her?

Late night phone calls weren't unusual in John Rosen's home. It was part of the lifestyle of a divisional police superintendent.

Margaret Rosen, fifty years old, pleasantly plump, was a placid woman who cast a calm and steady influence across the private world of the senior policeman. She flashed a glance at her husband as the phone rang, a glance that effectively said, 'It'll be for you.' She'd used that look for many years, one of the many silent snatches of communication that pass between a man and a woman after a quarter of a century of marriage.

It was 9.45 p.m. Rosen hadn't been home more than an hour after another hectic day. He pushed his newspaper aside, rose from his favourite chair and reached for the cell phone on the coffee table. When he heard the muffled voice on the other end he shifted his body so that his back was to his wife. He didn't want Margaret to see the expression on his face.

'Rosen. We need to talk.'

'Hold on. I'm going through to the den.' The glance to his wife was the one she knew as "police business". Private. Won't be long. He went through to his study and gently closed the door behind him. 'What do you want this time?'

'Lady luck must be on my side,' the caller said. 'You've been placed in charge of the garrotte murders case. I couldn't have asked for better.'

'Why?' Rosen felt the prickle of the hairs on his neck. He sucked his cheeks in, expunging air through his nose with a quiet, indignant rage. It was several months since he'd first heard from the caller. He'd hoped never to hear from him again.

'I need you to frame these garrotte killings on someone.'

'What? This is beyond the pale. I can't ...'

'You can and you will.' The muffled voice was final. 'I can't have this investigation go on. Wrap it up very quickly. Pin it on someone.'

'But who ..?'

'Who the hell cares who? Pick a homeless bum who drifts around Central Park every night. Or some petty criminal. You're the copper, you find someone.'

'But the media is going berserk. When the murders keep happening -'

The phantom voice cut across his again. 'They won't. That will be seen to.'

'But how?'

'Not your affair, Rosen. It shouldn't have happened but it has. It will be fixed. We'll make certain of that.'

'Who -?'

'You know better than to ask that, Rosen.'

Rosen tried to stifle his anger. 'I've done what you asked up to now. You assured me-'

'... That you wouldn't hear from us again,' the mysterious caller completed the sentence. 'True. But shit happens. We couldn't foresee the current sequence of events. You must act quickly on this, Rosen. We don't want the real killer caught. We will deal with that.'

'And if I refuse?'

The muffled voice boomed down the line, angry now. 'We've had this conversation before. Do you want your wife, and your superiors, to know about your particular little vice.'

'Of course not.'

'Then move quickly, Rosen. Understand?'

'It will be difficult.'

'Find a way. I don't think you could live with the alternative.'

There was a click and the voice was gone, but in the wake of this threat even the dull tone left on the line carried an air of menace. Rosen wiped his brow and found he was drenched in sweat.

A couple of hours after the dinner with Conrad Becker, Henry Kaplan, Roger and Masterton returned to the offices.

'Deep in thought,' Harold Masterton noted, entering Kaplan's office a little later in the evening.

Kaplan turned away from the view of the city skyline. From up here it was a quiet world, dancing in neon. He faced his long time CFO. 'Yes. I don't think I'll be sleeping much over the next few nights. That's why I'm here. And you?'

'The same. Where's Roger. Home?'

'Probably stalking the corridors himself. We're all tense.'

'Yes. But I'm confident it's a foregone conclusion. Aren't you?'

'I'll kick back once the deal's set in stone. Not until then.'

'Becker will buy,' Masterton said. 'He can't resist a killing like this. The price is too good. He'll play the game for a few days because he enjoys it too much not to. By the end of the week we'll be back on the rails.'

'You keep giving me these impromptu little speeches. Sure you aren't trying to convince yourself?'

'Part of my job description.' He grinned and was pleased to see he'd raised a smile in Kaplan. 'I'm not just here haunting the halls, though. I have something for you. That discreet matter you asked me to look at. I had our legal department get onto it and this report was on my desk this evening.' Masterton offered a matt finish black folder to Kaplan, but the latter waved it away. 'Just tell me what's in it. This is the dossier on Rory McConnell?'

'Yes. We had to dig back twenty years to really come up with something. When he was sixteen years old, McConnell lived on the north coast, a small town called Forthworth. He was a suspect in a murder case.'

'What!' Kaplan's head snapped to attention. 'Murder?'

'Bunch of teenagers at a beach party one summer night. The following day one of the girls, fifteen years old, was found buried behind a sand dune. Her throat had been cut.'

'And the police thought it was McConnell?'

'He was the last one seen talking to the girl. She was pretty keen on him and he had a reputation for chasing the ladies. He also had a bad boy image, small town rebel. The police questioned him several times but no arrest was ever made. No evidence. Time of the girl's death was 1.40. McConnell's mother said her boy was home at around 12.30.'

'Was the murder ever solved?'

'Five years later a truckie was arrested for three hitchhiker murders. The police believed him to be responsible for several other killings, including the one in Forthworth, although the guy never admitted to any one of them.'

'Where is he now?'

'Still in prison.'

Kaplan stroked his chin. 'So it could have been McConnell?'

'Could have been. Whether it was or not, it's hardly the sort of thing he'd want known nowadays.'

'I was looking for a skeleton in his closet,' Kaplan said, 'something I could use if I needed to.'

'You don't trust him?'

'Since when do I trust people? What else did you find on him?'

'Not much. He came to Sydney, landed a job as a cadet journo on a daily newspaper, went freelance about ten years later, writing for these indie rags like People Power. Got involved in underground socialist groups, greenie groups, anything that attracted the ratbag element.'

'Women?'

'Hard to get much on his personal life. He's had a succession of girlfriends, four that we know of. Each lasted about a year. Career girls, earning good money which he appears to siphon out of them for one of these causes he supports. The latest is -'

Kaplan beat him to it. '...Carly Parkes.'

'Nothing more,' Masterton concluded, 'except that his family background was poor. Father shot through when he was ten. His mother raised him and she's still living in Forthworth. A bit of a drunk, apparently. But, you've got the closet skeleton you wanted.'

'Not the one I wanted. I wanted something juicy, but not as juicy as suspicion of murder.'

'Because of Jennifer Parkes' daughter?'

Kaplan nodded. 'Exactly. What if McConnell did slit that girl's throat all those years ago? For Chrissakes, Harold, he's living with young Carly.'

Henry Kaplan lived in a split-level, fifteen-room house in the elite Sydney suburb of Vaucluse. Heavy with greenery and very private, it was set well back from the street and had spacious grounds and harbour views.

Helen Shawcross had lived with him for eighteen months. She loved the house and its grounds; the fleet of prestige cars; the expensive gifts; and the attention she received from high society. She might have loved Henry Kaplan had she been capable of real love. As it was, she was tiring of Kaplan just as she'd tired of all the men she'd been with. And she was aware, with Kaplan holding off bankruptcy, with an appeal hearing pending, that the good life might not continue. Not to the extent she'd known it. Of course, it wouldn't be a problem to find another sugar daddy: they lined up for a woman like her.

She was in no hurry. The idea of a fleeting affair with a bohemian type like Rory McConnell appealed. Something different. Something exciting.

Helen was aware that Kaplan kept a stack of old personal records in a number of archive boxes in his basement. Knowing he wouldn't be home until very late, she'd spent the entire evening going through those papers. If it hadn't been for the dust, causing her to sneeze several times each hour, she would have thoroughly enjoyed this clandestine invasion of his privacy. She knew how guarded he could be about his background. He rarely even spoke to her about Roger, his only son, whom she'd only met, briefly, on a few occasions.

Helen imagined how much more exciting it would have been if Rory were here with her now. She felt a pang of desire for him, a fever in her loins.

She found what she wanted - communications between opposing lawyers over the issue of Kaplan's divorce from his first wife thirty years before. She photocopied the relevant information on the copier in the study. Rory would grin like a Siamese cat when he saw these documents. None of it had ever been made public.

Helen wasn't totally surprised by what she'd found. There was a side to Kaplan she'd caught glimpses of from time to time. This information confirmed there was even more than she suspected. She'd never seen a picture of Kaplan's first wife. Until now. There were a number of faded photos of Henry and Monica Kaplan in the boxes. Before she left the basement, Helen gazed with curiosity at the dark haired young woman as she was in the 1980's.

It was the middle of the night when Kaplan arrived home. Helen reclined on the living room leather couch. Wearing a long, black negligee that accentuated the smooth, sleek lines of her body.

'Still up?'

'Couldn't sleep,' Helen replied, rising gracefully from the lounge to place a kiss on his cheek. 'You're not the only one stressed about the current predicament. It affects me too.'

'I know.' He took her by the hand, squeezed it. 'I'm sorry I haven't been around much lately. But I warned you it would be like this for a few weeks. When this sale to Becker is closed, we'll get away for a weekend.'

She licked her lips. 'Mmmm ...' She snuggled up close to him.

He smiled at her, stroked the beautiful head of golden hair, and then slumped down on the sofa. 'I'm bushed.'

She sat beside him. 'I think you'll find I can take your mind off business for a while.'

'Business isn't the main worry I have at the moment, believe it or not.'

Helen eyed him curiously. 'You're kidding, right?'

'Not at all. I've had some disturbing news regarding Rory McConnell.'

'Carly Parkes' boyfriend?'

'Yes. I'm worried about her.'

'Why?'

Kaplan told her about the incident in Forthworth. She listened, expressing surprise, but was careful not to show too much. Was Rory a killer? She'd sensed something dangerous about him. That was part of the attraction. He liked playing it rough and his lovemaking could be kinky. But murder? She listened as Kaplan told her of his intention to discuss the information with Carly's mother as soon as possible.

Rory may have a wild streak, but he's no killer, she decided. She was thrilled she had something extra now to tell him. She'd make sure he earned his information by pleasuring her the way she liked for as long as she could stand it.

Kaplan removed his coat and placed his feet up on the coffee table. Helen tucked her legs up beneath her, kneeling beside him on the sofa. 'Don't underestimate me,' she teased, 'I can even take your mind off a worry like that.' Her fingers moved with a slow, seductive rhythm over his body. As she worked to arouse him, she thought of the documents in those archive boxes, of the faded photographs of Monica Kaplan.

It pleased Helen that she was not like that woman. When it came to powerful men like Kaplan, Helen was the one in control. She had what Henry Kaplan needed. She had what Rory McConnell wanted. She intended to enjoy the next couple of days as she played one against the other, ending one affair, igniting the next.

TWENTY ONE

Jennifer phoned her office at 8.30 a.m. the following morning. 'Cindy, I'm going to be tied up most of the morning with police matters. Can you take the reins?'

'That's what I'm here for,' Cindy said cheerfully. 'Don't worry about us. You do what you have to do.'

'You're priceless. Thanks, Cindy.' Jennifer hung up. It occurred to her that when this matter was resolved, she should take some time off. For years she'd had an expert team in place, quite capable of running Wishing Pool Fashions in her absence. Perhaps she just never wanted to consider her company running without her. The fact was, she could afford to take things a little easier. A trip away - with Carly - would be perfect, if she could persuade her daughter to be in it.

Carly had stayed overnight. She wanted to be there when Stuart James arrived.

They'd watched TV together and done a little talking.

Part of Jennifer's morning would be taken up, with Carly, assisting Stuart James with the files in the garage. James had already phoned to say he was running a few minutes late - and to advise Jennifer he'd sent a copy of Brian's photo and particulars to all the youth preservation groups on Gleitzman's list.

The rest of her morning would be taken up with a visit to the police forensics lab. Neil Lachlan had phoned only minutes before to ask her to accompany him, hence Jennifer's call to Cindy. Lachlan had offered to pick her up. The lab visit was to follow up on Lachlan's request that she take a closer look at Brian's clothing.

187

With both Stuart James and Neil Lachlan working the case, Jennifer felt more positive.

God, how she wanted to put all this behind her once and for all.

Jim Howell was a short, wiry, bespectacled man and clearly passionate about his forensic work. His hands moved continuously, illustrating his words in frenetic movements that Jennifer found distracting.

'Fascinating case,' Howell commented. He gestured to the articles of clothing, neatly folded and placed on the bench beside the wall. 'A thorough testing of the fabric shows that the material has had only a short period of ageing due to usage or exposure. The same is true of the leather of the wallet and of the printed items in the wallet.'

Lachlan turned to Jennifer. 'Did you recognise these clothes, at the morgue, as those your husband wore the night he vanished?'

'I didn't take particular notice at the morgue,' Jennifer said. 'But yes, they did look the same.'

'Take a closer look,' Howell suggested. 'Take your time.'

Jennifer gazed down at the neat piles. Lachlan and Howell stood by patiently. Neither spoke.

Jennifer would never forget the last time she'd seen Brian alive - walking out the door into the driving rain of that blasted storm. She could still picture the white shirt with its blue stripes, the coat, the navy blue trousers, the water streaming in rivulets down his cheeks. 'As best I can remember,' she said, 'these were the clothes he wore.'

She recalled the report Lachlan had typed the day the body was found. It had stated that the clothes were damp. 'It was raining heavily the night I last saw him,' she added.

'Which ties in with the state of his clothing when he was found,' Lachlan said.

'The suit was an Excelsior brand,' Howell said, 'manufactured by StyleSet. I've confirmed they haven't been in business since the late 90's.'

'How can a suit made at least eighteen years ago show no more wear than if it were made just a few months ago?' Lachlan asked Howell.

'Only by ensuring the articles had no contact with the environment. For instance, sealing them in air-tight plastic bags.'

'But the clothes were still damp,' Jennifer pointed out, 'and it didn't rain during the night before Brian's body was found.'

'Any unusual properties in the water in the clothing?' Lachlan asked.

'No. Just plain, pure water.'

Jennifer sifted through the clothing, focusing intently on each item. Something niggled at the back of her mind, staying just out of memory's reach. 'There's something not quite right.'

'What is it?' asked Lachlan.

'It's on the tip of my tongue. I just can't seem to ...' Her voice trailed away as she strained her mind, searching for mental pictures of that night from so long ago.

'Take your time,' Howell repeated.

Jennifer went to the chair beside Howell's desk and sat down. It was hard to think on the spot, under pressure, like this. Think back. Go back to that night. Heavy rain. Lightning. Brian at the door, still drenched. She'd urged him to take a hot bath; she didn't want him to catch a chill. She remembered that much. What had he said? 'I'm out of fags. The shop will still be open. A few more minutes won't make any difference.'

She looked down at the clothes again, the wallet, the money inside it. The five-dollar notes were still crisp. Like the items you'd find in a time capsule. Remnants of another age. But something was different, missing. What was it?

Why, oh, why in God's name can't I remember what it was?

'Where would you like me to drop you off?'

'My place,' Jennifer said. 'I've got things covered at the office.' She clicked the seat belt in to place as Lachlan pulled out from the curb. He drove on to the distributor spanning Darling Harbour, which linked directly to the Harbour Bridge, heading north. 'If anything does come back to you, day or night, call me. Don't worry about the time.'

'Okay.'

They drove in silence for a while. Presently Jennifer said, 'I'm actually starting to wonder if my husband did fall through a hole in time. Crazy, eh?'

'That's strictly Doctor Who stuff. Listen, we're going to get to the bottom of this.'

'We're no further advanced than we were a week ago when Brian's body was found.'

'Not true. You have Stuart James working on this. Your angle on the youth preservation movement is worth following.'

Jennifer shook herself out of her moment of self-doubt. 'Yes ...'

'There's more,' Lachlan said. 'I didn't mention this on the way over because I didn't want to distract you before we met with Howell. Five other people went missing eighteen years ago, and they've also turned up over the past month or so. The main difference is these others were murdered by garrotte. Now, there may not be a connection ...'

Jennifer's head snapped about, her eyes connecting with Lachlan's. 'Others. Like Brian. You knew this?'

'I found out late yesterday,' Lachlan explained. They were on the bridge. Sunlight glinted off the steel girders. It was a bright day, the water in the harbour a vibrant blue. Lachlan moved the car into the left lane, following the Pacific Highway exit. 'I saw the deputy police commissioner late last night which is why I'm back on the case. I'm just starting to put it all together. The last one was a girl named Monique Brayson. I've organised her clothing to be analysed today.'

'You're expecting the same results?'

'Yes.'

'These others-'

Lachlan cut in, anticipating the question. 'There doesn't appear to be any connection between these people with each other, or with your husband. Nevertheless, I'm running checks all over the place to make doubly certain, Ms Parkes.'

'Please, detective, call me Jennifer.'

Lachlan nodded. It pleased him that they were communicating so well.

'Did these others also appear to have remained - young?'

'I'm looking into that. But from my initial enquiries - yes, it seems so.'

190

'No clues? Nothing?'

'No. Well, there is one thing of interest. The other five all vanished from Sydney's north-west. Your husband was the only one from the other side of the city. There may be nothing in that ...' He left the sentence incomplete.

Lachlan turned left off the Pacific Highway and less than a minute later the heavy traffic and endless line of office blocks seemed a world away. The streets of Chatswood were wide, leafy avenues, with well established homes, quiet and serene.

Something else occurred to Jennifer. 'Those two murders over the past week. The woman and the old man. They were garrotted.'

'There could be a connection,' Lachlan conceded, pulling in by the curb outside Jennifer's house. 'There's two common threads. First, all appear to be random killings; second, the killing method is the same.'

'But those two never went missing years before.'

'That's the one, major puzzling difference.' Lachlan would've liked to reveal more. But he couldn't tell her about the eyewitness to Bill Dawson's death, or that the police knew they were looking for a male jogger. That was strictly police business.

Jennifer stepped from the car. 'Stuart James feels certain he'll find something among Brian's old business records.'

'I'll compare notes with him later,' Lachlan said. 'And remember, if you recall anything in the meantime ...'

'I'll let you know.'

She watched as he drove away, and reflected on the fact that he was the total opposite to Rosen. Neil Lachlan might be a little rough around the edges but he had an easy, earthy charm and a straightforward manner. Jennifer liked him.

Carly hung up the phone as Jennifer entered. 'I've been trying to get hold of Stuart James,' Carly said. 'He hasn't been back to his office, though, since he left here.'

'Something wrong?'

Carly pointed to a handful of folders on the coffee table. 'He left those behind when he left. He seemed to think he'd found something of interest in those records and he intended taking them with him.'

'Did he say what he'd found?'

'No. He was in a rush to make another appointment. He said he'd phone later and took off. He had several of the old business files with him, but he left these, which he'd deliberately singled out, on the table.'

Jennifer thumbed through the pages of the files. They were audits on several companies - Marco Plastics, Sharvan Glass, Winterstone Pty.Ltd., none of which meant anything to her. She placed the folders back on the table and wondered what it was that James had found.

It never rains but it pours, thought Stuart James. A fortnight earlier he'd had very little work. In the space of the last week several new briefs - including two very large assignments - had come his way. All urgent.

He'd agreed to squeeze Jennifer Parkes into his suddenly busy schedule, thinking it wouldn't require too much work too soon. Something he could get his teeth into the following week, when he expected to be quiet again. It wasn't working out that way.

He stopped off briefly at his Australia Tower office. There was a message from Carly Parkes. He wondered why she was calling so soon, and he made a mental note to return the call later. Right now he had an important meeting to attend with a major client. He told his secretary, a plump, teenage Italian girl named Rosa he wouldn't be back until late.

Neil Lachlan strode into the reception area as James was scurrying out. Their eyes connected. 'Mr James ..?' Lachlan started.

'You've got him. But I'm afraid I'm running late for an appointment, Mr ..?'

'Detective Senior Sergeant Neil Lachlan, Homicide Squad.'

'Walk with me,' James suggested. 'I'd stop and see you, but -'

'Not a problem.' Lachlan fell into step beside him as they headed down the corridor to the lift. Lachlan explained that he was heading the investigation into the disappearance and deaths of six people, Brian Parkes among them.

James' interest was piqued. 'Others ..?'

'Yes. I'm aware your services have been retained by Ms Parkes and I believe it would be a good idea if we were to compare notes on a daily basis.'

'Agreed.' There was a shrill ping as the lift arrived. 'I'm in the basement car park,' James said as they entered the lift.

Lachlan explained the similarities between the cases. He'd had plenty of experience dealing with private investigators from his days in the Drug Squad. Most of them liked to play things close to their chests. Lachlan's approach was to give them some police-gathered information - the more startling the better - then go in with his own set of questions. He wanted an initial get-together with James without Jennifer present, which is why he'd dropped by unannounced. 'Ms Parkes advised me you're looking through her late husband's accountancy practice files. Anything of interest?'

They alighted from the lift and walked briskly past the rows of parked cars. 'Eighteen years ago Kaplan Corp hired Brian Parkes to conduct the routine annual audit on a few of their Australian based companies,' James replied, 'one of these was a shelf company called Winterstone Pty. Ltd. Kaplan Corp had purchased this business name not long before that. Winterstone was used to purchase a warehouse on an industrial estate in Sydney.' They reached James' car, and he fumbled for his car keys. 'It was a storage warehouse with space for hire.'

'Nothing strange about that.'

'Not at all. What is strange is that it doesn't appear to have been used for any commercial storage purposes. What's more, Winterstone paid a million dollars to a United States company and took delivery of a shipment from that company at around the same time.'

'What kind of shipment?'

'The bill of lading simply stated parts. Could've been anything. The even bigger question, though, is where did the money come from? Winterstone had no income and no operating capital when purchased. There is no record of a deposit into Winterstone's account, but the money was there. According to Brian Parkes' handwritten notes, attached to his audit-in-progress, there were several large discrepancies in the balance sheets of the other Kaplan companies he'd been auditing.'

'Money had been transferred from those other firms?'

'Secretly, not openly,' James pointed out.

Lachlan thought back to an earlier conversation with Jennifer. Brian had been hired by Roger Kaplan. They were buddies. Lachlan offered that information to James.

'I believe that to be the case - yes,' said James, 'but Roger Kaplan didn't purchase Winterstone or the shipment from America.' He got into his car. 'I really have to go, detective, but I'm happy to get together with you later.'

'When are you back?'

'Tonight. Around ten I'm afraid. It's going to be a long, detailed meeting.'

Lachlan handed the private investigator his card. 'Call me when you get in. We'll arrange to get together.'

James nodded and switched his key in the ignition. The motor roared into life.

'One last thing,' Lachlan said. 'If Roger Kaplan didn't set up the Winterstone operation, then who did?'

'The name on the shelf company forms,' James replied, 'was Kaplan Corp's senior financial director, Harold Masterton.'

It was late afternoon, the sun sinking quickly beneath the western skyline, when Helen Shawcross arrived at Rory McConnell's apartment. She had dressed seductively in a figure hugging, light green chiffon dress that fell just above the knee.

'You're a sight for sore eyes,' he said, embracing her.

'How about a drink?' She pushed past him, headed for the kitchen.

'Way ahead of you. They're already poured.'

They sat, glasses of white wine in hand, looking over each other like hungry lovebirds. 'This is a guilty pleasure, getting to see you again so soon,' Helen said. 'What's going on with little Miss Parkes?'

Helen's attitude toward Carly amused Rory. He'd always loved playing one woman off against another. 'Been camped at her mother's place the past day and a half. Called by around mid-day for a change of clothes. It's all to do with this business of her father being found, murdered, after eighteen years.'

'I know. Henry told me all about it.'

'Carly's mother hired a private investigator and the three of them have been getting their heads together.'

'Yes. Henry heard about that from his son, Roger. Strange business.'

'But it's worked out to our advantage.' He moved closer to her, placing his wine glass to his lips with one hand, using the other to massage the nape of her neck.

'Mmm. Feels good.'

'What's all this you mentioned on the phone? Lots of news for me about Kaplan's first wife.'

'I photocopied a heap of papers stored in his basement archives. Her name was Monica and she divorced him for beating up on her. She'd lodged medical certificates as proof with her lawyers. Henry's got copies of them. Seems it was kept pretty quiet though. As far as I know, even Roger wasn't aware his parents were divorcing. Of course he was only a boy at the time.'

'What happened to her?'

'She was a manic-depressive. There are psychiatric reports among Henry's papers, attesting to that. Seems she took a really bad turn when the meetings between the lawyers were getting nasty. Henry and his doctors had her committed to a loony asylum. Then he went ahead and divorced her.'

Rory whistled. 'Juicy. Character assassinations in print are always helped along by family secrets like that.'

'This Mata Hari stuff is going to cost you. Tonight you do the things I want, not the other way around.'

Rory's grin stretched from ear to ear. 'I'm flexible. But I don't think you've told me enough. Where's Monica Kaplan now?'

'I don't know. All I can tell you is she was sent to the Hillsdale Hospital for psychiatric treatment thirty years ago.'

Rory pressed his fingers down harder against the flesh of Helen's neck and shoulders. She groaned with pleasure. 'You should have been a masseur,' she sighed.

'Tonight I'm whatever you want me to be,' he promised, a mischievous smile playing around his lips. Harlan Draper at People Power would love it. More importantly, Rory expected it to give him the ideal entree for syndication to the major newspapers around the country, while making him the champion of the alternative media journalists.

'That's the good news,' Helen said.

'There's bad?'

'Uh huh. Henry hasn't just blindly trusted you as you thought. Seems he's done some digging into your own past.'

A shadow crossed Rory's eyes. He kept massaging Helen's back, but she felt the sudden tension in his fingers. 'Go on.'

'He knows that the police questioned you about a murder when you were sixteen.'

'How the hell did he find that out?'

'Didn't say. One of his people must have done some talking to someone in Forthworth. The local cops? Your mother?'

'My mother would never say anything about that.' Rory spat the words out. 'It was almost twenty years ago, for Chrissakes. Someone else was guilty.'

'Hey, relax. I know you didn't do anything. I just figured it would be good for you to know my boyfriend is checking you out. He may have agreed to the article, but he's wary.'

'The bastard's got nothing on me. But I've got plenty on him. Plenty.' Thoughts raced through his mind. Had Kaplan hired someone to look into his background? A private investigator? If so, was it the same one Jennifer Parkes had hired? She was close to Kaplan so that would make sense. Had Jennifer Parkes put Kaplan up to the idea? He thought he'd swayed her with his charm. Now he wasn't so sure.

'What's this all about, anyway?' Helen asked, excited by the idea of her two lovers secretly sparring against each other. Idealist versus capitalist.

'It's about exposing the system and its financial captains for the dirt they really are.'

'You're sounding agitated, lover. I think I'd better massage your back.'

'No. I'm fine. You did well to find out as much as you did. But now it's fun time.' Skilful fingers loosened her blouse and slipped it from her.

'Yes *please*.' She breathed heavily as his fingers went to work.

TWENTY TWO

It was one thing to find the time, early mornings and evenings, to select a victim, stalk them, decide on the right time and the right place to strike. It was quite another, the jogger found, to put aside as much time as possible, immediately, to kill a specific person who posed a sudden threat. This was a totally different function, nothing like the killings he so enjoyed. This was business, pure and simple. It didn't give him the same pleasure - that's why he'd performed only one other murder like it.

There was a reason for this kill because his prey was a link that the authorities could question. He shuddered at that thought.

Seated in his car, the jogger waited outside the city block that housed Stuart James' office. He glanced at his watch - 9.50 p.m. Earlier he'd driven to the suburb where James lived. He'd moved stealthily around the exterior of the house. No car in the driveway or garage. No lights. Frustrated, the killer drove into the city. He didn't have much time to spare. He entered the Australia Tower parking bay entrance with the use of a security key. Earlier in the day, a phone call and an obscene amount of money had secured him a copy of the key from one of his contacts. Not difficult when you knew the right people.

James' car wasn't there. The jogger cursed under his breath, then reminded himself to keep calm. If it couldn't be tonight, then tomorrow. He'd find a way.

He returned to his car. On impulse, he decided to wait a few minutes. Less than five minutes later James' Ford Falcon passed by and turned into the parking basement.

With several hours to fill before the expected call from Stuart James, Lachlan returned to the Hurstville Police station to process some of the paperwork he'd been avoiding. A detective, Dan Royle, stopped by his desk. 'You handling the Parkes case again?'

'Yeah.'

'Figured as much. Saw the reports out on your desk again.' A grin danced across Royle's face. 'I reckon you want that case because you fancy the widow. Very nice piece of ass.'

'All the ladies are very nice pieces of ass, according to you,' Lachlan retorted.

'True. But this one's a real looker. I'd say you're a bit of a dark horse, Lacho.'

'I wish.' Later, back at his Glebe apartment, Lachlan's thoughts returned to Jennifer Parkes as he fixed dinner: grilled cheese on toast with tomato and a few sticks of celery thrown in.

Why hadn't she ever remarried? Wedded to her business, perhaps? In between relationships?

Lachlan didn't believe in becoming personally involved with the people in his cases. When this investigation finished though, he wondered whether he'd get up the nerve to ask her for a date. It had been a long time since he'd done anything like that. He knew he needed to start circulating more.

And he hadn't been able to get Jennifer Parkes out of his mind from the moment they'd met.

On a more realistic note, he doubted she'd have any interest in a homicide cop. She'd have a lot more in common with men from the corporate and fashion worlds.

The phone rang. Todd's excited voice spoke like rapid fire. 'Dad. Guess what? Grandpa's getting better.'

'That's great news, tiger. How are you and your mother getting along up there?'

'Okay. It's a bit like a holiday. We're flyin' home the night after tomorrow. Mum wants to know if you could pick us up at the airport.'

'You bet I can.'

'Ace. We'll see you then.'

'Hold on, matey. What time does the flight get in?'

'Uh ... Mum's not here right now. Hold on.' There was some frantic shuffling away from the phone. 'Mum wrote the details on a pad earlier. Here it is. Flight 911. Arrives in Sydney at quarter past six.'

'Which airline?'

'Oh ... uh ...'

Lachlan laughed. 'Don't worry. I can figure it out. See you then, tiger.'

'Bye Dad.'

Lachlan hung up the phone and laughed again. Kids. He went back to his meal and it occurred to him that this was the first time since the separation that Marcia had asked a favour. Was this a good sign?

At 9.45 p.m. he received another phone call. Stuart James. The private investigator, driving back to his office, had called on his mobile phone. He suggested Neil meet him at the Australia Tower building.

The jogger left his car and sprinted to the parking bay stairwell. He'd noted the space allotted to James when he'd been in here minutes before. Level Two. He headed straight for it and moved quickly, cautiously, not wanting to be seen, a large iron crowbar in his hand. There were cleaners moving around the building.

James was parking his car at the far end of the level. The jogger wondered, briefly, why the investigator had returned to his office at such a late hour? Whatever the reason, the jogger's impulse to hang around for a few minutes had paid off. For once, luck or intuition or both, were on his side.

There was still the odd car scattered around the level. The jogger raced to the older of the two vehicles nearest the stairs, one that he was certain did not have an RFID chip. He removed a slotted screwdriver from his pocket. Tonight he was dressed in a staid, nondescript business suit, which served the purpose of helping him blend in with the city streets and offices.

Modern cars could not be hotwired in the old fashioned way, but the jogger was aware of the little known fact that a screwdriver could sometimes work when there was no RFID chip. He had done this before.

With the crowbar he smashed the driver's side window, pulled open the door, leapt in and quickly manipulated the screwdriver into the ignition. He jiggled until he managed to turn it. The motor spluttered into power and the lock on the steering wheel snapped.

Luck is with me, the jogger thought. If the screwdriver trick hadn't worked, then he would have had to find another way, perhaps another time.

Stuart James was locking his car door when he heard the sound of smashing glass. His head whipped about, his eyes scanning the other cars. At first he couldn't see any disturbance. Then he noticed a shape moving in the interior of the red car at the far end of the level. James figured a theft was occurring. Instinctively he sprinted towards the other vehicle.

The wheels screeched as the red sedan shot forward and headed towards the exit. James ran after the car, trying to glimpse the driver, wondering how the thief intended to get out of the parking level. Did he have a security key?

The jogger spun the steering wheel. Without warning the sedan made a sudden turn, wheels still screeching, rubber burning across the concrete. Stuart James was caught unawares and without cover. The nose of the sedan ploughed into him. There was a sickening thud as his body lifted into the air and was thrown aside like a rag doll, arms flailing.

He came down hard on the concrete. Another thud. The snap of breaking bones boomed in his ears. In a state of shock, he regarded his predicament as someone might from afar. Blood poured from his nose and mouth and he raised his hand to his head as though that might stem the flow.

There was a monstrous ache in his neck and shoulders - piercing, but he sensed further danger. He tried to push himself to his feet but the pain down his left side and through his left leg was excruciating. Broken leg, broken ribs, he thought dazedly. The roar of the engine and the screech of wheels filled the air again. He cocked his head to the right, saw the shadow fill his vision, the grille of the car hurtling towards him at breakneck speed.

The car smashed into him, carrying him along pinned to its grille. It squashed him like some rubbery figure as it hit the brick wall, its entire front end crumbling into a mass of twisted metal and glass, meshed with human limbs.

The jogger stepped from the car. He didn't bother to cast his eye over his victim. He ran to the other end of the level. James' car key remained in the door of the Falcon. The jogger took the key set and examined the others. It appeared that the office keys were on the same ring, just as he'd hoped.

Then his eye caught the box of folders on the back seat. He leaned in for a closer look. There was no doubting it, these were the business records James had taken from the Parkes house.

The killer swept the box up under his arm and walked briskly to the stairwell exit. He passed a cleaner at the next landing and kept his head down so his face wasn't seen. Not that there was any need. The cleaner didn't even glance at the commonplace sight of a business executive on the stairs. If they had, they would have seen the subtle but triumphant grin. The jogger's task for the evening had been successfully completed. He no longer needed to go to the private detective's office. James had obliged him by leaving the files in the car. The jogger had what he wanted.

At the same moment the jogger's car turned right out of George Street, Lachlan pulled up across the road from the Australia Tower building. He was pressing the night security bell at the lobby doors when he heard the scream.

A small, Filipino woman burst out of the stairwell doors inside the lobby area. 'Help. Please, help!'

Lachlan banged on the glass door, holding up his police badge.

The woman activated the security button on the inside wall and the lobby doors sprung open automatically.

'Level Two,' the woman croaked, gagging on her own words. She dropped to her knees, dry retching.

Lachlan bounded down the steps. As he approached the red sedan he saw the mangled remains of Stuart James. Bile rose in his throat. He stopped, sucked in air, and ran forward. As he did, he realised there wasn't a single thing anyone could do to help the private detective.

It was late and the jogger was tired. He hurled the folders at the wall in a fit of rage and paced the floor like a wounded animal. He'd hoped to kill two birds with one stone tonight. James was dead but the records he wanted weren't among the folders he'd taken from James' car.

Perhaps this could be handled another way. He resolved then and there to make the most unexpected move of all. He would go to the home of Jennifer Parkes - and end her meddling once and for all. He was determined, one way or another, to sabotage the investigation of Brian Parkes' disappearance and murder.

TWENTY THREE

'The word around the Kaplan Corp office,' said Rory, 'is that the sale of Southern Star will go through by the end of this week or the beginning of the next. That's why we need to change the schedule.'

'Bloody shame,' said Harlan Draper. 'I liked the idea of a series of three articles. The first two outlining Kaplan's background and achievements, with the hint of something darker suggested. And then the final installment, with the personal and professional exposé that we'd supposedly uncovered in the meantime.'

Rory nodded his agreement. 'Yeah. Would've been great. But I had no idea just how powerful the exposé would become, or how quickly Kaplan was moving to clinch this sale and save his shoddy empire.'

'Agreed.' Draper rubbed his hands together in delight. 'A bashed wife he committed to an asylum and strong evidence he interfered with the inquiry into the asbestos poisoning at the mine. You want the whole thing out before the sale goes through.'

'People deserve to know the truth, including Conrad Becker. I expect he'll pull out of the deal, at least for now.' Rory had been on his feet since his arrival ten minutes earlier. Impassioned by the material he'd gathered on Kaplan in the past twenty-four hours, he began to pace back and forth in the small, cluttered People Power office. 'Kaplan Corp is big news right now. Once this issue is out, the media will jump on it. For once, Harlan, you'll be leading the way.' He chuckled. 'Think of it, one of the dreaded alternative papers scooping them on a big news story.'

'Those high and mighty bastards won't come to us, though. They'll just steal what they want from our published piece and send their own boys in to dig further.'

Rory smiled inwardly. Not quite, old boy, he thought. He intended to be right in the midst of the action, selling his services to all and sundry as a freelancer. It would bring in the bucks and hand him the platform for a reputation. 'Doesn't matter,' he said to Draper, 'what matters is we're setting the agenda here, sending the tabloids off on Kaplan's scent, setting one self-serving capitalist mob against one of their own. Poetic justice, don't you think?'

'Find a space and put the finishing touches to the article,' Draper said. He reached for the phone. 'I need to call the printer and hold 'em off making plates.'

As he punched in the numbers, his eyes roamed over the beginning of Rory's first draft, the pages of which were strewn across his desk. It read:

Skeletons in a Multi-Million Dollar Closet.

For the past thirty years well-known Australian entrepreneur Henry Kaplan has built a business empire, with a diverse range of interests here and overseas. Kaplan is not, however, the man his publicists would have us believe.

Medical records obtained by this paper show conclusively that his first wife, Monica Kaplan, was the victim of constant bashing which led her to file for divorce. That action, hushed up at the time, was not completed before her husband had her committed to a hospitable for the mentally disturbed. People Power asks: is this the real face of the man who presents himself to the public as a champion of enterprise and a supporter of popular charities?

The article then shifted to industrial matters, detailing the evidence that suggested Kaplan had killed off the asbestos investigation after he'd bought a controlling interest in Southern Star. It was strong stuff and Draper beamed unashamedly. He enjoyed nothing more than bringing the fat cats down.

Mid-morning. John Rosen walked the streets aimlessly. Shattered. His head was filled with the moment of his suspension that same morning. The deputy commissioner had come straight to the point. 'I'm in possession of evidence, John, that indicates you've deliberately suppressed information that links these garrotte murders with those odd missing person cases.'

'What evidence?' asked Rosen.

Razell told him about Lachlan's visit, and about the enquiries both of them had made. 'I need an explanation.'

'There's nothing to explain, Ed. I'm on top of both cases and I'm not convinced there's any link.'

'This is hardly a set of coincidences, John.'

Rosen was silent. He simply avoided Razell's stare.

'Come on, John,' the deputy commissioner pressed.

Rosen's eyes were glazed, his expression one of a man who had lost his spirit. Suddenly he didn't have the steel to fight for himself. He knew the game was up. A part of him was glad, but it wasn't something his pride would allow him to admit. 'I don't believe there's a connection there,' came the lame reply.

'For Chrissakes, John, you've given the families of these victims the runaround and kept the facts from them.' He stood. After a brief pause he spoke again. 'Help me out here. We're on the same side. Tell me what's really going on?'

Rosen also rose to his feet. 'I've given you an answer.' His voice lacked the fire Razell would've expected. 'I'm not prepared to say anymore without legal counsel.' He headed for the door.

'Then I've no choice but to stand you down pending an inquiry by Internal Affairs.'

'Do what you have to do,' said Rosen.

He'd walked out without further comment and wandered the streets. Returning home he said nothing to Margaret. How could he hurt her now after so many years? The truth was simply too painful. He couldn't fool her, of course, and didn't even try.

'What are you doing here at this time of day? Something wrong, dear?' she asked.

He grunted, then continued to ignore her. No doubt she expected he'd confide when ready, as he had so many times before. Only this time it was very, very different. This was the one thing John Rosen could never confide to anyone.

The phone rang at 10 p.m. that night and Rosen knew, before he lifted the receiver, it was his phantom caller. He checked over his shoulder to ensure that Margaret was out of the room before he replied. 'I can't help you anymore. I've been suspended.'

The muffled voice at the other end of the line was angry. 'There's been no such announcement!'

'It happened today. The commissioner will probably keep it quiet for the time being.'

'Don't play me for a fool, Rosen. You know what to expect.'

Rosen checked the doorway again. No sign of Margaret. He heard the rattle of pans in the kitchen. 'I've helped you up to now, haven't I? For Chrissakes, they know I've been suppressing information.'

'You must do what I've ordered.'

'I can't-'

'You know the alternative,' the mysterious voice cut across him. 'Tomorrow, the world learns what kind of man you really are.'

'Look, give me more time.' Rosen heard the click on the line. He raised his handkerchief to his brow, dabbing the cold beads of sweat. He turned and his eyes connected with his wife. Margaret stood in the doorway, regarding him with a mournful, puzzled expression.

Rosen looked away and shuffled awkwardly from the room, closing the door behind him as he entered his study.

Those scenes replayed in his mind the following morning, as he walked the streets until his legs ached. He returned home. He'd tell Margaret he was too ill to go to work and that he'd be resting in the study.

He wondered whether he had the courage to go ahead and do what was on his mind.

'You haven't heard an early news report this morning?' Lachlan asked as Jennifer opened the front door to him.

'No. Why …?'

Lachlan followed her into the house. 'Stuart James was run down and killed last night in the basement of his office building.'

Jennifer sat, ashen faced, as Lachlan relayed the events of the previous evening. 'A businessman was seen on the stairwell by a cleaner, though he couldn't give a good description. The general appearance, though, is of a man of average height and weight. I believe this to be the same person responsible for the deaths of the missing people.'

'And who ran Brian down in Claridge Street last week?' Jennifer wondered.

Carly came in with coffee for the three of them. 'But why Stuart James?'

'I expect the killer knew James was searching through Brian's old files,' Lachlan surmised. 'And to have known that, he has to be someone close to either of you, or to someone else you told about James' investigation.'

Lachlan didn't like the vacant stare on Jennifer's face.

'If I hadn't retained his services,' she said, 'he'd still be alive.'

'You can't blame yourself,' Lachlan was quick to point out. 'James knew the risks involved with private investigations.'

'What could possibly be in those files?' Carly said.

Lachlan told them about his conversation with James, and the facts surrounding Brian's audit of Winterstone Pty. Ltd. 'James phoned me from his car to say he had the files with him,' Lachlan concluded, 'but there was nothing in the wreck. I'm presuming the killer took the files.'

'But Mr. James accidentally left some of those files here,' Carly said. She brought the files over and she, Jennifer and Lachlan flicked through them.

'Here,' Jennifer turned up the file on Winterstone. 'It seems this psycho lucked out on getting the file he really wanted.'

'Roger Kaplan employed Dad to run the audit, didn't he, Mum?' Carly asked. Her mother nodded. Carly looked to Lachlan. 'He should be able to shed some light on Winterstone.'

'I'm heading into town now to interview both Roger Kaplan and Harold Masterton,' Lachlan said.

'Masterton?' Carly's tone was curious. 'Why him?'

'Because,' Jennifer found the appropriate document in the file, 'he purchased the Winterstone business and set it up as a small subsidiary of the Kaplan group.'

'I have to stress,' said Lachlan, 'that the killer is very possibly someone close enough to either of you to have known about Stuart James being hired. He doesn't want anyone to know about Brian's suspicions regarding Winterstone. You could both be in danger.'

Jennifer's emotions were doing backflips as she tried to grasp the situation. She was horrified by the manner of Stuart James' death, and felt sick to the pit of her stomach. Neil Lachlan was certain this killer was someone who knew her. Who knew Carly. The blood drained from her face. Surely this couldn't be? And yet, it appeared logical. How else could the killer have known about Stuart James or about the files?

Perhaps it was a passing acquaintance? Someone who'd been watching them closely? The thought unnerved her and suddenly she felt incredibly insecure. And afraid.

'But this killer couldn't know that Stuart James told you about the Winterstone file,' Jennifer said to Lachlan, 'therefore he doesn't know Carly and I have been told.'

'Exactly, and we need to keep it that way. So, you're to discuss this with absolutely no one. Is that clear?'

Jennifer and Carly nodded in unison. Carly reached out and grasped her mother's hand. Their eyes met. 'It can't be someone close to us, Mum. I mean ... who ..?'

'I want to come with you to talk to Roger and Harold.' Jennifer turned her attention back to Lachlan but he was quick to deter her.

'Absolutely not. I'll be questioning both of them about Winterstone. When I said no-one is to be aware what you and Carly know, I meant no-one.'

'Surely you don't suspect Roger or Harold,' Jennifer protested, confused by the possible link between a Kaplan company file and this murderer.

'I don't have any suspects,' Lachlan admitted, 'but I don't want any chance of this leaking out - through anyone.'

They saw Lachlan to the door. It was humid. There was heavy cloud and a light rain had started.

'Looks like a storm could be brewing for later on,' Lachlan commented, walking to the driveway.

'Did I ever tell you,' Jennifer said to Carly as they went back into the house, 'there was a massive electrical storm the night your father vanished?'

'No. Only that he went out to buy a packet of cigarettes.'

'I wanted him to give them up,' Jennifer recalled. In her mind's eye she recreated the scene yet again. *Brian coming through the door. 'Blasted train ran late,' he said. His curly hair plastered down by water. 'It only takes five minutes to walk to the shop, less if I run.'*

There was something else.

One thing that had been just out of memory's reach since the forensic lab visit the day before. Something to do with Brian's clothes and personal effects. The comment about the approaching storm had pricked her memory. But the answer was still out of reach. *Damn.*

'I'm heading to the flat for another change of clothes,' Carly said.

'You're coming back later?'

'If that's okay.'

'Of course it's okay. I'd much rather have you here with me right now.'

'I really don't see how Detective Lachlan can be right, Mum, about this killer being someone we know. Do you?'

'I ... really don't know.'

'But you're scared. I can tell.'

'Yes. For both of us. But at least we're starting to get somewhere.'

'I might just as well be here while this investigation is going on. Otherwise I'll phone up every five minutes to find out what's happening.'

Jennifer wondered if that was the only reason, or whether Carly was avoiding Rory. Was she tiring of him? God, she hoped so.

Outside, the rain suddenly became a downpour.

'Mind if I borrow one of your brollies?' Carly asked.

'Go ahead. You'll find one in my bedroom cupboard.' Jennifer waited by the door as Carly went to fetch the umbrella. There hadn't been a cross word between them since she had been staying at the house. Was this the softening up Jennifer had longed for? Carly came bouncing along the hall and Jennifer caught just a glimmer of the carefree girl of yesteryear.

'Back later.'

'Okay.' And then, as Jennifer watched her daughter step out into the rain, she remembered what was different about Brian's belongings. She knew what had been missing.

TWENTY FOUR

Hans Falkstog did not believe in things supernatural, but he'd always felt he had something inside him that could sense trouble. He'd recognised the familiar sense of foreboding on many occasions. It had helped him avoid situations that were potentially destructive to him. It had a lot to do with his success, a lot to do with his power.

He felt it this morning, on a cool, clear day when he should have been feeling positive. He had stripped down to his swimmers and gone jogging along the beachfront. Everything was as he liked it: the open, blue horizon, the crisp air against his skin, the crash of the surf. This was always such a tonic to him, an alternative to his other activities. He did his best thinking, his most effective strategic planning, at moments like this. But this morning the sense of trouble was too strong, it dragged him down like the undertow of a storm-tide.

He remembered the first time he'd felt this way, many decades before.

He'd returned home to find that his father had left his mother and run off with another woman. Hans Falkstog was a hard and emotionless man, but to this day he'd felt his mother's pain at that betrayal. The following years had been grim and hard.

Why was his foreboding so strong this morning? He could only conclude it stemmed from the recent changes. It was always a concern when the structure of things altered after a long period of time. And eighteen years was a very long time.

He'd made enquiries over the past twenty-four hours, discovering that Brian Parkes' widow was making waves. He didn't like that. He ran

211

harder and faster, working up a sweat, and determined that he would be ready to meet the impending threat, as he had many times before.

It was Lachlan's first meeting with Roger Kaplan. The first thing he noticed was the resemblance to the father - a strong physical resemblance but one that lacked the older man's presence.

'I won't keep you long,' Lachlan said. 'What can you tell me about a firm called Winterstone?'

'Winterstone? Small firm, falls under the umbrella of our local professional services division. Odd division, lots of little firms, variety of services, not all that profitable.' Roger paused a moment, giving further thought to the question. 'You understand I don't have much to do with that division, but let me think - storage facility if I remember correctly. Why do you ask?'

'Brian Parkes was auditing the Winterstone books when he disappeared. According to his notes, he had some concern about a large discrepancy in the books. A sum of money secretly transferred from another division and spent on an equipment purchase from America.'

'I didn't know that. Are you sure?'

'Stuart James advised me of the notes before he was killed. I believe he was murdered because of the files he'd taken. So, anything you can tell me will be of great assistance.'

Roger cupped his chin between his thumb and forefinger and stroked it slowly. 'Well ... I don't actually know anything about it at all. It's administered by our clerical division. As I said, a commercial storage unit, mostly utilised by our other divisions, I expect.'

'The equipment purchase eighteen years ago?'

Roger frowned. 'No idea.' He spread his arms in a gesture of futility. 'Not much help, am I? Perhaps Harold may know more.' Roger called his secretary and asked her to locate Masterton. Lachlan didn't tell Roger that his next visit would have been to Masterton's office anyway.

'I'll want to see all the business records for Winterstone from its inception to the present day,' Lachlan said.

'No problem.' Roger gave the appropriate instructions to his secretary. Then he turned his attention back to Lachlan. 'It's hard to believe the answer to Brian's disappearance could be connected to one of our companies. The idea never occurred to me.'

'No reason why it should.'

Harold Masterton arrived. Roger introduced the finance director to the detective senior sergeant. Lachlan repeated much of what he had already told Roger.

Masterton showed the same element of surprise Roger had. 'Winterstone? Just a small storage warehouse.'

Which you set up, Lachlan wanted to say aloud, but he checked himself, preferring to see how things developed. He didn't want to let on that he'd actually read the file, which was at Jennifer's home.

Why hadn't Masterton offered the fact that he'd set up the company?

Masterton glanced at his watch. 'Can't stay long, detective, I'm currently going through a rolling series of meetings with the finance men from the Becker group.'

'Driving us all mad,' Roger added.

Terry Carter, a short, plump man who was head of the clerical services division, arrived with a slim file marked Winterstone. Lachlan leafed through it. Very little documentation there for a firm that had been in operation almost nineteen years, just the occasional use of space by one of the other local companies owned by Kaplan. There was no bill of sale for the purchase just under two decades earlier. 'I'll need to take this with me for closer inspection,' Lachlan advised the two men. 'It will be returned in due course and in the meantime the department will issue you a receipt.'

Both men mumbled their understanding. Lachlan noted that Masterton didn't look pleased.

The Police LAC in Sydney's Goulburn Street was a conservative structure, betraying no sign of the bustle within. A rabbit warren of non-stop activity, surroundings part modern, part older style, but housing in each section some of the most advanced electronic systems in Australian policing.

Lachlan's visit to the Superintendent's Special Task Force was a hurried one. He deposited the Winterstone file with senior detectives

Ron Aroney and Max Bryant. Lachlan had chosen these two men to assist him on the case. Now he briefed them on the document.

'There's nothing there to indicate the name of the American company from which Winterstone made the purchase. Get on to Customs and track down their paperwork and the name of the company. I also want you to gather as much background as you can on Harold Masterton, the financial director of the Kaplan Corporation.'

Before he left, Lachlan listened to Bryant's update on the investigation. 'Interpol have absolutely nothing on file from any member countries that fits the description of Brian Parkes. And forensics couldn't identify the make or model of the hit/run vehicle in that killing. There are no stolen car reports, either, to tie in with the night or the area in which Parkes was hit.'

'Another dead end,' Lachlan said more to himself than to either detective. 'One further thing,' he added, 'assign a team of uniformed men to a round the clock surveillance of the Winterstone warehouse. I want photos of anyone seen entering or leaving the building. Except me.' He smiled. 'I'll be conducting a search out there later today.'

Before he went to the storage building on the industrial site at Dural, Lachlan had one more stop to make.

Margaret Rosen hugged him, told him it was good to see him again. She smiled but behind the smile Lachlan was aware of the sad, wistful eyes.

John Rosen appeared at the doorway to his study. 'Saw your car pull up. Come on through.'

Lachlan entered the den, a sedate room of dark colours. 'Before you say anything, Neil,' Rosen said, 'I want you to know there's no resentment. Not on my part. You did the right thing going to Razell. In a way I'm glad.'

'Why, John?' Lachlan's voice was plaintive, not what he might have expected of himself. But then, he wasn't there as the head of the homicide investigation, he realised that now. He was there as the pupil, shattered by the betrayal of the teacher. He had simply come to ask the question, as much for himself as for any other purpose.

214

Rosen's eyes flittered about the room, avoiding Lachlan's and he leaned against the narrow desk. 'Four months ago,' he said, 'I received a package of photos in the mail. I would never have believed in my wildest dreams, Neil, that anyone could have known about me, had me followed and taken those pictures with a tele-photo lens.' He paused for a moment, searching for the right words to continue. 'That same night I received a phone call. I have no idea of the caller's identity. I was told to do as ordered or copies of the photos would be sent to Margaret, the commissioner, and the press. I practically threw up all over the phone while I was listening.' Another pause, longer than the first.

It tore Lachlan apart to see his old friend and father figure like this - broken, beaten, shamed. He spoke gently. 'Go on.'

Rosen sighed deeply. 'I was told that a number of people who'd been missing for eighteen years would be found, all would be dead. I'd receive a phone call just as each body was likely to be found. They'd all be located in north-west Sydney, except one.'

'Brian Parkes, the odd man out.'

Rosen nodded. 'I was told to use my position to take over each case, ensure they were kept isolated so that no one made the connection between them. It was also made very clear that my investigations of these cases should go nowhere. But that's not all, Neil. The caller assured me that after six had been found, that would be all, and I wouldn't be contacted again.'

'And the recent garrotte killings?'

'I was contacted again. Told to frame someone for those murders. The caller told me there wouldn't be any more, that something was being done about it.'

Lachlan shook his head. 'Doesn't make any sense.'

'No,' Rosen's voice was a croak, 'no sense at all.' His face was longer than usual, drawn, the cheeks and jowls sagging as though weighed down by the burden of guilt. 'So, you have the answers you came for.'

'John, couldn't you have found another solution-?'

Rosen didn't let him finish. 'We're not talking about another woman here. The pictures would have ruined me, but then I deserve that. It's Margaret, Neil. I couldn't do it to her. She must never see the pictures.'

'John ...?'

215

'Please don't ask me any more. Not about that.'

'Okay,' Lachlan conceded. 'About the case. Did you unearth any clues at all? Surely you have something. A theory ...'

'Very little. I pursued some matters, on my own, I was too curious not to. I spoke to the police psychologist, Hawkins, presenting it as a hypothetical case. Two interesting bits of information came out of my talk with him. He theorised that if five people vanished from the same area, then turned up eighteen years later, then there had to be something beneficial about that area to the killer. Less distance to travel maybe? Less chance of discovery? He also theorised that if a sixth victim wasn't garrotted like the others, then it could be because the killer knew him personally. The other five were snuffed out for the thrill of it. But if the killer knew Parkes, perhaps even liked him, then he wouldn't be able to murder him in the same vicious manner. Much less personal to run him down in a car.'

'Hawkins didn't suspect these talks were about a real case?'

'I was too clever for that, Neil. I dressed the details up differently. Spoke to him about different aspects on two separate occasions.'

Lachlan realised the theories made perfect sense. And now something else gelled for the first time. He told Rosen about Parkes' audit of Winterstone. 'Winterstone owns a storage warehouse in Dural, smack dab in the middle of the far north-western suburbs.'

'There's a connection there,' Rosen agreed. 'And if Brian Parkes knew something then the killer would've wanted him out of the way. If the killer was connected in some way to the Kaplan Corporation then he most likely knew Brian, hence the difference in the mode of killing.'

'What about the fact that the victims hadn't aged? Did the psychologist have any theories on that?'

'No. He suggested an intensive autopsy would confirm the actual chronological ages of the bodies, and whether drugs or surgery were involved. But we've already been down that road with Parkes and the others and there is no evidence of that with any of them.'

Lachlan glanced at his watch. 'I'll have a word with Hawkins myself. We need a full psychological profile based on the current information.'

'I'm glad you're on the case,' Rosen said. 'You're every inch the cop I always knew you'd be.'

Lachlan offered his hand. They shook. 'Why didn't you tell the commissioner you were blackmailed?'

'That means I'd have to come clean about the nature of the photos. It's best left in the dark, Neil.'

'Tell him, John. And tell Margaret. Give them the chance to show they can forgive. Margaret deserves that.'

Rosen cleared his throat, gave an almost imperceptible nod. 'Maybe ...'

Lachlan was heading across the Harbour Bridge when he received the message from HQ on the police car radiophone. Call Jennifer Parkes urgently, the dispatcher told him. He pulled over to the side of the road to make the call on his cell.

He felt a stab of anticipation as Jennifer came on the line and said, 'Neil. I know what was different about Brian's belongings when I saw them at the morgue ...'

It could have been any one of a thousand warehouses on any one of a thousand industrial estates around Sydney. A squat, lengthy red brick building with a few small windows on each side. It had a loading dock area and a long, wide driveway at the rear.

The interior had seen little use. A vast expanse of smooth concrete floor, multi-level rows of industrial shelving, dust and cobwebs and a thick, musty air which hung like an invisible veil - a shroud to the long years of secrecy. In the front of the building stood a glass cubicle-cum-office with a desk and an old-style telephone. The phone was disconnected and the dust covering everything made Lachlan sneeze several times.

Lachlan had the feeling it was a long, long time since anyone had been in this part of the building. To the administration section of Kaplan Corp this was a forgotten relic, buried among the files of the clerical archives.

He walked the length and breadth of the warehouse. Without the interior lights being switched on it was a dark, seedy, subterranean place. Lit up, the phosphorescent glow bounced off the brick walls, and cast shadows behind the willowy cobwebs.

The loading dock was the usual recessed area of floor into which trucks could back up to unload materials. More dust, more cobwebs. Lachlan glanced around the dock, then turned to leave. A flash of colour glinted in the corner of his vision. He turned back, focusing on a spot at the far end of the curved concrete mini-wall, around the recessed floor.

The object was dotted with thick, sooty specks of dust and partly obscured by the curvature of the wall. Lachlan stepped down into the recessed area and walked towards the object. With each advancing step he heard Jennifer's words replay in his mind. 'Neil ... I know what was different ... something missing ...'

The night Brian Parkes had left his home he'd borrowed his wife's small yellow umbrella, a token shell against the rain. And here it was, lying in the corner of a disused warehouse owned by a company that was a forgotten entity among the dozens of firms owned by the Kaplan Corporation.

Lachlan knelt before the umbrella. It was clearly in near-new condition. He looked back at the scattered pattern in the dust where he'd walked across the floor of the dock. A similar pattern appeared on another section of the floor, stopping in front of the large double panel doors of the building's rear exit.

Lachlan's earlier impression had been wrong. Someone else had been in the warehouse recently. Had Brian Parkes been there? Or the men from Kaplan Corp who'd known Brian? Had one of them been to this lonely place?

Lachlan used police gloves to place the umbrella in his car. He'd take it to the forensic lab for analysis. As he drove back towards the city another sensation crept over him. The distinct feeling that there was something else about the Winterstone warehouse that he'd missed.

The moment he'd freed himself from one of the long, drawn out meetings with the Becker people, Harold Masterton stormed into Roger's office. His nostrils flared like those of an angry bull, his face as red as his thatch of rust coloured hair. 'What the hell is this about Winterstone?' he demanded.

Roger looked up from the papers on his desk. 'What do you mean? You know as much as I do.'

'I seem to remember signing papers concerning Winterstone. It's starting to come back to me. Did you ask me to handle the paperwork for you? A straightforward shelf company purchase. I've barely given it a moment's thought since.'

Roger shook his head. 'That's strange. I don't recall that. I've always thought it was one of your little projects, supervised through the admin section.'

'The last thing we need right now is some cockamamie cop trying to link one of our buildings with a murder investigation. Think, Roger. Has anyone else been involved with this damn warehouse?'

'Maybe Carter in admin can shed some light on it. Hell, it was a long time ago, Harold. You certain you don't remember any more about it?'

Masterton paced. 'Well, there is something ...'

'Go on.'

'I've checked our records and verified this. It was during the same twelve month period Winterstone was set up that your father first employed Hans Falkstog as a management consultant.'

'Falkstog? His company's been on retainer for years and years. But he's never been involved in running any of our-'

Masterton cut in. 'Not now. But for a short while back then he consulted on some special projects. I never liked him, thought he was an arrogant, manipulative dickhead-'

'You think Falkstog might've had something to do with Winterstone?'

'I signed a hell of a lot of documents in those days that you and your father shoved in front of me. But I seem to remember Falkstog being involved in one or two that the rest of us didn't pay much attention to.'

'Have you asked Dad about this?'

'No. That's next on my list. For Chrissakes, Roger, we've got to put a lid on this before it gets out of hand.'

'I'm still not convinced there's a connection, Harold,' Roger said. 'Lachlan could be barking up the wrong tree. Winterstone is nothing: a shelf title that owns a warehouse. Someone would've noticed if funds were being diverted to it. If not you or I, then certainly Dad. And he had private detectives hunting for any lead as to what happened to Brian.'

'But think about it, Roger. If Brian Parkes discovered something amiss in his audit, he would've come to you or your father. He vanished before he got the chance. Lachlan's theory makes sense.'

'Christ,' Roger muttered. He watched Masterton leave the office.

It struck him that he'd never seen Masterton on edge like this. The finance director was showing a desperate side, one that Roger hadn't seen before. But Harold was right: the timing couldn't be worse with Conrad Becker in town and the sale of Southern Star looming.

Was it just that? Or was Harold Masterton particularly sensitive to the fact that his signature was on the Winterstone papers?

When Carly entered the apartment she heard the running water of the shower.

Rory's home, she thought. The lazy bugger. She was glad she hadn't seen much of him the past few days. She'd come to realise she needed a breather from the intensity of the relationship. It had begun to concern her the way Rory pushed her into the modelling assignments she detested more and more, and that he was continually borrowing large sums from her.

She wanted to be *involved*, but not just as some capitalist clotheshorse who contributed her earnings to ragtag organisations she never saw. It hadn't gone unnoticed, either, that since she'd been staying with her mother she'd received no phone calls from Rory to see how she was, despite the fact that he knew she'd been upset about the discovery of her father's body.

Nevertheless she was feeling horny. She decided to surprise Rory by joining him in the shower. She stripped out of her skirt, blouse and stockings, draping them over the back of the three-seat lounge, then tip-toed into the bathroom.

Through the frosted glass of the shower screen she saw two figures, limbs entwined as the needlepoint spray danced across them. Carly forgot her nakedness, her lust frozen away by the shock.

Rory's back was to her. Even through the frosted pattern of the glass Carly could distinguish the features of the woman embracing Rory. Their eyes met, and a smirk broke out across Helen Shawcross' face, a smirk distorted and made hideous by the dual effect of the patterned screen and the steam from the hot water.

'Want to join us, sweetie?'

Rory looked around, and as his face registered his surprise, Carly turned and ran. She slammed the door behind her with such force that the impact made the bottle of aftershave on the corner of the vanity unit crash to the tiled floor.

Rory slid the screen door open and stepped from the shower recess to give chase. He stopped and groaned aloud when his foot came down on a sliver of broken glass. By the time he pulled the splinter from his foot and hobbled from the bathroom, Carly - and her clothes - were gone.

Robert Dreydon was a weedy, wiry man with dark, slicked back hair and even darker, hawk-like eyes. Not physically strong, he didn't project an air of authority and spoke softly. Anyone who had ever met him, though, knew instinctively not to get on the wrong side of him - they knew, somehow, that he was dangerous.

Dreydon sat in the small, cluttered office across the desk from Fred Hargreaves. Hargreaves, large, beefy, round cheeked, always wearing a smile or the hint of one. He reminded Dreydon of a travelling salesman, or of a kid's favourite uncle at a backyard barbecue.

Hargreaves was, in fact, one of the best known, underworld middle-men in the Kings Cross district. The Cross, which occupied the eastern sector of the city, looked at a glance like any other city region during the day with its endless line of shops and high-rises - but on closer inspection the high number of bars, nightclubs, sex aid shops and street walking women in raunchy outfits revealed its other identity. At night, gaudy neon signs and throngs of party people brought it to life as the city's major meeting place for a myriad of sub-cultures.

Hargreaves indicated, with a sweep of his hand, the documents on his desk. 'The photograph in the folder is of a man named Barry Doolan. Miner. Works in the Southern Star mines at Red Hills in north-west Queensland.'

Dreydon looked at the picture. 'The man doesn't know how lucky he is. Fifty grand, you say?'

'Fifty grand,' Hargreaves confirmed. 'And this bloke won't say no. He'd probably accept less. He's in financial straits with a sick child and another on the way. One of his best mates is dying too. Believed to have suffered asbestos poisoning in one of the mines which they've since closed.'

'So he hates his employer.'

'With a passion.'

'But he has no knowledge of explosives.'

'He doesn't need to,' said Hargreaves. 'The unit will be ready made, packaged, easy to handle. All he has to do is plant it, set the timer, and then walk away whistlin' Dixie, a king for a day, because that's about how long his fifty grand will last him with his problems.' Hargreaves couldn't help but chuckle.

'And my job is to make sure he's fully briefed and that he agrees to go through with it.'

'Easiest assignment you'll ever have. Just make sure Doolan is clear about the objective here. To cause extensive damage and unfavourable media attention to Southern Star. Doolan will like that.'

'And your client?'

'It is essential to my client,' Hargreaves explained, 'that the sale of Southern Star Mining to the Canadian buyer doesn't go ahead. My client is certain the explosion at the mine will stop the sale.'

'Why?'

'The damage should be enough to dissuade any potential buyer. To cap it off, anonymous calls will be made to the media by my people, informing them that the bomb was planted by an activist group protesting the cover-up of asbestos poisoning at the site.'

'Who is this client?' Dreydon asked, fully aware he wouldn't get an answer. He just enjoyed stirring Hargreaves.

'You know better than to ask that.' Hargreaves laughed. He always enjoyed Dreydon's bare-faced cheek. 'Even I don't know who the real client is, and I couldn't give a fuck anyway. That way, he can't be traced.'

'Someone who's really got it in for the Kaplan group,' Dreydon said, 'and who's got enough inside information to come up with Doolan's name and circumstances.'

'Never mind all that. The important thing as far as we're concerned is timing. It's essential this explosion happens tomorrow. Move like lightning on this one, Dreydon.'

The small man with the grim countenance flashed a snake-like grin. 'Then you'd better tell me who I see in Queensland to pick up the device. I've got a plane to catch.' Later, as he left, Dreydon wondered what else this mysterious client might have done to cause trouble for the Kaplans.

John Rosen spent several hours that afternoon cleaning up the papers in his study, sorting them into a number of neat files.

At 4.25 p.m. he took a dozen photographs from an unmarked packet and threw them on the fire he'd started in the small, metal fireplace built into his study wall. He then took the .45 automatic handgun from his desk drawer, looked about at the familiar surroundings one last time, then placed the pistol in his mouth. The taste of steel was on his tongue, his lips enfolding the smooth hardness of the barrel.

Margaret Rosen was on the back porch when she heard the bang. Fear stabbed at her insides like a prod from a smouldering iron. She ran into the house, flung open the door to the study.

By the time she knelt down, weeping hysterically, beside the body of her husband, the last photograph had curled up and crumbled to ash. The image on that photo, of John Rosen in a compromising position with a smooth skinned teenage boy had been erased forever, unseen, only existing now as a suspicion in the mind of Neil Lachlan.

Jennifer went inside and opened the envelope delivered by the courier from the Stuart James Detective Agency's secretary. It contained hard copies of the emailed replies from the immortalist groups. Jennifer was surprised that all the groups contacted had responded. Names such as the L.A. Youth Preservation Society and the Younger-Longer Society ran past her eyes as she scanned the copies.

As she moved from one reply to the next, frustration welled up inside her. Not one of the groups had ever seen or heard of Brian Parkes or anyone matching his description. And not one, despite their knowledge of advanced medical procedures, shed any light on the strange incision to Brian's jugular vein.

TWENTY FIVE

Dear Mother,

He knows. He's known all along and now that I've realised it I wonder how I could've been so blind. It seems so obvious, the only real explanation.

If I'd figured it out before I could've taken steps to be free of the surveillance. I don't know how but I would've found a way, just as I'm doing now to ensure the watching doesn't start again.

That's not all though, mother. I'm taking steps to ensure the last remaining links between me and my needs are eliminated, along with the two people closest to stumbling across the truth. I wanted you to know that, whatever happens, I won't be caught – or stopped. I'll be okay.

My new beginning – which started with the Van Helegen woman – won't be cut short. In many respects it's just getting started. A new life, unlike anything I've known before.

I won't be able to write again, not for a long time, at least. It's simply too dangerous now – neither of us can run the risk of someone seeing these letters. You have been destroying them, haven't you?

If all goes well over the next twenty-four hours then the people getting too close will be gone – effectively ruling out the possibility you'll be tracked down, or your belongings searched. But, as a precaution, make sure all your copies are gone.

I'm sure you understand. The letters were fine when no one actually knew about the murders – before the victims returned to the places from which they'd vanished – but from here on in that secrecy is a thing of the past. Circumstances dicate that.

Don't worry though that you won't be hearing from me. You'll still be able to follow my handiwork. I intend to continue, sizing up each situation in the guise of a jogger and using the garrotte method on the chosen ones. My Van Helegen and Dawson killings made big news. I'm famous now. The police and the public expect another and I won't keep them waiting too long.

The murders aren't a secret any more, they'll make big news, and you'll be able to follow them in the media.

I know it's not the same as a personal letter, but it'll have to do for now.

I admit I'm feeling a little heady about my newfound notoriety. They call me The Garrotte Killer.

It's different to the way it was years ago, when no one knew about the killings. It was a lot safer that way but, strangely enough, I don't miss it.

Just as I don't miss the rotten surveillance that kept me miserable for so long. The one responsible for that is about to suffer. And you'll be glad to know they will suffer in the manner that will hurt them the most.

There's one final thing I need to say. I've never blamed you for any of the bad things. Consequently, I know you don't blame me for the path I've taken.

I chose power over weakness.

And now the upper hand is mine once more.

Wish me luck, mother. My return has only just begun.

TWENTY SIX

It was the kind of story every newsman dreams of. The sudden, inexplicable suicide of the man running the state-wide hunt for the garrotte killer.

The 5 p.m. news spots on every Sydney radio station broadcast the few facts known. The 6 p.m. tv news and their websites gave blanket coverage, including the brief press conference given by the chief commissioner.

Deputy Commissioner Ed Razell also fronted the media, offering his condolences to Rosen's family. He expressed the force's admiration for their colleague's long and distinguished career - and announced that the hunt for the garrotte murderer would continue with another senior man stepping in to the breach.

No speculation was given for Rosen's suicide, apart from the inference that he'd been under great stress.

The jogger absorbed the news over the radio as he drove at a discreet speed past the home of Jennifer Parkes. He saw Jennifer's car in the driveway. As he'd suspected, she was spending more time at home since the investigation of her husband's death. Did she have the specific Winterstone file he'd expected to find in James' car? He expected it must be in the house somewhere.

There were three things he needed to do to end any chance of discovery. First, get hold of the Winterstone audit file - the file he had never suspected had been kept, with the others, all these years. The second and third objectives were to remove both Jennifer Parkes and Neil Lachlan from the scene. They had already circled too close to the truth, even if they weren't aware of it at this stage.

The jogger's plan for Jennifer Parkes was perfect. He would do the totally unexpected: kill her in her own home. Another random strike by the garrotte murderer. At the same time he'd search the premises for the Winterstone audit.

He drove to a nearby café for a bite to eat and a cappuccino. It would feel very strange - *eerie* - to snuff out the life of this woman, as he had so many years before to her husband.

Perhaps it had always been destined.

It wouldn't be long before night fell. As soon as darkness descended over the city it would be time to unleash his alter ego once again.

Minutes after the jogger turned his car out of the street, Carly Parkes entered from the opposite end. She drove into the driveway of her mother's house and entered the lounge room, sullen faced, quiet.

Jennifer had the radio on in one room and the television blaring from another. A news flash was just ending, the shock news of the suicide quickly replaced by a thirty second commercial for a new soft drink. Healthy, vibrant young people cavorted in the surf.

'John Rosen shot himself,' Jennifer told Carly. 'I knew something was very odd with that man.'

'I heard it in the car,' Carly replied.

'How's Rory?'

'Okay.' Carly's reply was cold, dismissive.

'Something wrong?' Jennifer sensed that something was very wrong. It registered with her that as well as appearing withdrawn, her daughter had returned without the change of clothes she'd gone to fetch.

Carly shook her head, walked out of the living room and through to the back of the house. She wasn't in the mood to reveal to her mother what she'd found, wasn't certain if she ever would be. She didn't care for the old "I told you so" look in the eyes.

If anything, she was intrigued to find that she herself was not all that surprised. She'd half known she'd been fooling herself about Rory all along. His social conscience was something he brought forth only when it suited him. His passion for political change was dwarfed by his passion for anything in a skirt. Today, Carly realised, she'd simply seen, more clearly, the colours Rory had exhibited all the time.

'How long will Daddy be away, Mum?'

'Another three days, honey. Now, please don't ask me again. You've asked that question four or five times a day for the past week.' Meg Tanner sighed and kept stirring the pot of vegetable soup. She didn't like Don being away any more than the kids did. Don was a systems analyst for a large engineering firm. For the third time this year he'd been asked to undertake a trouble shooting project on one of the firm's sites in New Guinea.

Eight-year old Jason shrugged, then bounded out into the back yard making loud, whelping Indian noises. *Dances With Wolves* had made a big impression on him.

Her daughter, Samantha, fifteen, wandered into the kitchen and peered over her mother's shoulder at the brew. 'Smells wonderful.'

'Back off, vulture.' Meg suppressed a laugh. 'I'll be another ten minutes yet.'

'Late again. Typical,' Samantha replied with a wink. She sauntered back into the lounge room. Meg watched her, glad her daughter had inherited the long, lean limbs and dark hair of her father.

She focused her attention back on the boiling brew, or meant to, but from the corner of her eye she saw Jason balancing like a trapeze artiste on the fence at the back of the property. She was about to call out to tell him to get down, when he suddenly misjudged his footing and toppled down into their neighbour's yard. She didn't see him hit the earth on the other side, but she felt the falling sensation in the pit of her stomach. Silly boy. How many times had she warned him? She didn't expect the blood-curdling scream that followed.

'Oh, God, Mum, tell your son to stop making such disgusting noises,' said Samantha from the other room.

Meg didn't reply. She felt a stab of intense fear as the scream continued. Dropping the wooden spoon into the soup she raced out. As she approached the back fence she could see, through the thin space between the palings, the garden rake left in their neighbour's yard. Its sharp, steely spikes were facing the sky.

She launched herself up the side of the fence, clambering over the top. 'Oh my God!' she cried out as the other side came fully in to view.

The Southern Star colliery, 500 kilometres north west of Brisbane, had become one of Queensland's major coal producers and was also one of the most modern mining complexes in Australia. Since its inception it had continually promoted itself as one of the safest of all mining projects, with stringent safety precautions and an enviable record.

The exception, though Barry Doolan, was the health of the workers. In the last fifteen years, over fifty men had been forced by ill health into early retirement. All had serious lung, throat and heart disorders. Some had inoperable cancers. The bastards didn't promote that.

All had worked in Shaft Number Five, which maintenance crews suspected of asbestos leaks from the underground ventilation system. The union, in association with the local health authorities, had forced an inquiry from the Government. A year after Kaplan Corp had bought into the mine the inquiry had stopped. By this time Shaft Number Five was permanently closed, its uses fulfilled. Newer, deeper tunnels and underground galleries had taken its place. There were many personnel changes around the same time. A new maintenance team was appointed.

Doolan worked the 3 p.m. to 11 p.m. shift in the newest and deepest of the tunnels, Shaft Number Twelve. When he'd come on duty this afternoon, no one had any reason to suspect that the duffle bag, which usually contained his lunch box, newspaper and towel, also contained a compact black box. A sophisticated, miniature explosive device.

Doolan took his usual place in the open rail transport car with a group of men from his shift. As it descended along the makeshift track into the mouth of the shaft, Doolan thought back to the visit he'd received earlier in the day.

His visitor had been a small, dark haired man with a dangerous look. He'd called himself Smith and said he was a life insurance advisor sent by the union. They strolled into the back yard of the tiny fibro cottage, out of earshot of Doolan's wife, Sandra.

Dreydon came right to the point. 'We know you're in a dreadful financial state, Barry,' he said without a trace of sentiment.

'We?'

Dreydon raised the palm of his hand. 'Hear me out. Too much money on the horses, not enough put aside for the bills.'

Doolan became agitated. He always did over money matters. 'Man's got a right to some relaxation.'

'We can put an end to your money worries,' said Dreydon, grinning like a shark. 'We have a little job we'd like you to do.'

'Who are you?'

'Relax and hear me out. I have a client who wants to cause the Kaplan Corporation some real financial pain, a mission I'm sure you can relate to. Not for your own satisfaction, but for the memory of your mates, the ones from Shaft Number Five, and the ones who are still suffering.'

'I don't know ...'

'Fifty thousand dollars, in cash. In advance.'

Doolan's eyebrows shot up in to perfect arches. 'Fifty grand.' He whistled. 'When ..?'

'Right now. Suitcase is in my car out the front.' Dreydon paused for effect. 'There's no danger to you, Barry, and no one needs to get hurt. We have a very sophisticated explosive device–'

'Explosive!'

'You simply hide it, set the timer, walk away. Easier than operating a Blu Ray Player, Barry. I understand the last shift finishes at 11 p.m. Set the timer for 3 a.m., dead middle of the night, and leave it towards the centre of the shaft you work in.'

Dreydon stopped and waited for the full implication of all he'd said to sink in. He loved this kind of work and felt like laughing out loud, but restrained the impulse. He could almost hear the cogs shifting in the neanderthal brain of the down and out compulsive gambler before him.

'Middle of the night,' Doolan repeated, mumbling. In his mind's eye the fifty thousand dollars shone like gold at the end of a rainbow. 'And no-one gets hurt.'

'That's right.'

Dreydon saw the subtle shift in Doolan's expression. A decision had been made.

'Switch if off,' said Lachlan. Bryant leaned across the table and pressed the "off" panel on the department's TV set. The news report faded from the screen. Lachlan sat, unmoving, staring at the blank screen.

'Hard to believe he's gone,' said Aroney.

'Why the hell would he do such a thing?' Bryant wondered aloud. 'John never showed any signs of depression or anxiety. Wasn't the type.'

'Whether he was the type or not,' Lachlan snapped, 'he's gone.'

The other two looked at him in surprise. Neil Lachlan was one of the most contained men they'd ever known, and even the mildest expression of emotion was out-of-character

'I'm sorry.' Lachlan leaned back, sucked in deep lungfuls of air. 'It's such a blasted shock. I knew John for twenty years.' His mind wandered back over two decades of memories. How could something like this happen to someone you thought you knew so well?

Bryant stood up and paced the room. 'This damn thing gets weirder and weirder. Rosen takes on the missing persons cases, sits on 'em, then you're brought in and Rosen goes and…' He didn't finish making the obvious statement, reminding himself of Lachlan's long association with the superintendent. 'Is there a connection?'

Lachlan told them about his final conversation with Rosen.

'So someone out there knows who the killer is, and blackmailed John to ensure the police investigation ran into a dead end,' Aroney summarised. 'But they also said the killer would be taken care of. What do you think they meant by that?'

'Sounds as though it's a vigilante thing,' Bryant pointed out.

'I'll follow that through with Internal Affairs,' Lachlan said, 'they'll be investigating the suicide. In the meantime we carry on, full steam ahead. John would have wanted that. Winterstone ..?'

Bryant pushed a sheath of papers towards him. 'Despite all they say about the public service, the customs boys had their paperwork in order.' He indicated the spidery scrawl on the faded document.

'February, 1993. One container, total weight three tons, received at the docks for Winterstone Pty.Ltd. Classification of goods: Electrical equipment.'

Lachlan read the name of the sender out loud. 'Lifelines Incorporated. From Burbank, California. What do we have on them?'

'Nothing yet,' Bryant replied. 'Nothing relevant comes up when you google it. There's a contact phone number on those Customs records. I've got a call to the US booked for later tonight, 9 a.m. their time, to see if I can raise that number or whether the local authorities over there can assist.'

'Ring me at home, no matter the hour,' Lachlan said, 'the moment you know anything about them.' He swung towards Aroney. 'That warehouse is bugging me. It was too empty. No clues. Except for the yellow umbrella Parkes had with him the night he vanished. Ring the local council, Ron. I want the original building plans for that warehouse.' He rose to leave. 'I'm going to the lab with the umbrella. But first I want Jennifer Parkes to make a positive ID of it.' He had one last thing to say before he left. 'For the first time since I started on this case I feel there's a solution. And it's within reach.'

Bryant and Aroney voiced their agreement. Like distant lights in a thick fog, a pattern was slowly beginning to emerge.

Jennifer heard the car come screeching into her driveway. She peered between the drapes and was surprised to see Meg and her daughter rushing up to the front door.

She went out onto the front landing. 'Meg ...' She was shocked by the sight of her old friend, chalk-white face, eyes glassy and wide with distress.

'Just left Jason at the hospital,' she blurted out, 'but I don't want Samantha stuck there with me all night. Could she stay overnight with you?'

'Of course.' Jennifer led the two of them into the house.

'I didn't like the idea of her being at home on her own, y'know. Not with this garrotte killer loose in the city.'

'Meg, what happened?'

233

'Jason fell on a rake in our neighbour's yard. Impaled his left leg.'

'Good God.'

'It was terrible,' Samantha added. She sat on the lounge, visibly shaken. 'His screams sent shivers right through me.'

Carly came in. 'Thought I heard voices. Hi.'

'I've got to get back,' Meg said.

'Ring us. Let us know how he's doing,' Jennifer said. After Meg left, Jennifer went to comfort Samantha, explaining to Carly what had happened. The girl melted into Jennifer's arms, weeping, and Jennifer, still reeling from the deaths of Stuart James and John Rosen, couldn't shake the nagging feeling that everything was going horribly, terribly wrong.

Kaplan arrived back at his office at 7 p.m. after spending much of the afternoon with Becker. Harold Masterton sat in Kaplan's office, waiting.

'Becker is ready to fly to Queensland with us tomorrow to look over the mine,' Kaplan announced excitedly. 'He's ready, Harold. We're almost there. I can't wait to see the look on that blasted liquidator's face.'

'What's all this about Winterstone, Henry?' Masterton snapped, oblivious to Kaplan's comments about the impending sale.

'Winterstone? What's that?'

'A business name we own. We hold the real estate for a storage warehouse in that company's name.'

'So?'

'That cop, Lachlan, thinks there's a link between Brian Parkes' disappearance and a Winterstone audit he was carrying out eighteen years ago. I don't know a damned thing about it and it's not looking good, Henry.'

'Calm down.' Kaplan went to his desk and lit a cigar. 'Whose name is on the company papers as director?'

'Mine, damn it, and one of my assistants at the time who's long since left.'

'You remember signing them?'

'Vaguely. I'm certain the directive must've come from Roger or yourself or one of the other directors at the time. Or even Hans Falkstog, who was consulting on certain projects back then.'

'I don't recall anyone ever mentioning it.' Kaplan drew on the cigar, savoured the aroma, then released it. He often had a cigar in the evening when he was feeling positive about a business negotiation. 'I'll speak to the other directors, and get in touch with Falkstog. Let me see if I can shed any light on it.'

'We don't want any hiccups now, Henry, with Becker about to sign.'

Kaplan noticed that sweat had broken out on Masterton's brow. 'I'm sure there's a satisfactory explanation to the whole thing. Let me worry about it.'

Masterton nodded, but the haunted look in his eyes told Kaplan that the finance man was in for a sleepless night. What was he most worried about? Kaplan wondered. The possible effect on the sale of Southern Star? Or the implication that he was involved in the murders being investigated?

And why had he brought up the name of Hans Falkstog?

The killer who strikes again and again normally has a preference for his victims to be male or female. The jogger was different in this respect. His focus had always been on the right place, the right time, the routine of the chosen, *not their gender*. For him, the thrill was the same, regardless.

Except when he had to kill for a purpose. The excitement was replaced by pressure that wound itself around his temples, like a steel band. It was essential that nothing go wrong, that he wasn't recognised. It was imperative to be successful. He didn't enjoy that kind of pressure.

That's how it was tonight with his planned attack on Jennifer Parkes, and how it would be tomorrow for his blow against the meddling detective. The jogger promised himself that after that he would kill simply for pleasure again - and quickly. His killings should be a thing of pleasure, not of business.

He drove by the house and saw the Parkes bitch at the mailbox, removing flyers and catalogues. She was wearing the blue nylon jacket with the red trim. He'd seen her wear it before.

The rain, which had been drizzling down throughout the day, momentarily stopped. An occasional roll of thunder crackled in the distance. The streets were wet, shiny. It was twilight, minutes away from total nightfall, and the jogger knew he was too far away to be identified. Despite this, he tilted his head away and allowed the peak of the sports cap to slip lower, shielding part of his face.

His vehicle wasn't one she would know. It was his second car, always kept garaged, used only when his darker half went out to hunt and kill.

He turned the corner, parked half way along the connecting street, alighted and began to jog. The fall of night was complete now, the shadows of the late afternoon transformed into long, deep stretches of ebony between the pools of light cast by neon. He passed two other joggers.

Perfect. He liked it best when he could blend in completely with the environment. It was a good omen.

He knew Jennifer was in the house, alone. The plan was crystal clear in his mind. All he needed to do was to lure her outside and strike swiftly from behind. He didn't want to see her face. He didn't want to think about who she was.

He'd thought long and hard about this. He would pretend she was a stranger, a victim chosen at random. Perhaps if he could force himself to believe that for just a few minutes, if he could ignore the pressure he felt to be successful, then he'd be able to enjoy the sensation after all.

After Carly had moved her car into the garage behind her mother's, she'd announced she wasn't hungry and that she was turning in early. Jennifer had looked in on her twenty minutes later. Carly was fast asleep. Unlike her, Jennifer thought. Something about Rory was really troubling her. It was as though placing her car in the double garage signalled her intention to stay awhile.

'I can't eat either,' Samantha said. 'But don't worry about me, Mrs P, I'll just sit here and flake out in front of the tele.'

236

'I'll be buzzing around the place,' Jennifer said. 'Just holler if you need anything. If we haven't heard from your mother a little later on, we'll phone up to see if there's any news.'

'Thanks.'

The rubbish bin, close to a metre high and army green in colour, stood between the side of the garage and the rear right corner of the house.

The jogger stepped from the footpath and onto the driveway, still jogging. He could have been just another fitness freak returning home to the eyes of any passer-by. The houses on either side were quiet.

He took the bin in both hands, tipped it on its side until it was almost horizontal, and then slid it along the ground, leaving it on its side in the middle of the driveway. Next, he knocked firmly on the side door entrance before retreating to the rear.

Jennifer didn't hear the knock. She had decided to take a shower and at the precise moment the jogger rapped on the side door, the warm, refreshing needlepoint of the spray was gushing over her.

Samantha lay sprawled on the lounge, attempting to concentrate on an American sitcom. Her mind kept wandering and every time it did she could hear her brother's high-pitched screams.

The knock at the side entrance came as a welcome intrusion. She opened the door, peered out, saw the bin lying across the driveway.

'Dogs ...' she muttered to herself. She assumed there'd been no knock, that she'd just heard the clatter of the falling bin. It had started raining again, heavier this time, so she reached back, grabbed hold of the blue nylon jacket Jennifer had left draped across the back of the lounge, pulled it on and stepped out to pick up the bin.

At the rear right hand corner of the house, the jogger saw the tall, slim figure with the long, dark hair and the blue jacket with red trim. The wire lay at the ready in his hands.

Quick. Clean. Just don't look at the face, he told himself. Pretend it's a random victim. A thrill kill. No purpose. Just pleasure.

But the steel band, already in place around his skull, squeezed tighter and he felt no sexual high. Just the pressure to complete his business, then flee.

He moved with the stealth and speed of a jungle cat. That hadn't changed. This was his natural persona, had been ever since that afternoon in the alley with Vinnie. This was the one time, the only time, that he felt that the power was rightfully his.

Samantha bent forward towards the bin. The jogger was upon her instantly, the wire looped around her throat and then drawn tightly, blocking off her air supply, piercing her flesh.

She tried to scream. No sound. No air. Couldn't breathe. In vain she attempted to jerk herself free. She was held too tightly. Her arms shot upwards, her fingers desperately clawing at the wire but she had no leverage. No hope.

Pain seared through her entire body. Her vision blurred.

She would have been dead within sixty seconds if it hadn't been for the sudden, blinding light that filled the driveway, illuminating them.

The car swung in and pulled to a stop. Lachlan switched off the motor but left the headlights on as he jumped from the driver's seat.

The jogger released his grip, simultaneously withdrawing the wire. He flung Samantha violently against the wall, leapt over the bin and ran.

Jennifer stepped from the shower, towelled herself dry, pulled on a fluffy white terry-towelling robe and walked into the living room. She saw that Samantha wasn't there, that the side door was open, the glare of headlights. She ran outside.

Her breath caught in her throat when she saw Samantha sprawled on the ground, a stream of blood circling her neck. Lachlan charged up, glanced down at the girl and then at Jennifer. 'Get her help,' he yelled, 'I'm going after him!'

The rain crashed down. The jogger slipped on the grass in the backyard but regained his footing quickly. He hurtled towards the back fence, jumping and clearing it but coming down hard on his side in the neighbouring property.

He was too desperate to feel pain. On his feet again instantly he raced across the yard, leaping another fence, then out onto the street and into the properties on the other side. The copper was hot on his tail. He could hear Lachlan's footsteps and his breath, hard and heavy, as he leapt the same fences. He didn't think Lachlan had fallen over and he knew his pursuer was stronger and more agile.

Why the hell had the copper arrived at the house this evening? The jogger hadn't considered that possibility. Lachlan was fit and relentless, he wouldn't give up. He'd chase him to the end of the world and back.

Another house. Another driveway running along the side. The jogger sighted one of the large rubbish bins pressed up against a side fence. He slowed, grabbed the bin with both hands, and rolled it back at full force down the sloping driveway behind him.

Lachlan ran at breakneck speed, just entering the driveway. He saw the bin tumbling towards him, tried to avoid it, but it delivered him a glancing blow to his right leg, knocking him off his feet. He sprawled on the concrete, gashing his cheek.

He sprang back up, oblivious to the blood. The jogger was out of sight now but Lachlan presumed he'd gone over the back fence. He raced to the fence, clambered to the top of it, scanned the landscape beyond. Heavy sheets of rain obscured the view.

His policeman's instinct pricked at him. All was not as it seemed. He jumped back into the yard and ran back the way he'd come. Just a hunch but he knew, if he'd been the one running, he would have circled around the other side of the house.

Back on the street he knew he'd judged correctly. The killer was half way to the next cross street. Lachlan pressed on. He wondered why the murderer had stayed on the footpath, in full view. If he'd dashed into another garden, leapt another fence, he would have been out of sight. Gone.

And then he saw the reason why.

Nearer the corner, just visible to Lachlan through the haze and mist of the rainstorm, a car pulled over. A middle-aged couple climbed out of it. He partly saw, partly assumed what happened next. The killer knocked the man and the woman to the ground with a vicious sweep of his arm, grabbed the keys and dived into the car.

Lachlan reached the corner as the vehicle, a wine coloured Toyota Celica, sped away. 'You all right?' he asked the couple.

'Son of a bitch stole my car,' the man said as he helped the woman to her feet.

Lachlan patted his pockets and realised he didn't have his cell phone on him. It was in his car.

'I'm a police officer,' Lachlan said. 'You live here?'

'Yes.'

'I need to use your phone quickly, sir. There's every chance we can still stop him.'

Less than ninety seconds elapsed before the message was broadcast to every police patrol in the metropolitan area.

Twenty minutes later Highway Patrol Officers Patresi and McCormick found the Celica parked outside an apartment block, seven streets away. Ten minutes later a further five police vehicles arrived and combed the area. The jogger, they believed, had abandoned the car to return to his own vehicle somewhere in the immediate vicinity.

The rain beat down in a deluge now, combining with the distorted glare from the city's lights to reduce visibility to almost zero. An hour later the search was called off.

Doctor Susan Chan was a petite, dark-eyed woman, fortyish, with an intelligent and compassionate face that inspired confidence. Jennifer was glad, for Meg's sake, that the doctor wasn't one of the cold, clinical, arrogant types sometimes found in the frantic halls of a city hospital.

Jennifer, Carly and Lachlan waited with Meg as the doctor approached, striding through the double swing doors of the emergency room. Meg, functioning entirely on nervous energy, was the first to snap to attention.

'Mrs Tanner?'

240

'Yes.'

'Your daughter is very lucky to be alive, Mrs Tanner,' Susan Chan said. 'I'm afraid she's far from being out of danger. She has extensive bruising and swelling of the larynx, causing great difficulty in breathing, and she's severely traumatised.'

'Oh, my God.'

'But she's responding well to treatment and we've stopped the internal bleeding. I'm keeping her in emergency for the time being and the next twenty-four hours will be crucial. Your daughter has been sedated but you can go to the ward to see your son. He's out of theatre and he's going to be fine. I've already explained that he won't be playing football for quite some time, though. He's going to need all his energy for his physiotherapy sessions.'

Lachlan introduced himself to the doctor and asked when he'd have the chance to question Samantha about her assailant.

'Not until morning, I'm afraid. At the earliest. If you'd like to phone then, ask for me personally.'

Jennifer and Carly accompanied Meg through to the ward.

'I wish you could stay with me for the next week,' Jennifer said to her long-time friend, 'to give you some good, old fashioned mothering to help you through this. But it's hardly a good idea in light of the circumstances. It's not the safest place to be, with the police watching over Carly and me.'

'They think Carly's in danger as well?'

'Detective Lachlan does. We can't be sure how much this madman knows, or thinks he knows. We didn't expect him to come after me. As far as we're aware, he doesn't even know that I know about Brian's audit.'

'That's what this is all about, this ... Winterstone thing?' Meg had picked that much up from the snippets of conversation she'd heard between Jennifer, Carly and Lachlan.

'Apparently,' Jennifer replied.

They walked out to the lobby. Outside, an ambulance pulled in to the outpatients express driveway.

241

'God, Meg, I'm so sorry.' Jennifer's words almost caught in her throat. 'If I hadn't stirred up all this business over Brian ...' Her voice faded.

'This monster has to be found,' Meg said matter-of-factly. 'Just make sure you two look after yourselves. *Please.*'

TWENTY SEVEN

'I'm glad you called. I came straight over. You're okay?'

Jennifer hugged Kaplan, ushered him in. 'I'm fine.'

'Someone tried to kill you?'

'The same person who killed Stuart James. He attacked Samantha Tanner, thinking it was me.'

'That explains the police out the front,' Kaplan said.

'Carly and I are both under protection.'

'And Meg's girl ..?'

'Samantha's still on the critical list.' Jennifer paced, which was unlike her. She peered through the front window drapes, then strode back toward him, arms folded. 'Henry, I think you may be able to help us. I called you over to ask you about Winterstone.'

'I'll do anything to help, you know that.'

'Stuart James believed there was a connection between Brian's disappearance and his audit of one of the companies in your group.'

'I know about that. Detective Lachlan spoke to Roger and Harold about it.'

'That file is now in the hands of the police, but the killer probably didn't know that. We think he thought the file was still here, that I knew about it, or that I may have found out. That's why he came after me. Carly could also be in danger.'

'Lachlan told you this?'

'Yes. He believes the same killer is responsible for six missing persons found dead, and the recent garrotte killings.'

'Six missing persons? Christ.'

'What's going on, Henry?'

'I don't know, Jennifer. It makes no sense. I can see that the evidence points to a connection with our Winterstone firm, but I can't see any reasons. None of us would get involved with a killer.'

'What about Harold? He purchased the Winterstone name and set up the warehouse operation. He might know something that could be of use, but just doesn't realise he knows it.'

'I'll question Harold further about this myself. If there's a link I'll get to the bottom of it.' He took hold of her hand, squeezed it. 'I promise you that.'

'If ever I needed your help, Henry, it's now.' Jennifer was terrified that, despite the precautions being taken, something could happen to Carly. The attack on Samantha was evidence of that.

Jennifer had been determined to solve this case - but now it appeared she'd let the demons out of Pandora's Box and everything was spiralling out of control.

'Are you sure you'll be safe here?'

'As well as the police watch outside, Neil Lachlan will be staying in the house overnight. He insisted and he's due back any minute.'

'Then I'll wait. There's something I want to speak to him about, and it's something you should hear. But I'd prefer that Carly didn't.'

'Carly's in her room, trying to sleep.' Jennifer was curious but she didn't prod further. She heard the sound of a car pulling up out the front. Neil Lachlan had arrived.

It was after 1 a.m. when Lachlan finally lodged the umbrella with forensics. Jennifer had identified it earlier after they'd left the hospital. Lachlan had checked in on Bryant at HQ but was disappointed that while Bryant's call to the US had gone through, there'd been no answer on the Lifelines phone number, and he was now waiting for a return call from the California State police in the hope they might be able to shed some light on the Lifelines name.

Lachlan had now arrived at Jennifer's home ten minutes after Kaplan, and as Jennifer motioned him in she told him that Kaplan wanted to discuss something.

'What's this all about then, Mr. Kaplan?' Lachlan asked.

Jennifer seated herself on the sofa. The two men remained standing. All were tired. It had been a long day and an even longer night.

'I gave Carly's boyfriend, Rory McConnell, permission to write an authorised article about my corporation. He's had access to my people for interviews, background info, that sort of thing, and he's been into our main office on a couple of occasions over the past week. Naturally, I had my legal department conduct an investigation into Mr. McConnell's own background.'

'Is that normal practice for you?' Lachlan asked.

'It's business, detective. I like to know what sort of people I'm opening up my people and my files to. I was disturbed by what I found.'

'Disturbed?' Jennifer repeated, clearly worried.

'He was a suspect in a murder case, in the town of Forthworth, in the early 90's. The victim's throat had been cut. He was never charged, and the police now believe someone else - another killer - was responsible. I might not have thought too much of it. But it appears this garrotte killer is someone close enough to Jennifer to know about the private investigator and the search through the old files. McConnell approached me about inside access to my organisation just after Brian Parkes was found. I got to thinking. It occurred to me that McConnell arrived in Sydney around the same time period that Brian went missing. The connections are loose but they started worrying me so I thought I should mention them.'

'They worry me too,' Jennifer said.

Lachlan turned to Jennifer. 'Carly lives with McConnell?'

'Yes, but she's staying with me for the moment.'

'I'll look into this Forthworth business further,' Lachlan told Kaplan. 'You were right to tell us what you'd learned.'

'Call me if there's anything more I can do,' Kaplan said. 'Rest assured, Jennifer, we'll get to the bottom of this whole damn mess.'

This was the Henry Kaplan Jennifer knew so well, so certain, so strong. But was there anything he could really do to help? For the first time ever, she wondered if he actually had the absolute control over his companies she'd always thought he had.

245

It wasn't a night for sleeping.

Jennifer, restless, invited Lachlan to join her for a drink in the back room overlooking the garden.

'No booze for me,' Lachlan reminded her. 'I'm on duty.' He didn't reveal the other reason, his determination not to slip back into the heavy drinking of his Drug Squad days.

Not for the first time he felt strongly that he'd like to start his new life by seeing more of Jennifer Parkes. He just wasn't sure how to broach the subject. The timing certainly wasn't right, with a madman on the loose and a police guard stationed outside her home.

Jennifer showed disappointment he couldn't have a drink. 'You don't mind if I have some wine. I need a nightcap after a night like this.'

'Go ahead. Coffee will be fine for me.'

It was hard to believe that only a few hours earlier a violent rainstorm had raged outside and Lachlan had chased a killer through the streets. The storm had passed and now all was calm. The wall length glass door at the rear allowed a panoramic view of the surrounding garden showing that the night clouds had passed overhead to reveal a full, bright moon. Its light glinted in magical slivers off the shiny wet leaves of the trees. A chorus of approval came from the night birds now that the rain had gone. Their chirpy, melodic warble filled the air like the evensong of a church choir.

Jennifer set the drinks down on the coffee table. 'I often sit out here and listen to them,' she said of the birds.

'I could happily listen to them all night,' Lachlan remarked. 'You could forget there's a world of crime and criminals out there.'

'Does the job get you down, detective?'

'You know what, I think it would be a hell of a lot more comfortable for both us if you just called me Neil.'

'Okay.' She smiled warmly at him. She liked this man a great deal, and for the first time, and despite everything that was happening around them, it felt good to admit that to herself and just go with the flow.

'It's like any job. There are times when it gets you down, there are times when it doesn't. On the best days there's a feeling of satisfaction, of having done something useful.'

He asked about her fashion business and was intrigued to learn about the garden rockery wishing pool Brian had built, the tradition of the five cent coins, and how years later Jennifer had called on that memory when naming her company.

She told him about Brian. 'He was a whizz with figures. It came naturally to him and he worked hard. But away from work he became your ordinary, average guy. He played squash a couple of times a week. Loved dining out and movies and building and renovating around the house.' She took a sip from the wine. 'What about you? You know, I've never known a policeman before.'

'Then we're even because I've never known a fashion designer. Believe it or not, detectives are just ordinary people too. I'm separated. I have a ten year old boy named Todd who I see every second weekend.'

'That must be hard.'

'Incredibly hard.'

'You know, you're different when you're alone with someone like this.'

'Am I?'

'You're usually so intense. Which is normal, I guess, when you're on the job. I hadn't pictured you with your feet up, relaxing with a coffee.'

'Like I said, some of us are just normal people.' He returned the smile.

'I'm sorry. I'm probably being very naive with such inane comments. Of course policemen are normal people. I guess it's difficult though, switching off from the job when you do go home?'

Lachlan's drug squad days flashed before his eyes. He'd lived, breathed and slept the job. It was the nature of the narcotics division. And he'd lost his real life. 'It's something you have to learn to do,' he admitted, 'sometimes it's a hard lesson.'

'I'm glad you're here tonight, Neil. Thanks for staying.'

'Least I could do. I should never have assumed the killer wouldn't see you as a threat if he thought you didn't know enough. Clearly, even the chance you'd get suspicious about the file was too much for him.'

'At least it showed us how desperate he is.'

247

'You should try and get some rest.'

Jennifer frowned. 'Won't be easy. But you're right.'

'I'd like to see you again when this is all over,' Lachlan said, surprising himself. 'Perhaps we could get together for dinner. I could keep showing you how normal I really am.'

'Sounds good.' They exchanged tentative smiles.

Jennifer had been laying awake in bed for over an hour.

She couldn't switch off.

And she was feeling ridiculously horny.

She hadn't stopped thinking about Neil Lachlan. She hadn't been attracted to a man in this way for a long time, so why now? The timing sucked.

There was something about his strong but laid-back command of things. And that partly raffish, partly amiable smile that offered a glimpse of another side.

She got up, padded through to the kitchen to pour a cool drink, and then stepped out onto the back balcony. Insomnia wasn't new to her and when she couldn't sleep, for whatever reason, this was her routine.

She was still in her negligee.

Lachlan was supposed to have retired to the guest room.

But he was also on the balcony, unable to sleep, sitting in the easy wicker chair and watching the stars.

Jennifer was startled when she saw him. 'Oh…I…' She blushed. 'Sorry. I'm not supposed to be out here.'

'I guess you couldn't sleep either.'

'No.'

'Head full of the case?'

'Yes.' Actually, that was a lie. His head was full of her but he kept that point private.

They made small talk for a while, and then Jennifer turned to leave. 'I know I said this before, but I really do appreciate your staying over tonight and the personal interest you've taken in the case. So, you know what, I'm going to let you have the balcony for as long as you need it, and I'll head back in.'

'No-'

'No, really Neil, it's absolutely fine. Try and get some rest, after all, you have your guys stationed outside...'

He realized, sheepishly, that he was staring at her curves through the flimsy cotton of her negligee, and she'd noticed. 'Sorry, I'm...'

She made light of it. 'It's okay. Actually, I'm flattered.'

'You are?'

Their eyes locked on one another. And that was the exact moment when everything changed, when something electrifying passed between them.

Lachlan rose. 'Your balcony, all yours. I'm going to hit the bed again, see if I can get at least a few hours, big day again tomorrow.'

She eased back as he squeezed by.

Her heart thudded at the closeness of him. Once again their eyes fixed on each other's, and then, impulsively, Lachlan leaned in and gave her a light kiss on the lips.

She didn't kiss him back. Contained herself. The old restraints kicking in.

He pulled away. 'Sorry...that was unprofessional.'

'I'm not complaining.' She felt herself opening up, allowing her bottled-up emotions to run free.

She placed her hand to the back of his neck, eased in closer and returned the kiss.

There was a sudden thundering crash and the two of them pulled apart and whipped their heads around in alarm, Lachlan positioning himself into a protective stance in front of her.

The next-door cat had leapt from the fence onto the fibreglass roof of the balcony. It ambled along and then jumped down onto the opposite fence.

Jennifer laughed nervously. 'Talk about tension.'

Lachlan followed her back into the house. She locked the back door behind them and then they headed to their rooms.

Outside the door to her room she said, 'Thanks.'

'Try and get some sleep.' Lachlan turned toward the guest room.

There are moments in all our lives, Jennifer conceded to herself later, when we throw aside our inhibitions and act in the heat of the moment.

She reached out, took Lachlan's arm and turned him back toward her. 'Permission granted to stop being so damn professional,' she said.

Lachlan's head told him to turn away. He was a detective on the job. But for once he threw all caution to the wind and responded to the ache that he felt for this beautiful woman.

Their mouths came together, exploring.

Lachlan didn't even recall slipping the negligee from her body as he cast his shirt aside.

The next thing her knew he was in her room, the door pushed shut behind them, both naked now, clinging to one another as they eased onto the bed. Everything about her was soft and sweet and intoxicating and under her caresses he felt every inch of his body exploding with new life.

Jennifer tingled and shivered from head to foot at the natural, husky aroma of him. His tongue and his fingers traced her neck and her breasts, moving lower, and she felt a liberating freedom and an ecstasy that she hadn't felt for a long, long time.

Later, in the afterglow, they lay on the bed facing one another, fingers entwined.

'You can go and start being professional again,' Jennifer said, grinning.

'Yes. I think I should.'

'I do have one favour to ask, though,' Jennifer added. 'I don't want to be stuck here, a prisoner in my own home, until this killer is caught. There's something in particular I want to do.'

'I'm listening,' Lachlan said.

Jennifer was pleased that Lachlan agreed to the idea and accompanied her the following morning to the home of Thomas Brayson.

She spent an hour with the old man whose daughter had been missing eighteen years, the two of them exchanging their memories of the loved ones they'd lost.

Lachlan marvelled at the depth of compassion with which Jennifer reached out to the old man, and her commitment to keep in touch, to look in on him on a regular basis.

That was the moment he knew he was in love with Jennifer Parkes.

TWENTY EIGHT

Earlier that morning, at 3 a.m., the bomb exploded at the far end of Shaft Number Twelve. The force of the blast pulverized tonnes of coal, sending it drifting in clouds of black dust through the tunnels and galleries of the mine. The dust, mixing with the air, caused a second, even greater explosion that was heard throughout the entire Southern Star complex and into the townships beyond.

The blinding, deafening detonation sent a fireball screaming through hundreds of metres of tunnel. Everything in its path was incinerated.

In the shed at the entrance to the shaft, four men played cards and drank Tooheys beer. On any other night they wouldn't have been there. Tonight was an exception.

These four men were about to take a couple of days leave for a fishing trip. At the end of their shift, they'd decided to celebrate and relax with a few drinks and a game of poker. Three hours later their impromptu get-together showed no sign of ending. They were merry with the beer, loud, jovial, and enjoying their game.

The instant the fireball leapt from the mouth of the shaft, like the fiery breath of some mythical dragon, the shed and its four occupants were blown to pieces. In the days that followed pieces of their bodies, meshed with metal and timber, were found in an area of up to three hundred metres away.

The resulting fires spread quickly to the cluster of buildings centred around the adjoining mineshafts.

Southern Star's rescue and maintenance teams were on the site within ten minutes. They worked furiously to seal the shaft and fight the fires breaking out all over the complex, but they were driven back repeatedly by heat and fumes and exploding chemicals.

By 4.30 a.m. an eighty-strong group of firemen, local police, miners and rescue professionals joined the operation.

Arriving on the scene, Mines Manager, David Hansen, was confronted by an eerie, otherworldly landscape.

Piles of twisted metal, falling rods, intense heat and clouds of carbon monoxide, illuminated by the angry red glow of the flames.

On the perimeter of the disaster area, news vans rolled to a halt and crewmen set up their equipment. And as the first light of dawn crept over the horizon, the TV news helicopters swept overhead.

At 5 a.m. several men working for Fred Hargreaves phoned the news desks of every major metropolitan newspaper and television station across the east coast of Australia, claiming responsibility for the bomb. They identified themselves as members of a new activist group called AVO (Asbestos Victims Organisation).

The mission to sabotage the sale of Southern Star Mining was complete.

News of the disaster coincided with the publication, that same morning, of the People Power edition with its exposé of Henry Kaplan, the man, and his corporation.

Rory McConnell expected to attract attention to his journalistic talents with the article. He'd arranged to send copies of the article to the editors of the major papers and websites. Whatever attention the article might have generated was now increased tenfold. His phone didn't stop ringing. One editor after another asked for Rory's input regarding Kaplan's knowledge of the asbestos issue. The current affairs TV programs lined up to interview him.

At 9.15 that morning Conrad Becker called an urgent meeting with his senior advisors. He fumed with anger that Southern Star Mining had been the target of terrorist attacks by an activist group. All were alarmed by the inference that Kaplan had used his influence to stop the asbestos inquiry.

During the first hour of trading that morning on the Australian Stock Exchange the value of Southern Star shares dived by a whopping forty percent.

Flanked by aides, Becker stormed into Henry Kaplan's office. Kaplan, shattered by the news, sat helpless and listened to the tirade of abuse from Becker. The Canadian tycoon made it clear, there was now no chance whatsoever of the sale going through. For Henry Kaplan, it became the final nail in the coffin of his life's work.

'Hey, Neil, two visits in one week, I've never been so popular.'

'It's one of those "can you do me a favour" visits again,' Lachlan said as he took a seat alongside Teddy Vanda.

'I'm wounded,' Vanda deadpanned. 'And you still haven't spilled the full story behind your last visit.'

'You'll have to put up with my silence on that a little longer.'

'You're just no fun anymore.'

'Maybe I can be. I'm looking for something pretty unusual.'

'So what else is new?'

'There's a link between those missing persons and the recent garrotte killings. But as you know there's an unexplained gap of eighteen years. I want to establish if this garrotte killer was involved with those disappearances - and where he's been since.'

'And here I was thinking you were going to ask something difficult for a change.'

'I want you to run a search for garrotte murders, or attempted garrotte attacks, Australia wide.'

Teddy grimaced. 'I suppose you want me to run a check all the way back to the year dot?'

'Let's go back twenty years. For starters.'

'That all? Lucky for you I owe you one, eh?'

'Lucky.' Lachlan relaxed and allowed himself a laugh.

The jogger was up early that morning and tuned in to the television. The first newsbreak concerning the bombing went to air at 5.53 a.m. The jogger's face broke into a self-satisfied grin as he watched the aerial footage of the pandemonium across the fire-ravaged site.

Later, he phoned Fred Hargreaves. 'You've done well,' he said. 'So well you've given me an idea. I need one of those explosive devices for a project of my own.'

'No problem,' came the reply. 'You deliver the cash, we deliver the product.'

The jogger made the necessary arrangements and then hung up. His aborted attempt on Jennifer Parkes' life had left him fearful that his plans were falling apart. But he felt much better this morning after watching the scenes of carnage on his TV screen. A new plot was hatching in his mind, one that made far more sense and solved all his remaining problems with one decisive blow.

TWENTY NINE

Earlier, on his way to Police HQ in Parramatta and his visit with Teddy Vanda, Lachlan had listened to the radio news about the Southern Star bombing. Why had this happened now, at the very same time his investigation showed a link between the missing persons and the garrotte killings to a company owned by the Kaplan Corporation? Co-incidence?

After seeing Teddy, Lachlan went to the special unit in the Sydney CBD. 'I was expecting an update call from you,' he said tersely to Max Bryant, referring to Bryant contacting the Burbank police in the U.S.

'Still no luck, Neil. I left a message. No return call as yet so I've emailed a request for any info Burbank can give us- or find out quickly- on Lifelines Inc. I'm following that up with repeated calls.'

Ron Aroney had been on the phone. Concluding his call, he approached Lachlan and Bryant. 'Those council plans arrived first thing this morning. I put them on your desk,' he said to Lachlan. 'According to the original design the building had a large basement, with a lift and stairwell access.'

'No sign of that when I was there,' Lachlan replied, 'but that's not to say they hadn't been sealed off.'

'The obvious question then,' said Bryant, 'is what the hell is down there that had to be sealed?'

'And,' Aroney added, 'who sealed it?'

The deputy commisioner took the anonymous call at 9.45 AM. 'Someone on the phone, won't give his name,' his P.A said, 'says he has vital information on the Southern Star bombing.'

It was unusual for Ed Razell to take such a call. Usually he directed something like this to one of his senior detectives. But the nature of this call changed that. He'd already had a call earlier from the Federal Minister for Industrial Affairs, requesting a full enquiry into the allegations of the asbestos cover-up. Although the incident had occurred in Queensland, the HQ of the Kaplan Corporation was in New South Wales and the minister wanted the authorities in both states involved. 'I'll take it,' Razell said.

'Who is this?' he said gruffly.

'The phone calls to the press from these AVO crazies are fake.'

Razell had heard similar voices on the phone before, handkerchief over the mouth to disguise the voice. The sign of an amateur.

'There's no such organisation.'

Razell had expected as much. He already had several men looking for information on any such group. 'You need to identify yourself,' Razell demanded. A useless question but one that had to be asked.

'Consider me a friend. The bombing was organised by someone who had a lot to gain by casting attention on Kaplan today. Have you seen that rag People Power this morning, Razell?'

'No.'

'Then go get a copy. Couldn't have been better timing for the journalist who wrote the exposé on Kaplan.'

There was a click and the line went dead.

It made sense.

Razell had already considered the possibility that AVO might be a smokescreen for someone bombing the mine for a totally different purpose. He pulled out the report he'd received that morning from Lachlan.

Rory McConnell, freelance journo for indie paper People Power, had been added to the list of suspects in the missing persons murders. Razell pondered the fact that these two names kept cropping up. McConnell attacking Kaplan in print, while Kaplan fed information on McConnell's dubious past to the police. What was it with those two?

Razell marched out of his office. 'I'm paying Detective Senior Sergeant Lachlan a visit,' he informed his P.A.

'I got the shock of my life when I ran the data on aborted violent attacks, with garrotting as the main selection criteria. I expected maybe two or three unrelated attempts over the twenty year period.'

'And?' Lachlan was impatient.

Teddy Vanda, recognising the anxiety of the moment, shifted his internal gears effortlessly from light-hearted into deadly serious. 'The computer came up with twenty-six attempted garrotte killings, all in the north western suburbs of Sydney, at staggered intervals in the mid-90's. Some were a few weeks apart. Towards the end of the cycle they were up to six months apart.'

'Twenty-six attempts,' Lachlan repeated, stunned.

'Twenty-six over a period of a couple of years. Then nothing since. And that's not the interesting part. In each and every attack, the intended victim reported being saved by the intervention of two men.'

'Who?'

'Unknown. In each reported attack, the victim told an identical story. They had no idea who their attacker was, and no idea who their saviours were.'

'Were they always the same two men?'

'Apparently not. Descriptions of the two men varied, Neil. But they were always large, powerful looking characters.' He allowed himself a light moment. 'Like me.'

'The link between these attacks was never noticed,' Lachlan assumed.

'The reports were made to different stations, depending on the exact locale of the attack. Local detective Constable Ron Nicholls recognised the pattern and instigated an investigation. It went nowhere and was relegated to the back burner after the attacks stopped.'

'So, the reason this guy stopped killing was because someone else was stopping *him*.'

258

'In order to be on the spot like that, someone had to undertake twenty-four hour surveillance of the killer, or of his intended victims,' Teddy suggested. 'You'd find those skills in security specialists or private detectives. I programmed the computer to compile a list of companies involved in that kind of work.'

'I knew there was a reason I kept hanging around you,' said Lachlan.

Teddy raised his right eyebrow appreciatively. This was the Neil Lachlan with whom he'd always had camaraderie. 'And I ran a cross check of those company names against Winterstone for a possible connection. Nothing. Zero-ville.' Teddy paused, held up his finger to highlight his next comment. 'Then I did something I rarely do.'

Lachlan was intrigued but kept his impatience in check. 'The suspense is killing me.'

'I left the computer alone, picked up the phone, and did some old fashioned police work called talking to people. You've piqued my curiosity. Must have, for me to do stuff like this off my own bat. I may have come up with something.'

'On Winterstone?'

'Not exactly. On the parent company. The Kaplan Corporation hired a private investigator, a Swede named Hans Falkstog, back in the 70's, to watch over Kaplan's son during a kidnap scare.'

'You got this from Falkstog?'

'Are you kidding me. It's nigh on impossible to get information from these security specialists. Too secretive. I phoned the accounts division at Kaplan Corp. and asked for a list of security firms and private investigators that had ever been on a retainer. I said I was from Corporate Affairs. The accounts woman was very obliging. Falkstog Security Systems had been used by the corporation since the incident in the 70's. They supplied a variety of services, patrolling offices and factories that Kaplan owned, advising on the installation of electronic security systems, that sort of thing.'

'Falkstog? I've heard of him.' Lachlan searched his memory. 'Ex-military. The Federal Police called him in to advise on a couple of difficult cases a few years back.'

'He's not so popular with the feds these days,' Teddy said. 'The local vice boys investigated Falkstog a couple of years ago. He's suspected of illegal surveillance practices, of running drugs, and of operating a prostitution racket.'

'They couldn't pin anything on him?'

'Right. Smooth operator, covers his ass brilliantly.'

'I wouldn't have thought prostitution his style.'

'I remember talking with one of the Vice Squad boys about that. Falkstog has a quirky, vicious side to him. That's the reason they think he got into brothels. Vice believe he acted as a client. Whenever a new girl joined she'd be sent to Falkstog for a session.'

'Trying out the goods himself?'

'That's what the vice guys thought,' Teddy confirmed. 'But surveillance tactics are Falkstog's specialty. And that fits in perfectly with the surveillance that appears to have been placed on this garrotte killer, or his victims.'

'But most likely surveillance on the killer.'

'Yeah. I was about to come over and see you with this, Neil, because I thought you might be able to make something of it. So your visit's saved me the trouble. You're considerate that way.' He flashed a grin, but was equally as quick at getting back to business. 'Maybe there's a connection in all this. Or maybe I'm dreaming. Stuffed if I know.'

'No dream.' Lachlan ran his fingers through his hair. Lack of sleep was catching up and the strain was showing in the lines around his eyes. 'Someone with inside info on the Kaplan Corporation knows who the killer is. He hired Falkstog's firm to follow the killer and intervene whenever an attack occurred. That's the kind of scenario that leaps immediately to mind. It would cost an arm and a leg, but it's something a corporation like Kaplans could afford.'

'But there's nothing irregular in the accounts. They fitted in with payment for the regular security patrols and consultations.'

'It's probable,' said Lachlan, 'that funds were diverted to a personal account and paid that way. Harold Masterton has shaped up as the main suspect in this. He set up Winterstone in the first place and ordered the equipment.'

'What equipment?'

'We don't know yet, but never mind about that.' There would be time enough later to fill Teddy in on all the details. 'In the meantime, mate, could you run an investigation into the personal cheque accounts of Harold Masterton, Henry and Roger Kaplan and other members of the board, for starters. We're looking for any amounts made out to Falkstog Security Systems.'

'I'll need warrants to access the records.'

'You'll have them in an hour.'

'You realise that if someone has been paying Falkstog they could have been using cash.'

'Could have. But large amounts of cash, as often as they'd need paying, could be messy. Personal cheques would be easier and wouldn't be subject to company audits.'

'Your optimism is showing.' It was the cheeky Teddy again.

'Not as much as I'd like it to be.'

When Teddy Vanda called Lachlan- four hours later- he had the information Lachlan wanted. Through his personal cheque account at National Combined, Henry Kaplan had raised a cheque to Falkstog Security Systems for one hundred and fifty thousand dollars per month, for as far back as non-archived records were held. The last cheque had been issued three months earlier, just prior to the initial bankruptcy proceedings.

Masterton wandered the halls, listening to flashes of radio news from different offices. The entire building was abuzz with the events of the morning. Becker's words still echoed in Masterton's mind. He ambled into Roger's office. The boss's son had just hung up the phone.

'What on earth is happening to us?' Masterton croaked. 'First the police connect Winterstone to those murders. Now that God-awful bombing. And Becker's pulled out of the deal.'

Roger threw his hands up in dismay. 'I don't know. I've never even heard of this AVO mob before. Where the hell did they spring from? And as for that bastard McConnell and his lefty rag article...'

'I spoke to the Herald editor a few moments ago,' Masterton said. 'Apparently a copy's been faxed to them and to every major newspaper in Australia.'

'The bastard,' Roger repeated. 'Every paper in the country will be after him for more info. If he gets onto this link with Winterstone and feeds that to them...You haven't been talking to him, Harold, have you?'

The blood rose in Masterton's cheeks. 'I don't know the first thing about McConnell or that blasted warehouse.' He was interrupted by Henry Kaplan, who burst into the office unexpectedly. 'Harold. Leave us please.'

'Henry...?'

'Leave us!'

Masterton glowered from Kaplan to Roger and then, swallowing his anger and his pride, stormed out.

'Only someone with inside knowledge could have organised the bombing at Southern Star,' Kaplan told his son. Fury had distorted his features, changing his face from the one that beamed from the covers of so many business magazines, twisting it into something that revealed the darker, hidden side to his nature.

'You don't think it was Harold?' Roger asked.

'Someone with something to gain by the bankruptcy going ahead.'

'What would Harold have to gain?'

'Nothing. His career, like mine, is over. But yours isn't, is it?'

Roger's brow furrowed with lines of confusion. 'Dad...?'

'You're happy to live on the money you have stashed away, aren't you? The hidden accounts. The easy life. You don't give a stuff about the company, you never have. What is it, Roger? It doesn't satisfy you like your other interests?'

'What the hell is this all about?'

'Don't play dumb. Not now. You don't need to worry, do you, now that the corporation and its money are gone? Christ, you're actually pleased.'

Roger swallowed hard. He glared at his father, fists clenched. Then, with his finger pointing and stabbing at the air, said, 'You were always the big shot, always the superstar. Never me. I was never good enough. I never did it right, did I? Well, it's all gone now and as usual you're blaming me.' He charged toward the door.

'I'm not finished with you, Roger,' his father warned.

'I'm finished with you,' Roger retorted, slamming the door behind him.

From its exterior it appeared to be an ordinary leather briefcase, and neither the case nor the man carrying it attracted so much as a second glance. The jogger was conservatively dressed, dark business suit, striped tie.

The plan for collecting the briefcase had been child-like in its simplicity. He had delivered a cheque for twenty thousand dollars, made out to one of the many business names used by Fred Hargreaves. That cheque was handed over to the front desk clerk in a back street Kings Cross hotel. The clerk had been instructed to hand the briefcase over to the bearer of that cheque.

Back in his car the jogger inspected the contents of the briefcase. Several packets of blasting explosive were wired to the detonator mechanism, which consisted of an alarm clock, a battery, a light bulb and a head-screw. A simple but effective form of bomb making, Hargreaves had assured him on the phone, modelled on the compact, home made bombs used by terrorist groups all over the world. This particular version detonated only when it received a signal triggered by the plunger. The plunger was no larger than a cell phone and shaped to look like one from a distance. It featured a lever, which needed to be pressed down firmly to set the electronic impulse in motion.

He imagined the moment in which he stood with the plunger in his grasp, his target within sight.

The jogger drove to the large, sprawling estate. The house, nestled in an area largely shielded by hedges and overhanging trees, had beautiful, landscaped grounds. Everything was quiet. The jogger scouted the area, making doubly sure. Neither the cleaner nor the gardener was due today...and the house was empty.

The jogger went to the rumpus room on the west wing of the second floor, an airy room filled with natural light. The double glass doors opened onto a balcony that overlooked the front garden. Light filtered through the canopy of trees in a patchwork pattern. The jogger placed the briefcase on the table, standing it against the left wall.

Now that he was in the house with the explosive in place he felt a growing sense of confidence. This would work. Curiously the idea had only come to him that morning, as he'd watched the news broadcasts. It seemed a logical progression to what had gone before.

He felt a familiar tingle in the hairs on the back of his neck, and then the swell began to surge through him. The sickly sweet sensation of the dark power. He had no qualms about destroying this house. It represented everything he hated. Money and property and bravado and bluster. This house, with its plush pile carpets throughout, the polished mahogany furniture, the painting and antiques and the great, vast emptiness of it all. Like the soul of the man who owned it.

The jogger took the coil of wire from his coat pocket and held it tightly. He hadn't expected to feel the thrill, but it was there, coursing through him, even though this was not one of his random thrill killings.

He'd eliminated the chance of the watchers coming back. Hadn't he? Soon he'd be free of those who were closest to discovering his secret. Perhaps that was why the excitement surged within him.

He thought of Jennifer Parkes. Perhaps her death, at his hands, had been destined. After all, she was one of *them*. She'd built a company, played at the business of being in control.

He snapped the wire taught in his hands.

THIRTY

The deputy commissioner's visit to the special unit room was a hurried one. He told Lachlan about the anonymous call suggesting Rory McConnell was behind the Southern Star bombing. He wondered if it could be mere coincidence that McConnell was once a suspect in a murder case, and that he was close to the Parkes family.

Razell knew Harold Masterton was still the only link Lachlan had in the Winterstone investigation. 'Could there be an unknown connection between McConnell and Masterton?' he'd asked.

Lachlan asked Bryant to run a check on that. He then brought Razell up to date on their suspicion that there'd been a strange surveillance on the garrotte killer. And that possibly Henry Kaplan or Hans Falkstog were involved in some way.

These thoughts circled in Lachlan's mind. He advised Bryant to call him as new developments arose, then left with Ron Aroney for the drive to Dural. First, he needed to see the hidden basement at the warehouse. He'd arranged for the police rescue's demolition men to meet them there.

And then he wanted to meet with Hans Falkstog.

The rescue team used sledgehammers and blowtorches to knock down the brick wall that hid the basement in the Winterstone warehouse.

The two men had a knockabout, larrikin air to them, despite the gravity of the work they were normally called for. 'There you go, mate,' one called to Lachlan. 'Gateway to Hell. All yours.' He grinned, gave the thumbs up sign, then they took off for their next assignment.

'Doesn't know how right he could be,' Lachlan commented to Aroney.

'Is there anything those rescue blokes can't do?' Aroney wondered as he inched forward into the darkness of the basement.

'They can't bring back the dead,' said Lachlan.

Aroney explored the wall with his fingers, found the switch and the room beyond was bathed in a pallid glow. Neither man was prepared for the sight that next greeted their eyes.

Jennifer tried to ignore the presence of the constable in the front room - his was the latest in a series of shifts watching over the house. She sat in the kitchen and listened to the radio news reports about the Southern Star bombing.

Carly appeared in the doorway, a welcome diversion to the battery of bad news. 'You look as if you could use something to occupy the mind and I've got just the thing.'

She led her mother through to the study and she booted up Jennifer's PC.

'One of the girls I know from modelling – Marcie – showed me this very cool website. She knows the guys who are putting it together. It's called 'Fever For Fashion' and it's a comprehensive collection of images, year by year, from the 1900's through to today, showing the fashions from one era to the next.'

'Okay, sounds like fun.'

'That's not the half of it. It's interactive, so you can actually play around with the images, taking elements from one picture in one era, and mixing and matching them with items from another era. And it does it all by company, so there's an image stream of fashions through the ages from Givenchy, and another stream for Ralph Lauren, and it's all kinds of clothing brands, and accessories, and cosmetics. Runs the full gamut.'

Jennifer looked over Carly's shoulder as her daughter accessed the site and entered keywords, bringing up a gallery of images. 'You're right, it's cool. Very cool.'

'And it has a complete history of each of the companies and their products,' said Carly. 'I have to admit, I love this site, even if I am done with the whole modelling charade. Take a look at this, for instance, did you know the L'Oreal company in the U.S. was originally called Corsair, and that they changed the name of the holding company because its L'Oreal brand was the name with which the world identified?'

'Yes. Back in 2000. Seems so long ago now.'

'I never knew that. Imagine, back when you started your company, Mum, if someone else had owned the Wishing Pool Fashions name. You would have had to call the business something else. Anyway, time to play. Pick a brand.'

Silence.

Carly turned around to face Jennifer. 'Come on, Mum, pull up a seat, pick out a brand name. Any-' She stopped mid-sentence, noting that her mother was standing very still, her eyes on the screen but her mind a million miles away.

'Mum....?'

'Corsair changed its company name to L'Oreal,' Jennifer repeated.

'Yeah...?'

'Not at all unusual for companies to change their name.'

'So? Mum, let's play-'

'The police haven't been able to find out anything, as yet, about the Lifelines company that supplied goods to Winterstone. Nothing on the internet. What if that company's name was changed?'

'Okay. Good point, I guess.'

'Probably nothing in it, but worth investigating.'

'I suppose, but how would you do that?'

'There's a thousand and one databases out there with all sorts of information, particularly when it comes to the corporate world. Let's try a search for business name change information. Google it.'

Carly typed in 'lists of company name changes.'

The Search Results screen listed several websites.

The 'famous-business-namechange' website had a wealth of information and lists. Jennifer and Carly trawled through it.

'They've got to be kidding,' Carly said with a giggle, scanning the site, 'Google was called BackRub when it launched in 1996, and changed its name to Google two years later, just as it was taking off and revolutionising the whole search engine industry.'

'This is interesting,' Jennifer said, reacting to items she was seeing on the site. 'The iconic tobacco firm Phillip Morris Inc., a household name in the latter half of the twentieth century, changed the name of its parent company to Altria in 2001, and some believe it was to disassociate itself from the growing negative image of cigarettes.'

'Crazy,' said Carly.

Jennifer pointed out another item. '1996. A U.S. airline company, ValuJet, was grounded after one of its planes crashed in the Everglades. Massive bad publicity. It merged with a smaller airline, Airtran, and adopted that as its new name to distance itself from the tarnished Valujet brand.'

'Nothing here on Lifelines.'

'Go back to the Search Results.'

Carly backspaced.

There were a number of commercial sites, and a national archives web page, that listed company name changes for the stock exchanges and the wider marketplace.

'Try this,' Jennifer said. 'Back to Google. Type in "Lifelines, Burbank, California, company name change," let's see what comes up.'

Seconds later the search results showed "Lifelines name change, legal challenge," and the link led to a cached article on the United States National Archive website.

In the mid 90's a wealthy family had taken out a legal injunction against Lifelines Inc. The case had gone to court where it was subsequently dismissed by the presiding judge, but not before a wave of bad publicity and media coverage had engulfed the firm.

Later, the company moved its operations to New York and changed its name to Longer Life.

Jennifer pulled a chair up and searched for that company name.

A link to the company appeared at the head of the page and Jennifer clicked on.

'What do you think Longer Life is, anyway?' Carly asked. 'One of those youth preserving alternate health mobs?'

'No idea. But hopefully we're about to find out.'

The basement room was long and wide, ample floor space, low ceilings, stark bare walls - the light provided by low-hanging fluorescent tubes somehow didn't disperse the shadows still hovering on the ceiling and in the corners.

The gazes of both men were drawn to a row of long, metallic cylindrical caskets standing along the far end of the eastern wall. Lachlan subconsciously found himself counting. Eleven.

'Jeez - us.' He heard Aroney breathe, an unlikely tremor colouring the word, which produced a responding tingle at the base of Lachlan's spine.

Both drew closer to observe the wires and tubes, which connected each casket to individual controls built into the wall.

The room was deathly silent, but Lachlan imagined the steady mechanical hum which would have emanated from these unearthly appliances had the power still been feeding to them. Raising his eyes, he saw also that at the top of each cylinder was a large metal lid. Six were open. The other five were closed ... and - six missing bodies had turned up recently. Okay, Lachlan mentally steadied himself. Just what in hell were they going to find in this Godforsaken place?

'You ever seen anything like this?' Lachlan said. He needed to break the silence closing in on him like something tangible. '... Ron ..?'

Aroney jerked his eyes from the canisters back to Lachlan. 'Uh, yeah. Yeah, I have.' His head nodded jerkily, looking from Lachlan to the canisters and back again, as though gripped by a sudden surge of hyperactivity. 'Just can't remember if it was one o' them sci-fi TV shows with freakin' aliens snoozin' away in them, or the last remake of Frankenstein. This supposed to be some sort of laboratory?'

Aroney's comment voiced both their thoughts.

'Maybe.' Lachlan felt a shiver bite at the nape of his neck as he climbed up to peer down into the first cylinder.

It was empty.

Aroney watched silently as Lachlan checked each of the remaining five open cylinders - all empty, as he'd expected.

A sense of foreboding came over the two detectives as they now contemplated the closed cylinders. 'You going to open 'em?' Aroney muttered.

'Unless you want the privilege.'

A gust of wind found its way through the smashed brickwork where they'd entered, dislodging something at the opposite side of the room, which fluttered as it hit the floor. Both men started, instinctively drawing their guns and swivelling in that direction. A moment later, each flushed with embarrassment as they realised the absurdity of their actions. No one living could have remained in that sealed-up basement ... and guns would be of little use against ghosts.

Aroney laughed shakily. 'And we're supposed to be a couple of hard-assed coppers. Let's get on with it. I say we take half each.'

'Done,' Lachlan agreed, thinking: how do you halve an uneven number? Why an odd number such as eleven? The question niggled at him.

Aroney opened the first of the remaining five - empty.

By unspoken agreement Lachlan took the next - also empty. Their apprehension began to abate a little as the third also revealed vacant space.

'I've got a feeling I've seen something like this before,' Aroney said as Lachlan opened the fourth closed canister. 'I mean, I just can't - put my finger on it. You got any idea what these things are?'

'There is something ...' Lachlan began, searching his memory.

Aroney reached across and put his weight into lifting the metal lid of the final canister, heaving it back with a flourish. Lachlan saw the detective's head suddenly snap backwards, his other hand flying up to cover his nose and mouth.

'What the ..?' Lachlan started, hurrying over to him. His partner seemed to be struggling for breath. Reaching the canister, the insidious stench rose to meet him. Overpowering. Unmistakable. The sick, rancid odour of decomposing human flesh. 'Oh, God,' he croaked, looking away.

Aroney buckled over, dry retching, forcing himself to keep the rising bile down. Lachlan quickly covered his mouth and nostrils with his handkerchief. Coughing, he inched closer and peered into the capsule. It was hard to tell exactly how long this body had been left to rot. It could have been weeks, maybe longer.

Unseeing eyes bulged from a ghastly white, bloated face. The hair hung in lank, yellow strands. The corpse was a naked female and the skin, peeling away, was covered in the ugly green and purplish stains of putrefaction. Liquid trailed from the nostrils and mouth, and the features had long since begun to liquefy.

Lachlan slammed the lid shut. No point corrupting the air further until they'd organised the removal of the body.

'I say we get the hell outta here,' said Aroney.

'No argument here.' Lachlan indicated the rest of the basement. 'But we need to give the rest of this place a thorough search. Find out just what this is all about.' Looking about as he spoke, he noticed the body size sack, made of foil type material, that lay nearby.

'Oh, my God.' Jennifer gave Carly an incredulous look as the first page of the Longer Life web site filled the screen

She read and then re-read the heads and sub-heads to the opening section:

Your introduction to death and its aftermath: suspension as a life alternative. The beliefs and mechanics of cryonic suspension.

'Long term frozen bodies,' Jennifer muttered in realisation.

'Is that what cryonics is?' Carly asked.

'Yes.'

'Do you know much about it?'

'No. Not much at all.'

Carly sucked in a deep breath. Jennifer saw tears forming in the corners of her daughter's eyes.

'So Dad wasn't alive all these years. He was killed eighteen years ago, then frozen. And hidden.'

Jennifer gripped her daughter's arm. 'I know it's a shock but hang in there. We've got to see this through, for your father's sake.'

'I know. I'll be okay.'

They squeezed each others hands in a gesture of support, then turned back to the computer screen and the first page of the text:

It began in 1964 with the publication of The Prospect of Immortality by American physicist, Robert Ettinger. He began developing his theory after investigating the work of a French biologist who had used glycerol to freeze frog sperm.

Ettinger proposed that human beings could be frozen with a minimum of cellular damage. Be perfectly preserved until, in some future time, they could be revived and cured of whatever illness caused their death. Ettinger's book was not simply a cold clinical essay of scientific facts and theories, he had the stamp of the visionary. Ettinger envisaged a future society where immortality was commonplace.

There was no support from the scientific community, but Ettinger's book sold well and became a Book Of The Month Club selection. Ettinger's idea took hold, briefly, with the general public: people near death from illness or accidentally killed in accidents, frozen and kept in suspension until the medical world could cure them or bring them back to life.

Ettinger's use of the term cryonics found its way into the language of the mass media but the physicist did not get involved personally in setting up any organisations. Those he inspired later formed the Eastern Cryonics Society. The group was established to develop and produce cryonic suspension techniques, and to promote the cause as widely as possible, but to this day the practice remains mostly unpublicised.

And one of those groups, thought Jennifer, was Lifelines Inc., later to become Longer Life.

'It's like the modern world's answer to the ancient Egyptian mummification process,' Jennifer said to Carly.

272

The information in the article was comprehensive, complete with diagrams and photographs. Cryonics was clearly the immortalists' extension, some would say flight of fancy, from the actual science of cryobiology. The cryobiologist studied the effects of cold temperatures on living creatures. Cells, tissues and organs had successfully been frozen and preserved. Those applications had particular use in surgery, and the past two decades had seen rapid growth world wide in cryosurgery.

Outside the established scientific and medical communities, the cryonicists trod their own maverick path. They believed that once a person died, immediate freezing would preserve the body in a near-life state.

The first client had been a seventy-four year old American lung cancer patient named James Bedford, frozen at the moment of clinical death in 1967. Since then thousands of people had signed up for the service with various suppliers. Thus far more than fifty had been cryonically frozen.

The court case in the 90's was due to a family that legally challenged their father's will. He had wanted his head cryonically frozen by LifeLines Inc. The children were against it. The case was overturned but not before local media headlines about frozen heads had cast a gruesome public image on the cryonics firm. They'd changed their name and location, for a fresh start.

Jennifer wondered what it would be like to awaken, cured of your illness and brought back to life, to continue living in a far flung future society. She didn't believe it was possible. Surely a human being, whether dead or alive at the time of freezing, couldn't re-awaken after centuries, or even decades. But these people not only believed it, they were committed to it as an alternative approach to life and death.

What possible connection, she wondered, had Brian had to any of this?

273

THIRTY ONE

Rory McConnell tapped away on his computer keyboard until he heard the knock at the door. Helen Shawcross stood there, wide smile, dressed suggestively in a tight fitting cotton blouse and denim shorts fashionably frayed around the edges. Two small suitcases stood beside her.

'What are you doing here?' Rory snapped.

Her smile crumbled. 'Nice to see you too, lover.'

'Well?'

'I've had it with Henry. Couldn't spend another day in that mausoleum he calls home. I decided - what the hell - to move in with you for a while. Your other friend won't mind, will she?'

'For God's sake, Helen, it's over. I was going to text you today. Break the news.'

'Text me?' She glared at him.

'It's been a lot of fun but it's run its course. It's over. We're done.'

'Done? You used me to get what you wanted, information for your hot shot news stories, then you tell me it's over!'

'Don't make me call the cops and have you cited for stalking, Helen. Leave with a little dignity, eh?' He slammed the door.

She stood there, fuming, clenching her fists. She wanted to kick the door in, scream at him, throw whatever she could lay her hands on at him. Instead, she picked up the suitcases and walked away. She could get back to the house at Vaucluse, unpack, and Henry would be none the wiser. He wasn't fun anymore, and he was fast losing everything that made him useful, but he'd have to do for a little while longer.

'Sure you don't want to take a break from this?' Jennifer asked. 'Leave me with it awhile.'

Carly's eyes had dried but her expression remained grim, her body stiff with the tension of their extraordinary discovery. 'No, Mum, I want to read on. I need to know how and why this happened. And who was responsible.'

Jennifer gave her a re-assuring smile. It took every ounce of her inner strength to remain calm, to focus on the information. She was glad Carly was with her. Her hand moved to the mouse again and she clicked to the next page:

'This is the cryonics process -

The body is placed in a watertight sack of strong thin material. In order to prevent cellular damage, the body is perfused with an anti-freeze Ringers lactate solution. The perfusion is performed with a surgical pump. It continues until the blood, draining from the right jugular vein via a tube is colourless.'

This, thought Jennifer, explained the puncture to Brian's throat, not evident with the other victims because of the garrotte wounds to the same area. Draining the blood and replacing it with an anti-freeze solution minimised the damage to the body's fluids.

'A second perfusion is then performed with a cooled solution of glycerol in the lactate solution.

The next step is to wrap the bloodless body in heavy-duty aluminium foil, preventing ice crystallisation and external cell damage. Strapped to a slab, the body is then inserted into the capsule.

The capsule resembles a giant thermos flask, eight feet tall and thirty inches in diameter. Inside it, the body floats vertically in minus 320F liquid nitrogen, which must be replaced once a month. The body can be preserved like this indefinitely.

It is not the goal of cryonicists to simply reverse the freezing process once a body can be medically revived. It is equally important for the patient to be fully restored to good health - to return to an active, satisfying lifestyle.'

Jennifer wondered whether the cryonics societies could have imagined that their extraordinary system, would be used by a demented killer for an entirely different purpose.

She reached across the desk for her cell phone. 'We should let Detective Lachlan know what we've discovered.' She phoned the special unit.

Max Bryant answered. 'He's out of the office, Ms Parkes,' he said gruffly. 'But he's on the mobile and asked to be called with anything important.'

'It's Jennifer Parkes,' Lachlan said to Aroney, 'but I can barely understand her. Too much interference. I'm going outside.' With the phone pressed to his ear, he retraced his steps to the area immediately outside the warehouse basement.

Despite his amazement, he listened without interruption as Jennifer quickly outlined what she and Carly had learnt so far.

'That explains what Aroney and I have found here,' he responded. 'Listen, Jennifer, I can't stop and talk right now. Can you phone Bryant back and give him that web address for Longer Life?

'Consider it done.'

Lachlan rejoined Aroney, who was poking around at the wall opposite the cylinders. Aroney had identified a pile of canisters marked liquid nitrogen.

There were several tables with packages of foil. Once again Lachlan thought of the hum that would have once pervaded this room, the quiet, sinister energy of the machines. The thought unnerved him. He told Aroney what he'd learned from Jennifer about the cryonics.

Aroney whistled. 'Explains how those missing people hadn't aged. I remember reading something about cryonics in the papers, years ago. That's where I've seen pictures of these containers. I didn't realise how much it had grown over there in the US. So what do you think, Neil?

Brian Parkes and the others were murdered in the 90's and have been here, perfectly preserved, until just recently?'

'Yes. At which point the killer reversed the process, then re-dressed them and dumped them back where they were last seen.'

'And the body over there?'

'My theory is that the cylinder was faulty. That body began to decompose, very, very slowly, over the years. When the killer found out, he simply left the body there.'

'Why go to all this bother and expense?' Aroney said. 'Shit, why not just bury them somewhere in the bush in the first place?'

'Perhaps because they'd have been found, eventually,' Lachlan suggested. 'No chance of that here. Who'd come scrounging around the basement of a little used, Kaplan owned warehouse? But I expect there's more to it than that. This killer is in it for the thrill, there appears to be no other motivating factor. By freezing his kills and storing them here he had his own private trophy room.'

Aroney winced. 'Sick bastard. It's as if he was trying to go one better than someone like Ted Bundy.'

They walked across to the rows of metal filing cabinets at the far end, and began to rifle through the drawers.

'Air tight plastic bags,' Aroney said. 'To keep everything in its original condition.'

'Every eventuality was planned for, Ron. Containers over there stored the blood ...' Lachlan had seen such containers at the Red Cross blood bank, refrigerated units that could cryo freeze blood, in liquid nitrogen. The blood was treated with a special coolant, used for the long-term storage of rare blood types. 'The cryonicists didn't necessarily keep the blood, in some cases they didn't even keep the whole body, just the head. But this demented killer has gone the whole hog - bodies, blood, clothing, items, preserved thanks to LifeLines/Longer Life.'

Lachlan paused a moment, allowing the facts to settle in. Then he continued: 'The more I think of it, the *perfect* trophy room for a psychotic mind like this one. And he prepared everything he needed to put the bodies back - those containers of fresh water ...'

'Yeah. To douse Parkes' clothing, recreating the conditions of the night he vanished. But why thaw out the original six now? Where's the killer been ..?' Aroney's voice trailed off. 'What's this?'

Lachlan joined him and looked into a draw full of standard size envelopes. Many had been opened. All had been posted at varying intervals over the years. Aroney pulled out the typewritten page from one. 'Letters?' he said with a note of puzzlement. He read aloud:

'Dear Mother,

They're still watching me, you know. After all these years, even though it's a long time since I've tried anything. Sometimes I wonder how I've managed to remain sane. Of course, the girls who are sent help ...'

He stopped, looked at Lachlan. 'What in blazes!' He was lost for words. The letter had been posted over a decade before.

Lachlan rummaged through the pile, checking the postmarks. So Falkstog had supplied his prostitutes as well as the surveillance. All the envelopes were addressed to Ms M Rentin, c/- Winterstone at the Dural address. 'The earliest was posted eighteen years ago,' he remarked. He opened it and scanned the contents.

'Dear Mother,

I had an intriguing thought today, one I wanted to share with you.

Just think of the crimes - all the crimes committed by all the men and women throughout history –'

'If the killer wrote these letters to his mother then why'd he send them here?' Aroney wondered aloud, peering over Lachlan's shoulder. 'Unless ...'

'I've a hunch about that name - Rentin,' Lachlan said. 'I'm going to phone Bryant, get him to follow through on it from his end. But right now, we should pay Falkstog a visit. My gut tells me he holds the key.'

'You go,' Bryant said. 'I'll stay and keep the place off limits until the forensics boys get here. But tell 'em to hurry, will you?' He glanced about at the bare brick walls, the bizarre array of canisters and caskets. 'This place gives me the creeps.'

THIRTY TWO

Hans Falkstog lived in a colonial white, double storey mansion, set in lush, green landscaped gardens. The rear of the estate, complete with an Olympic size swimming pool and tennis courts, backed onto a private strip of beach where its owner jogged most mornings.

This wasn't just the home of a wealthy, enigmatic businessman. A top-secret operation was housed within. Lachlan had found that private security firms were a mushrooming business, preferring to run their offices from private residences rather than city blocks. And, they guarded their own confidentiality as closely as that of their clients.

The elite security professionals came from a variety of backgrounds; they were commandos, ASIO agents or military officers. Many were martial arts experts. Lachlan knew that a growing number of these bodyguards were former policemen.

Falkstog Security Professionals employed its people on a freelance, project-by-project basis. It also called on computer programmers, electronics experts, locksmiths and lawyers. The lion's share of its assignments these days were for executive bodyguards - the fastest growing area of the industry.

Sounding irritated, Falkstog agreed to a brief meeting when his secretary buzzed through to say a Detective Sergeant Lachlan was waiting in the reception area. Falkstog was tall and athletic, with the finely honed, muscular physique of a much younger man. His sandy hair had receded and he had the sky blue eyes and porcelain smooth skin of a Swede. He ushered Lachlan into his study and listened, poker faced as Lachlan asked about the nature of his work for Henry Kaplan.

'I can't discuss private client business,' said Falkstog with a cool smile. 'I'm sure you understand that.'

'I appreciate your position on this. But you're not a doctor or a lawyer ...'

'That doesn't rule me out on having principles, detective.'

'Mr. Falkstog, this is a multiple homicide investigation. I believe the information you hold on your client is vital to that investigation. If you won't talk now I'll have police lawyers subpoena you and your files to appear in court.'

'What in blazes!'

'I'm sure you don't want certain aspects of your business dragged before the public.'

'This is outrageous.'

'I don't have time to be stonewalled like this.' Lachlan was tired, short on patience. His anger showed. 'There's a killer out there, and he's ready to kill again. I'll see you in court.'

Falkstog showed a weary indignity. He shrugged. 'I suppose I might as well talk to you now, detective, and save us both that sort of trouble. Let me assure you I have no desire to hinder an important investigation. At the same time I'm required to protect the safety and privacy of my clientele. How can I help?'

'Over twenty-five years ago, Henry Kaplan received a kidnap threat against his son. He employed the services of your company.'

'Yes. Some disgruntled employee tried to scare the shit out of him. The coppers nabbed the guy a few weeks later.'

'Since then your services have been retained by the Kaplan Corporation?'

'That's right. Security patrols for his business premises, cleansing his boardrooms of industrial bugs. That sort of thing.'

'Some years later, Kaplan also employed you on a private basis.'

A cloud crossed Falkstog's eyes. 'Yes. He was adamant it should remain a confidential matter. Not that anything illegal was involved. It was simply a matter of some embarrassment to him.'

'Embarrassment?'

'Private matter, Lachlan.'

'For Chrissakes, he paid you $150,000 a month, every month, for many years? For a private matter that was embarrassing to him?'

'Round the clock surveillance. Not as outrageous as you might think. These days there's more than a few wealthy people, usually a select group of chief executives, who have themselves or families or important staff members watched night and day. Visiting pop superstars and actors, even a few who don't really need it, do the same. It's been a growing trend, ever since John Lennon. And it's lucrative, incredibly so. Perhaps you should consider a change of career, detective?'

'So, for more than a decade your people carried out round the clock surveillance on Henry Kaplan?'

'No,' said Falkstog, his face impassive, eyes cold. 'I'm afraid you haven't got it quite right.'

Jennifer's phone call to Max Bryant was brief. She gave him the details of the Longer Life website. She no sooner replaced the receiver than the phone rang again.

'Jen, It's Roger.'

There was no mistaking the anxiety in his voice. 'Roger, I'm glad you called. I heard the news reports ...'

'Jen. Dad's a mess. I've never seen him like this. It's not just the mine disaster. Becker's pulled out, everything's collapsing. And this business with Winterstone and Brian. Dad's devastated. It seems Harold Masterton was involved. But Dad came charging into my office, blaming me for everything - so I left.'

'Oh, God.'

'When I calmed down I went back. Apparently he'd stormed off, smashing things, babbling. Went home. Can you meet me there?'

'Of course.'

'It's just that I know you'll be able to calm him down ...'

'Roger, I'm on my way.'

'What's going on?' Carly asked as Jennifer hung up the phone.

'Hold on.' Jennifer ran into the adjoining room. 'I've got to rush over to Henry Kaplan's place, constable,' she said to the policeman on watch. 'Family crisis. You'll make certain Carly's okay here?'

281

'Of course, Ms Parkes,' said the young man. 'But I'm under orders to watch you as well. I can't allow you to go off -'

'Detective Lachlan made it clear that I'm not a prisoner in my own home,' Jennifer cut across him with steely resolve. 'I need to go now. Urgently. Look, why don't you arrange for another unit to meet me at the Kaplan home in Vaucluse?'

'You're driving straight there?'

'Yes, constable. Straight there.'

'Hold on. Let me phone through and clear it with my superiors.'

He made the call on his cell and Jennifer stepped back into the corridor.

Carly trailed her mother to the front door. 'Be careful, Mum.'

'I will.'

'And Mum?'

Jennifer paused at the front door, giving Carly an enquiring glance.

'I'm sorry about ... before. Not trusting in you. About Dad. About lots of things.'

'It's in the past. Forget it, okay?'

'Okay. And Mum, shouldn't you be waiting for the all-clear about heading off.'

'I'm sure it will be fine.' And she was gone.

Carly turned as the constable, having completed his call, stepped into the corridor.

'Apparently Detective Senior Sergeant Lachlan's orders were strictly that your mother stay within watch at all times,' he said to Carly, looking toward the front door. They heard the sound of the car backing onto the street and then heading off.

'The detective should know my mother better than that by now,' Carly said. 'If I were you, constable, I'd see to it that a back-up unit meets her at the Kaplan place, wouldn't you?' The constable, frowning, hurriedly made another call. Carly grinned, and it occurred to her that she'd sounded exactly as her mother would've sounded in the same situation. Funnily enough, that didn't bother her at all.

For a moment she stood by the door, looking out, and said a private prayer for her mother. *Lord, keep her safe.*

She closed the door and went back into the living room to wait.

282

Hans Falkstog knew that if he turned Neil Lachlan away, the detective would be back within hours with a search warrant and a small army of back-up coppers. He couldn't expose his clandestine operation to a situation like that. So for the moment he had to treat Lachlan with kid gloves. Co-operate. Reveal more than he wanted to.

And then, when the coast was clear, he'd deal with the meddling policeman. At the rear of Falkstog's multi-level home was a special command room, built as an extension to the main house. He took Lachlan through to where banks of sophisticated electronic gadgetry were housed. It had been Falkstog's idea to do this, a ploy to maintain some control over this unexpected meeting. He'd already argued with Lachlan that he couldn't reveal the identity of the person he'd had watched for so many years - that, Falkstog insisted angrily, was a matter of professional discretion and client privilege.

'As I'm sure you're aware, security companies like mine are a growing industry. In fact, we represent a wide-reaching international civilian espionage network. Nothing illegal, you understand. Mostly gathering information, or protection. We offer a kind of secret service, if you like, to businessmen and others who can afford us. Not to mention government departments and even the federal police who have engaged my services from time to time.'

'All the more reason I'd expect your full co-operation in this matter,' said Lachlan.

Falkstog gave a wry smile. 'I'm just not convinced you're on the right track here, Detective.'

Falkstog employed two operators per shift in his control room - three shifts every twenty-four hours to monitor the equipment. A video system and an ultra-high frequency radio network transmitted pictures and sounds from various field agents with mobile gear. The material gathered was then stored on the hard drives.

Lachlan wasn't an expert on electronic surveillance - but he felt certain that some of the equipment in the room was highly classified military and police hardware - not for sale or use by civilians. That however, was a matter for later. And there would be a later. He intended to come back, with Ed Razell's endorsement, and raid Falkstog's premises. 'And this is how you carried out the monitoring?'

'Yes,' said Falkstog, his voice betraying a trace of pride. 'I had two operatives in the field, working in shifts around the clock. Usually they were stationed in a car or small van with video and audio monitoring equipment, always within reasonable striking distance of the subject. In addition, all operatives carry long range, night vision binoculars.

'Audio micro bugs were placed in the subject's car, his apartment, his office, his briefcase - and, of course, at the warehouse.'

Lachlan raised his eyebrows at the complexity and thoroughness of such surveillance. And yet, to men like Falkstog who ran such businesses, this was routine. 'All these years you knew this man was a vicious serial killer, yet you sat on the information -' The sudden anger in his voice couldn't be mistaken.

'Absolutely not!' Falkstog interjected with equal anger. 'I already explained on the way down, Detective Lachlan, that neither my agents nor myself had any reason to believe this man might have been a killer. I was told, and I believed, he had a psychological condition, that he could be dangerous to himself or to others, so he needed to be watched for that reason. And you have not produced any physical evidence to the contrary. If there was any proof ...'

Falkstog was unaware that Lachlan knew of the many killings that had been prevented by Falkstog's men.

Lachlan didn't want to reveal any more or provoke Falkstog any further. The element of surprise was his best option now – to return within the hour with a warrant to seize Falkstog's records.

Falkstog himself, Lachlan decided, would keep until later.

For now, he needed to quickly connect Falkstog's surveillance with the findings at the Winterstone warehouse - and link them definitively with the man he was now certain was the garrotte murderer.

After Lachlan had left, Hans Falkstog picked up his phone and called the number he thought of as the hot line. It was a long time since he'd used this number, a long time since he'd spoken to the man on the other end of the line.

Falkstog said, as the call was answered, 'I have a code one, repeat code one situation here.' He explained, quickly and briefly, about the visit from Lachlan, and about the information Lachlan possessed. 'I had to play along for the moment, but this detective will blow the whistle, within hours I'd say. He must be eliminated - *fast*.'

The man on the other end of the line, Commander (retired) Malcolm Addison, formerly of military intelligence, sat in his Canberra office, a 40-minute flight away in the nation's capital. 'We can't do that,' he said.

'Did you hear me right -' Falkstog began.

'Lachlan is the senior man on this garrotte killer case,' Addison cut across him. 'There's massive government, police and media focus on that case. It's simply too dangerous, too sensitive an issue to take Lachlan out.'

'Then what can -?'

'Listen to me,' said Addison, 'listen very carefully.'

THIRTY THREE

'Phones haven't stopped ringing,' Ron Aroney said as Lachlan entered the Special Unit room. 'Razell's phoned back three times wanting to know what we found at the warehouse, and whether we'd had McConnell in here yet.'

'I'll call Razell in a minute. McConnell?'

'I sent a car for him but there's no sign of him at his flat or at that newspaper office. Perhaps it doesn't matter. Max had better luck checking on that name from those letters, Rentin, and your hunch was right.'

'Where is she now?' Lachlan directed this to Max Bryant.

'Died eighteen years ago. Body released to her son for a private burial. But there are no records of any such burial.'

'So, that's how it began,' said Lachlan.

'There's more. I just got off the line from the contact number on that Longer Life website. A guy named William Potter answered, got him up in the middle of the night. He wasn't too pleased when he found out it was police in Australia.' Bryant handed Lachlan the printouts from the website. 'Fascinating stuff. All the guff on this cryonics, and on the Longer Life company.'

Lachlan flicked briefly through the pages. Lifelines Inc had been started twenty-two years before by a Californian millionaire industrialist named John Gallagher. He'd become interested in cryonics but didn't want to sign up with any of the existing cryonics societies of the time. Gallagher liked to do things his own way so he'd started his own organisation. His was a commercial enterprise, signing up clients as well as building and selling the necessary equipment to others.

He had since died and been frozen. His son, Stephen Gallagher oversaw the organisation, and a retired colleague, William Potter, ran the company as a part time interest. It was the younger Gallagher and Potter who'd relocated the company and changed its name.

'Potter was eager to help, though, when I told him we suspected a killer of using the cryonics gear,' Bryant continued, 'he told me one of their men, Clyde Fritzwater, came to Sydney for two days in the mid-Nineties as part of the sale arrangement with Winterstone.'

'Why?'

'To instruct Harold Masterton on how to operate the equipment and prepare bodies for freezing. One-on-one training, including how to make the surgically precise incisions needed. Apparently it's possible for one person to carry out the procedures alone, though certainly not ideal.'

'So Masterton bought the equipment,' said Lachlan, puzzled.

'Hold on. I got Fritzwater out of bed too. He confirmed that he made the trip. But even back then, Harold Masterton would've been a lot older than the man Fritzwater described having met. And there's been no further contact in the years since between Longer Life and the man who made the purchase, the man he believed was named Masterton.'

'A younger man? That ties in with what I suspect from the Falkstog surveillance.' Lachlan picked up the phone. 'No sign of any problems at the Parkes home?'

'All quiet,' Bryant said.

Lachlan wanted to make certain, and to bring Jennifer up to date. He called her landline number. 'What's the name of the guy currently posted there?'

'Baltin,' said Aroney.

Carly answered. 'I'm fine, Sergeant Lachlan,' she replied to his initial question, 'and your Constable Baltin is right here. Do you think it would be all right if he took me to the hospital? Meg called and she needs the support right now. Samantha's still critical.'

'Not right now. Could you put your mother on?'

'She had to go over to Henry Kaplan's place. Roger called. Some kind of emergency. The constable's arranged for a man to meet her there.'

Lachlan drew a sharp breath. 'Listen to me carefully, Carly.' The sudden steel in his voice alarmed her. 'You're to stay right where you are. Tell Baltin that no-one - friends or otherwise - are to be allowed in. *No-one*. Understand?'

'Yes.' Her voice was a whisper.

Lachlan slammed the phone down unintentionally. 'Come on,' he called to Aroney as he ran for the door. He stopped for an instant at the front desk of the section dispatcher. 'Put out an APB. All available cars, in the vicinity, to the Kaplan house, Vaucluse. Radio through the address. Pronto.'

Roger opened the front door as Jennifer stepped from her car and ran up the front steps. 'Jen. Thank Christ. Thanks for coming.'

'Don't be silly. Of course I'd come. Where's Henry?'

'Upstairs, in the old rumpus room.'

'What happened?'

'Hard to say. I don't think it's a breakdown, otherwise I'd have called the medics. He just seemed to go off the deep end.'

'God knows the two of you didn't need this bombing on top of everything else.'

'Or that miserable article by Rory McConnell.'

'I could strangle him for that.' Jennifer clenched her fists at the thought of how they'd all been duped.

'Dad's calmed down a bit now. But I'm worried –'

'Let me go in alone and sit with him. He's got to be made to see this isn't the end of everything. I thought that once, after I lost Brian.' She headed up the stairs.

'Third door on the left,' Roger said.

'I remember.'

She slipped quietly into the room and looked about, puzzled. The room was empty. The wide, glass balcony doors were closed, the drapes pulled across, leaving only a soft half-light. Then she heard the door close behind her and the click of the lock.

Across town, Masterton was cleaning out his desk when Kaplan entered.

'I'm sorry I snapped at you before,' Kaplan said. He slumped down in the chair facing the desk.

Masterton saw a worn-out shell of the man he'd known for so long. His energy drained, Kaplan appeared drawn and shrunken. 'I understand. Father and son stuff. It's not like I haven't had a front row seat to it all these years.'

'I need a favour.' Kaplan said. There was a tone of resignation in his voice.

'Name it.' Masterton observed Kaplan's hands closely. They were shaking. In over three decades he'd never seen Henry even close to shaking with nerves.

'I'm in no state to drive right now, Harold. But I need to get across town to police HQ. To see that detective. Lachlan.'

'Why don't you just phone him?"

'This needs to be in person.'

'No problem. I'll drive you,' Masterton said. 'What's this all about Henry?'

'Something I should've done a long time ago.'

Masterton waited for an explanation. When there wasn't one, he asked, 'What?'

'I can't talk about it right now, Harold. Maybe later. But I need to see Lachlan now.'

They were half way out the door when the phone rang.

Roger pocketed the key to the rumpus room and retreated along the corridor to his father's bedroom. He picked up the phone beside the bed and punched in the number. 'Henry Kaplan, please. It's his son. Urgent.' He waited. 'Dad?'

'What?'

The reply was angry, confused. Good, thought Roger. 'I'm at your place. Jennifer's here.'

'What's going on, Roger?'

289

'She's agitated, losing control. Knows about your involvement with Brian and Winterstone.'

'What the hell-'

'No time to explain further. I've called the cops. Can you get here?' He hung up without waiting for an answer.

While he'd been talking, Roger hadn't heard the crunch of tyres on gravel outside, or the footsteps moments later on the front steps.

'Change of plan,' Kaplan said to Masterton. 'I've got to rush home.' He headed for the doorway.

'Was that Roger?' Masterton asked.

'Yes.'

'For God's sake, Henry, *what* is going on?'

'Can't talk now.'

'You're in no state to drive, you said that yourself.'

'I'll be okay.'

Masterton took chase, following Kaplan to the lifts. 'I'm driving you, Henry,' he said.

Jennifer went to the balcony doors and peered through a parting in the drapes. Splinters of sunlight sparkled against the framework of bark and leaf that surrounded the house. The doors were locked. What was Roger doing? Was Henry even here? A cold uneasiness traced ghostly fingers up her spine.

She heard the click of the lock again and turned. Roger stood in the doorway. He closed the door behind him.

'Roger ..?' The loop of wire in his hands sent an electric jolt of realisation through her. The implication was obvious. Samantha, attacked by the garrotte killer. Once again she heard Neil Lachlan's words, someone close enough to your family to know you'd hired Stuart James. But Roger? For a sickening moment she thought her bladder would betray her.

'It has to be this way, Jennifer.' His voice was calm, impersonal.

'What's this all about, Roger?' She struggled to sound forceful. In control.

He began to tingle all over, bursting with the urge to kill. He hadn't expected to feel this way. Not with someone he knew so well. Not with Jennifer. Yet the sensation was there, deeper and stronger than ever. Is it because of my newfound freedom? he wondered.

This was the other, hidden side to him, freed now to become the dominant part.

My new life. It doesn't matter whether I know the victim or not.

'My father's on his way, but I can't take the chance that you'll warn him in some way.' He inched forward, beads of perspiration glinting on his forehead.

Terror gripped her like a physical thing, vice-like, crushing the breath from her lungs. 'Warn him? Roger ... stop this.'

All at once he lunged at her, cat-like, eyes alive with a darkness she hadn't seen before. She reacted quickly, leaping back, arms raised protectively - but he lunged again, snapping the wire coil into place around her neck and stepping to the side, twisting the wire as he did.

'Dear God -' The words were ripped from her as the wire closed on her larynx, hard and cold against her flesh.

He positioned himself behind her, maintaining the rock solid hold on the wire. From this position it was easy to apply the final pressure while keeping the victim completely restrained.

He felt her body go rigid, every muscle and nerve-end tight with tension, trying to pull against him. Her hands had flown up to her throat, her fingers prying at the wire. It was a gesture he knew well.

So natural. So utterly useless.

He forced her onto her knees, his own knee pushing into the small of her back. She was fighting for breath now. Desperate. He allowed the tautness of the loop to slacken a little, giving her just enough breath. He had time enough to play and he wanted to experiment, draw it out. And talk. He wanted to boast - and to explain. After all, this was no stranger. Jennifer Parkes was part of the history of all that had happened.

Someone who would understand, as she died.

Jennifer gulped tiny mouthfuls of air. Not enough. 'Roger ... please, no ...' Her voice was a croak, her vision blurring fast.

'You shouldn't have interfered,' Roger told her. 'I can't take the chance of others learning about Brian's audit.' His breath was heavy, hot against her ear. 'No-one would have been any the wiser if you hadn't hired that detective.'

'The constable at my place ... knows you called me ...' The words squeezed between her clenched teeth. 'They'll ... know ...'

'They won't even suspect,' Roger said triumphantly. 'There's a nice little explosive device in that case on the table. Same as the one that tore into the mine. When I'm finished here I'll watch from outside for my father to arrive, then I'll detonate. The police will think you both died at the hands of the Asbestos Victims Organisation. A ratbag group that doesn't even exist. And I'll have eliminated two birds with one stone.'

The noose tightened again. 'You ... did that?'

'Yes. Eventually they'll figure there's no AVO, but I've allowed for every eventuality. I made an anonymous call to that deputy commissioner, pointed him in the direction of Rory McConnell. That article of his came in very handy, it will help to make him look guilty.'

'Why ..?' Despite the pain and the struggle for breath, Jennifer's mind grasped for a plan. Keep him talking. He wants to talk.

'I had to stop the sale. Without his precious corporation cash flow Dad couldn't keep hiring the men who stopped me.'

'I don't ... understand.' She was taking short, regular breaths, reminding herself mentally to stay calm at all costs. Her vision had improved.

Don't move, don't panic him. He has to think I'm totally at his mercy and he has to keep talking.

'Time's up. I think you understand enough. And this makes perfect poetic sense, doesn't it? First the mine, then the house of the man who owns the mine, while you just happened to be here.' His voice had taken on a strange, dream-like quality.

'Roger. We're ... friends.'

'You shouldn't have tried to take control, the way you always do. Like Brian. I thought a friend like him would keep his mouth shut about the secret money transferred into Winterstone. That's why I hired him. But oh, no, not Brian.' A short, incredulous laugh escaped his lips. 'He wanted me to go to Dad, come clean about stealing the funds.'

'Oh ... God. You ...'

'No. Not like this. I ran him down.' All of a sudden he jerked her head back and tightened the wire. 'But that's enough. Perhaps you shouldn't have resisted my advances years ago, Jennifer. Things might have been different.' He pulled tighter and tighter.

This was more intoxicating than any other "kill". He had a searing heat in his loins, a lightheadedness, and he realised there would be time not just to garrotte Jennifer slowly but to rape her, disfigure that beautiful face with the edge of the wire - a greater power, a more all-encompassing control than he'd ever exercised before.

He could get better and better at this.

He realized now that erasing Jennifer Parkes was the final step in leaving his old life behind, and beginning the new.

And he could tell Jennifer, as she died, more about the detail of his killings. In particular his murder of Brian; how much he'd enjoyed the monthly ritual of maintaining the cylinders, housing the bodies and the containers that stored their blood; how he'd open the lids and look at the bodies, laughing and hugging himself as he thought of her anguish and the others who never knew what had become of their loved ones.

He loosened the wire again, allowing tiny breaths of air into Jennifer's exploding lungs. Not nearly enough, just an amount to tease. He put his mouth to her ear, whispering harshly, 'Let me tell you all about my game, Jen. Once I knew we were going to lose the warehouse, along with everything else, I knew I'd have to get rid of my frozen trophies. So I put the bodies back where they'd last been seen, knowing full well it would baffle the police - and annoy the hell out of the bastards who watched me all those years.'

Then he pulled the wire tight again, without warning. He would tell her his story bit by bit as he drew out the agony of her death. The trick would be keeping her at death's door long enough before she was gone forever.

Sheer panic coursed through Jennifer. The air that had found its way into her lungs was gone in just a few seconds. She couldn't breathe at all now. The wire had cut the surface of her flesh and she felt a thin line of blood pulse from the incision. Her fingers groped hopelessly around the outer rim of the wire, unable to find even the tiniest space for leverage.

Her vision disintegrated into formless shapes and darkness descended. It was as though the moon was shifting across the sun, for a total eclipse.

THIRTY FOUR

The squad car sped through the streets of Sydney's eastern suburbs, heading for the elite, tree-lined avenues and stately homes that backed onto Sydney Harbour.

Lachlan glanced distractedly at his watch. Aroney talked as he drove.

'Damn good hunch, Neil. Working out that M. Rentin was the maiden name of Henry Kaplan's first wife, Monica. You reckon the son froze her too - after she died? In one of those cryo chambers?'

'Yeah. But he obviously didn't think of her as dead. He probably really thought she could be brought back one day.' Although Falkstog had refused to reveal the name, Lachlan was certain Henry Kaplan's paid-for surveillance had been on his son, Roger. He'd explained this to Aroney. And he was now just as certain that Roger's call to Jennifer was part of a new attempt to kill her.

'So he wrote all those letters to his deceased mother, telling her what a wonderful little murderer he'd turned out to be. Kept her and the letters right there with his frozen body collection. A total whack job.' Aroney shook his head.

'The worst kind,' Lachlan said, 'because he wears two faces. He could go to work, run companies, socialise easily with the wife of a man he'd run down because that man was probing too much. As though the dark side of him was someone else altogether.'

Aroney braked hard, blasting his horn at a cab, which changed lanes suddenly in front of him. Lachlan swore.

'And the father knew?' Aroney continued.

'Oh yeah ... he knew all right. He hired Falkstog Security to run a round the clock team of watchdogs to stop his son from indulging his taste for killing people. Then, when Roger started putting the bodies back, Henry Kaplan found a way to blackmail John Rosen, forced him to cover up the obvious link between the bodies. Henry Kaplan is responsible for a lot of things, just one of them being John's untimely death.'

Aroney nodded, acknowledging the bitter edge to Lachlan's voice. 'So ... why d'you reckon Roger would take the bodies out of the deep freeze now and put 'em back on the streets?'

'Watch it,' Lachlan snapped, lurching forward against his seatbelt as Aroney braked again.

'Bloody bike couriers. Think they own the friggin' road.' Unperturbed, Aroney hit the horn, accelerating roughly into the right-hand lane. He switched on the car's siren.

Lachlan reached forward for the radio mike, the uncomfortable sweatiness of his palms having nothing to do with the near-miss. The trip was taking too damn long. Making contact, he demanded the position of the squad cars headed to the Kaplan house. The slap of his fist against his thigh was an expression of frustration that even Aroney could not miss.

'Tell them to pull their fingers out. We're trying to prevent another possible homicide here!'

He slammed the mike back into its cradle.

Aroney stole a glance across at him. 'You okay?'

'Seems all cars, including the one Constable Baltin requested, were called to another APB just before mine. A domestic in Bondi has turned into a siege.' Lachlan seemed to visibly straighten himself out. 'What was it you were saying?'

'Wonderin' why, after eighteen years with his trophies in deep freeze, Roger Kaplan suddenly started shoving bodies back onto the streets.'

'The same reason he could start killing again after eighteen years. The money was gone. Frozen by liquidators. That was before the appeal and the potential sale of the northern mine. Henry Kaplan couldn't keep paying for the surveillance, not until he became solvent again. Roger knew he couldn't keep running the cryonics equipment or hold onto the warehouse.'

'So he started dismantling the whole thing,' Aroney surmised. 'Pumped the blood back into the bodies, unfroze and redressed them and put them back, knowing everyone would be thrown by the age discrepancy.'

'Better than leaving them in the basement,' Lachlan pointed out. 'Decomposition would have set in. The smell would have attracted attention eventually and he didn't know how long he could keep the place off limits before the receivers put it up for auction. My guess is, he was running out of time and couldn't figure out how to dump all the hardware down there. So he sealed it. But he dropped the umbrella when he was moving Brian Parkes.'

The car slowed. 'Blasted traffic.'' Aroney scowled. Despite the siren's wail, the jam ahead left no spaces for the cars to move aside. 'Bugger this.' He spun the wheel and jerked the car onto the median strip, bypassed the cars in front of them, then manoeuvred the vehicle back to the correct side again, weaving through the traffic with skilled precision and at high speed. 'And Jennifer Parkes still thinks that psycho's her friend?'

Lachlan winced at the thought and his heart pounded harder. What had Roger Kaplan said to Jennifer to entice her over to his father's estate? What if they were already too late?

Helen Shawcross fumbled with the key, realised as she did that the front door was unlocked, then pushed it open and dragged the suitcase over the threshold. What a fool she'd been, throwing herself at Rory like that.

She heard a voice, somewhere on the floor above. Was Henry at home? His car wasn't in the driveway and she hadn't recognised any of the cars in the street. Who then? Someone with a key. Roger?

She bounded up the stairs, heard the voice clearer now - yes, Roger's voice - coming from the rumpus room at the far end of the hall. What was he doing here? Henry must be with him, she thought.

Oh, God. Mustn't let him see the suitcase.

First, though, she needed to find out what was going on. She walked along the hall and burst into the room.

And stopped, her mouth dropping open, her breath caught in her throat.

Lachlan glanced frantically at his watch. It was taking forever to get to Henry Kaplan's home.

As they wove in and out of the traffic, Aroney filled Lachlan in on more of Max Bryant's conversation with Bill Fritzwater. Bryant had learned that Roger Kaplan's initial order had been for twelve cryonic chambers. No doubt Roger had ordered these so he could commence freezing and storing his victims. He would've ordered more as he needed them, as he was able to arrange the money. But he hadn't finished filling the original twelve before the long surveillance began.

But Lachlan and Aroney had found only eleven canisters in the Winterstone warehouse. Lachlan recalled that there'd been one empty space at the end of the row. He now had no doubt that had been the resting place of Roger's mother.

So where was it now - the twelfth canister with the frozen body of Monica Kaplan?

The moment he saw Helen in the doorway, Roger's fevered brain switched into crisis mode. He couldn't - *wouldn't* - allow his plan to be ruined now - not by one unexpected circumstance.

He cast Jennifer aside like a rag doll, reluctantly releasing the wire from her neck. He could tell she'd lapsed into semi-consciousness. He'd finish her off in a moment. He sprang to his feet, every nerve primed for action, his eyes blazing with single-minded purpose.

Snapping out of her split-second of shock, Helen's instinct for self-preservation took over rapidly. She spun on her heel and ran full pelt back along the hallway.

Roger darted after her. He reached her at the top of the stairs, looping the wire around her throat with both hands. Helen screamed and struggled wildly. Twisting in his grip, she brought her knee up hard, partly connecting with Roger's groin. He cursed in agony, losing his balance and toppling back, the wire loop falling from his grasp.

Helen flew down the stairs, but Roger, blocking out the pain and quickly regaining his balance, snatched the wire from the floor and hurled himself bodily down the stairwell. He smashed into Helen from above, sending her crashing to the floor at the foot of the stairs, sprawling across her. The wire fell from his grasp again.

He launched himself onto his knees, his arms springing out, his hands locking onto Helen's throat.

'Get off me you bastard!' Her scream was cut off as his fingers pushed down heavily into the flesh of her neck, blocking her air, crushing her larynx. She twisted her body about, trying to gain some leverage, but he was too heavy for her.

'Stupid bloody bitch!' he yelled. The anger inside him was volcanic. The deep, dark thrill had never been greater, soaring through him at fever pitch, bursting for release. He jerked her head violently, banging it several times against the floor with every ounce of energy he possessed. The sickening crack of her skull smashing against the polished marble caused his sexual excitement to explode, the juices flowing freely from him.

Then he applied the final pressure to her throat, his fingers so deep now he could feel the supple pulping of her organs. Her body went limp beneath him.

'Helen's here as well,' Kaplan exclaimed, clearly surprised, as they pulled into the driveway. Her car was at the far end, near the house. 'I expected her to be out most of the day.' He leapt from the car.

Masterton reached across, gripped Kaplan's arm. 'Let's not go racing in. A dramatic entrance may not help.'

Kaplan considered this momentarily. 'The voice of reason.'

'Yes, I am.'

'Very well. We'll do it your way.'

Jennifer lay on her belly, sucking in draughts of air. Every breath was an effort as it strained for passage through her heavily bruised throat. Blood welled from the incision and ran in tiny rivers to the carpet.

She felt disorientated; her vision still cloudy, but with each long breath the fog lifted from her brain and her inner resolve fought its way back up. The need to survive was like a living thing, marching up her spine.

She heard his footsteps above the thumping of her heart before he appeared in the doorway. Her hair had fallen across her eyes and, forcing herself to keep them open slightly, she saw he was like a man possessed - a demon. Nothing like the Roger she thought she'd known. And ...

Oh, dear Jesus ... please God, help me.

The murderous, bloodied length of wire was still in his hand.

I've got to fight him. Somehow.

She lay still and deathly silent.

If he thinks I've died ...

He prodded his foot hard into her side. Testing. The pain was like a red-hot knife ripping through her, but she bit down hard on her lip and remained still. Roger, uncertain, used his foot to roll her over.

Jennifer squeezed her eyes closed. She had never felt so vulnerable and an icy fear stabbed even deeper, to the core of her heart. She didn't think her ruse was going to work.

At that moment she heard a car pulling up, doors opening, footsteps on the driveway.

Roger moved quickly to the balcony doors. 'Damn it.' His father was entering the house with Masterton. He turned and fled from the room.

There was still time for his plan to succeed. Jennifer lay limp on the floor. Whether she was dead or unconscious didn't matter now - if she woke there'd be no chance to warn his father. Roger raced down the stairs and out the rear exit. He pulled the hand-held detonator device from his pocket as he ran.

Jennifer heard Roger run from the room. She opened her eyes warily, looked around, breathed a sigh of relief and pushed herself to her knees. What had disturbed him? Henry? She heard the front door open.

The bomb.

She had little energy in her arms or her legs. She summoned up every last reserve of strength, breathing deeply and rapidly like a drowning woman brought back once more to the surface.

Kaplan and Masterton reached the foot of the stairwell where they were confronted with Helen's body. She lay face down in a pool of blood.

Kaplan knelt, his hand reached feebly for her head. He didn't need to feel for a pulse to know she was dead. He felt nothing but a curious sense of detachment, as if this was someone else's house, someone else's girlfriend. *Someone else's son.*

He averted his eyes from the corpse, looked around. 'Jennifer ...' he croaked. He started towards the stairs.

Outside, Roger ripped the plastic casing from the device, freeing the plunger, and placed his thumb over it, at the ready. He would allow sixty seconds for his father to reach the room on the first floor and then he would activate the bomb.

His mission was almost complete. He no longer felt that he should worry about the copper, Lachlan. Let the investigation continue and the connection with Winterstone be made. Over the years he had placed enough circumstantial evidence to point the finger at Harold Masterton. It was a bonus that Masterton had arrived with his father.

He moved past the pool and the paved barbecue area, across the landscaped gardens, to the rear of the property. A slope led to the embankment along the harbour shore. Now he was far enough away for safety's sake.

Jennifer grabbed the briefcase and moved as fast as she could, wobbly but determined, into the hall and across to the bedroom opposite. She tried to open the window but couldn't lift the frame.

Damn.

Taking hold of the stool beside the vanity unit she hurled it at the glass. The window smashed and Jennifer lunged forward, throwing the case out with a sudden final burst of energy.

She turned and ran back across the hall.

Roger checked his watch. Now, he thought. He raised the detonator in his hand and looked towards the house.

Jennifer had reached the doorway to the rumpus room when the world went mad.

The briefcase was two metres from the window and falling, another four metres below the level of the first floor when Roger Kaplan's thumb pressed down firmly on the plunger. As he did so he averted his gaze, catching just a glimpse of the blinding white light that otherwise would have filled every corner of his vision. The force of the blast blew him off his feet and ripped the device from his grasp, sending it spinning through the air.

The explosion could be heard, a deafening crack to some, a low boom further afield, up to a radius of fifty kilometres.

A hole, ten metres in diameter, was torn into the rear wall of the Kaplan mansion. The wind from the explosion caused fractures to appear in every wall, floor and most items of furniture.

Jennifer was thrown violently across the room and onto the floor. Her ears rang with the roar. Her cheekbone cracked as she hit the floor and blood burst from the torn skin of the wound.

Fractures rippled through the floorboards, spitting carpet and handfuls of timber, concrete and dust into the air.

Jennifer placed her palms down flat on the floor, tried to push herself to her knees, but she had no strength left in her arms and jolts of pain stabbed all over, like hot knives. Her head dropped, her breath coming in short, sharp gasps as she fought against the darkness.

Kaplan and Masterton were hurled across the room beneath a flying wall of debris. Kaplan was sure he screamed yet he heard no sound, other than a deafening boom, which rang and rang and rang in his ears, an endless echo. The air around him filled with swirls of dust, churning like storm clouds, and a steady shower of masonry and slivers of brick drizzled across the room.

Nothing looked familiar. The house had become a shambles, every nook and cranny transformed into something twisted and grotesque.

Pain pulsed from everywhere. Kaplan was aware of enormous pressure on his chest, and he moved his arm to the area of pain. Looking down and across his body, he saw he was drenched in blood. He'd never seen so much blood.

'Oh ... God.' He groped about, squinting through the grey cloud. 'Harold!'

Masterton appeared beside him, dishevelled, bloodied. He hooked his arm around Kaplan and painfully dragged him towards the door. 'We've got to get out, Henry.'

'Harold ... what has he done? What - has my son done - to us?'

THIRTY FIVE

Moments before, the police car had screamed to a halt on the street outside. Lachlan and Aroney looked at the cars in the driveway and exchanged glances. 'Henry Kaplan's here,' Lachlan said, 'but who else?' He didn't know Helen's car. They were about to open their doors when the roar of the explosion filled their heads. The car rocked.

They looked to the house. Every window had blown out, sending a stream of shattered glass over the front lawn. The front door had been ripped from its hinges.

'For Christ's sake,' shouted Aroney, 'he's bombed the bloody place.'

Lachlan darted from the car and raced into the house, Aroney on his tail. They entered a virtual war zone. A burning, acrid smell, dust as thick as a winter fog, furniture twisted into tortured shapes and scattered piles of metal and brick. One dead body. Masterton scrambling for the door, supporting a badly hurt Kaplan.

Sirens wailed from the street outside. The first of the squad cars belatedly reacting to the all-points bulletin.

'Where's Jennifer?' Lachlan stopped in front of Kaplan and Masterton. The once powerful tycoon was a mere shell now. He stared up at Lachlan with a broken expression that said I don't know.

Lachlan stepped past them, mounted the stairs. The banister, still holding until then, shifted with his weight. Part of it began to crumble. He moved cautiously along the first floor hallway, aware of the danger of falling debris. He coughed. The dust was thick so he took his handkerchief from his pocket to cover his mouth. He glanced into each of the rooms as he passed.

'Neil!' Aroney's voice came from below. 'We've got to get out. Gas fumes, coming from the kitchen. She's gonna blow again.'

'Sweet Jesus,' Lachlan muttered under his breath. Where was she? He reached the doorway to the rumpus room, saw Jennifer sprawled on the floor. A trail of blood circled her.

He felt for her pulse. Found it. 'Thank God.' He lifted her over his shoulder and retraced his steps quickly. As he passed through the remains of the ground floor living room, a gaseous aroma filled his nostrils. He fought back nausea.

Aroney had helped Kaplan and Masterton across the lawn and was heading back down the driveway when he saw Lachlan. 'Hurry,' he called frantically.

Lachlan stumbled through the doorway. He was almost to the driveway's end when the second explosion rocked the grounds. He lost his footing. Jennifer slid from his shoulders and crashed to the lawn.

The blast blew a small hole in the front wall of the house. The escaped gas inside had ignited with sparks from the electrical wires. It sent another wave of red-hot flame through the house, shooting from the windows and all the cracks.

Jennifer opened her eyes, raised her head to see Lachlan, kneeling beside her. He clasped the palm of her hand in his.

'You okay?'

'Okay,' she rasped. Her hands flew to her neck, her fingers gently trailing the ugly red welt. 'We've got to go after Roger.'

'Where is he?'

She banked her head towards the house. 'Must've taken…the rear. He had …' She stopped briefly, gulped in a lungful of air. '…a remote device for the bomb.'

More sirens. Several cars screeched to a stop along the street. The footpaths were lined with residents, all gaping in astonishment at the wreckage of the Kaplan home.

Lachlan sprang to his feet. Three police officers ran towards him.

'You all right, sir?' one asked.

'Fine. Is an ambulance on the way?'

'Yes, sir.'

He pointed to one of the men. 'Stay with Ms. Parkes.' He cocked his head towards the other two. 'Come with me. The bomber is at the rear of the property.'

'Be careful,' Jennifer called after them, but her voice was barely a croak. No-one heard her.

The young officer's hand came to rest on her shoulder. 'Take it easy, Miss. The medics will be here in a moment.'

Jennifer's thoughts, however, were on Neil Lachlan. She watched him race around the side of the shattered building and said a quiet prayer: *Please, God, don't let anything happen to him.* And in the fantasy realm of her mind's eye, she dropped a five-cent coin into the old wishing pool.

After the first explosion, Roger scrambled to his feet. The rear of the property didn't have the extent of damage he'd expected. He feared that Jennifer and his father might not have been killed in the blast. He had to be sure.

If I can get back in, I'll finish them off before the emergency services arrive.

He sprinted across the garden and up the steps of the wide round patio. Chunks of timber and metal and glass lay everywhere. He heard Neil Lachlan's voice from inside.

'Where's Jennifer?'

Damn him to hell, thought Roger. What was he doing here so soon? The explosion had only just occurred. Was he psychic? Whimpering sounds came from Roger's father.

He turned and ran full pelt back across the property, down the slippery embankment to the water's edge. He ran along the shoreline, under cover of the thick brush and overhanging trees. There was practically no beach here, just a thin stretch of sand littered with seaweed and stones.

He heard the second explosion.

The flag of freedom had, until now, been flying high in his expectations. An undiscovered country. Freedom from his father. Freedom from the watchers. Freedom to kill.

Sirens wailed from the street. Now, instead, he'd been discovered; his plans foiled. Now he was the hunted.

He reached a grassy knoll. It stood at the point where the houses stopped and a bend in the shoreline created a natural reserve. He paused to catch his breath.

All's not lost, he told himself. He simply had to alter his plans. The money was still there, untraceable. Underworld contacts such as Hargreaves, who'd helped him in the past, could assist him in escaping to a new life.

'It's over, Roger.'

Roger's head whipped about. Lachlan was approaching, several metres back along the strip of land. Two other police officers were coming up behind him.

Roger felt an overwhelming desire to squeeze the life from Lachlan. The meddling copper had been a thorn in his side for over a week now, always arriving on the scene at the wrong time. Was there something between him and Jennifer? That might explain it.

Roger threw his hands in the air, a gesture of defeat. 'Okay, okay.' He began marching, shoulders slumped, back towards them. 'I don't have a weapon,' he called out.

When he made his move it was sudden and swift. He shifted direction with a violent twist of his limbs, propelling himself into the water at a run, diving when he felt the sand give way to greater depth.

'Stop!' Lachlan's reflexes were equally quick. He drew his gun but immediately saw it was pointless. He cast it aside and ran into the water, feeling the sudden steep slope away from the shallows. He dived.

Roger was a strong swimmer. He hurtled through the water. He didn't intend to outswim Lachlan - that wouldn't work. What he did intend was to swim to a point where the current changed, then across, coming back into a stretch of shore on the other side of the point.

But he didn't want Lachlan on his tail the whole way. He was a dozen metres out when he stopped. He yanked the loop of wire from his trouser pocket, and then dived again. He opened his eyes. The salt stung them and the light was dim. The shadow cast by Lachlan's form cut a swathe along the surface. Approaching rapidly.

Roger swam in a sideways pattern, attempting to position himself beside or behind the advancing swimmer. His lungs screamed out for air but he figured he could last a few seconds more. If he broke the surface directly behind Lachlan, applying the garotte instantly, then he knew he'd win. He'd force the copper down and his victim would be in the weaker position, grappling to maintain equilibrium in these depths. The survivor would be the one with the most air in his lungs.

Lachlan reached a spot roughly above his prey. Roger was slightly to his opponent's left now, just a half a metre below him. His lungs were about to burst but the adrenalin surge kept him going. His vision was a blur of shadows and shapes, dark and shifting, silhouetted by a thousand points of shimmering green light.

Now.

He pushed himself to the surface, thrusting the loop of wire blindly towards Lachlan. His aim was off, missing by a hand's space. Lachlan banked to the side, whipping his head about to face Roger, but the killer had slipped beneath the surface again, his body brushing against Lachlan's legs. He surfaced again almost immediately, to Lachlan's rear once more, and this time the wire snapped into position around his quarry's throat.

Despite the sharp bite of the wire, Lachlan arched his body into a backwards flip and pivotted. Kicking his legs up, he placed them in a scissor grip around Roger's neck and pulled him forward. Surprised, Roger's grip on the wire faltered and was lost. It fell away into the depths.

Roger allowed himself to fall forward and sink into the ocean under the force of Lachlan's pull. Then he jerked his body free and propelled himself away. He had no choices left. He had to beat Lachlan to the shore at the far side of the point.

He could hear his pursuer thrashing through the water behind him. Roger dived, kicking furiously. Perhaps he could outdistance the copper if he swam underwater for long stretches at a time.

He saw long stems of reed and fern rise like tentacles from the ocean floor, tangling with chunks of seaweed. A school of fish, bright vibrant colours, darted away as he approached. He looked back. Lachlan had also submerged and was gaining on him.

308

An incredible tiredness gripped Roger. His arms and legs felt as though they were weighed down. He expected that Lachlan was feeling the same but he knew the copper wouldn't give up the chase. He'd follow until they both drowned.

Stupid, arrogant copper.

I'll have to go back with him.

As the reality hit him, that he'd finally lost to Lachlan - game, set and match, Roger registered surprise at reconciling himself to the fact. He felt almost calm. Philosophical. He needed air so he stopped swimming and pushed upwards. His body began to rise but then, a sudden jerk, and he stopped. Something was tugging at his left foot. He looked down and could see nothing but ferns and flowers and the tentacles of a thousand colours, billowing in the shadows.

He tried to pull his foot free but it wouldn't budge. Lachlan was beside him now. Roger looked into the pinched, distorted face of his nemesis, eyes open just a slit and smarting against the sting of the saltwater. Their eyes made contact.

Lachlan recognized the terror in Roger's face. The language in the killer's gaze cried out for help.

Both men bent down, searching for the source of the problem. Roger's hands grappled furiously at the trapped foot. A thick, fibrous stem of a sea plant had coiled itself tightly around his ankle. The coils, looped like a tight fish, allowed no slack.

Lachlan's lungs were aflame. He rose quickly to the surface and sighed with relief as air filled him and noted that they were approximately a hundred metres from the shoreline. The two police officers were in the shallows, waiting and watching for a sign. Lachlan waved frantically, gesturing for them to come in. Perhaps the three of them could free Roger Kaplan before he drowned. Lachlan had begun to fear, though, that they would need a chainsaw to hack through that tentacle.

Roger Kaplan was a psychotic madman and a sociopath, but Lachlan couldn't leave him to drown. The thought of him down there, lungs bursting, the ocean pouring into his throat, sent a chill to the very core of his soul.

He sucked in as much air as he could, held it, dived again.

Jennifer raised her head and looked to where Henry Kaplan sprawled nearby on the grass. Masterton sat a little further along, conferring with two police officers. She thought she heard one of them say something about internal bleeding and that an ambulance was coming.

She was worried about Henry. He had so much blood on him and he lay so still. Despite the pain searing through her limbs she pushed herself over to where he lay. 'Henry.'

Slowly, he tilted his head to face her. 'Thank God ... you're okay.' His voice was a croak, his face distorted by pain. '... My fault.'

'You can't blame yourself for Roger.' Their eyes connected and Jennifer read the anguish in his expression.

'I should've ... stopped...' he paused. Coughed. ' ... him.'

Jennifer's hand came to rest on his shoulder. 'Don't talk. Rest. The medics will-'

'I have to explain.' He took a deep breath. 'Eighteen years ago I took a call from Brian. He told me ... Roger was interfering with funds. Wanted me to talk to Roger- about ...'

'You knew?' Tears stung the corners of Jennifer's eyes. Her hand withdrew from the shoulder.

Kaplan's voice wavered, his breath coming in short gasps. 'Before I had a chance to confront Roger ... Brian vanished.'

'Oh, my God.' Jennifer buried her face in her hands. She felt a sinking sensation deep inside - the gut wrenching anguish of knowing that the world as she knew it had gone - a lie, smashed now by the brute force of a secret revealed.

'I followed Roger to that blasted warehouse one night. After he left I went in. Found the equipment. The bodies...' His voice cracked. His eyes searched hers for understanding. 'He was my son, Jennifer. My heir. All I could think to do was to keep him safe ... and to stop him ...'

'How?'

Haltingly, he told her about Falkstog's surveillance teams.

'But Roger started again.'

310

'The blasted bankruptcy. Couldn't pay Falkstog ... I hoped Roger wouldn't realise ...'

'He knew you were behind it?'

Kaplan groaned and clutched his chest. His body rocked with a spasm, then slowly calmed. 'He must've known ... towards the end.'

Jennifer looked to the burning house, then back again. 'I don't understand - how Roger could have done all this. *And you knew ...*' A chill swept through her with unexpected force. She'd always thought of Henry and Roger as part of her family. But who - or what - were they? Monsters? Nothing seemed real ...

Kaplan's hand reached feebly for hers. 'My son, Jennifer ... still my son.' His eyes pleaded for forgiveness from her. 'Can you ..?' All of a sudden he coughed up blood. Another spasm shook his body, sucking the air from his lungs. He went limp, his head lolling to the side.

Jennifer heard the ambulance siren approaching rapidly. She was numb with shock, unable to bring herself to touch the body. Tears streamed freely down her cheeks. Then, her shoulders sagged and she lay her head down on the grass.

At first he felt a terrible panic as his lungs screamed for air. He was sure his body was going to burst.

Then, slowly, a strange dream-like state descended on him. He saw faces in the shadowy depths, floating, staring. One of the faces bobbed closer. It was Vinnie. His first victim. What was he doing here? Waiting? Waiting for his vengeance?

Then the faces blurred to nothingness and the myriad blue-green colours swirled about him in slow motion. He knew what was happening…He wasn't going to join his victims, that had never been his destiny. The light faded and he could feel the ice cold liquid surging through him.

His time had come. He was being prepared for suspension, and he would lay in wait alongside his mother. Together they would sleep, preserved, until they were re-awakened in the world of the future.

THIRTY SIX

The newsbreak cut into the programs of all channels Australia-wide. On the Twelve Network, Racine Gordon, an elegant brunette who spoke in crisp, clear tones, appeared on the screen. 'In an extraordinary series of events, police today discovered that the bombing this morning of Southern Star Mines was the work of one man, the same man now believed to be responsible for the garrote killings that panicked the city of Sydney this past week.

'Police have yet to identify the killer, but our sources indicate that a special unit, reporting directly to the police commissioner and led by Detective Senior Sergeant Neil Lachlan, has identified the killer at the scene of yet another bombing.'

In his grandparents' home in Brisbane, Todd Lachlan lay on the floor in front of the television. He sprang to his feet and looked for his mother. She was moving their packed suitcases into the hallway, ready to leave.

'Mum! Didja hear that? They said Dad's name on the tele. He caught that bad man!'

Marcia stopped. Leaning against the sofa, she placed her hands on Todd's shoulders. 'Shoosh. Listen. There's more.'

'We cross now, live, to the Vaucluse home of fallen entrepreneur Henry Kaplan. Rory McConnell, the investigative reporter whose exposé on Kaplan appeared today in an independent newspaper, has joined the Network Twelve team for this report. He joins us from the scene. Rory ...'

The studio set dissolved quickly and Rory McConnell's face filled the screen. Behind him, emergency service personnel raced around the burning ruin of the two-storey mansion. 'Thank you, Racine. As you can see, bedlam has broken loose here. There are two fatalities at the house - Henry Kaplan and his female companion, Helen Shawcross.

'The big news, though, is the identity of the bomber, also believed to be the notorious garrote killer. We've just been notified that it is Henry Kaplan's son and erstwhile heir - Roger Kaplan - who drowned in the harbour while trying to escape police.'

'Wow!' said Todd.

Marcia squeezed his shoulder, glad the killer had finally been stopped. And she felt good that Neil had played a part. She couldn't deny he was a committed, hard-working cop - he deserved this.

The amazing thing about the trip to Brisbane was that it had cleared her mind, freed her from the anger and the guilt she felt about the past. She'd read that distance from your troubles could do that, but she hadn't expected the sudden, gratifying feeling of release. It had helped her make a very clear decision. She was going to spend more of her time on weekends with the man she'd been seeing, give herself a chance to find out how she really felt about him.

Todd could spend more weekends with Neil. Both would like that, and they deserved it. For the first time she felt they could all get on with the next phase in their lives. She determined that there would be no more hurt, no more recrimination.

'We are still waiting for the official line from police,' Rory continued, 'but I believe the police commissioner will hold a press conference within the hour ...'

In the waiting room of Sydney's North Shore Hospital, Meg Tanner watched the news broadcast. *Roger Kaplan?* The facts refused to settle in her mind. They stayed just out of reach, circling like a plane without a clear place to land. She hadn't slept all night and she was like a zombie. How could Roger Kaplan be responsible for all this? He was Jennifer's friend. He'd been Brian's *best* friend.

Doctor Susan Chan approached her. 'Mrs Tanner, you daughter is awake and, she's off the critical list.'

'Oh, thank God.'

313

'She's going to be fine. And she's asking for you.'

Meg breathed a sigh of relief as she followed the doctor into the emergency ward.

The raid took place at six a.m. the following morning, while the city slept, and the sun's first light crept across the skyline.

Armed with a warrant and the full backing of the police commissioner, Lachlan had assembled a team of six men, Bryant and Aroney among them.

Lachlan felt certain Hans Falkstog had been fully aware, all those years, that the subject of his firm's surveillance was a cold-blooded killer. Lachlan was also certain Falkstog had operated equipment outlawed for commercial enterprises, and that many of his practices were illegal. And it followed that if Henry Kaplan had employed Falkstog to watch his son, then he would have used the same resources to blackmail and use John Rosen.

Just hours before Lachlan had confirmed that suspicion. He'd obtained the phone records for Falkstog's address and found that several calls had been made to John Rosen's number.

Less than twenty-four hours had elapsed, since Lachlan had been in the two storey beachside house, but what he found on the raid came as a complete shock.

When they received no response at the front door, they broke in. Inside they found an empty shell. All the interiors were gone. Falkstog's huge office was bare.

Lachlan led the way to the electronics control room at the rear. Empty, stripped of its bank of sophisticated hardware. There was no indication - *nothing* - that such an operation had ever been housed there.

'Clearly you were right about Falkstog,' Ron Aroney said. 'And he wasn't takin' any chances on you coming back here with a search party.'

'But to have moved everything out,' said Lachlan, 'all the house contents, the heavy duty gear set up down here, literally overnight - in a matter of hours...'

314

'Practically physically impossible, unless you have massive help.' Aroney scratched at his short, unruly mop of hair. 'This guy wasn't just your average security executive. Who the hell was he?'

That question burned in Lachlan's mind as they moved back through the house. It would have taken a highly professional group, trained in speed and stealth and with far reaching resources, to have moved in so quickly and erased all sign of Falkstog's activities. It reeked of government, but legitimate authorities wouldn't get involved to that extent with a man like Falkstog. Would they?

Just what kind of covert connections did Hans Falkstog have?

THIRTY SEVEN

The Winterstone warehouse was cordoned off and guarded by a police unit.

'Good morning, detective.' The constable nodded his head as Lachlan entered the dock area with Jennifer. She wore a silk scarf to cover the wounds on her throat. The only other signs of her ordeal were the gash on her face and a limp, the result of a badly bruised hip and thigh. They went through to the basement.

For several minutes Jennifer stood silently as she ran her gaze over the room: the imposing, alien looking metal caskets; the wires and tubes; the blood storage units; the cylinders of liquid nitrogen.

'I had to see this,' she said. 'Just once.'

'I understand.'

'What will happen to it?'

'Once the department's finished with it, the equipment will be released to the receivers along with everything else. I expect it's the first time cryonics units have been under the liquidator's hammer anywhere in the world.'

'I guess I've seen enough.' They returned to the dock area, Lachlan falling into step beside her. She didn't look back. She'd heard the police psychologist's assessment of the case and she remembered his words now. 'Of the male serial killers profiled by America's FBI, many were eldest sons who had a strained relationship with their fathers. Theirs are disturbed minds, lacking self-esteem, and with a corresponding lack of courage. They kill for power, or sexual gratification, or both, and it becomes their drug.'

'This isn't going to be an easy thing to get over,' Lachlan said to Jennifer after the warehouse visit. They were walking back to Lachlan's car. 'Have you given any thought to the psychologist's suggestion?'

'Counselling?'

'Yes.'

'I'll be okay, Neil. I'll never understand how Roger could've done the things he did, or how Henry could've known and said nothing. Neither of them were the men I thought they were - but it's in the past and I'm damned well going to bury it and get on with my life.'

Lachlan took her hand in his. They were brave, determined words, exactly what he'd expect from the feisty Jennifer Parkes. But he intended to keep a close eye on her, and on Carly, for the immediate future.

Words were one thing. Living them was another matter entirely.

'One thing I've wondered, though,' said Jennifer, 'is what I might've done if I'd been in Henry's position, if Carly had been the one doing such ... things? And I don't know the answer. I really don't know and it frightens me.'

'Hard as it might be, nine out of ten parents would give in to common decency and go to the police. Especially when the lives of others are threatened. I know you well enough to know you're one of the nine.'

They reached Lachlan's car at the end of the double driveway.

'I'm going to sell Wishing Pool Fashions.'

'Why? Because of all this-'

' I want to start something new, something that doesn't have a past connected to the Kaplans. Carly wants to be part of it.'

She flashed him a smile, the first he'd seen from her since the bombing ordeal three days earlier.

'Although with Carly on board it'll have to be something with a social conscience.'

'Environmentally friendly fashions.' Lachlan returned the smile.

'If there's one good thing that has come from all this,' Jennifer observed, 'it's that it's brought Carly and I close again. That's something that Brian would've wanted.'

'You and Carly are going to do just fine.'

'Another good thing,' she said, smiling again, 'is...well, you and I. ' She gripped his hand.

'I agree,' he said. 'In spades.'

The sun's rays held a warm comfort. From the moment she'd walked out of that warehouse, Jennifer felt a weight lift.

She hadn't felt this light of being for a long time.

EPILOGUE

In Queensland, in a fashionable suburb of Brisbane, Wim Vanderkirk, the man previously known as Hans Falkstog, stood with his arms folded as he watched the transmission coming from a hidden camera, far away.

The woman on the screen wasn't known to him, neither was the young man she cavorted with in the expensive hotel suite. Falkstog knew this woman's husband. He was a senior figure with a government agency. The man would be furious when Falkstog confirmed his client's wife was being unfaithful.

This woman could not imagine how her life would be turned upside down. Falkstog knew the bizarre vengeance his client planned. He would cast his wife out of their home, cut her off financially, and ensure that this boyfriend, and any other men that she met, were scared off by threats from Falkstog's menacing phantoms.

She would find it impossible to get decent legal representation in the divorce.

She would become a distraught and lonely woman, struggling to survive.

Falkstog strode into his office at the far end of the hallway. He liked the layout of his new premises, and the way in which the operation had been set up. He felt good. With his darkly dyed hair, green tinted contact lenses and plastic surgery, he was a different man. He intended to ensure it was a long time before he faced such an upheaval again.

The phone rang and he immediately recognised the voice of the powerful figure on the other end.

319

'Yes,' said Falkstog, 'ready to go into action again - as always. Who's the subject?'

As he listened to the reply, he swivelled to his computer keyboard and began to tap the keys. 'No, no problem. A full scale surveillance can be underway within hours. Money talks, my friend, any language you want.'

At the far end of the continent, a man known to most Australians replaced the handset and settled comfortably back in his chair. A grim smile of satisfaction flitted momentarily across his features. He was glad Falkstog/Vanderkirk had been successfully relocated. He was still the best independent operator of his kind and the right one for this assignment.

Falkstog's covert investigations for certain government officials meant that he attained and stored highly sensitive data.

Information that could not fall into the hands of the regular authorities.

The problem was that, as a freelancer, Falkstog had a range of wealthy clients, and his illegal work for just one of them – Henry Kaplan – had brought his entire operation to the attention of the police.

There could be no more unfortunate incidents such as the one to which they'd just been exposed.

If and when that happened, Falkstog's operation would be dismantled and Falkstog removed- permanently.

It was a wintry morning in upstate New York. A cold, bitter wind had reduced the temperature to below freezing.

Donald Simms pulled the collar of his woolen coat closer round his neck as he waved the freight company's container truck into the receiving dock.

He'd worked for the Dreamhaven Cryonics Society for the past three years as the day shift technician and caretaker. Sometimes he thought he'd go mad in this job, stuck in this quiet place for long, lonely hours with the caskets of frozen dead bodies.

He'd stayed because jobs were scarce. He'd only got this because of his relatives. His nephew, a successful dentist, had died four years earlier. He'd been at this plant, in cryonic suspension, ever since.

As the truck backed up, Simms went to the filing cabinet in the corner cubbyhole-cum-office and pulled out the corresponding paperwork. It was rare for an already frozen patient to be admitted. It had happened only once or twice before, but never with a client from another country.

This one had been sent, after eighteen years suspension in Sydney, Australia, because the family member - a son - was planning to come to live in the US. The logistics of shipping this chamber and its power supply must have been horrendous, Simms thought.

These whacko immortalists had more money than sense.

The woman's name, he read, was Monica Rentin.

A trust fund had been set up in New York several months earlier, and the annual proceeds from that would pay for the on-going suspension of the frozen old cow.

Simms chuckled to himself. *More money than sense ...*

He wondered how much dough this woman's family had - and whether they'd be prepared to pay if the casket with the woman went missing, held for ransom. It was an interesting thought.

What would they pay?

How hard could it be to put one of those damn caskets onto a truck and spirit it away to a hiding place?

The freight man jumped down from his cabin. 'Where do you want me to put this thing?'

'Straight through the double doors behind me and to the right of the morgue,' Simms said.

'Morgue?'

'That's what I call it.'

Simms glanced through the paperwork as the hydraulic forklift moved the casket. Strangely, there'd been no further contact from the son since he'd arranged the shipping three weeks earlier.

Simms put the papers aside and daydreamed, as he often did, of grand fortunes attained from clever crimes, and his escape from this twilight world of the frozen dead.

He went through the double doors to hook the chamber and its mobile power unit up to Dreamhaven's permanent systems.

In the cold, clinical operations room, Monica Rentin/Kaplan's long suspended, perfectly preserved body began its untraced and indefinite stay.

***

2594616R00162

Printed in Great Britain
by Amazon.co.uk, Ltd.,
Marston Gate.